OFF THE BENCH

OFF THE BENCH

#UofJ4

ALLEY CIZ

HOUSE OF CRAZY
PUBLISHING

Also by Alley Ciz

Stay connected with Alley

Sign Up for Alley's Newsletter

Bloggers Join Alley's Master List

Join Alley's Facebook Reader Group

**@UofJ411: What's happening here? #TheyDoSayOppo-
sitesAttract #WhereAreAllThePost-its**

On a scale of one to ten, Quinn Thompson is a fifteen.
Gorgeous. Fiery. A cheerleader so far out of my league it's
embarrassing that I even fantasize about her.
I need to find a way to shut down the dirty thoughts she inspires
before it's too late. If I don't, this whole new life of mine is at risk.
Easier said than done when temptation lives right down the hall.

For such a smart guy, CK can be surprisingly clueless.
Sweet. Shy. The star of all my naughty nerd fantasies, but utterly
blind to my flirtations.
Giving in to his plea to be his love coach may seem drastic, but
I'm *desperate* for the chance to come off the bench.
Too bad the friend zone was a hell of a lot safer for my heart.

Paperback ISBN: 978-1-950884-27-8

Ebook ISBN: 978-1-950884-26-1

Cover Designer: Julia Cabrera at Jersey Girl Designs

Cover Photographer: Lindee Robinson Photography

Cover Models: Andrew and Alyssa

Editing: Jessica Snyder Edits, C. Marie

Proofreading: My Brother's Editor; Dawn Black

❀ Created with Vellum

To all those friends who love us for who we are. Even when they get a million random voice messages during the day
#FoundFamily #SquadGoals

Author Note

Dear Reader,

OFF THE BENCH is the 4th book in the #UofJ Series but it can be read as a stand-alone. CK and Quinn are side characters in the original trilogy.

#UofJ Series:
Cut Above The Rest <—Freebie. Download here

1. Looking To Score (Kay and Mason)
2. Game Changer (Kay and Mason)
3. Playing For Keeps (Kay and Mason)
4. Off The Bench (Quinn and CK)
5. #UofJ5 *Preorder, Releasing 2022*

IG Handles

CasaNova87: Mason 'Casanova' Nova (TE)
QB1McQueen7: Travis McQueen (QB)
CantCatchAnderson22: Alex Anderson (RB)
SackMasterSanders91: Kevin Sanders (DE)
LacesOutMitchell5: Noah Mitchell (K)
CheerGodJT: JT (James) Taylor
TheGreatestGrayson37: G (Grant) Grayson
TheBarracksAtNJA: The Barracks
NJA_Admirals: The Admirals

Playlist

- "This Is How We Do It"- Montell Jordan
- "Ooh La La"- Goldfrapp
- "Woman"- Kesha
- "The Trouble With Love Is"- Kelly Clarkson
- "Plastic Hearts"- Miley Cyrus
- "CAN'T DANCE"- Meghan Trainor
- "Here Comes The Hotstepper"- Ini Kamoze
- "El Chico Del Apartamento 512"- Selena
- "Amor Prohibido"- Selena
- "One Margarita"- Luke Bryan
- "Good Times"- Cassadee Pope
- "Visiting Hours"- Ed Sheeran
- "Tequila Makes Her Clothes Fall Off"- Joe Nichols
- "Shivers"- Ed Sheeran
- "Word Up!"- Little Mix
- "Classic"- MKTO
- "Mean"- Taylor Swift
- "Jaws Theme"- Jaws
- "Move"- Little Mix
- "Fly"- Maddie & Tae
- "Tattoo"- Hunter Hayes
- "Happier Than Ever"- Billie Eilish
- "Hoedown Throwdown"- Miley Cyrus
- "Sit Still, Look Pretty"- Days
- "Crazy Girl"- Eli Young Band

- "Ironic"- Alanis Morissette
- "Fuck Up The Friendship"- Leah Kate
- "Love Lockdown"- Kanye West
- "Jesus, Take The Wheel"- Carrie Underwood

FIND PLAYLIST on Spotify.

QUINN

"HE'S GOT to be kinky in bed, right?" Liquid spills over the rim of my Solo cup as I throw my arm out toward where the man in question stands.

Whoops.

I lick the tangy, sweet margarita off the back of my hand while my two best friends eye me like I've lost my mind.

In their defense, I am teetering on that precipice.

It's not my fault though.

Eight months.

Eight *flipping* months.

You would think a time frame that is almost long enough for a person to gestate an entire human being would be enough time to get the guy you've been crushing on to pick up all the things you've been throwing down, right?

Yeah…

Not so much.

I'm sure you're asking yourself now, but Quinn, why wouldn't you just move on if he's not interested?

Harrumph. Lord knows my mother would rather I did so.

Ay dios mío.

I can't even *begin* to imagine what she would say to me if she knew I was sitting here pining over an adorkable nerd and wallowing in my unrequited feelings.

It wouldn't be good.

Pinche mierda.

She already thinks I've wasted my first two years of college by not locking down one of the *many* athletes my school, the University of Jersey, or U of J for short, churns out to the pros like Nabisco shelves Oreos.

Don't even get me *started* on how she considers working toward a bachelor's degree a "waste of time."

Freshman year, she asked, "Quinny, *linda,* are you sure you won't consider joining a sorority? You know that's how I met your father."

If her beliefs were rooted in how, like many others believe, a college degree isn't necessarily needed for a job nowadays, it would be one thing. But, unfortunately, it's not. And worse? She can't respect that my degree is so much more than a fancy piece of paper for me—it's a stepping-stone for a career that will be all *my* own.

This past year it was, "How are the boys at the school ever going to notice your pretty face if you keep it buried in a book, *linda*?"

Of course, she wouldn't care about my grades. To her, the only degree I should be focusing on is my MRS. Preferably with one of those athletes I mentioned earlier.

I love my parents. It's obvious they adore each other, but I don't want my looks to be the only thing others see as valuable about me. *Mamá* wanted me to cheer for the social status it gave me, but I continued with it because I saw it as my free ticket to a top-notch university.

Oof. That's *way* too heavy of a topic to be thinking about right now.

Tequila will fix that.

Margaritaville it is!

Mamá would be praying to *La Virgen María* if she knew that while my studies may have been the reason behind the tunnel vision my freshman year, it's the cute blue-eyed boy with the Clark Kent-style glasses who has prevented any other guy from capturing my attention for the last. Eight. Freaking. Months!

"Who are we talking about?" Emma leans to the side, bracing her forearm against the cushion of her lounge chair, attempting to get a better vantage point from which to view the cluster of sexy beasts across the balcony from us and effectively knocking me out of my mental musings on things better left packed away.

On my other side, with her cup poised in front of her face, eyes peering into its depths, Kay mumbles, "I'm going to need to be another margarita deep if you expect me to give up the deets on Mase."

Emma and I snort, our heads coming together to make *Is this biotch serious?* eye contact.

"Umm…" The weight of Emma's body presses into my side as she folds hers over to peer around me for an unobstructed view of our delusional friend. "I know the master suite is separate from most of the penthouse, Kay, but it is *not* soundproofed."

"Nor are you quiet, babe." I hide my *Yeah, you get the good dick, girl* grin behind my cup.

Color blooms across Kay's pretty face. "You guys suck," she grumbles before downing a healthy swallow of her margarita.

"Nuh-huh," I counter, twisting around and leaning back into Emma, who props her chin on my shoulder like my own gorgeous brunette parrot. "From what I overheard this morning, that honor goes firmly to you." I poke my tongue into the side of my cheek three times, simulating a good knob slob.

"*Ohmigod.*" Kay flops forward, her long curly locks obscuring the burning cheeks that match the recently re-added pink streaks in her hair.

"Your embarrassment is adorable but *highly* unnecessary." I pat Kay's back. "Hell, if I were you, I'd be strutting around this place like a motherfucking peacock." I pause, my face scrunching up in thought. "Though I guess it's hard to strut when you're walking funny."

Emma snorts again, and I have to press my lips together to restrain a laugh. As the daughter of a state senator, it's a goddamn miracle the impulse to release such an unladylike—her mother's words, not mine—sound hasn't been trained out of her.

"An awkward gait isn't always in*dic*ative of good sex." The pointed emphasis Emma puts on the second syllable of indicative has Kay straightening, and both of us tap our cups to Emma's in punny cheers.

The three of us all nod in agreement. This is true. I may be in the middle of a human-growing, about-to-be-infant-birthing dry spell, but I have experienced a hitch in my giddy-up thanks to chafing caused by a round of overeager jackhammer humping before.

"Though by the way that boyfriend of yours practically had you singing an opera with his name, I think it's safe to say Mason is *all* about tasting *your* rainbow, babes."

"Skittles pun." Emma does a *Yes!* arm pump. We have far too much fun with Mason's choice of pet name for Kay.

"I hate you guys." Kay buries her face into her hands, despite being used to the constant teasing.

"No, you don't," Emma and I chorus together just as a shadow falls over our little cluster of chaos.

"Skittles?" Both concern and amusement tinge Mason's tone as one of his dark brows hits the edge of his backward ball cap when I whisper a "Whoop, there it is" then hiss when Kay connects an elbow to the side of my ribs.

Totally worth it.

Objectively speaking, Mason Nova is one sexy beefcake. The six-foot-five football god could practically have my bestie coming on the spot with the simple twinkle in his seafoam-green eyes and a flash of his matching set of dimples. But...that's not why all of my girly girl parts are sighing dreamily as he continues to glower at us.

Nope.

It's not his looks that have the plastic of my cup giving an ominous crinkle as I clutch it tighter in an effort to keep myself from visibly swooning.

Nuh-huh.

The thing that has me and, much to my friends' acute displeasure, the UofJ411, our school's gossip Instagram account, captivated by them, is the intuitive and instinctive way Mason Nova is aware of all things Kayla Dennings.

Like right now.

There Mason was, standing clear across the massive thousand-square-foot deck, in the middle of his own conversation with our five other roommates—yes, you heard that right: there are nine of us living here in our own U of J reboot of *The Real World*—and *still* he was aware of his girlfriend's growing mortification.

"Caveman," Kay mumbles into her hands, keeping her face hidden.

Mason's lips quirk at the twin sighs Emma and I let out at Kay's use of the other half of their cutesy pet names. Yup, I totally get UofJ411's obsession with my friends because when witnessing #Kaysonova in action, there's no denying that they embody everything that defines #CoupleGoals.

Actually…

I slip my phone out from under my thigh and snap a quick pic of the look of adoration on Mason's face as he looks down at his girlfriend. Maybe when Kay's done being embarrassed by us, I'll be able to convince her this should be one of the things she allows him to post to his own Instagram account. Letting the world see how much he loves her can be a powerful tool, despite her abject disdain for all things social media.

Despite his amusement, Mr. Alpha-Man is not having the distance from his girlfriend anymore. Mason scoops my friend from the lounger, claiming her seat himself and settling in with her on his lap.

Emma retakes her parrot perch on my shoulder, and without an ounce of shame from either of us, we watch as Mason crooks a finger under Kay's chin before smoothing his thumb over the curve of her cheek. "Now you've got me curious what you ladies were talking about with you blushing like this, Skits."

"Is it too late to get new friends?" Kay asks instead.

For a split second, Mason's eyes shift to us before he drops them to Kay's hands, lifting one and kissing the jeweled birthstone bands—the ones that represent those who mean most to her—adorning her fingers. "Yeah, babe, I think it's safe to say it's too late."

Kay growls, and Mason kisses the tip of her nose, chuckling at how adorable he thinks she is. He's not wrong. At under five feet tall, Kay is more like an angry puppy than anything else.

My gaze once again finds its way back to the person responsible for the current deluge of debauchery.

Shit!

Maybe I should start praying to baby Jesus like *Mamá*, because if that man doesn't start looking at me as more than Quinn, his friend, *me voy a volver loca.*

"Ahhh." Kay's gray eyes sparkle with intrigue when she pops out of her Mason love bubble. "That's whose shade spectrum you were speculating about."

"Now there's a tongue twister for you," I joke in an attempt to take the heat off me.

"*Annnddd* we're back to oral sex." Emma holds a hand up for a high five. "Nice."

Mason perks up, his muscular torso rippling beneath his *Property of U of J Football* tee when he shifts so he can see all three of us at once. "Oral sex?" He quirks a brow, intrigue now bleeding into his tone. "Skit, are you telling them about that thing I did with my tongue thi—"

Kay cuts off the rest of Mason's sentence by smacking a hand across his mouth. "Only *you* would wanna know if I'd been bragging about your bedroom skills when we should be focusing on how our darling Q is musing about if our sweet, shy CK is a closet dom."

"You know what it does to me when you roll your eyes, babe." Mason's comment only has Kay rolling her eyes a second time before they both, unfortunately, focus on me, and he says, "Well, this just got interesting."

Sonofabitch.

I down the rest of my margarita in one go, slamming the side of my fist to my forehead at the stinging bolt of pain slicing through my brain when it momentarily freezes. Guess that's the price I pay for avoidance via frozen tequila.

Annnnddddd…it didn't even work.

Nope.

Three sets of eyes are still trained on me like they're waiting for me to premiere a new cheer for the U of J's Red Squad.

"As the only one here not in possession of a vagina—"

"A fact Kay is most *certainly* grateful for."

"I'm going to need you to break this down for me," Mason continues, as if Emma never spoke.

"Huh?" I ask, not necessarily playing dumb but not entirely clear on the actual question.

"What makes a chick wonder if a dude keeps whips and chains hidden in his closet?"

It's my turn for my cheeks to heat, and I curse the depths of my empty Solo cup for not magically refilling with some liquid salvation.

I close my eyes and peel one open to check again.

Still empty.

Damn.

And you know what else?

There are still six curious eyeballs waiting for an explanation.

Double damn.

You know what?

Whatever.

I'm a big girl. If I can dish out the teasing about my friends' sex lives, I can certainly take it when they turn the hedonistic tide on me.

But first…

I'm gonna help myself to Emma's margarita.

Noting the perfectly sculpted eyebrow arched at me when I hand her back her empty cup, I clear my throat and say, "It's not so much whips and chains as I picture a collection of rulers and neckties."

Mason makes a rolling *Explain* motion with his hand, and then Kay uses his body to play defense when I eye her margarita.

Jerks.

"Just…just…*ugh!*" I throw my hands up and thread my fingers into my hair as my words jumble together. "Look at him," I finally end up shouting, and then I fall backward when everyone, and I mean *e-ver-y-one*, looks my way.

Fan-flipping-tastic.

Oh, dear sweet, sweet chubby-cheeked baby Jesus, thank you for the easy distractibility of college co-eds, because by the time I sit up and shove my red hair out of my face, I only have the original Three Stooges to contend with.

"Do you *may-be* wanna try that again?" Emma asks.

"And *may-be* try pretending like you're not on the sidelines at a Hawks game?" Kay adds in the same teasing singsong.

God, these bitches are lucky they are my sisses from other misses, or I'd hate their asses.

I clear my throat and try again. "Do you see him?" I jerk my chin, then bounce my eyes in CK's direction when my friends don't automatically look his way. "He's got that quiet, reserved demeanor and those yummy sexy glasses."

"Yummy?"

"Sexy?"

"Glasses?"

Em, Kay, and Mason ask in order, and I nod. "Uh…yeah. Dudes aren't the only ones who can have fantasies triggered by eyewear."

"Are we talking slutty secretary, naughty librarian-type stuff?" Mason asks the question to me, but winks at Kay.

Oy. That's more detail than I needed to know about their role-playing preferences.

"Yup. Though in my case, it's more I'm the naughty schoolgirl, and CK is the dominating professor ready to *personally* see to my detention."

Aww, look at me joining in the TMI sharing.

My *abuelita* would make herself go hoarse reciting *Ave Marías* if she knew the number of times I've imagined CK's blue eyes blazing at me from behind those lenses as he instructs me to bend over a desk to "teach me a lesson."

Oh yeah, even now, my go-to masterdate is enough to have me squirming in my seat.

I jackknife up, my back going ramrod straight as a sudden thought slams my body like my bases dropped me after a basket toss.

Oh shit!

If we can hear Mason and Kay doing the hippity-dippity, does that mean everyone and, more importantly, *CK* is able to make out the buzz of my vibrator when I'm loving myself up thinking about him?

Oh…

Wait…

Did you not realize?

My bad. *says in best Cher *Clueless* voice*

Let me back up a sec.

Remember those eight months I was bitching about earlier in the night?

Yeah…

Well…

Those are going to feel like child's play—pun most definitely intended—with the months to come if this man doesn't buy a clue like contestants on *Wheel of Fortune* buy a vowel and notice I. Want. Him.

Why?

Because not only is the man in question constantly trying to avoid me…

Now…

There's no escape for him.

Or for me and the sexual frustration he causes to build up inside my body.

Again, why?

Because not only is CK, Mr. Christopher Kent, my clueless crush.

No.

Nope.

Now he's also my roommate.

CK

#CHAPTER2

FOR ABOUT THE dozenth time tonight, I find my mind wandering.

It doesn't matter that I'm standing in the middle of a group of people or that I'm literally mid-conversation; the inevitability of that pesky, *How is this my life?* thought popping in to interrupt is precisely that—inevitable.

The number of times I've experienced this existential crisis since accepting my admission to the University of Jersey two years ago is unquantifiable.

Though...

I guess the true *What the fuck?* change to my life happened a few months later when Kay Dennings all but forced her friend-ship upon me.

And no...that's not an exaggeration. I honestly can't find another way to define it. Kay may lack height, but she sure as hell doesn't lack what my gramps calls grit.

That said, now I'm not sure how I would survive without her or the others in my life.

"CK...bro. Come back to us. It's your turn."

It's not the fingers snapping an inch from my face that yank me back to the present and have me focusing in on the towering form of the second person to crowbar their way into my life.

No.

It's those two letters, the C and the K, that do it. Simple initials I could never have anticipated would hold such a significant role in my life.

Yet…

They ended up being the catalyst for…

All of this.

Seriously? This can't possibly be my real life. A part of me keeps expecting everyone to yell sike and reveal that this is all one big joke, a prank to toy with the geeky nerd.

But…

Two years?

That would be one hell of a long game, even for the most sociopathic.

I shake off those thoughts and concentrate on the three-foot block tower in the center of our circle instead. We're deep into our fourth game of Drunk Jenga, making both the arrangement of the two-by-three blocks more precarious and my cognitive abilities a tad bit fuzzy.

Tongue pinched between my teeth, I select one of the side pieces as my query and carefully slip it free.

"Social," I call out, and all around me, cups and beer bottles are lifted in a toast before everyone takes a sip as the game piece directed.

"You were thinking it again, weren't you?"

My shoulders slump the second after I finish gently placing the block on the now swaying tower. Does it make me an ass that I hate that Grant knows me well enough to *know* where my mind went? Is it wrong that I was also hoping he would forget?

A knowing chuckle reaches my ears, and there's a matching amused twinkle in the dark eyes looking down at me when I turn his way. And no, before you start getting defensive on my behalf —though I appreciate the effort—I mean that in the most literal sense. At six foot eight, Grant Grayson, or G to those of us in our makeshift family—and that's a whole other thing—looks down at ninety-nine percent of the American population.

"I don't know what you're talking about." I feign ignorance, not wanting to dig into the heaviness of my insecurities.

Not here.

Not now.

Not with someone who has become a vital addition to my life.

"Aww, it's cute when the smarties try to play dumb," JT Taylor, the first two letters in the alphabet soup of mashed-up family Kay has collected, comments as he hip checks his way forward to take his turn at Jenga.

"Yet, they can never really pull it off, can they?" Grant finishes, leveling me with a *Stop trying to pretend I don't know you* eyebrow arch.

I tip my beer at him, conceding, shifting my attention to the Jenga block JT pulls free. I focus on the…*creative*—I'm talking smiley face, sloppy pubes, and excited jizz spewing from the tip —rendering of a penis drawn on it, hoping Grant will let the other issue go.

It works, and every person possessing a hopefully-less-colorful-and-animated version of the dick lifts their cup and takes a drink as instructed.

Thank god.

It's bad enough I had to promise my friends I would start putting myself out there. I don't need to hear another one of their lectures—ones I could probably recite by heart at this point— about how it's time I *finally* realize and recognize how awesome I am.

That's easier said than done.

The game continues with the standard practice of pulling and placing Jenga blocks, one after another—except, this is Drunk Jenga. With each piece pulled and each quantity of alcohol consumed, the volume of our voices grows and the gesticulating of our movements becomes more erratic until, finally, a rogue arm swings into the tower.

There's a loud clatter as the blocks hit the deck to a chorus of "Ooo, party foul" and tittering giggles.

It doesn't bother me. I've shockingly grown used to the chaos. Plus…it helps me fade into the background where I'm more comfortable.

Again there's that whisper of *How did I get here?*, and by here, I mean both theoretically and physically. Except this thought is quickly followed by a much older and even more familiar *You don't belong here.*

Sadly, despite all of my friends' efforts, I can't argue with it.

Looking around, it is blatantly obvious that one of these things is not like the other, and that thing that's different? It's not Kevin bowing with a flourish or Alex telling him to save the sacking for the quarterbacks, not our backyard games. No. The different thing? It's me. I'm the odd man out…in *every* sense of the word.

Am I an athlete? Nope.

Was I popular? Only if the category is the favorite choice to be picked on.

To make a long story short, jocks, cheerleaders, and me…we don't get along.

Yet…

Now I'm living in a houseful of them.

Ahh…now you get why I'm constantly asking myself how this is my life.

"Dude." A gust of air whiffs across my face as Grant claps his dinner plate–sized hands in front of it. "Oh no, no, no," he continues as I shove a flop of hair out of my eyes with a glare. "You're doing it again, and that shit needs to stop."

"What's he doing?" Another blond head I've grown used to butting into my business leans into the middle of our conversation before I'm meeting the mischievous smirk of Travis, the U of J's star quarterback and, yes, one of those new roommates I mentioned. "Ooo, is he finally withholding his mysterious video game from you too?"

"It's not mysterious," I grumble.

"Mmmhmm." Trav hooks an arm around my shoulders, but it's not to headlock me or pull me in for a noogie like the football players of my past. No, instead, it's filled with a brotherly camaraderie I've been trying valiantly to grow used to. "So tell me then, is it a real-time strategy, first-person shooter, role-playing…" He makes a rolling motion with his free hand. "Stop me if I guess correctly."

He hasn't. The game I've spent the last few years of my life coding and developing falls into none of those categories. But… even if he did guess correctly, I wouldn't tell him.

I'm far too protective of it.

It's far too *personal* to me.

"Come on, CK," Trav whines, and a surge goes through me.

Sure, he isn't one of the jocks who made my life miserable growing up, but to have something he wants, to feel like I'm sorta in a position of power here…it's heady.

"Leave my CK alone, QB1." Kay's voice rings out from across the deck, and I can't help but smirk at the easy way she claims me as hers. It's not in the romantic sense—no, that position has been declared loud and proud by the behemoth she's sitting on— but it's an assertion nonetheless.

"Bullshit," Trav shouts, his face contorting into a scowl when I tease him about Kay loving me more. "Short Stack, tell him that's not true."

Kay only rolls her eyes because that's her signature move, which in turn has Mason cackling and the rest of our crew tossing out their own colorful insults about how Trav is acting like a whiny bitch.

There's manhandling, and JT jumps onto Trav's back, smacking his ass like he's a horse he's trying to urge to go faster. Alex and Kevin are leaning against each other, and Grant is wiping a tear from his eye.

With JT still on his back, Trav kneels in front of Kay, his hands clasped in front of him as he pleads with her to make him her top choice for "brother" with promises of undying love and laundry-doing servitude.

"Your Lysol-needing hands aren't going anywhere near my underwear, QB1." Kay puts a finger to the center of Trav's forehead and shoves him backward, leaving JT sprawled like a flattened pancake beneath Trav's body.

"You got that fucking right," Mason growls, giving his best friend a death glare.

"Can we start a pool on how long we think it will be before Mase finally ends up killing Trav?" Noah, the only staple from our group who won't be living with us, takes out his phone like he's ready to start drafting.

"Bro." Alex chuckles, shaking his head. "You're not even going to be here."

"Damn, man." Noah mimes being stabbed in the heart. "That's how it's gonna be? Out of sight, out of mind?" He wiggles his hand on his chest. "Harsh."

"You act like DC is so far away," Kevin says dryly.

"Yeah, bro, you know we'll be visiting to scope out the food sitch." Grant pats his stomach, forever thinking with it.

"Glad to see it's your stomach that will bring you to our nation's capital and not the opportunity to see me play." Noah hums. "Yup, *really* feeling the love," he complains, as if we would actually allow him to have his NFL debut without us being there to cheer him on. Even I, the most reluctant member of this family, know that's not how we work.

"You wanna feel the love, No?" A feminine voice from across the deck calls out, obviously listening in because *none* of us are all that known for minding our business.

Emma Logan, or Em as I've always known her, completes the trifecta of unexpected friendships that altered my life in ways I could have never have imagined during all the time I spent shoved into lockers.

Her red Solo cup is raised in the air, and she starts to sing the chorus to Luke Bryan's "One Margarita". Kay joins in the off-key crooning, but still, it isn't either of them that has captured my attention.

Instead, much to my dismay, I find my gaze homing in on the redhead sitting between them and completing their karaoke trio.

Quinn Thompson.

Perky.

Bubbly.

Cheerleader.

So damn beautiful it hurts to look at her, but it's actually more painful to force my gaze away.

Except…

No amount of personal growth will change the fact that she's so fucking far out of my league that even fantasizing would be an embarrassment.

Noah walks over to the built-in bar in the corner of the balcony and pulls out the premade pitcher of margaritas from the mini-fridge. He joins in on the singing as he fills the ladies' cups, swinging his hips side to side and dropping it low, much to their amusement.

Never one to give up, Trav makes another play for Kay's top-brother spot, taking her hand and pulling her up to two-step with him.

Mason growls, hooking an arm around Kay's hips and

tugging her back into his lap. "How many times do I have to tell you to stop flirting with my girl?"

That sets off another round of drunken giggles from the ladies and another eye roll from Kay.

"I think you should have CK put you on that dating app his summer class is testing," Em says to Trav.

"Yeah, maybe if you have a girlfriend of your own, you'll leave mine alone," Mason grumbles.

"Oh, ho, ho." Trav chortles with an arm banded over his middle, body folding over exaggeratedly. "Look at our Casanova." He gestures to Mason, spinning to look at the rest of us with a flourish. "He gets wifed up, and now he's the poster boy for happily ever after."

Mason flips him off, then looks to me hopefully. "CK, help a brother out." His hands come together in prayer. "Get this loser on that app with you." He hooks a thumb at Trav.

Heat creeps up my cheeks. It's bad enough I let Emma convince me to use the app my computer engineering class is testing and debugging, but now everyone else knows. *Thanks, Em.*

"Umm…" I grip the back of my neck. As if I haven't already felt like a loser. "I don't think you want me to do that. The algorithm is all off." *Or at least I hope it is.*

"Why?" Em tilts her head, a furrow tugging between her brows. "Only being matched with the crazies?"

I study the contents of my cup, watching the last of the foam bubbles pop, wishing to be anywhere but here.

Ugh! This sucks.

Having to admit this just proves how much I'm not like the rest of them.

Blowing out a breath, I adjust my glasses before finally admitting, "I haven't had any matches."

The heat in my cheeks burns hotter as all around me, jaws drop. *Ah, yes, see? Your CK is a loser.*

"That can't be true," Quinn challenges, holding out a hand and wiggling her fingers. "Give me your phone."

Is she insane? I know I already said she's out of my league, but she wants me to hand over *proof* of that? No way.

"CK," she says with another *Gimme* finger wiggle.

I don't move. Not gonna happen.

She huffs and clumsily pushes to her feet. There's a distinct weave to her steps, but it doesn't take away from the enticing sway of her hips.

The sweet scent of coconut fills my lungs a second before the tips of her sandals butt up against the toes of my Vans as she invades my personal space with zero shame.

That's Quinn for you, though. Confidence radiates out of her pores.

One manicured finger taps my chest until I tuck my chin enough to meet her dark gaze. An itch forms beneath my skin from her nearness.

"Do you need me to get your phone myself?" Her hiccup takes the intimidation factor she's going for down a few notches.

That doesn't stop me from shuffling on my feet at the thought of her hand sliding inside the pocket of my shorts. Given the amount of beer I've consumed while playing Jenga, I might do something embarrassing like moan if she did.

That's the only reason I can think of for why I finally give in and give her what she wants.

Quinn shoves her Solo cup at me, and I've barely gotten it pinched in my grip when she almost smacks me in the face, holding my phone up to it to unlock it with Face ID.

She hums as she navigates through the apps until she finds the Greet Geek app.

"Greet Geek?" She pauses, thumb hovering over the screen, her dark eyes scanning me from head to toe. "You are so perfectly geek chic."

She's not the first person to use that descriptor for me, and it's one of the reasons I gave in to the others' prodding about trying out this particular app. It's geared toward matching me up with others who consider themselves in the geek camp.

"Oh my god, Superman." Quinn pops me in the chest with a backhand, and I try not to preen at the nickname she bestowed upon me months ago. "You *barely* listed *any* of your best qualities."

I roll my eyes, because yes, Kay has rubbed off on me. The exaggeration in how Quinn expressed that statement was a bit much, even for her intoxication level.

My profile lists many of my academic achievements, my

major, and that I like to design video games in my spare time. What else would people want to know?

"We *need* to fix this." She clucks her tongue, shaking her head. "Hold, please."

Grant snorts, propping his elbow on my shoulder as Quinn walks away and huddles with Kay and Em on their original lounger.

I can honestly say I'm not quite sure what just happened.

QUINN

THE ENTIRE U of J marching band plays inside my skull, and I roll over with a groan, smothering my face deeper into my pillow.

I've just found goose-down bliss when the creak of door hinges sounds, and I'm jostled by ninety pounds of canine jumping onto my bed.

Any other day I love how Herkie, Kay's yellow Labrador, seeks me out in the mornings. Lord knows his mama damn near goes into anaphylaxis when it comes to her reaction to hours in the a.m.

This particular morning, however…not so much.

Herkie doesn't give two Scooby Snacks about the hangover high stepping through my brain. He needs to pee, and he needs to pee now.

Still…

I don't move fast enough for the pooch and get the doggy equivalent of a wet willy when he all but shoves his tongue into my ear canal. With considerable effort, I flop my head around on the pillow, sputtering all manner of bed head out of my face, and glare at my incredibly rude alarm clock.

With a *harrumphing* body adjustment of his own, followed by a lick across the tip of my nose, all my mad melts away. I'm such a sucker for Herk's soulful brown eyes. Grunts and curses in Spanish—both from me—fill the silence of my bedroom as I untangle myself from the mass of blankets, attempting to keep me with them.

The temptation is real.

But...I wouldn't be a good dog aunt if I didn't let him outside to do his business.

The buzzing of my phone has me hunting around in my pillows. But when I find it, there aren't any notifications, and... where the hell is that buzzing coming from?

Welp, that's a new hangover symptom.

Again, I go searching, wondering if maybe Emma or Kay left their phone in here last night. Tossing pillows like I'm hunting for treasure left behind by the Tooth Fairy, I freeze when I find my query.

Umm...

What?

Why is the phone on my bed not in a case with Skittles or a cartoon coffee cup on it? Why am I staring at an old-school Game Boy?

Only one person living in this penthouse has a case like that. But why do I have it?

Hmm...

Does anyone want to fill me in here?

I'd like to buy one of those vowels, or maybe a clue.

A wet nose pushes into the back of my leg, and my fuzzy brain remembers we have more important things to worry about —he needs to pee.

As expected, none of my other roommates are awake as Herkie and I make our way through our home until we reach the doors leading to the balcony. I'm supremely grateful for the section of fake grass Mason had installed in the far corner of the deck when Herkie is able to just trot outside on his own to do his doggy business. It leaves me free to try to piece together whatever bad decisions led to me having my crush's phone.

How do I know they were bad decisions? I had *a lot* of tequila last night.

So...

Just trust me on it, y'all.

Standing in front of Emma's bedroom door, I make the sign of the cross and pray to whoever is *Abuelita's* favorite patron saint when she worries if I'm safe or not. I'm going to need all the protection I can get if I'm going to survive the task of waking up a non-morning person.

Not to be outdone by the starlight projector on her bedside table, a beam of sunlight illuminates my slumbering friend like she's a goddamn Disney princess.

Naturally, I do what *any* best friend would do when confronted with a scene like this.

Balling my hands into fists, I brace myself on the shelf my knuckles create, leaning forward to place a smacking, wet kiss on Emma's forehead. I duck just in time to avoid the arm that comes swinging my way.

"The apartment better be on fucking fire for you to be waking me this early, Q," Emma mumbles into her pillow before lifting it to cover her face.

My heart rodeo lassos like it does almost any time I get called Q. It's such a simple nickname, yet I know the true significance of being labeled a letter to those closest to Kay. Hell…I don't even call Emma *Emma* anymore. She is strictly Em, now and forevermore.

"Listen, biotch…" I climb onto her mattress and flop down beside her with a dramatic flair. "We have *way more* important things that need to be addressed than the time of your wake-up call."

I don't wait for Emma to answer or, hell, even to pull her pillow away from her face before I'm thrusting my hand at her, CK's phone clutched tightly and upside down in my grip.

Perfectly manicured fingers wrap around my wrist, lowering my arm enough to make it possible to actually see what I invaded her space with.

It takes four blinks and one hell of an impressive crane of the neck before Emma asks, "Why do you still have CK's phone?"

"*Still* have?"

Emma nods, and now I'm even more confused than I was when I first found the unexpected snuggle buddy stowing away in my bed.

"Why did I have it in the *first* place?" A hint of panic creeps into this question. None of this is making any sense.

"You—" A yawn cuts off whatever Emma was about to say, and I'm *this close* to shaking her in *I gots to know* impatience. "Didn't believe him when he said he wasn't getting any matches on that dating app."

Whatever alcohol still hanging around in my gut like a clingy one-night stand swirls in loop-de-loops at the mention of CK dating. When's he going to take *my* flirting seriously? I swear I've all but donned a whipped-cream bikini trying to get him to realize *I'm* into him. Yet...*nada*.

"Oh-kay." I roll my lower lip between my teeth, racking my muddled brain for *why* I continued to hold on to it. "And...what? I kept it so I could delete any of the matches I saw after proving him wrong?"

That actually sounds like a brilliant plan. I'm already mentally patting myself on the back when Emma metaphorically dumps the football team's Gatorade cooler on me.

"Your marketing major side took over, and you went all *Oh em gee, Superman, you didn't tell them all the things that make you a super sexy hot nerd dreamboat*," she mocks in an exaggerated falsetto and Texan drawl.

All of those are accurate descriptors for one Mr. Christopher Kent, and yes, I have said them out loud before, but...

"One"—I boop Emma on the nose, sound effect and all—"I don't sound *anything* like that." Yes, you can tell I'm from Texas, but my accent is slight. "And, two, *shut. Up. I did. Not* say that." I pause, rolling my eyes up with a blink, as if sorting through my memories. "Did I?"

The first vestiges of a smile start to tug up the corners of Miss Grumpus's mouth.

Well...

At least one of us is amused.

"Not in those exact words, no." She shakes her head. "But you did tweak our shy guy's dating profile."

Mierda.

Freaking tequila.

"What did I put?"

If Mr. Cuervo was involved, I'm liable to have

put *anything*. Hell, it's a damn miracle it was CK's phone that ended up in my bed and not my person in his.

Ooo, that's a strategy I haven't tried yet…

"I don't know." Emma reluctantly sits up, the blankets pooling around her waist as she shrugs, rubbing the heels of her palms against her eyes, moaning about needing coffee.

Sure…let's take care of her caffeine fix. *That's* what's important here. It's not like I'm completely panicking about the possibility of blowing up any potential future of a love life or anything.

"*Emma*," I whine. My use of her full name has her arching one of her perfectly sculpted brows at me—seriously, those suckers could make Ellen Pompeo weep at their altar.

"*Qué pasa, chica?*"

I bite the inside of my cheek to keep from laughing. This is *not* a laughing matter, but Emma Logan dropping the Spanish on me? Yeah, it's like *Abuelita* is here with me, waiting for the daily gossip.

"I *need* to know what I wrote." My nail aggressively taps the screen, lighting it so the Greet Geek notifications show. Their mere existence mocks me. They are a visual reminder that I am, in fact, not the type of girl CK is looking for.

All of it…freaking *all* of it is made all the more annoying because I can't even open them to see what they say. *Freaking passcodes.*

Hmm…

Would it make me a total creeper if I tried to tiptoe into CK's room for a Face ID?

"Worried you confessed your undying crush in written form?"

I narrow my eyes, my mouth pressing into a flat line. "Are you *trying* to get me to hide all the coffee in this house?" I arch a brow. "Because I'll do it."

She smacks a hand over her heart, flopping back onto the mattress like she's reenacting her performance of Juliet's death from her high school production of *Romeo and Juliet*.

"You're a *monster*, Q," she whisper-hisses.

"And *you're*"—I poke her twice in the belly—"being a. Bad. Friend." I wave the phone around—again. "Help. Me."

Emma takes the phone from me, tapping and swiping across

the screen, only to end up growling and tossing it when she realizes what I already knew—it's locked.

My hopes plummet, and it feels like I have one of my poms shoved inside my throat.

What did I do?

What did I flipping *do*?

Guess eight months is my official limit. One too many margaritas and a dating app were what it took to finally break this cheerleader's back.

Except…

Now instead of just having to deal with a clueless cutie, I have to contend with my own overzealous stupidity.

"You know wh—" Emma's hair goes flying around her face as she viciously shakes her head. "Nope. Even I know that's a bad idea."

"What?" I all but shout as I clutch her forearm like she's a life preserver in this stormy sea I created for myself.

No more tequila for me.

Dammit, why couldn't my brain cells channel Joe Nichols and just make my clothes fall off instead?

"Chill, babes." Emma twists her arm and reverses our grips until she's the one holding on to me. "I was just going to say that Kay might—*might*—know CK's passcode. But…"

She trails off, but I don't need her to finish.

It was one thing for me to bust in here and wake her up; it's an entirely different level of insanity to even consider doing the same with Kay.

Plus…there's the whole she-sleeps-next-to-her-own-personal-alpha-caveman thing.

Do I…?

Don't I…?

Holy shit.

Estoy loca.

Fuck it!

I'm doing this.

No.

We're doing this.

Yup—I'm invoking girl code and forcing Em to be my backup.

Here's hoping Kay and Mason don't sleep in the nude.

#CHAPTER4

A COLD NOSE touches my cheek, and I blindly reach out for the furry head I know is there as I'm roused from sleep.

"Hey, bud." I give Herkie a good scratch between the ears and get a face full of tongue and dog breath in return.

My canine companion ditches me as soon as I'm awake, leaving me to get ready by myself while he goes in search of his next victim to rouse. The dog has made it a habit to wake anyone and everyone he can in the morning since his mama avoids them as often as college student—or, in Kay's case—humanly possible.

Blindly, I feel around on my nightstand, slipping my glasses onto the bridge of my nose and blinking at the empty space where my phone should be.

Dammit. Quinn still has it.

What the hell happened last night?

What did I drink?

Too much.

Way too much drinking.

I need coffee.

I can't believe I let her take my phone last night.

No. Wait. Scratch that.

Yes, I can.

There's very little I wouldn't give Quinn if she asked. It's one of the many reasons why I try to keep my distance from her.

And now I share an apartment with her. I glare at my bedroom wall like I have the X-ray vision of the superhero she's nick-named me after and can see her out in the living area.

My head swims as I whip my gaze to the left, my laptop taunting me, tempting me to pull up my profile on the Greet Geek website.

What changes did Quinn make to it?

What did she say about me?

I…

I don't want to look.

Shit.

I need out of this room.

I need out of this room *now*.

Staying here will only lead to more overthinking of the *hows* and *whys* of last night.

Hastily pulling on a rumpled T-shirt and sweats, I beat feet to the bathroom. Then I curse myself around the toothbrush shoved in my mouth for not pulling on socks to protect me from the chill seeping through the soles of said feet as I stand at the sink.

The evolution of last night's events has me choking on Colgate suds. My mind stutters like the rainbow wheel of death that likes to taunt me when my MacBook tries to give me a heart attack.

Freaking Kay—this is *all* her fault. Sure, it was Emma who suggested I agree to be one of my class's Greet Geek users, but it was Kay who pushed me over the undecided line.

She just *had* to go and fall in love with Mason.

You know what?

Mason is actually the one I should blame. Kay was nowhere near this pushy until he inserted himself into our lives. It's because of him that Kay wields new softly uttered sentences to break down more of my walls.

"You know *I* know *how scary it is to put yourself out there."* She typically says this one with a squeeze to my forearm.

"Remember how hard you fought being our friend?" This one usually has her wiggling fingers in my face, making it so the light reflects off the emerald birthstone ring she wears to represent

how important I am in her life. I especially hate when she does that. It makes me all emotional and uncomfortable.

"Sometimes, the risk of stepping outside your comfort zone comes with rewards you never expected." The googly heart eyes she gives Mason—the complete antithesis of any kind of love match she would have ever said she wanted for herself—whenever she says this one could make a person ill with how sickly sweet it is. Thankfully I am usually too busy choking on the implication of that statement to puke.

I can never admit how much Kay's urgings make me want to give in.

It's too much of a risk.

Sure, Kay put her anonymity in jeopardy by being with Mason.

But…

Doing something crazy like admitting my feelings for Quinn…

Yeah, that's only asking for my whole world to blow up. I cannot, absolutely cannot, risk losing my friends by potentially putting them in the position where they would have to choose between one of us. Especially not when I fear I would come out the loser in that scenario.

The rich aroma of coffee drifts beneath the bathroom door, hitting my nose and breaking me from the mental musings chasing me like the ghosts in *Ms. Pac-Man*.

Ugh!

I exit the bathroom and pad down the short hall, my steps coming to an abrupt halt when I find all of my roommates scattered about our living room.

Rubbing the sleep from my eyes, I blink at the scene in front of me, questioning if I fell back asleep or am having some sort of hangover hallucination.

What in the…

Trav twirls side to side, the ends of a neon green and hot pink hibiscus flower Hawaiian print shirt clutched in his hands. "You can't tell me I don't look fly as fuck in this."

Mason groans and chucks one of the throw pillows at him. "We should have never agreed to let you come," he mutters, shifting Kay around on his lap and helping himself to a sip of her coffee.

Kay's awake? How late did I sleep?

Trav dodges the projectile pillow and blows a raspberry at Mason. "You're just jelly I pull this shit off better than you ever could."

"Yeah, that's it," Mason responds dryly.

It's only been a few weeks since the nine of us moved into the penthouse Mason purchased near campus, but scenes like this are quickly becoming the new normal.

"CK!" Trav shouts, perking up at the sight of me. Herkie may be the yellow lab in this house, but Travis McQueen can be like a damn Golden Retriever with all his energy.

Yeah…

I massage the ridge of my brow, desperate for that coffee if I'm going to deal.

"CK," Trav whines, and someone—I think it's Alex—mutters about him being a tantruming toddler not getting attention.

"What's up, Trav?" I drop my hand from my head and force my attention to him.

"Tell your friends to stop being haters."

"My friends?" I arch a pounding-along-with-my-heartbeat brow.

Trav folds his arms across his chest, a look of determination overtaking his features. "I refuse to claim ownership of Mase when he's acting like an asshole."

"And what makes today different from any other day?" My question sets the others off on a series of *oohs* and shouted *burns*.

"The disrespect in this house is unreal," Mason complains, but the smile curling at the edges of his mouth is all I need to see to know he didn't take offense to my teasing.

"You'll live." Kay pats his cheek, then squeals when Mason growls and covers her mouth with his own.

A collective groan filters throughout the room, and more than one person mimes gagging at the lovebirds.

"*Blah!*" A streak of red hair whipping through the air has my gaze tracking to Quinn sitting cross-legged on the floor, her torso folded over her legs from her dramatic flop forward. How do I know it was dramatic? Well…she's now tipped over onto her side, back of her hand pressed to her forehead with a sigh. "*Dios mío.* Get a room."

Distantly I hear Kevin add a deadpan "There's one right

upstairs," but all my attention is homed in on the knee waving around in the air thanks to Quinn's still bent leg. It's all *Look at me! Look at me!*

Dammit!

I *am* looking at it. I'm looking at it and the long bronzed leg with a thick toned thigh and lean calf bracketing it.

Clearing the lust suddenly clogging my throat, I hook a thumb at Kaysonova—their ship name, in case you were wondering—and croak out, "When are those two not sucking face?"

My question garners a round of finger guns from the room because it's true. The PDA in this penthouse is definitely on the high side of the spectrum.

"You fuckers may have jokes, but the only reason Kay and I are even down here and *not*"—Mason arches a brow and points at the open door of the master suite visible in the loft-style floor plan—"up there is *because*"—his finger drops accusatorially at Quinn—"our bed got a bit too crowded this morning."

"Oh shit." Trav rushes toward the wall of glass that makes up the apartment's outer wall, glancing up at the sky with a hand shielding his eyes. "I think I just saw a pig fly." He turns back to the room with a dropped jaw and comically wide eyes.

"What the hell are you going on about?" Mason asks, almost reluctantly.

"What? I'm just saying..." Trav pops a shoulder, lumbering back to the group. "I would have thought we'd see flying swine before we *ever* heard about *the* Casanova complaining about having multiple women in bed with him." He winks, and Mason flips him off while Kay just rolls her eyes.

I'm missing something here...

My gaze bounces around the room, trying to figure out just *what* that something is, but I get distracted by the blush now staining Quinn's cheeks.

"Yeah, right." Emma snorts, attempting to cover the distinctive sound by smothering her face with one of the throw pillows. "I think we could all safely say Mase is too damn *caveman*"—her mouth pulls into a smirk over the edge of the barely lowered pillow at the use of his pet name from Kay—"to share Kay with anyone." She lays the pillow across her lap, angling her body to face Quinn. "Even if that person is our smoking-hot *mamacita*."

Quinn folds her hands over her heart, bunching her shoulders up in an *Aw shucks* manner. "Love you too, booboo." She pops up to her feet and strides over to lay a smacking kiss on Emma's lips.

"Where the hell is my kiss?" Trav flounces the open sides of his shirt out, flexing his muscles in a way that now has Em joining in on the *Toss the Pillow at the Quarterback* game.

Quinn skips over to Trav, who welcomes her with open arms, tugging her in close as she rises up on the tips of her bare toes, which I remember being painted a vibrant turquoise, and presses a kiss to the side of his cheek.

Her open affection is all part of her charm, and the instances when it is turned my way have become my guilty pleasure. I hoard them in my memory because I know nothing will ever actually come from them.

"You guys are in *rare* form this morning." I finally finish making my way into the kitchen, resuming my java mission, searching the cabinet for my preferred mug.

A whiff of coconut floats my way, causing the blood to rush through my veins faster. "They've been like this all morning." Quinn leans in close, the soft curve of her breast pressing tight to my side.

"Kay and Mase?" I step to the side and out of touching distance. Or so I thought.

"*Pfft.*" A bolt of electricity shoots down my spine as Quinn playfully bumps her shoulder into me. "Like you said…" She gives me a conspiratorial smile. "When are those two not sucking face?"

The grin she flashed me is gone as quickly as it appears, and for what feels like the first time since we've met, Quinn seems… nervous around me. She tucks her chin into her chest and starts to fidget with various items on the countertop.

Before I can ponder what she could be nervous about, her smile is back, and she turns toward me, long lashes fluttering—*Is there something in her eye?*—a mug, *my* mug, lifted toward me. "Coffee, Superman?"

I force myself to focus on the image of the original Game Boy printed on the side of the mug and not the woman who has it cradled between her hands, her body heat bleeding into me, that sweet scent of coconut filling my lungs as she angles in another inch closer.

It doesn't work.

Fuck me, she's pretty.

Face scrubbed clean and free of any makeup.

Hair tousled and messy from sleep.

An oversized T-shirt hanging down one arm and exposing the graceful slope of one bronzed shoulder.

Tiny sleep shorts that showcase toned legs better than even her cheer skirt does.

This is torture.

It's like the universe is using this...using *her* to keep me in check, as if it knows I'm getting too comfortable in my new life.

Why? Because every day, I'm confronted with an image similar to this.

Quinn.

Here.

In my house.

Where I live.

With her.

Where she's close enough to touch yet somehow remains just out of reach.

I don't mean physically. I would only have to lift my arm an inch or two, and I could cup a hand over her hip. My fingers would slip under the hem of her shirt, making contact with skin I know from past experience when she's been close is warm and soft.

Except...I can't.

It'll only be a tease.

I may be CK to my friends here, but I'll always be Christopher Kent at my core.

"Aww, look who it is. Little Chrissy Kent, the nerd mascot."

"I didn't know the U of J had an adopt-a-nerd program."

"Do you trade tutoring lessons for pity kisses? We all know that's the only way you'd get anything from a cheerleader."

I squeeze my eyes shut, that memory of how easily I was reminded of that fact when I went home for Christmas still all too fresh. And Quinn Thompson? She firmly and solidly belongs to the CK side of my life—aka the fantasy, *not* the reality.

I know this.

She knows this.

I mean…

Sure, she flirts with me. But…she flirts with everyone. It's just a part of her personality. Remember how she acted with Emma and Trav minutes ago?

Shit.

The Game Boy image starts to blur in front of me, and that's when it clicks.

Dammit. How could I forget again?

Quinn still has my phone.

And…

Fuck! Is that what she was nervous about?

I bet whatever tweaks she made didn't change anything. I bet I *still* don't have any matches for my profile and she's not sure how to break the news to me.

I knew it.

Whatever. It's fine. Quinn can keep my phone for all I care.

Plus…it serves to prove my point that she isn't interested in me *that way*. If she were actually serious about wanting to be with me, she wouldn't have offered to help tweak my dating profile, right?

Are you going to stop staring at the girl like a creeper and take the coffee from her? a voice whispers from the back of my brain.

Quinn's dark eyes widen, and she sucks in a breath when I finally accept my mug from her after a muttered "Thanks." I can't tell if it's from my fingers brushing hers when I do or if it's because she notices that her nipples are poking my chest. She may not, but I sure as shit do.

It may be common for her to be all up close and personal with people, to casually touch them, but it'll never be *normal* to me. The worst part? She is utterly oblivious to what her nearness does to me.

"But I meant Trav." Quinn points at the flapping-the-ends-of-his-shirt-open-and-closed quarterback. "He's spent the last ten minutes subjecting us to his vacation-looks fashion show."

"And with every outfit he struts out in, his obnoxiousness grows," Emma says around a yawn, coming over and reaching out grabby hands for her own coffee, laying her head on the island for the thirty seconds it takes Quinn to prepare it.

"You guys suck," Trav complains, then he bellows for JT, who comes lumbering out of the one guest room we keep for people like him.

"You better get this rude wake-up call shit out of your system before Hawaii—" JT's words break off with a yawn as he scratches at his bare stomach. "Otherwise, I'm asking the hotel staff to put me on the other side of the resort from the quarterbacks."

"Quarterbacks? As in plural?" Kay asks as JT plops down beside her and Mason.

JT gives her a look. "You're trying to tell me B wouldn't be just as bad as this one?" He bounces a finger at Trav as he references Ben Turner, the quarterback of the Baltimore Crabs.

"Good point," Kay concedes. She knows Ben better than any of us, seeing as he's both teammates and best friends with her older brother Eric.

Massaging my temples, I pray for the Advil I took to kick in faster. I'm going to need all my faculties to deal with the way the four of them are now clamoring to talk over the other.

"You guys are going to be so bored without all of us here," Emma muses, propping her chin on her fist.

I jolt, a sudden realization washing over me.

Em has family obligations to fulfill this summer.

Kay, Mason, and Trav are going on vacation with Kay's family —JT included.

Grant is hopping a train for the Bronx tomorrow, his mama ready and waiting for both her boys to be home to spoil.

And Kevin and Alex are headed to DC to help Noah get settled in before he has to report to training camp.

Sure, we'll still see them, and they'll be around periodically, but…

For the most part…

Everyone is leaving.

Everyone *except* Quinn and me.

"Oh, I don't know…" Again Quinn steps into my personal space, this time to reach up to smooth hair away from my face. "I think we can find ways to entertain ourselves."

Why does she always have to touch me?

Why do I have to like it so much?

More importantly, why do I want to ask her to never stop?

It's dumb. Pure stupidity. My IQ and grade point average tell me I'm smarter than that.

Yet...I want to.

Then I remember, again, the lack of responses—as in none—from Greet Geek. If I'm being rejected by my own kind, it's impossible to even consider trying to date someone like Quinn.

It's one thing to be rejected by countless faceless women. But rejection from Quinn? I doubt I would survive.

So...

No.

Nope. I'll rein in my crazy and keep my feelings to myself. Sorry, Kay. I know you found your happy and only want the same for me, but some risks just aren't worth taking.

#THEGRAM

#CHAPTER5

UofJ411: *REPOSTED—CasaNova87: Talk all the shit you want about me being wifed up, but how can I not love the crap out of this chick? #ShesAllMine #LuckyToCallHerMine—picture of Mason mooning over Kay*
Gah! The way our @CasaNova87 looks at her is everything *heart eyes emoji* #Kaysonova #CasanovaWatch #CoupleGoals
@therandybookworm: I swear this man just gets hotter and hotter #CasanovaWatch
@the_librariansdaughter: *fire emoji* *drool emoji*
@Maggs328: She's got that love lockdown #WeddingBellsAnyone

UofJ411: *REPOSTED—TheBarracksAtNJA: When our legends like @CheerGodJT bring their friends to work, things get interesting—reel of Kay, Em, and Quinn working on stunts at The Barracks*
Anyone else hoping these two can convince @CasaNova87 queen to join the Red Squad? #CasanovaWatch #Kaysonova #WeWantThatNationalTitle
@mimi_reads: Is she coming out of retirement? #AskingForAFriend
@ramblings_of_a_bookbrat: Damn, that's impressive. #LookAtThoseStunts
@katslovesbooks: I mean...don't you wanna cheer on your man? #FootballPlayersAndCheerleaders #Kaysonova

UofJ411: *picture of everyone sitting around a table at Jonas*
Rumor has it, this is the last meal these new roomies will be sharing
before most of them go their separate ways for the summer
#TellUsYourPlans #ComeBackSoon
@the_romance_reader_gal: Aww, look at how cute @CasaNova87
and his BAE are. #CoupleGoals #Kaysonova #CasanovaWatch
@amandashaner17: I heard @QB1McQueen7 got teary-eyed in his
goodbye speech to @LacesOutMitchell5 #WeWillMissYouGoldenToe
#TeammatesForever

**UofJ411: *REPOSTED—CasaNova87: Aloha vacation!
#FriendsAndFamily #MaiTaiMadness #MakingMemories—
boomerang of a group of glasses toasting***
It may be summer break, but we'll still have updates on all your
campus faves #NoRestForTheWicked #WeSeeYou #CasanovaWatch

**UofJ411: *REPOSTED—LacesOutMitchell: Stopping for
sustenance on the way down to DC with my boys
#CityOfBrotherlyLove #WelcomeToPhilly
#TheBromanceNeverDies—picture of Noah, Alex, and Kevin
mid-bite***
Anyone else in the mood for a cheesesteak? #nomnomnom
@mamakate1873: Who's up for a road trip? #FootballPlayerFinder
@simplygraceplanning: I make a mean playlist. #RadioDJ
@prykegirl119: I grab the snacks #LoadedUpWithGoodies

QUINN

"MIJA!" My *abuelita's* signature fuchsia-painted lips spread into a megawatt smile the second my face comes into focus on the screen. I love how not even technology can take away the impact of the happiness and love radiating off her. *"Como estás?"*

The familiar husky lyrical lilt of *Abuela Lupe's* voice infuses my system, washing away the stress I've been carrying these last few days.

This is what I needed.

For close to a week, I've been on tenterhooks waiting to see what would come from my drunken meddling. Of course, it doesn't help that I have absolutely no idea what exactly that meddling was.

Freaking universe. Couldn't throw a girl a bone? Seriously, Jesus, I thought I was your homegirl.

Dammit, Kay. Why couldn't you wield your skill for picking the perfect punny shirt for a person to guess their passwords? What good does a T-shirt that professes being besties with the son of God do when it doesn't yield results in our time of need?

I'm usually not one to complain when a person willingly chooses to add to my wardrobe, but fashion is not the area I needed help in. Nope. It was the passcode for CK's phone I needed.

Shit. Maybe we should have had a *Star Wars* binge for our last few movie nights because my pint-sized friend could have taken a few notes from Mr. Luke Skywalker if we did. Didn't she know I needed her to be my only hope? And you know what happened? *Chica* failed.

Yup...I totally don't feel guilty about waking Kay up the other morning. If I have to suffer, she has to suffer. Misery loves company and all that.

Except...

Now I'm all alone, my friends have scattered around the country, and I still don't know if Emma was correct or not. Did I or did I not declare my undying love for CK all over a dating app?

I don't think pimping out your crush to your fellow co-eds is what Kay meant when she said you would have to be the one to make a move if you wanted CK.

Ugh! That particular thought is not the *least* bit helpful.

Whatever. What's done is done. Daddy likes to say if you lie with dogs, you get up with fleas. Welp, in my case, it's if I drink the tequila, I'll wake up with competition I inadvertently invited in to play for CK's heart.

Rapid-fire Spanish flows between *Abuelita* and me as we fill each other in on all the things that have transpired in the days since we last spoke.

Unlike when I talk to *Mamá*, there are no pointed digs or leading questions about if I'm making the most of my time being around all the elite athletes at my school. Questions like those are why I don't feel comfortable using the fancy video chat system installed on the large flat-screen TV in the living room and opt to use my iPad and AirPods. The quickest way to find myself homeless would be for Mason and Kay to think I'm using them to social climb.

When Mason first broached the subject of us all moving in together, I didn't hesitate to accept his plan for our new living arrangements. Having our own place off campus instead of the dorms allows me to hang around Jersey for the summer and avoid *some* of those less-than-pleasant parental conversations.

Abuelita is getting up there in age. She doesn't need the added stress or increased blood pressure a dust-up with her daughter would incur.

Ay. I can still hear the faint echoes of their last fight.

"Quinn es mi nieta," Abuela Lupe shouted as she thrust an arm out in my direction.

"Sí, Mamá, y ella es mi hija," Mom retorted as she squared off against her mother.

I stood rooted to the spot, my gaze ping-ponging between them as they fought.

Abuelita's body goes in and out of frame as she moves around the kitchen of my childhood home. I hate how a place that once held so many of my best memories is now tainted, stained by the harshness of her parting shot from that day. *"Sí, y pensé que te crié mejor que eso."*

Even now, I have to dig my knuckles into my chest against the pang of regret it causes.

I shake my head to rid myself of the melancholy before it can really set in. We may not be together, cooking side by side like we were last summer, but I let the familiar soundtrack of the snick of knives hitting cutting boards and the sizzle of oil heating in a pan chase the last of my blues away.

Now's not the time to be thinking about how witnessing the two most important women in my life fighting *because of me* made me feel. Not unless I want to listen to yet another lecture from *Abuelita* about the importance of living my life for me and nobody else.

"Sonofabitch." Salsa flies in a red arc across the kitchen when I jump at the sudden shadow stepping into my peripheral.

Forgetting all about the now-empty bowl clutched in my grip, I slap my hand to my chest, the glass causing me to grunt from the impact.

Holy shit.

My pulse is erratic, and I rip one of the AirPods from my ear, cursing them for making it possible for me to be snuck up on.

"I'm sorry." The apology from CK is quick to come and wholly unnecessary. It's not his fault.

I lift my gaze, about to tell him as much when the words die on my tongue, my mouth suddenly going dry at the sight in front of me.

Ay dios mío.

Gone are his glasses, those bright cerulean blues completely unobstructed from view, hitting me with their full impact.

Sweat dots his hairline, falling from his dark, disheveled locks and making me suspect he must have come from the gym located in our building.

A furrow pulls between CK's dark brows as I stare at him like a lust-drunk fool.

To be fair, that's precisely what I am. It's like I'm one giant hormone. The longer I stand here and stare, the closer I get to grabbing my pom-poms from my bedroom in the hopes that if I shake them hard enough, maybe he'll *finally* hear the *Oh my god, will you just kiss me already* plea my body pretty much sings whenever he's near.

The veins of his arms stand out in stark relief, roping down and over the muscles still swollen from his workout, taunting me to run my fingers over them like braille.

The silence grows between us as my gaze tracks lower, my breathing hitching as I take in the sweat-soaked material of the shirt clinging to his torso. There's a darker panel of gray running down the center of his chest, bisected by a ragged slash of, you guessed it, red salsa.

"Oh shit." I ignore the halfhearted chastising ringing through the one AirPod still in my ear at my cussing and round the kitchen island with a dish towel in hand.

The diagonal line of salsa starts just under CK's armpit and cuts at a downward angle across his stomach.

I should have stayed on my side of the counter, because the second the terrycloth makes contact with the mess I made, my brain stutters to a stop.

Channeling their inner Carrie Underwood, my hormones make like Jesus and take the wheel.

My palm flattens, making as much contact as humanly possible with the hard chest beneath it, my fingers flexing to dig in harder when CK sucks in a shuddering breath.

Somewhere in the deep recesses of my brain, I have enough presence of mind to maintain my grip on the towel. Then, with it firmly in hand, I use it as an excuse to feel up CK in a way he would never normally allow.

His shirt is one of those tanks with the drop arm cutouts, allowing my fingertips to make direct contact. There's a slickness to the warm skin, and I don't know what it says about me that I want to lick him.

I run my thumb over the bumps of his ribs before dragging the towel along the reddish-brown stain, brushing away the chunkier pieces of tomato and onion clinging to the cotton.

He may not be as bulky as the other guys who live with us, but I'm still able to make the ridges of a…

Two…

Four…

Six!

You're telling me he has a freaking six-pack hidden under his clothes?

Something brushes my bare foot, and I jump, only to realize it's the towel pooling on top of it.

When did I drop that?

Oh shit!

I probably dropped it around the same time I brought my other hand around to join in on the muscle counting.

Inhaling a deep breath, I attempt to get my undersexed, touchy-feely self under control, but it backfires in spectacular fashion.

Why?

Because instead of bringing with it the pungent scent of body odor, all I get is the musky scent of his sweat. Of course, CK doesn't smell like BO. That would be too easy. At least I'm not already overwhelmingly attracted to him or anything.

Oh…

Wait…

Yes, I am.

"Do you want a taste of me?"

CK's eyes widen, and his cheeks pinken. What is he embarrassed—

Dios santo!

Please tell me I didn't ask him if he wanted to taste me.

"I mean, do you want a taste of the *chilaquiles* I *made*?" I all but shout.

Distantly I register the husky timbre of *Abuelita's* laughter, but it's drowned out by the booming beat of my heart.

Madre mía!

I'm forever bumbling over my words when it comes to this

man. It's been less than twenty-four hours since the last of our roommates departed, and already I'm inadvertently coming on to CK.

I mean, sure...do I want him to *taste* me? Uh—*yeah!* I'd strip naked and lay myself out on this counter, right here, right now, if I thought it would put an end to the tension that's thick enough to scoop with my homemade tortilla chips.

How the hell am I supposed to survive the summer without the buffer of our friends?

#CHAPTER7

I WANT to say the saliva filling my mouth stems from the rich aroma of spices and savory meat lingering in the air, but that wouldn't be the whole truth.

No, the other half of the equation is the woman currently standing in front of me, trailing her hands down my body like she's studying the topography of my torso.

Fuck me.

Quinn touching me always ends up causing all kinds of below-the-belt issues for me. I'm a twenty-year-old man and routinely find myself praying for impotence in an effort not to embarrass myself.

What the hell is wrong with me?

"Do you want a taste of me?"

What the fuck did she just ask me?

"*Dios santo!*" she whispers, and my penile problems only continue to grow.

Sonofabitch. It's hot as fuck whenever her Spanish slips out. There's just something sensual about the way it rolls off her tongue.

Quinn jumps in place, whipping around, the bowl that used

to hold the salsa I'm now sporting like a fashion accessory clanging on the counter as she hastily scrambles to pick up a white serving platter. "I mean, do you want a taste of the *chilaquiles* I *made*?" The way she practically shouts the question at me has the first vestiges of a smile tugging at the corners of my mouth.

My dick twitches as if looking for an answer buzzer. If it were up to him, he would reply *I'd like to choose option one for a thousand, Alex.* Clearly, I watched one too many episodes of *Jeopardy* with Gramps growing up.

Luckily, my stomach is the faster contestant, beating out that wayward piece of my anatomy by rumbling loud enough for the whole room to hear.

Thank god, because I'm not sure what would have come out of my mouth if I tried to use actual words to answer. Though, honestly, I should be used to it by now. Wondering if my hormones will finally stage a revolt and cause my brain-to-mouth filter to fail is a daily worry.

And right now? Yeah...I'm a hairbreadth away from that actually happening because yes...

No...

Wait...

Scratch that—the answer is an unequivocal *fuck yes*, I want to taste Quinn.

The number of times I've fantasized about doing so, about swiping my tongue across her plump lips to discover the flavor of her lip gloss, about suckling on those nipples that live to torture me to see if it's possible to return the favor or lapping at her center until she's a writhing mess while satiating my need for her is unquantifiable.

"CK?" Quinn asks, a furrow forming between her brows.

"Oh." I grip the back of my neck, my hand sliding across the sweat coating it. "Um...sure...I'd love some."

Dammit. My cheeks heat, and I pray she'll attribute it to my workout and not my rising stress level regarding coming across as some creeper who stares.

A beaming smile overtakes Quinn's face, and she lets out a squeal, bouncing up and down on her toes, the plate knocking into my stomach in her excitement.

"Shit, sorry," I say, rocking back on my heels because, of course, I haven't moved away. Why am I so awkward with her?

Quinn giggles, happiness radiating off her like it always does. "I should probably put this down before you end up wearing the entire meal."

She sets the dish down, muttering a "Hush you" as she circles the counter, leaning onto her elbows and sending a pointed glare at the propped-up iPad. "No one asked you," she adds, or at least I think that's what she said; my Spanish isn't as fluent as Em's.

Quinn's dark eyes flit my way before she rolls them and returns her attention to the iPad. "Yeah, yeah, yeah, *te amo*." She pauses a beat and finishes with an "*Adios*."

I feel another smile forming as her cheeks puff out like a blowfish, and I have to snap an arm out, laying my hand down to stop the AirPod she sends bouncing down the granite.

"*Abuelita?*" I jerk my chin at the iPad, my pronunciation far less perfect than Quinn's hypnotic flow.

"The old bat is such a smartass." A grin tugs at her lips, removing all complaint from her words.

"You say that like we don't live in a houseful of smartasses," I comment before inhaling a whiff of the utter deliciousness she places in front of me.

Sure, I can admit that there are many, *many* things that make it difficult for me to live with Quinn, but her propensity for taking over the kitchen and cooking up all kinds of delicious culinary feasts is not one of them.

"Oh my god, Q." I groan, an explosion of flavors bursting along my tongue as the homemade tortilla rips between my teeth.

"Good?" The way her eyebrows rise high on her forehead could make a person think Quinn is actually worried about me liking the dish, but the rolled back set of her shoulders gives away her confidence.

This chick can cook, and she sure as shit knows it. That doesn't stop me from covering my mouth with a hand and mumbling, "So good," as I enjoy the spicy heat of diced jalapeños and the soothing chill of the sour cream.

"And yes…" Quinn picks up our earlier vein of conversation as she starts to busy herself by cleaning up. "We may live with more than half a dozen people who could all double major in sarcasm, but"—she leans forward, close enough that the warmth of her breath blows across my cheek, her eyes dancing with humor—"*Abuela Lupe* gives me shit in two languages." She wiggles two fingers in my face, my blood heating more from the small taps of her fingertips on my chin than from the hot peppers mixed into each bite of the meal I'm consuming.

"Em does in three languages," I point out after swallowing down both another bite of *chilaquiles* and the healthy dose of lust her touch inspired.

"It's actually four when you factor in that she also knows how to sign."

I nod. "Our friend is full of hidden talents."

"What an overachiever. Bless her heart."

I snort, sinus cavities instantly burning, eyes immediately watering as a pepper shoots up and out my nose at the Texan–Valley girl tone Quinn adopts.

"Thanks." I accept the outstretched napkin. "So…" I cough, clearing away the last of the misplaced food. "How come you didn't use that for your call?" I gesture to the television hanging in the living room behind me. If she had, I wouldn't have accidentally scared her.

A tightness forms around Quinn's eyes, but it happens so fast it was probably just a trick of the light. "Eh, it's easier to talk while I cook if I have *Abuelita* right here." She frames out a space on the island with her hands. "It also lets me pretend she's standing next to me like she would be if I were home."

"Do you regret choosing to not go home for the summer?"

No one was more shocked than I was when Quinn announced she would also be staying in Jersey for the summer. My family may not be why I'm avoiding going home, but Quinn is *über*close with hers. She talks to her *abuelita* almost daily.

"Not really." She shrugs. "The summer classes I'm taking will help make my workload easier for when cheering starts again." Her mouth opens like she's going to continue, but she clamps it shut instead.

That's odd. Quinn is always so open. The fact that it feels like she's not telling me the whole story is…strange. Especially so when she opts for a subject change.

"Besides the gym"—her gaze takes another pass over my

sweat-soaked shirt—"what else do you have planned for the day?"

"Not much," I offer with a shrug as my phone buzzes on the counter, drawing our attention to it.

The easy smirk on Quinn's pretty face slips when she spots the bright blue Greet Geek notification lighting the screen.

My muscles bunch, my shoulders drawing tight as the unexpected elephant in the room sits between them. Neither of us has broached the subject of how she revamped the dating profile I was coerced into creating, or how those tweaks have garnered responses I hadn't previously received.

Except…

None of the interactions have yielded anything more than a handful of texts before they all inevitably peter out. Rehabilitating a profile on screen is one thing. Following through and living up to what was advertised is entirely another.

The silence in the room grows until it's its own physical entity, with only the occasional squeak of the chew toy Herkie is working on decimating to break it up. It's a three-way standoff with my cell phone, like Quinn and I have been transported into one of those old John Wayne movies Gramps is such a fan of.

"I take it whatever I did worked?" Quinn twists and pulls at her fingers to the point of her knuckles popping.

It probably makes me a special kind of asshole, finding comfort in her unease, but I can't help it. She is typically beyond confident in everything she does. Witnessing little pockets of uncertainty like this or her earlier flub of words proves she may actually be human beneath her high ponytail and oversized bow.

"Sort of." I blow out a breath, raking a hand through my hair and gripping the damp strands.

"Way to give a nonanswer, Superman." Quinn winks, her playfulness returning, though it does nothing to help ease the frustration brewing in my gut.

"I don't get it."

"What don't you get?" It should be a crime for Quinn to sound as calm as she does in the wake of my growly aggravation.

I wave a hand at my phone. "You utilized the writing

prompts from the app in a way that has had people messaging me—"

I think she mumbles, "Great," but since I don't address it, I'm almost certain it was some kind of wishful-thinking hallucination on my part.

"—but those conversations never manage to last more than a few text exchanges before they peter out."

I should probably get my ears checked with all these auditory delusions because now I'm pretty sure the squeal I just heard came from Quinn and not Herkie's toy.

"Umm…" Once again, Quinn glances around as if avoiding any eye contact, the kitchen suddenly becoming her sole focus.

My mouth opens to ask her what she was going to say, only to have it go dry as I watch her hurry around cleaning up the mess she made while cooking.

Holy shit. Just kill me now.

Sure, I'm used to seeing Quinn in the *I love cooking with wine… sometimes I even put it in the food* apron Kay gifted her with this past Christmas.

But…

That was mainly in the cooler months.

Now we're solidly into summer.

Why? Why does women's fashion have to trend toward smaller pieces of clothing to combat the heat and humidity of the weather? How am I ever going to survive living with Quinn when her summer wardrobe sometimes makes it look like she's naked beneath her apron?

Fuck me.

The last thing I need is anything actively making me think about Quinn naked. My imagination certainly manages that feat enough all on its own, thank you very much.

Hell, last night, I had to jerk off in the shower—twice—just to be able to lie down in my bed. It was either that or digging a hole in my mattress for my incessant boner to fit in.

Though I could do without the prickle of guilt that came from it. Why is whacking off to thoughts of your friend, your *roommate*, different than porn?

You might want to figure out how to get over that guilt; otherwise, you'll end up with an ulcer by the end of the summer.

I can't even argue with the chastising from my conscience. I thought last night's bright green camisole—or whatever you call those silky tank tops girls wear—was bad with only skinny straps curving over Quinn's bronzed shoulders. But today's body-hugging strapless yellow sundress?

Like I said: *fuck me.*

At least yesterday I could glance at Quinn's shoulders to snap me out of the raunchy musings my mind concocted while watching her dance around the kitchen cooking—not that it did much good. My hand still spent more time adjusting my pants to hide my unabating boner than it did lifting my fork to my mouth to eat the enchiladas Grant requested for his last night here before returning home. Talk about awkward as fuck.

Today I have no hope. Whenever Quinn turns to face me, my mind automatically forgets there's clothing beneath the well-worn and slightly stained from being abundantly used apron.

The scrape of a chair across the tile floor has my gaze snapping up to see Quinn settling into one of the barstools next to me. I pray it's because of her efficiency, not that I was lost inside my head so long that the kitchen is now clean.

Oh good, she took off the apron.

Because that dress is any better? my dick perks up to say.

Sonofabitch.

"You were starting to say something before," I prompt, effectively ignoring the sometimes-you-make-me-wonder-if-it-would-be-easier-to-be-a-eunuch appendage trying to stretch the limits of my mesh shorts.

"I was." Again Quinn's gaze isn't focused on me but instead on the steady drum of her fingers on the countertop. "But before I tell you, you have to promise not to judge me, because if you're gonna judge *any*body, it should be Em, because that biotch is the tequila instigator in this family."

Ah, yes, family.

You hear that, you horny motherfucker? I ask my dick. *We have a family here, one we cannot risk because you want to know what Quinn feels like on the inside.*

"That's debatable."

Quinn's dark eyes fly up to me, her jaw unhinged. "Oh my god, Superman." She pushes me on the shoulder, my skin prickling from the playful touch. "Did you just joke with me?"

My cheeks heat to the point that she could use them for cooking her next meal, and I dip my chin. "We joke around."

The flat press of Quinn's lips tells me she's less than impressed by my sullen teenager tone. "Not like you do with Em and Kay." She folds her arms over her chest. "Most of the time, you treat me like I have cooties." Her glare dares me to challenge her. "I promise you I've had my shot." She uncrosses her arms and draws two circles and two dots on her forearm.

I go to speak, but she throws her hands up to stop me. She draws another set of circles on her skin, then follows it up with two squares before finally holding her arms out to the side. "There, now you know I also have it everywhere."

I want to tell her she forgot the one with two lines that declares she'll have it for all time, but I refrain. For as much as she gives me shit for not treating her like our other friends, I simply can't. A close friendship with Quinn is just a slippery slope to getting my heart crushed by the inevitable rejection.

"Anyway…" She lays a hand on my forearm, leaving it there to see if I'll allow her recently confirmed cootie-free touch to stay. I do because I'm clearly a glutton for punishment. "I don't actually remember what I wrote in your profile." She chews on the end of her thumbnail.

"You're telling me I just blew my opportunity for you to forget about hounding me about putting myself out there by bringing the subject up myself?"

There's a beat of silence as Quinn freezes before she doubles over in laughter, her long red hair whipping me both on the way down and when she straightens. "Yeah, oh-kay." She wipes under an eye. "Because there's not like this many"—she wiggles all ten of her fingers—"people or so who would be asking or anything."

I concede with a nod. This is what I get for allowing Kay and everyone to force their friendship on me. Haven't these people heard of boundaries?

Without warning, Quinn scoops my phone from the counter. "No passcode needed, bitches," she singsongs as she thrusts my phone at my face to unlock it the same way she did the night she appointed herself as my matchmaker. I rub at the end of my nose and narrow my eyes as she throws her arms up in victory.

Jaw working side to side, lips periodically pursing, Quinn

hums, wiggling around on the stool as her fingers scroll through my phone, utterly unconcerned about the invasion of privacy. See what I mean about boundaries?

After two solid minutes of perusing my phone, Quinn's chest expands with a deep inhalation, and her shoulders release from their hitched state. I'd almost think she was nervous about what she could have said, but she's probably the most *I don't give a fuck what you think of me* lady of the trio that lives here, so I highly doubt that's it.

She twists around, her body contorting so she can look toward the dining room behind her, and calls out, "Alright, Jose, we can keep you. We are quite clever when we chill, if I do say so myself." She even goes as far as to toast the tequila brand with an imaginary glass, holding an empty fist in the air.

See what I mean? Zero hint of embarrassment if she's acting a fool. She owns who she is and lives life to the fullest.

Unlike me.

Her thumb is back to scrolling, pausing every so often, then tapping here and there.

What is she doing?

Please, God, don't let her be reading my messages. I don't need her to see my awkwardness in text.

"Can you stop," she scolds, holding my phone out farther when I try taking it back. "I'm basking in my awesomeness."

"Okay, now you sound like Trav."

"*Mierda*, don't talk to me about Shark Bait right now." She makes a cross with her pointer fingers, hissing at me like I'm Dracula.

"Shark Bait?" I ask, doing my damnedest to shift subtly in my seat to avoid her noticing my reaction to her Spanish curse.

"Don't even get me started." She slashes a hand through the air. "But"—she all but clucks her tongue, snapping the T sound—"I would like the record to show that if Mr. Quarterback ruins my chances of getting to stunt with *the* JT Taylor when they all get back from their little *National Lampoon's Vacation*, I will take a page out of Kay's book and shave him *bald* when they come home."

Her threat has me rubbing one of my eyebrows, remembering the story about the time Kay and Tessa Taylor shaved off JT's and Eric's.

"It's too early for shots, so careful with the fangirling," I joke, referring to the drinking game Kay insisted we invent because of Quinn's over-the-top cheer crush on her old stunt partner. It's either that or focus on the slimy and highly inappropriate jealousy I feel toward my friend over something he never asked for.

JT's better suited for her anyway.

Yeah, even I can't argue with myself about that one.

"Don't tempt me with a good time, mister." Quinn shakes a finger in front of my face. "I have to leave for The Barracks soon." The scowl she tries to put on melts after two seconds, then she's all boobs jiggling and panting breaths as she tries to scoot her stool closer to mine without getting off of it.

Stop staring at her chest. Your mama raised you better than that.

I drop my gaze from her bouncing bosom to her bare knees slipping around mine, but that's not any better. Nope, because as she spreads them enough to fit my leg in the V of hers, the hem of her skirt inches higher and higher.

"Now stop trying to distract me." She slaps my thigh, the muscle spasming beneath the playful touch. "These writing prompts"—the phone she's still somehow managed to not relinquish control of dances in her grip—"are meant to be icebreakers, a fun way to let somebody new learn something about you in a way that doesn't feel like pulling teeth." The arch of her brow adds the *Like you are with me* she politely refrains from tacking on.

"I get that." Her slow blink tells me *Uh-huh.* "I do," I challenge, her lips twisting to the side, clearly not believing me at all. Might as well get straight to the point. The sooner I do, the sooner I can escape to my room, putting an end to this uncomfortable inquisition and gaining some much-needed distance from an unattainable temptation.

"Can I ask you a question?"

"I love that you're asking permission like I have a choice in the matter," I deadpan, more than used to how my friends—especially the ladies—run roughshod over anybody when they're curious about something.

"Oh, be still my beating heart, Superman." I get a *You silly man* nudge as she really vamps it up, deepening her drawl. "I don't know how much more of this playful side of you I can take until I burst like a glitter-filled piñata."

I move to stand, but that only causes her to latch on to my arm like some kind of bubbly barnacle.

"Don't run away." The plea swimming in her dark eyes is the one that has had me doing precisely what she's accusing me of on multiple occasions because of how much power it could wield over me.

"I thought you said you have work."

Yes, work at a cheerleading gym because she is a cheerleader.

"I see what you're doing." She narrows her eyes but glances at the clock on the stove then curses softly.

Sweet freedom is in sight. It's so close I can practically taste the cool water spilling from the showerhead, the bathroom my sanctuary.

"Well, Mr. Smartypants, it seems once again you are correct and have somehow weaseled your way out of exploring *this*"— her expression shifts, crinkles creasing the ridge of her brow, her nostrils flaring like she smelled something foul—"further."

My prayers have been answered.

"But…"

Her pointed pause as she starts to walk away has me on guard. It takes everything in me not to cover my balls as if she's about to hit me with a junk punch despite the distance expanding between us.

"I'll help you practice evolving your conversation skills."

She mutters under her breath, but she does it in Spanish and is too far away for me to make out anything more than the lyrical rolling of Rs.

Still…something akin to premonition causes goose bumps to rise on my skin.

I walk over to Herkie, who's still chowing down on the couch. "I know your name isn't Toto, bud." His furry blond head tilts as it rises. "But maybe I would have been safer back in Kansas?"

Dozens of childhood bullies are starting to look like they might be small potatoes compared to one feisty cheerleader.

QUINN

THE BAREST HINT of light peeks through the slats in the built-in blinds, but I can't hold out any longer. Sure, what I'm about to do may incite a revolt and have my friends boarding planes, trains, or automobiles to murder me in my sleep, but it's a risk I'm just going to have to take for the sake of my sanity.

For reals, they will have to forgive me if they want me to continue to be their roommate. Because if I don't finally give in to the urge to text them, I'll be moving out of the penthouse and into a padded room somewhere.

I swear to Christ, the butterflies in my stomach must have called to the coffee flowing through my bloodstream like Snow White singing for woodland creatures. But, instead of collecting helpers to clean, they gathered up every lingering molecule of caffeine they could get their grabby little wings on. Seriously, those bitches have not stopped fluttering since I left the kitchen *yesterday*.

"Aren't you tired yet?" I lift the hand I have pressed to my belly, pointedly ignoring the eyebrow-scrunching head tilt Herkie gives me. And yes, dogs can totally eyebrow scrunch.

My canine companion flops back against me, more than

content to bask in the butt scratches I'm giving him with my other hand.

If only those butterflies weren't suspiciously unresponsive. Nope, they all but ignore me entirely in favor of hosting a rave in my gut.

"I'm totally screwed, Herk," I say to the pooch, not giving a single fuck that he's a dog. At least he acknowledges me, his nose pressing into my armpit as he readjusts his furry body to make eye contact. I'm going to miss having him around once Kay returns from vacation.

I know yesterday was one of the first times CK joked around with me—just me—without running away, but...*damn*. If this is the result of witnessing such a miracle, I'm going to be a frazzled basket case before the week is over.

Okay. That's it. I'm doing it. I'm risking life and limb and texting Em and Kay.

ME: I NEED YOU GUYS!

ME: CAW-CAW BITCHES!

I wait precisely point eight seconds before following up those two messages with a *caw-caw* GIF as a third. Doing some quick mental math, I figure I might get lucky and not get reamed out by Kay, since it's only midnight in the middle of the Pacific Ocean.

Otherwise, I might as well have handed her the pen to sign my death warrant.

KAY: OMG. *"Do you have a death wish?" GIF* Tell *Abuela Lupe* if I wasn't still awake from tonight's luau, she'd be planning your funeral right now.

Oh, man, Kay is totally my favorite. I've said it before, but I'll say it again—she was the best roomie reco ever!

EM: Is it wrong that I am HIGHLY amused by this?

KAY: WTF? I KNOW I WASN'T SLEEPING, BUT YOU'RE

SUPPOSED TO BE ON MY SIDE! A.M. HOURS ARE THE DEVIL'S PLAYGROUND!

I chuckle as Emma takes the brunt of Kay's ire and watch as more of those three dots dance on the screen.

EM: Calm your shouty capitals, woman! *Bad Boys* "Woooosaaahhh" GIF* I'm not saying I wouldn't help you hide the body for the obscene hour she chose to message us at. (If you're reading this, Matthew, thanks for picking up coffee this morning and just ignore the murder threats. Dad doesn't need to know, mmkay.)

Obscene? It's after six in the morning, our time. These non-morning people make me laugh.

KAY: Are you laughing at me? I swear I hear you laughing at me. If you are, I hope you snorted and now have butter pecan latte coming out of your nose. *"I said what I said" GIF*

ME: Who the hell is Matthew? And wait…you're already up, Em? *"Oh, shucks" GIF*

It's probably not wise to tease my unexpected ally, but if you can't tease your friends, how good of friends are you really?

KAY: Matthew is the name of the security guard she's stuck with when she's traveling with her dad's campaign. Em SWEARS he spies on her conversations.

EM: OMG, he TOTALLY does.

KAY: Just because he showed up at ONE Royal Ball does not mean he reads your text messages.

I know I texted them about something for myself, but seeing the name given to the parties Carter King—one of Kay's friends from home and Emma's refuses-to-admit-she-wants-him sorta-crush—has my Spidey senses tingling with this new piece of information.

Unfortunately—or fortunately, depending on how you wanna look at it—Em's text comes in before I can finish composing mine.

EM: Carter King is NOT a topic that can be discussed this early in the day…or ever.

KAY: Uh-huh, whatever you say, babes. I wonder if King says the same about you. Hold on, let me ask JT.

EM: KAYLA MICHELLE DENNINGS, DON'T YOU FUCKING DARE.

ME: Have I told you bitches how much I miss you lately?

KAY: Yes, but in the future, maybe refrain from doing so in the middle of the night.

ME: Middle of the night? It's MIDNIGHT. That barely constitutes a.m. hours.

EM: Did you not get your infusion of vitamin D today? *eggplant emoji*

ME: You might be onto something, Em-babes. She does get cranky when she doesn't get laid.

KAY: *"Grrr" GIF* I hate you guys.

ME: No, you don't.

EM: *"Fact" GIF* Peep your fingers if you need a reminder.

KAY: You assholes are lucky you each share a birthday month with somebody else I love; otherwise, I may have had to "lose" your birthstone bands in the ocean.

ME: Chillax, *mami*. We just want to make sure you're using ALL of your Caveman's athletic prowess to the fullest. *Ace Ventura humping the air GIF*

EM: *"Get it, gurl" dancing GIF*

ME: *The Waterboy* "You can do it" GIF*

EM: *Brad Pitt dancing GIF*

KAY: Guys, this is Mason. Can you stop poking the bear? Skit looks about three seconds away from her head spinning around like that chick in *The Exorcist*.

ME: Hey, Caveman! *"Hey there" GIF* But maybe scroll up in the convo for a bit, THEN let us know if you really want us to leave her alone *wink emoji*

KAY: I knew there was a reason I made sure you both could still be roommates with my girl. Okay…proceed.

Kay may not have wanted to date Mason when he initially pursued her, but homeboy is a winner in my book.

With the break in this conversation's unexpected detour, I let my fingers fly across the screen of my phone. There's nothing elegant, prolific, or even grammatically correct about how I tell them about everything that went down with CK yesterday. I pretty much word-vomit a freaking term paper's worth of details in one long run-on sentence.

My heart jumps into my throat like it's practicing stunts with the Red Squad as I wait to see what my friends have to say.

It doesn't take them long, their texts practically tripping over themselves in their haste to respond. My thumb can barely scroll fast enough to keep up with the flurry of messages moving the thread.

Here are some of the highlights:

EM: Well, at least you didn't confess your undying love like you feared.

KAY: Puh-lease. I love CK dearly, but that boy is so blind to how awesome he truly is, he wouldn't believe it if she did.

EM: Is it wrong I kinda want her to sign up for the app and catfish her way into making him fall in love with her?

KAY: If it is, then I don't want to be right. *crying laughing emoji*

I don't know why I waited to reach out, why I didn't text them right away. Lord knows it would have saved some of my stomach lining if I did.

Any time I really get down on myself, venting and purging to them—typically in drunken *Woe is me* fashion—they *never* make me feel like I'm crazy. Instead, they remind me how it's sort of become a running joke in our crew that anyone close to CK had to force their friendship on him.

I get it, given his history. He's practically been conditioned to dislike and mistrust all manner of jock.

It's kind of ironic how one of the reasons behind my mother signing me up for cheer was to make me *more* desirable of a love match, yet the guy I'm crushing on sees it as a negative.

Still…if two of the three people closest to CK don't think I'm off my rocker for holding on to my crush, who am I to give up?

ME: I'm not catfishing him.

EM: *Mean Girls* "Boo, you whore" GIF*

I don't know what would be worse, having CK fall for me because he thought I was someone, *something* I wasn't, or…losing him because of who I actually am.

EM: Damn, now I feel all guilty and shit.

ME: What? Why? I love that movie.

Mean Girls is a staple in the movie rotation of our girls' nights.

EM: Because I'm the one who suggested he sign up as a beta user for that app to help him grow and become more confident. Somehow I thought if he did, it would open his eyes to what's right in front of him. You know, YOU, Q.

Her words warm my heart.

ME: There's NOTHING for you to feel guilty about, babes. Did you forget I was the one who revamped his profile? You may have set the wheels in motion, but I took on the role of his pimp.

Oh my god, that's it.

I bolt up in bed, Herkie letting out a disgruntled snort as the blankets pool around my waist.

ME: Holy shit! Em, you're a genius. I could kiss you right now.

Here she is feeling guilty, but her plan actually worked. For the first time in eight months, CK and I had a full-on solo interaction without him running away or shutting down. I mean, sure, the topic of discussion was how he's failing at keeping *other* women engaged in conversation, but...

What if I take those same writing prompts he complained didn't provide any follow-through and use them for us to get to know each other better? Could doing it under the guise of the app accomplish what Em suggested?

I could probably beat out the Flash for the *Guinness Book of World Record*'s fastest texter with how quickly I type out my plan to the girls.

Now...

Where the hell are my Post-its?

#THEGRAM

#CHAPTER9

UofJ411: *REPOSTED—NJA_Admirals: The next great partner stunt duo learning from the best—reel of Kay and JT coaching Olly and Livi at The Barracks*
Le sigh Can we at least get your siblings to cheer for us if your girlfriend won't @CasaNova87 #CheerEnvy #SchoolSpirit #CasanovaWatch
@caligirlheartsbooks: Aww, look who's back from vaca #WeMissedYou #Kaysonova
@emilybunnyauthor: At least they keep it in the family #CasanovaWatch #Kaysonova #FamilyMatters

QUINN

I HAVE BEEN a morning person since the day I was born—at least according to *Abuela Lupe*. Sure, I may enjoy giving her hell for the fun of it, but I can't argue the fact that the day I came wiggling and screaming into this world, it was at the wee hour of 5:43 a.m.

So, yeah…that's me. I'm a regular morning glory.

Why am I telling you this? Well, outside of how this fact has earned me more knife emojis than I can count from Kay and Emma this past school year, my love for all things single-digit hours has *leans in and cups a hand around mouth to share this secret* grown.

Yup, you heard that right.

I, QUINN THOMPSON, LOVE MORNINGS *EVEN* MORE!

Move over, early bird! Your feathery behind has zero chance of snagging that worm now that I spring up in bed like that dad in the old board game *Don't Wake Daddy*.

Nope, now my legs are uncovered, and my feet touch the floor all before the devil himself gets the chance to mutter, *Oh, shit, she's up*.

I'm sure you're asking yourself, but why, Quinn? What changed to add a Pop Rocks-esque pep to your morning routine?

Well…it's simple—CK happened.

Yeah, yeah, yeah, I know my crush on him started embarrassingly long ago, but…

Now…

Oh. Em. Gee!

It's like all the months of unrequited love-fueled angst I lived with have been forgotten, overridden by the giddy excitement I've felt these last two weeks. Love notes from a crush will do that to a person.

Ugh! Okay, fiiine. If you're going to get all technical about it, they aren't *love notes* per se, but a pen pal-type exchange of *getting to know you* Post-its, scribbled with writing prompts specifically chosen and crafted to hopefully allow me to sneak past an overly guarded guy's defenses.

And…

If you *really* want to be a dick about it, I'll relent and admit that the exhilaration from CK actually opening up to me *may* have made me slightly delusional.

Whatevs.

Deluded or not, my plan is working. And before you even start with me, it's not like my plan is evil. I'm not some villain slowly spinning around in a chair, methodically stroking a hand down a cat as I dictate a plan for world domination.

For one, the only domination that interests me is seeing if my suspicions about CK's sexual preferences are correct. For another, my partner in crime during week one of Operation *Covert Amorous Correspondence*—or CAC for short—was a canine chomping down on a plushy taco toy the entire time I hemmed and hawed over what my opening question should be.

Does a wingdog, a squeaky toy soundtrack, and an arsenal of glitter pens and rainbow-colored Post-its scream evil to you? I didn't think so.

I'm perky and sociable, not diabolical.

Like the fourteen mornings before this one, I jack-in-the-box out of bed, but then I freeze when I step on one of the Barney-purple balls strewn all over the floor.

Balancing on one leg, I lift my foot, peeling the crumpled Post-it from the sole. I glare at one of the remnants of my indecision, its existence taunting me.

The three shots of tequila I downed for liquid courage last

night swirl around in my gut, trepidation skittering down my spine in the fresh light of day.

Ay dios mío.

What did I do?

Unfolding the paper in my hand, I smooth out the wrinkles and creases, staring at the now illegible scribbles I crossed out of existence. Based on the tiny hole punctuating one of the lines, I may have been a bit aggressive in all my vacillation.

There are seven similar paper balls scattered across the hardwood, and it suddenly feels like there's a land mine field between my bed and the door.

Maaayyyybe... I shouldn't leave my room today. Who the hell knows what's waiting for me outside of it.

Stop being a chickenshit, Quinn.

Rolling my shoulders back, I shake the bed head from my face and stride toward the door with purposeful steps.

Except...my hand hovers over the doorknob like it's a rattlesnake ready to strike. I glare, narrowing my eyes at the beam of sunlight reflecting off the chrome handle, my throat thick with indecision.

"It's been eighty-four years."

Okay, fine, it's been two and a half minutes, but kudos to my subconscious for nailing the old lady from *Titanic's* voice.

Still...

I can't force myself to move. My breaths grow labored, the heavy pants puffing out my cheeks and flubbering my lips. I sound more like I'm preparing to interview for a job running a Lamaze class than working on gathering the nerve needed to check what CK responded with.

Bawk, bawk, bawk.

I swear to you, the discarded Post-its behind me form chicken wings and flap them.

What the hell are you so scared of?

Oh...I don't know...maybe that out of the dozen or so writing prompts I've used throughout our notes, last night's question was without a doubt my boldest one to date.

No longer was I asking the easy starter questions like *My zombie apocalypse plan is...* Nor was this the slightly more "relationship-y" and considerably more self-serving *The secret to getting to know me is...*

Nope. This time, I flipped the script.

I didn't ask CK to tell me something about himself, but…to think about me.

I'd like to tell you I yanked open my bedroom door and stormed out of the room like a woman on a mission, searching out CK's note like a lioness stalks its prey.

But…

That would be a lie.

Instead, I put off the inevitable for as long as possible, showering and getting fully ready for the day before meandering into the kitchen.

Whoop, there it is.

Sitting dead center on the counter is the only purple Post-it to avoid last night's reject pile.

With heavy steps, I drag myself to the island, squeezing my eyes shut until colors bloom behind my closed lids. Then, with a fortifying breath, I slowly peel them open.

I glare at the words penned at the top of the paper in glittery silver ink: *I would fall for you if…*

I can just make out the top of CK's surprisingly neat penmanship in my peripherals, the black ink bold against the fanciful ink I favor.

The sight of his answer scrawled across the bottom has relief unknotting some of the tension from between my shoulder blades. I don't know what would have been worse—him ignoring me completely, or if his answer confirmed what I'm starting to fear may be the true cause behind his hesitation to my flirting: that *I'm* not good enough.

Oof. If *Abuelita* were here, she'd smack me with her *chancla* for even thinking like that about myself. With my biggest cheerleader in mind, I let the thought of her bolster my confidence enough to look.

You push me over.

Wait…

What?

My gaze jumps back up the paper.

I asked: *I would fall for you if…*

And CK responded with: *You push me over.*

What kind of horseshit is that?

Oh, no, no, no.

This just won't do.

I rip the note from the counter, the paper tearing from the force.

I damn near gave myself gray hair, psyching myself up to read what he wrote, and he leaves me with bullshit like this? I sure as shit hope Emma meant what she said about helping to bury a body because I'm about to murder an adorable nerd.

Paper clutched in my grip with an intensity I should probably be using to hold on to my sanity, my feet audibly *slap-slap-slap* against the floor.

"Wh—" CK startles awake at his door banging against the wall from my I-don't-give-a-single-shit entrance.

Later, when my fury isn't burning as bright as my hair color, I'll appreciate how cute he looks with his eyes squinting to see without his glasses, but not now. No, now She-Beast Quinn is at the helm of my actions, and with a flying leap, I land in the center of the bed.

"What kind of *utter* bullshit is this, Christopher?" My knuckles skim the tip of his nose as I thrust the slightly tattered paper in his face.

His dark brows fly up his forehead, those crystalline eyes meeting mine in all their unobstructed brilliant blue glory.

"I've been around you ladies enough to know better than to tell you to calm down." He leans back a bit, slowly lifting his arms in a *Don't shoot* gesture. "But what's with the Christopher-ing?"

"Don't go trying to be all cute and stuff right now, mister." I shake my finger at him. You heard that right; I flipping shake my finger at him. *Ay dios mío.*

He gives me a slow blink, the thick fringe of his dark lashes adding another point against him, because even with the two coats of mascara I put on, they are nicer than mine.

My breaths saw in and out of my lungs as we stare each other down, my chest heaving, my tantrum nowhere near close to waning.

With cautious movements, CK stretches an arm toward his nightstand. One eye remains on me like I'm some kind of rabid raccoon he's worried will strike at any moment. Honestly, the ferocity of my overreaction could have very well melted off my makeup to pool underneath my eyes.

He's silent as he slides those panty-melting black frames up the bridge of his nose.

Why, yes, professor, I've been a bad, bad *girl.*

Okay then. Looks like Hornball Quinn is shoving She-Beast Quinn to the side. At least my inappropriate horniness has the added benefit of dousing some of my temper. I'll take it as a win.

Without the fuzziness of frustration tingeing my vision, I'm able to appreciate the sight of a sleep-rumpled CK. His blue-black hair is flat on one side and in complete disarray on the other, an itch forming between my fingers with the urge to muss him up more.

That's not even the best part.

Nope, that honor goes to the fact that he's shirtless, as in, without the barrier of material to keep my eyes from feasting on all the deliciousness that is Christopher Kent.

Oh, looky—that *was* a six-pack I felt that day. I should have lifted his shirt and smeared salsa all over his stomach, then licked it clean. Damn. Talk about a missed opportunity.

Strong fingers curl around my wrist, and I jolt, unaware my arm was still lifted until CK lowers it to rest on the soft comforter covering his lap. You know, the same comforter that's pooled around his bare waist, the one that would only need to be shifted another inch or two to reveal if my crush is the type of person to sleep in the buff.

Sure…I know CK well enough to know that's an unlikely scenario, but a girl can dream, right?

He maintains his grip on me, which is probably a good thing, given my proximity to his crotch. Hornball Quinn would totally take over the controls and have me cupping him through the covers if I wasn't restricted.

Once again, completely unaware of my naughty musings, CK carefully works to liberate the homicidal-tendencies-inducing paper from my clutches.

"Umm…" His brows dip beneath the edge of his frames as he reads over the note. "I'm not sure I see the problem."

The uncertainty swimming in his eyes when he lifts them back to me has a wave of protectiveness rushing through me.

But...

This *chica* needs answers, so that instinct to put his feelings first can take a back seat.

"What kind of answer is *You push me over*?"

"A literal one," he says around a yawn, a teasing smirk tilting the side of his mouth after.

Oh, be still my beating heart. You would think I would be used to this side of CK by now, but you'd be wrong. It's the main reason why his literal response makes me grin like a fool despite my best efforts.

I narrow my eyes and snatch the Post-it from him, crumpling it into a ball and tossing it over my shoulder like I did with its predecessors back in my room. "Literal answers need not apply."

This did not go *at all* like I hoped.

"You practically act like a fangirl at a Shawn Mendes concert whenever I'm sarcastic with you. *Now* you're telling me you have a problem with it?"

"Oh, funny man's got jokes." I give his shoulder a playful shove, and sure, I may have snuck in a squeeze to the muscle. I'm a lovesick woman on the edge here, people. I'm allowed a covert grope here and there.

"These notes aren't the place for your sarcasm, Superman." My next sentence gets stuck in my throat, and I have to swallow twice before I manage to get it out. "You said you needed practice on how to evolve the prompts to an actual conversation. Sometimes sarcasm doesn't always translate through text."

Has perdido la maldita cabeza?

The status on whether or not I've lost my mind varies from day to day. To be honest, between the building sexual frustration and the guilt that comes with using a guise of...romance tutor?— *Is that what I am? Holy shit, I'm an idiot*—it's not just a possibility, but an inevitability.

"Umm...so..." CK rubs a hand across his mouth, and it takes everything inside me not to audibly sigh at the unassumingly hot gesture. "If someone responds to it with their own sarcastic response...would you consider that a good...or...bad sign for a future date?"

If the date is with me, it's a great *thing.*

Slow your roll, Quinn, before you scare him away.

Clamping down on my excitable tendencies, I take a beat. "Being compatible and having things in common are almost always good signs." I grind my teeth to restrain the excitable *We have so much in common* I badly want to tack onto the end of the sentence.

He blows out a breath, sagging back against the headboard. He may not have checked out my chest when it was all heaving bosom earlier, but you're *god*damn right I check him out. CK isn't like the other guys we live with who walk around shirtless with their muscles practically screaming *Look at me, look at me*. Don't get me wrong, I'm not complaining. I love the beefcake parade on the reg, but CK is *never* a participant. It's a crying shame given what he's been hiding, too.

Mami is going to enjoy him all stretched out in front of me for all it's worth.

"Okay...good." He glances toward his nightstand. "That makes me want to puke a little bit less over this date."

Umm...

Hold up.

I wiggle my ear, sure I heard him wrong.

He has a date?

Ermigod, what?

In the countless worst-case scenarios I considered, I *never* imagined...this.

Though...

I should have. A man like CK, one so obviously going places based on his own merit and accomplishments, would never settle for a woman who's nothing more than window dressing.

QUINN

CHAPTER 11

HE'S GOING ON A DATE.

C *freaking* K…

Christopher mother*fucking* Kent is going on a god*damn* date.

And…

Not only is it not with me, I also somehow inadvertently made myself the catalyst behind it.

How the fuck did this happen? How did my plan to get to know him better, for us to grow closer without him realizing and inevitably running scared like he's always been prone to do backfire so spectacularly?

I'm going to die alone.

Ay dios mío.

That's dramatic even for me.

"Ugh!" I tighten my ponytail to the point of making my scalp burn and set off across the mat in a frustration-fueled tumbling pass.

Not wanting to risk ending up sitting in the dark, lying in wait for CK to return home from his *date* like some creeper, I fled the apartment for safer ground.

I know I'm probably risking sounding like a broken record, but thank god for Kay and Em. I didn't know friendships like theirs existed in this world until the three of us and our fourth roommate, Bailey—don't ask—moved in together at the start of last school year.

Now? These fly girls are an extension of my family. We take our girl Rose's mantra of "You jump, I jump" to whole new heights. And no, I'm not talking about the air we get in our basket tosses.

Not once have either of them made me feel judged or even held others' actions against me when it would have been easy to lump me in with them.

Still...they didn't, nor did Emma block my number when she probably should have. Instead, she texted my neurotic ass until our communication was cut off by Captain Buzzkill Matthew commandeering her phone. Our group text thread with Kay may have been filled with swearing and sputtering voice memos after that, but him taking her phone was for the best. I'll already have to put in a few extra hours studying to make up for not paying attention in class while texting her.

Then there's Kay, the reason I have a place to escape to in the first place. The Barracks may not be the gym I spent my youth in, but there's nothing like bouncing on a blue mat while surrounded by large bows and high ponytails to chase the blues away or help a girl find her zen when her crush is out with *another* woman.

I rebound out of the tumbling pass with a solid pop, my ponytail whipping my back as I straighten, my arms rounding down to my sides, my hands slapping my thighs with a resounding smack.

Brushing away the strand of hair stuck inside my eyelashes, I look to the sidelines and see eight pairs of anime-wide eyes staring at me in disbelief.

Kay is the first to pick her jaw up off the floor, asking, "Umm...*excuse me*, what the hell was that?"

"And you call yourself our tumbling coach, PF," Tessa Taylor —JT's biological little sister and Kay's in every other sense of the word—says with a cluck of her tongue.

"*Ooo*, PF," JT joins in, dragging out Kay's gym nickname in a long *Pfff* instead of using the individual letters like everyone here does. "Coach Kris will take away your coach title if you're not careful."

Kay does what she always does and rolls her eyes. "You both suck," she comments, then she turns her attention back to me, her eyes wary as they watch me cross the spring floor to join them all huddled together. "You know I wasn't asking her to name the skills."

"Suuuurrrrre," JT drawls, and Mason shoves him until he topples over like some cross-legged stuck turtle.

"You's the best boyfriend ever." Kay twists in Mason's lap, looping her arms around his neck and placing a smacking kiss on his lips in thanks.

Tessa clasps her hands over her heart, falling into her bestie Savvy King in heart-eyed bliss, the latter giving an indulgent headshake. A sitcom-worthy *aww* rings free from Tessa and is chorused by Mason's younger sister, Livi, on her other side.

Three guesses which two future high school seniors in the room are the hopeless romantics.

"Your boyfriend is ruining all my fun, PF," JT grumbles, folding his arms across his chest. "How's a guy supposed to pick on his sister with a *hulking caveman*"—he adds a snooty flair to the description of Mason's pet name—"fighting her battles?"

"Puh-lease." Kay waves him off with a flick of her wrist. "I've *never* needed E to help me 'fight my battles'"—she adds exaggerated air quotes around the phrase—"and I sure as shit don't need Mase."

Mason growls, and Kay soothes him with a kiss to the underside of his jaw.

Folding my legs beneath me, I join my friends sitting on the floor. Tilting my head, I focus my attention on JT. "Did the washing machine ever get all the glitter out of your laundry?"

He rears back, hissing through his teeth. "Devil women." His arms flail as he tries to point at four of us at once. Tessa, Savvy, and I *may* have had a hand in helping Kay glitter bomb his and Trav's luggage before they left Hawaii.

"I much preferred when you likened my best friend to herpes than when you're cursing me with the herpes of the craft world, Short Stack." Trav pouts from his stretched-out lean, canting his head in Kay's direction.

Mason shrugs, utterly unconcerned with the razzing.

"Don't try to make me feel guilty for you getting the punishment you *more than* deserved." Kay arches a brow and drops the octave of her voice. "You *know* what you did, QB1."

Her deadpan delivery and the parent-level scold to her tone has our group whooping it up. Tessa and Mason's siblings Livi and Olly whine about how they missed out on all the vacation fun. Finally, after Kay suggests maybe they take a page out of Savvy's book and chill, she turns her attention back to me, squirrel moment officially over.

Welp, guess she didn't forget about her original question.

"So…you wanna tell me what has you adding double whips and Arabian double fulls in your tumble passes?" She eyes me with a pinch between her brows. "You don't typically throw stuff like that."

When I first realized *who* Kay was, I couldn't comprehend how one half of the best partner stunt pairings—JT being the other—wasn't cheering collegiately. Sure, all-star cheerleading is kind of its own self-contained world, but the partner stunt duo of JT Taylor and PF Dennings was the most famous one in our circuit. I still remember when they burst onto the scene in high school. The tricks they attempted were some of the most challenging and creative seen in competition.

But…

Now that I know her better, I understand why she opted to step away from competing to coach. She has this instinct for knowing her athletes, for picking up on their strengths and weaknesses by observing them. It's why she knows, without question, that was not a standard tumbling pass for me.

I shrug, shaking my hands out, then stretching my arms over my head. "I had some things to work out." You'd be surprised how easy it is to up the level of difficulty of your skills when working through personal shit.

"Do those things have anything to do with a certain shy roommate of yours?" Tessa asks knowingly, a hint of singsong creeping into her tone.

Of course she knows.

Everyone knows.

Everyone except CK, that is.

I huff out a breath and flop backward onto the mat, staring up at the hundreds of banners displaying NJA's accolades.

Wow, look at all those national and world titles they've won.

"If you think giving her the silent treatment will make her forget the question, you're sorely mistaken." Savvy sounds almost bored, as if her experience in their long friendship has desensitized her to Tessa's extraness. "Tess is like a damn dog with a bone when she smells the possibility of a love story."

I choke on my saliva, hope springing eternal inside me. "A love story?" I croak.

"*Ooo, YASSS!*" Tessa forward rolls, jumping to her feet and executing a textbook-perfect toe touch, complete with spirit finger waving hands thrown in the air when she's done. "You do know roommates/forced proximity is one of my top favorite tropes to read."

"Careful, Tess," JT cautions with a smirk, "your love extraness is showing."

"When is it not?" Savvy asks in the same tone as earlier.

"Do not hate on my love for romance novels, Jimmy." Tessa wags her finger at her brother then props her hands on her hips. "I'm a freaking fount of untapped expertise."

"You're something alright," JT mumbles, but not low enough to not be overheard if Tessa's annoyed growl is any indication.

The bickering commences in earnest, but it's nothing more than white noise as my mind whirls with the same thoughts that have been churning through it all day.

What's it going to take to make CK notice me?

I flirt with him *all* the time.

I smile at him.

I play with my hair.

I touch him any chance I get—his forearm, his hair. I sit as close as I can so our bodies brush against each other.

Still…

Nothing.

The man doesn't treat me any differently than he does Kay and Em.

No…

Wait…

Scratch that. He does.

Sure, he has these moments of shyness with my friends, but with me? With me, it's like he withholds himself…more.

It wasn't until everybody else was gone and I busted out my arsenal of trusty Post-its that things started to change.

They did change, right?

Covering my face with my hands, I let out a rebel yell, the sound not muffled nearly as much as I would have hoped.

Pushing up onto my elbows, I'm met with wide eyes and raised brows. "Don't judge me." I huff.

"We would never," Kay is quick to say, zero hint of sarcasm in her words. "But…" She pulls a face that has me pushing to sit up fully. Curiosity has a surge of adrenaline pumping through my veins when she trains her gaze on Tessa, who breaks into a beaming smile. "Maybe T has a few tips you could employ."

"OH MY GOD, YAAAAASSS QUEEN!" Tessa snaps and drag queen shimmies with her cheer, eyes shining brighter than all the overhead lights combined.

"Now you've done it," JT mutters. "She's sleeping at your place tonight, PF."

Tessa proves how much she could be Kay's sister and rolls her eyes. "Please, it's Friday." She holds a hand out to tack on the *Duh* missing from the statement. "I'm staying at Bitchy's."

Savvy nods in confirmation.

"Great, now I'm gonna owe King a case of beer."

Again, Savvy nods, this time a sly grin tugging on the right side of her mouth. "If that's how you pay back my brother for the shit we put him through, you're better off investing and buying a brewery. But fear not"—she pats JT's bent knee—"Carter isn't the Royal we plan on torturing tonight."

My gaze locks with Kay's, and that rush that comes from when you telepathically communicate with your bestie flows between us.

At her nod, I suggest, "Well…if you change your mind, you could always tell him how I lost one of my crisis negotiators because of *bodyguard*"—I bounce my shoulders and waggle my eyebrows—"interference."

Tessa drifts off on a tangent about her love of everything enemies-to-lovers, filling in some of the gaps for Trav about the tension all of us know exists between Em and Carter.

When she's done once again claiming how she called Kay and Mason's relationship from the start, Tessa plops down beside me with enough force to cause movement in the springs of the floor. "Now for you…"

Again, I chance a glance at Kay, who only gives me a *Sorry, not even I can control her* headshake but follows it up with a *Listen to her* chin tilt.

I make a rolling motion with my hand, and Tessa links her hands together, cracking her knuckles. If we could bottle even an ounce of her confidence, we'd be billionaires.

"Now…I'm not saying I don't *love* the little love notes in disguise you have going on…"

I hide a chuckle behind my hand. That's a new description I haven't used before.

"But…you've been neglecting the most powerful tool at your disposal."

The hairs on my arms stand on end. "Why am I afraid to ask what you think that is?"

"Because you've met her." Jaws drop, not at the unexpected comment—that's factually accurate—but at who the source of it is. Olly blinks at suddenly having eight sets of eyes on him.

Yeah, I know how that feels, buddy.

"I don't care if you'll be my sorta brother-in-law someday"— the point of Tessa's finger is aggressive as all get-out—"your colorful commentary is not needed, *mmkay*?"

"Jesus, T." Kay buries her face against Mason's chest. "We haven't even been dating for a full year. Slow your roll."

"And they did break up once, *sooo*…" Trav lets his sentence trail off with a *What are you gonna do?* shrug.

Mason flips him off. "Asshole."

"You shut your mouth, quarterback." Tessa goes practically feral. "And"—she whips her head back to Kay—"if you two"— she Vs her fingers to now include Mason—"aren't married by the time I graduate from college, I'll eat my cheer bow."

"Why does it always feel like we're having five conversations at once when we're together?" I ask, but that warm feeling of rightness from being reunited with my people cocoons the moment. This is what I needed today. I needed our ridiculousness to wash away my melancholy.

"Because we usually are," Livi confirms, dodging Trav's attempt to pull her in for a noogie.

Tessa double finger guns her, and then once again, I'm back to being her focus. "*Anyway...*" She sighs. "You gotta use your newfound forced proximity to your advantage. The notes are a good way to build that foundation of friendship CK has always stayed on the fringes of forming with you, *but*...now you need to remind him you're a woman."

"I'm pretty sure CK's well aware I'm a woman." I grab my more-than-a-handful boobs—thanks to the Bautista genes I inherited from *Mamá*—and give them a jiggle. "The issue is he doesn't want..." I finish my incomplete sentence with an *All this* wave of a hand down the length of my body.

Deep-rooted insecurity causes my throat to thicken with emotion, and it's harder to swallow it down than I would like. It's not about my appearance. One benefit of *Mamá's* mantra about using one's looks is that it has bolstered a healthy body image. If only it didn't come at the expense of my self-esteem. Her tunnel vision became the ideal breeding ground for all the other ways I didn't measure up to fester.

Who knows? Maybe if I was more than just a pretty cheerleader, CK would be on a date with me right now and not some mystery girl.

Sagged against the elevator wall, I watch the digital dial count off the floors on the way up to the penthouse. My body is drained, but my heart is close to bursting like it is any time I leave The Barracks.

Some of that feeling can be credited to the time I got to spend playing around stunting with my friends, but it's mostly from the hours before helping coach NJA's athletes. Sure, the job is cheerleading, but there's nothing like being valued for your expertise to make someone feel validated.

The *ding* announcing I've reached my destination has a mild buzz of apprehension forming beneath my skin. A part of me wonders if I made a mistake by not accepting Kay's offer to stay at her family home for the night, but I shake that thought off before it gets the chance to fully form.

Rolling my sore shoulders back, I stride out of the elevator with a confidence I don't wholly feel, but I am all about manifesting with a positive mental attitude. A *Fake it till you make it* approach has served me well for almost twenty-one years; why put a stop to it now?

Eager to wash away the dried sweat coating my skin, I make a beeline for the bathroom.

All thoughts of a shower hotter than Texas in July immediately cease the second I spot the light spilling from beneath CK's bedroom door.

What's he doing home?

Changing direction, I don't stop until the tips of the flip-flops I switched my cheer shoes out for butt against the wood of the door.

Lifting a hand to knock, I hesitate, my arm hovering in the air long enough to feel the strain in my already fatigued muscles.

Hazlo, Quinn.

Knock-knock.

I wait…

And then wait some more.

Did he not hear me knock? Does he have his headphones on?

Pressing my ear to the door, I hear the soft hum of his television playing.

Okay…so probably no headphones—

The door swings open unexpectedly, and since my body is pressed against it like a starfish on a fish tank, I go with it, falling to the ground with a grunt.

My cheeks burn as I flail around.

"Quinn?" CK stares down at me like he's not exactly sure what he's seeing.

Can't say I blame him. I've gone from starfish to turtle stuck on its back. Awesome.

He pushes his glasses higher on his nose and…

Oh my god! Did I just sigh? Sonofa—

Grr, I can't help it. It's such a simple action, one I'm sure he does countless times throughout the course of any given day, but *man*, it does things to my lady parts.

Straightening my legs and crossing them at the ankles, I prop myself up and lean back on my elbows.

Oh, great. Now I probably look like I'm sunbathing. Because that's not weird or anything, seeing as it's nighttime…oh…yeah…and I'm inside.

"What are you doing here?" he asks.

Was that—

Did he—

Oh my god, that rumbly sound was CK chuckling at me.

If I had any doubt about if my humiliation has my ears playing tricks on me, the twinkle in his baby blues confirms my suspicions. Guess this is the price I pay for him growing more comfortable around me.

"What am *I* doing here? What are *you* doing here?" I snap, practically accusing the poor guy as the culmination of the day's events procreates with my growing mortification. "I thought you had a *date*?" I hiss. I motherfluffing hiss like a damn feral alley cat.

All playfulness disappears as CK's expression falls, his eyes dimming, his mouth pulling down into a frown. There's a pained pinch between his brows as they dip below his frames, and the way his body seems to curl in on himself cracks a piece of my heart.

God, why does he suddenly look like I kicked his puppy?

"She bailed." He goes to shove his hands in his pockets, only to realize the mesh shorts he has on don't have any. He finally settles for folding his arms over his chest, his shrug coming across as *It's no big deal*, but I can read him well enough to know it definitely is a big deal.

"What do you mean?" I may have been less than thrilled about his plans for the evening, but I would never want him to seem this…dejected over the date's failure.

"You know…" He gives me another one of those shrugs, lifting his chin and staring off in the distance. "Our server had just delivered our drinks when she got a call from her roommate about a busted pipe in their apartment and had to leave."

"She *fucking* bailout called you?" I barely notice CK wincing at my screech as I start cursing this faceless bitch for pulling such a dick move on a guy as great as CK.

My words putter out mid-rant at the grin slowly forming on CK's mouth. It's microscopic, but it's there. I see it, and I put it there. *Me! Eep!*

"What?" My voice comes out all breathless, like I'm some kind of Latina Marylin Monroe.

Oof…actually…it's a pretty terrible impression. And now the heat is back in my cheeks. *Well, hello, old friend. I missed thee.*

"Umm…" CK drops his gaze, though I'm not sure what's so fascinating about the floor now that I'm not thrashing around on it. He clears his throat. "I…like how…umm…"

Aww, now I'm not the only blushing beauty in the room, as color stains the skin beneath his glasses.

He clears his throat for a second time, and if the budding of my nipples against my sports bra is any indication, I like the rasp that has crept into his voice. "When you get passionate about something, you…slip into Spanish."

Annnddd that revelation has my lady pop timers hard enough they could cut glass.

"Do you like the way I roll my Rs, Superman?" I singsong, sobering when he nods, well aware of how difficult an admission like that was for him. I say one more sentence in Spanish.

"All I caught of that was a bitch in there somewhere."

Now I'm grinning, shaking my head. Why is it everyone learns the curses of a foreign language first?

"It's not a perfect translation, but I said something along the lines of how that bitch didn't deserve to be out with you in the first place if she wasn't willing to put in the time to actually get to know you."

I mean…sure, he may be too good for me, but a bailout call? Classy—not.

"Maybe she just didn't like what she saw."

That crack in my heart expands, and my arms twitch to pull him into a hug when he points to himself. Those assholes he grew up with better pray they never run into me. My hair may be dyed red and not naturally that color, but I have zero qualms about embracing *every* stereotype about how we're crazy and opening up a can of whoop-ass on them.

"Don't be stupid." I press my lips together. "You know as well as anybody that first dates are awkward." He pulls a face, but I can't read this one. "It's like a general rule that you have to wade through the suck at the start to get to the potential toward the end."

"May—" He hesitates. "Maybe I need to practice."

"That's the essence of dating."

Oh my god, Quinn, shut up!

"Umm…" He's back to toeing the floor with his sock-covered foot.

"What?" I nudge him with my own foot.

Is he…

Is he going to ask me out?

"Would…you…teach me?"

Ermigah!

He.

Asked.

Me.

Out.

Elation is too tame of a word for what's rushing through my veins. I'm damn close to jumping into a toe touch like Tessa earlier when CK bursts my already-thinking-about-what-under-wear-I-would-wear dreams.

"Be…umm…my"—he juggles his hands up and down like a scale—"love coach?"

"Love coach?" I screech. Yes, I've turned into a banshee.

"Well…yeah…you know…" *Ay dios mío.* He *really* needs to stop adjusting his glasses while my brain is spinning like a top. "You've sorta been doing that already, but I thought maybe we can integrate a more practical approach…do a few mock date activities and stuff."

Every instinct inside me is *screaming* at me to say no, to shout NO!

But then a little voice that sounds suspiciously like Tessa whispers that this is a golden opportunity. This could be my chance to show CK what it's like to date *me* without any of the pressure that comes from dating.

The idea has merit.

What could go wrong?

#CHAPTER12

"CHRISTOPHER KENT, you have some damn nerve, you know that?" Quinn storms into the apartment, orange Post-it clutched in the fist shaking at me.

Ahh…I should have anticipated this would be her reaction when she found it stuck inside her philosophy notebook.

"I have some nerve?" I close the lid of my laptop, hiding away the current edits to the video game I've been designing, and swivel in my seat to face her fully.

"Oh, no. Put that smile of yours away." Her strides are long, her sandals slapping the floor with each angry step she takes. I should probably heed the warning in her purposeful approach, but my gaze is stuck on the sliver of bronzed skin peeking out above the waistband of her shorts as I watch the tantalizing sway of her hips.

A hand grips my head, fingers digging into my cheeks until Quinn has my mouth pursed into some sort of forced fish face.

My glasses slide down the bridge of my nose, but she slaps my hand away before I can fix them. "I will *not* be charmed by your adorkability right now, do you hear me?"

I have no idea what she means. I'm too distracted by…*her* to figure it out. Her sweet scent invades every inhalation. I'm well aware—painfully so in some places—of all the points where her body makes contact with mine.

I blink, and her gaze drops to watch the movement. I curse the fact that we're close enough to share oxygen. If she were outside of my I-don't-need-glasses-to-see radius, my dick wouldn't be millimeters from brushing the smooth skin of her thigh and then those blazing dark pools would be blurry.

"You know…" Cautiously, I reach up, curling my fingers around her wrist, my thumb brushing along her palm until she loosens her grip on me. "I never realized you hid such a fiery temper under your high ponytail."

Quinn blinks, her bottom lip pulling in as her teeth bite into it. She closes the last bit of space separating us, her arm laying on the curve of my shoulder, her forearm aligning with the back of my neck.

I'm damn close to purring when she starts to play with the hair at the base of my skull.

What is she doing?

"That's what happens when you keep a person at arm's length."

I dip my chin at her direct hit. I did that out of pure self-preservation. I've never understood why the others wanted to be my friend, but now that I've accepted their friendships, I couldn't handle losing them.

Quinn? She's easily the most social of all of us. She could befriend a paper bag if someone turned it into a puppet. Being friends with someone like me comes as easily to someone like her as brushing her teeth. I keep telling myself I need to remember this fact. Except…the more time I spend with her, the harder that becomes.

"And yet, what did you do as soon as I stopped?" Her eyelashes fan out when I finally fix my glasses.

Did she just hum?

Geez, I'm losing it.

I clear my throat. "Did you already forget how you barged into my room this weekend, whistle pinched between your teeth, the thing bleating in between demands that I get my mangy butt out of bed and drop to give you twenty?"

Quinn shrugs, not at all apologetic for her rude wake-up call. "You're the one who asked me to be your love coach."

I bark out a laugh. What the hell was I thinking? The entire dating endeavor was asinine to begin with. Directly involving Quinn? My scholarship should be revoked for such a blatant display of stupidity.

"I didn't mean it in the literal sense," I challenge. "I need help not scaring women off, not making the team."

"You sure know how to ruin a girl's fun, CK." She pouts, the pucker of her lips calling me to claim them.

I wonder how she would react if I kissed her right here, right now.

Nope. That's crazy.

Quinn's exuberant personality may have led to her playing drill sergeant the other day, but all joking aside, her help is strictly a platonic venture. She'd probably laugh in my face if I tried to kiss her.

"Now…" She steps back, and I pointedly ignore the part of me that's disappointed by this. "There are many, *many* things you do better than me"—*Doubtful*—"but you, sir, threw down the gauntlet with this note."

After I banished her coach persona from my room—which took two thrown pillows and me rolling myself up in the covers like a burrito—we reconvened at a more reasonable hour to discuss a plan that wasn't insane.

Once again, she tried to reassure me that first dates are awkward for the general population of the world. She reiterated how sometimes doing an activity one is good at instead of the traditional sit-down dinner could be an easy way to banish some of the nerves involved.

When I asked her for an example, she brought up how good I am at billiards. She suggested a venue like a pool hall could be an excellent alternative.

It hasn't escaped my notice how often I've caught someone—including Quinn herself—commenting on how different I've been with her. Of course, I could try to claim it's because our other roommates are gone, making Quinn the sole source of companionship around the apartment, but that would be a lie. Kay and the others may not be staying *at* the apartment, but both Quinn and I see most of them multiple times a week.

Hell, the night I had my date fail, she was with several of them at The Barracks.

So, no, that's not it.

I know how my inclusion has evolved into this big, almost inside joke of our group, but like when I had a class with Kay, living under the same roof as Quinn is what created a situation I'm not able to run away from and gave her the opportunity to take her turn at forcing her friendship on me. *That's* the change.

Unfortunately, unlike with Kay, Em, or G, I'm wildly attracted to Quinn. And getting to know her? *Fuck!* It makes that attraction all the more painful. I never expected to have so much in common with a girl like her. It's a slippery, slippery slope.

In a few of the Post-its she's left stuck in random places around the apartment, I could have taken the chance to hint at my feelings toward her, but I pussed out every time.

I'd rather suffer the pain of an unattainable crush than be crushed *by* her.

"Oh my god." Quinn pops me on the chest before taking the front of my shirt between her fingers, lifting and stretching it out to see the graphic printed on it better. "You little shit talker." Her gaze bounces between my face and my shirt, narrowing at the graphic of the original Nintendo console and the words *Classically Trained* circling it. "Forget the gauntlet. This is a declaration of war."

I buff my nails at said *declaration*. "If you can't handle the heat, stay out of the kitchen, Red."

We each suck in a collective breath at the spontaneous nickname.

Well…that's new.

Quinn's the first to recover, her tongue peeking out to slide across her teeth as she shifts her gaze to the kitchen beside us. "If you're going to quote presidents to step to me, pick one of the other forty-five who didn't use my domain in one of their famous phrases."

"You know that phrase came from a president?"

She freezes at my question, but I don't know why. I think it's impressive as hell.

"Yeah, President Truman," she says, her tone is clipped. "He also coined the phrase 'The buck stops here.'"

I nod, filing the fact away for future use. "I didn't know that."

Again, Quinn seems…almost cold all of a sudden. A few awkward seconds hang in the air like a lingering fart before she shakes off the weird mood and is back to her usual sunny self.

"I should stop sharing my cooking with you."

"No." I jump from my seat and latch on to her arm, going as far as dropping to my knees to lend weight to my pleading. *"Please* don't do that. I'll *starve."*

Okay…I wouldn't starve. I make a mean bowl of cereal, and it wasn't until recently that Quinn even had the time to cook, but her cooking is bomb. I may not be as over the top in my ass-kissing for it like Grant, but it's also not something I'll willingly give up if I can help it.

A divot forms in the center of Quinn's cheek like she's restraining a laugh. I'm so desperate for her to take back her threat, I don't even care if it's at my expense.

Whoa, if that doesn't show how much power she has over you, I don't know what does.

"Hmm…" She taps her chin, the corners of her mouth finally shifting up. "Careful, Superman, you just handed me your kryptonite."

I'd be scared, but her statement has *nothing* on my previous thought.

"Now come on"—she jerks a chin toward the living room—"let's go find out who the real M.D. is."

"Boo-yah!" Quinn mic-drops the Nintendo controller. "And that, ladies and gentlemen, is what you call a sweep." She body rolls and shoots me a wink.

Hanging my head in defeat, I know losing this round of *Dr. Mario* isn't going to be the most painful part. Neither are the permanent rectangle and circle imprints my thumbs are sporting. No, that honor goes to how my loss—a tournament loss at that—means I'm now subjected to *two* of Quinn's questions. She thinks she's slick, sneaking in getting-to-know-me questions, but I'm well aware of what she's doing.

You still answer them.

That's true. I do.

Hands rubbing together, Quinn shifts around on the couch until she's facing me, one of her knees knocking into my thigh when she refolds her legs beneath her.

Oh, great, she's really settling in this time.

Cheeks flushed, a smudge of mascara under her left eye, hair sitting in a lopsided ball on her head from hastily pulling it up after the first hour of us playing *Dr. Mario* passed, she's a mess. Not that she cares—pure joy from her victory radiates off of her.

Why does she have to be so goddamn beautiful? On a scale of one to ten, Quinn's a fifteen. Too bad it's not just her level of attractiveness that makes her out of my league. But it is what has me tugging on my shorts to create more space for the boner that refuses to quit.

"If you could get rid of *any* inanimate object, what would it be?"

And…this is why she pulls answers out of me. Throughout the two hours we've battled it out in the most intense *Dr. Mario* gameplay I've *ever* been a part of, she's thrown out some of the most random inquiries.

Who has an inanimate object they hate enough to wish out of existence?

Though…she did give me the perfect opportunity to fuck with her.

"Oh…that's an easy one." I move around until I mirror how she's sitting, a tiny kernel of guilt forming in my gut when she bounces excitedly. "Post-it notes."

She gasps, her jaw dropping and eyes widening. "You *monster*," she whisper-shouts.

She's so damn fun to tease. Her unfiltered reactions are adorable.

"You know what?" She huffs, her nostrils flaring as she crosses her arms.

Unfortunately, all that does is highlight the way her cleavage swells, the scalloped lace of her bra peeking over the scooped edge of her tank.

Why does it have to be lace?

Do her panties match?

Should I ask her next time I win and get to ask the questions?

Better yet, would she answer?

"—because of it."

Lost in thoughts of what Quinn looks like in her underwear —*I bet she looks fucking hot covered in lace*—I miss most of what she said. "Huh?"

"Wow…as your *coach*"—there's a pointed emphasis on the title—"I feel it's my *duty* to tell you that not paying attention to what your date is saying is bad date etiquette."

"Guess it's a good thing you're not really my date," I joke.

"CK!" Quinn's voice goes three octaves higher.

I can't help but chuckle. Damn…I was missing out all of these months. All that wasted time avoiding her when we could have had easy fun like this.

She flops forward, burying her face in the small diamond shape created by our crossed legs, shaking her head. Her voice is muffled, but I can still make it out when she speaks. "First you come for my precious Post-its"—she whips her head up, resting her chin on my calf muscle—"now you're gonna insult the awesomeness of this afternoon?"

Notching a finger under her chin, I press until she straightens, leaving my hand in place because…well…because she hasn't asked me to remove it. "I didn't mean to insult the day." And because I'm feeling bold, I stroke my thumb down the line of her jaw. Was she a little slower to open her eyes after that blink? "Can you forgive me, Red?"

She folds her lips between her teeth, but whatever smile she was trying to restrain breaks free within seconds. "You keep calling me Red, and I'll consider it."

"Good." Not wanting to push my luck, I drop my hand and pick up my controller, scrolling through the menu to start a new game. "Now tell me how you got so good at *Dr. Mario*."

"Oh no." She clucks her tongue. "I still get another question."

I bite my lip. Of course Quinn didn't forget. She's like a damn dog with a bone. Instead of skeletal remains from the ground, she drags answers out of me. So much for hoping she lost count.

I make a rolling motion with my hand for her to proceed.

"What character—whether book, television, or movie—were you inexplicably scared of growing up?"

I pause, my thumb hovering over the start button in the center of the controller, then crane my neck to see over her shoulder.

"What are you doing?" Quinn asks on a laugh, knocking the same shoulder I was trying to peer around into mine.

"I'm looking for your phone." I try one more time but don't spot anything. "You have to have a list or something on you— how else are you coming up with this random shit?"

"It's all up here, big boy." She taps her temple the same way the guy does in the GIF I've learned is one of her favorites to use any time she tries to convince me she's had a good idea. "Now stop stalling and spill the damn tea."

"That's not really what—"

She cuts off the correction with a *Stop talking* hand gesture. "Christopher," she warns.

Oh, this is going to be embarrassing. "You can't judge me," I caution.

"I would never." She lays a hand over her heart. "Even if you tried to denounce my prized Post-its."

I can't even with this woman.

"Okay…ready?" She nods. "E.T."

Her mouth falls open in a wide O.

She circles a finger in the air and asks, "What makes you afraid of a Reese's Pieces-loving alien?" To her credit, she doesn't laugh.

I swallow the lump that jumps into my throat. If I have nightmares tonight, I'm waking her ass up. "You know when he gets sick and turns all white and skinny?" My body involuntarily shivers as the image surfaces in my memories. "It freaks me out."

This time she does laugh.

"You have to answer now." It's my turn to bump her with my shoulder when her giggle persists. "You got out of the inanimate object question. I'm not letting you off the hook for two in a row."

"You did that to yourself, mister." She wags a finger at me, and I have the overwhelming urge to nip at her fingertip. I don't, of course. That's a level of teasing far too intimate for two people who are just friends. No matter how much I wish it could be different.

"Yes, yes"—I hold my hands up—"I insulted the Post-its." I mock bow. "I apologize to you and the people of 3M."

A new wave of giggles overtakes Quinn, and she falls against the cushions.

Wiping a tear from her eye, she straightens, reaches out, and taps one of my shoulders, then the other, like she's knighting me. "You are forgiven."

I shake my head at her ridiculousness, but my cheeks are sore from all the grinning I can't seem to stop.

"I'll honor your contrition by answering both questions." She clears her throat and holds up a finger. "The inanimate object I'd get rid of is the corner of my bed. That sumbitch always tries to break my toe when I get up to pee in the middle of the night."

I rub my pinkie toe as if feeling the phantom pain from the last time I did that myself.

"And my character is Jaws...or"—she shrugs—"well...I guess it's all sharks, but that fear stems from Jaws. She's my origin story."

"She?" I arch a brow.

"Uh, yeah." That ball of hair on her head loses the good fight at her vigorous head nod, the long red locks tumbling around her shoulders. Damn, that was sexy. "In the third movie, it's the mama shark seeking her revenge because the good people at SeaWorld let her baby die after it snuck into the park."

I rub a hand over my mouth, but Quinn's narrowed eyes tell me I'm not hiding a thing. "Sorry. I'm just surprised out of all the shark movies out there, it's the *Jaws* franchise that made you terrified of sharks. No offense to Spielberg, but it didn't even make for a convincing fish."

"*Oh*, because his *alien* is so much more convincing?"

"Touché."

I wrap an arm around her shoulders when she falls into me, holding her close as we both succumb to our laughter. So what if I sniff her hair?

"You're not wrong with your reasoning," she says when we finally catch our breath. "To this day, I can't watch a movie with a shark or water creature without lifting my feet from the ground."

"I do that too." My confirmation has her squeezing my side.

"But I think my irrational fear comes more from watching all the movies with my cousins on my *tia*'s waterbed than the movies themselves."

"Oh, no." I shake my head. "Tactical error, Red."

"I know."

We stay like that, with her snuggled against my side, neither of us in a hurry to move or start our next game. The casual cuddle isn't anything I haven't done with Kay or Emma, but with Quinn, it feels different. I can't help but wonder if I just made a tactical error of my own.

QUINN

THE SOUND of running water calls me to the closed bathroom door like a siren luring sailors to their doom.

Again, I find myself standing in front of it, my cheek pillowed against the wood without my permission.

Mierda.

This shit needs to stop. Crazy is not a good look on me.

I can't help it, though. The periodic interruptions to the steady stream keep putting all kinds of naughty visions in my brain. I wonder if this is how Harry Potter felt when Snape used Legilimency on him.

Back away from the door, Quinn.

Hands curling into fists, knuckles digging into the wood, I forcibly shove myself away before I barge into the bathroom. Imagining what CK looks like in the shower—dark hair slicked tight to his head, water sluicing down his body, soap bubbles catching on the ridges of muscle he keeps hidden—is bad enough. I doubt I would survive witnessing it in person.

Not to mention walking in without knocking would make you a Creeper McCreeperson, and that's putting it nicely. There is this thing called consent—it's kind of important.

Distraction. I *need* a distraction.

Shoving away from temptation, I all but run to the living room, diving onto the couch and rolling across the cushions like I'm some extra in an action movie and not just a cheerleader on edge.

Universal remote in hand, I slam my thumb onto the volume button until the sexy bouncing beat of Ed Sheeran's "Shivers" drowns out any sound of CK in the shower. Arms swaying and rolling, I dance them up my sides, clasping my hands together over my head, my hips joining in on the action as I settle into the rhythm.

Dancing around to music is one of my happy places, and I'm going to need all the help I can get if I want to keep myself from taking a trip to Broodyville later.

Unlike when CK went on a date last week, I don't feel nearly as *woe is me* about tonight. I don't know if it's knowing it was coming instead of being blindsided or if it stems from the role I helped play in it coming to fruition, but I'm not going to complain.

Not even all the *I told you so*s Tessa singsonged during the Marshals cheer practice this afternoon bothered me. Chick was spot-on in her advice. I may need to borrow a few of her romance novels for research purposes.

What would CK say if he knew his love coach had one of her own?
Whatevs.

CK and I have been bonding, and I take that as a win.

Though…

Does it make me an ass for hoping tonight's date illustrates how true that is for CK too? Asking for a friend. *whispers* That friend is me.

If it does, let's pretend I'm not hoping for that, at least for the sake of my karmic balance. I know how much of a bitch karma can be, and I don't need to face her wrath.

"Now, that's a damn sight better to walk in on than Noah balls-deep in some rando." The deep boom of Kev's voice has me whirling around, my dance moves stuttering at the unexpected return of two of our roommates.

"You got that fucking right, brother." Alex claps him on the back, his face pulled into a grimace. "I think the image of his pale white-boy ass thrusting like an overeager Chihuahua is permanently burned into my brain." He digs his fingers into his temples, the paper bag in his hand bouncing off his forearm as his eyes squeeze shut. "I'll be on my deathbed, senile and unable to remember my own name, but I'll have that vision playing on a loop."

"What are you guys doing here?" I rush them with a flying leap, jumping onto Kev at the same time the bathroom door opens.

With me still wrapped in his beefy lineman arms, Kev moves across the apartment until we're in front of CK, who's standing awkwardly in the doorway, dressed and ready for his…date.

"CK, my dude." Alex reaches out the hand not holding the grease-stained bag, and the two share this weird, complicated bro-shake. Alex steps back, his head tilting to the side as he studies CK's face. "I'll never get used to seeing you without your glasses, bro."

Patting Kev so he'll put me down, I unwind my legs from around his waist and skirt around Alex's equally as tall but not as bulky frame until I'm standing toe to toe with CK.

The fresh scent of evergreen tickles my nostrils, and I caution myself not to lean in and sniff him. *Ugh!* He smells as yummy as he looks.

Except…

Where are his glasses?

"Why aren't you wearing your glasses?" I ask, after scanning his body from head to toe a second time.

CK looks away, refusing to meet my eye like I've noticed he does any time he feels embarrassed by something. I yearn for the day when he feels comfortable enough to not give a fuck with me.

Not giving a damn about our audience, I pinch CK's chin between my fingers and bring his gaze back to mine. "Superman…" I give him the same eyebrow arch my mom gives me when she's waiting for an answer.

It works. CK blows out a breath then says, "I thought it helped make me seem a little less geeky without them."

My brows draw together. Why the hell would that be his worry for someone he met on an app named Greet Geek?

Wait…scratch that. Who the hell cares?

Rolling my eyes at the absurdity, I shoulder past him and

hunt for his glasses case. Spotting it on the counter, I snap open the lid and take out the black frames.

Alex and Kev are posted on either side of the archway leading back to the open-concept living space when I emerge from the bathroom. They're leaning against the wall, settled in as if they're about to watch a show. Again I ignore them.

Carefully unfolding the thin plastic arms, I flip the glasses around until they're facing CK and step a foot between his.

He sucks in a breath, his chest brushing mine as I move in even closer. It doesn't matter that he lets me invade his personal space on a daily basis; my girly bits shake their pom-poms any time we get all up close and personal with him.

My fingertips brush across the clipped hair of his sideburns before they skim along the top curves of his ears as I line his glasses up with his face.

His eyes remain locked on me the whole time, those blue pools burning me in their intensity. It's hard to swallow as I crest the tip of his nose and slide the glasses home.

Neither of us moves. My hands hover around his head, fingertips barely threaded through the soft strands of his hair, as if needing to touch but also unwilling to mess up the carefully styled locks.

Something, I don't know what, but... something *different* pulses between us.

My gaze falls to his mouth and his nostrils flare.

Gah!

I just want to grab his face and kiss him.

While I don't do that, I do end up pressing my hands flat to cup his face, but it's a gentle hold meant to garner every ounce of his focus. What I have to say is important. I don't want him to miss a word.

"Your *geekiness*"—I spit the word, mad he's twisting it as some kind of insult—"is one of the best things about you. Geek chic is a *compliment*, not an insult. And"—I rise onto my toes, trying to get us as close to eye to eye as our height difference allows—"if some chick can't *appreciate* that about you, she isn't worth your time."

Again, his eyes slide to the left, but he brings them back to me when I pinch him tighter. "If you say so," he whispers.

"I do." I drop back onto my heels. "Plus…who's the love coach in this relationship?"

Did I just insinuate that we have a relationship? Oof, talk about a Freudian slip.

"Love coach?" Alex asks before coming over and propping his face on my shoulder. I swear I must have been a pirate in a previous life with how often people take this parrot position with me. "Tell me more."

Mushing Alex in the face, I ease him away. "So nosy." I tsk.

"What if I offered a bribe?" He lifts the bag and points to it.

"Depends." I start down the hallway, turning to walk backward when the guys start to follow. "What's in the bag?"

"Cheesesteaks," he states proudly, and my stomach is not the only one rumbling.

"We swung by to see Alex's family on our way back from Noah's and know better than to return from Philly without them," Kev tacks on, setting the bag on the island with an audible thump.

"Umm…" I eye the bag that sounded more like it's holding a bowling ball than greasy goodness. "I know you guys tend to put in some serious work when it comes to food, but it sounds like you bought enough to feed an army."

Alex confirms my suspicions, and I stop counting somewhere around the time he pulls out the dozenth foil-wrapped sandwich.

"Who the hell are you feeding with all that?" I wave at the gluttonous feast stacked in a wide pyramid.

"It's cute you'd think we'd roll through without telling the others." Alex boops me on the nose, claiming the barstool to my right while Kev takes the left.

"I'm assuming the others are Kay and Mase?" I hear CK's voice, but it takes me a moment to spot him leaning against the end of the counter. He's put as much distance between him and us as possible, watching us interact in a way I haven't seen him do in weeks.

"And Trav…and JT…and I'm sure Tessa and Savvy will tag along," Kev adds.

I accept the sandwich in Kev's outstretched hand with a nod of thanks. The sweet scent of grilled onions and peppers makes my mouth water as I unwrap the foil, grease coating my fingers within seconds of lifting the sandwich.

I'm millimeters away from beefsteak and melted cheese sauce nirvana, the soft dough of the hoagie bread touching my lips, when something dawns on me.

"Wait...you told them you were coming home, but not us?" I bounce a finger between CK and me.

"Eh, we knew we'd see you guys," Kev mumbles around what I swear is half the sandwich stuffed into his mouth.

"Yeah, those losers are living the nomadic life this summer," Alex adds.

"Nomadic seems like a bit of a stretch," CK deadpans. "At least until training camp starts for E in a few weeks," he says, referring to Kay's older brother Eric who plays for Baltimore.

"Speaking of training camp"—Kev drops the arm not holding his cheesesteak around my shoulders—"what's the sitch with this love coach thing? Do you have a costume? Is it a seggsy thing?"

A man who's a veritable brick wall, capable of stopping anyone who dares to try to get to Trav on the gridiron, should not use the word *seggsy*. Nor should they waggle their eyebrows so animatedly they look like they could detach from his face.

"Ooo, if it is, can I sign up to be on your team?" Alex raises a *Pick me, pick me* hand. "What's a little friends with bennies between roomies, am I right?" He puckers his lips at me, and I roll my eyes, more than used to his flirtatious nature.

"I did find myself in bed with CK the first day I took on the role." I shoot CK a wink, color staining his cheeks.

Kev and Alex whip their gaze around, literally sitting on the edge of their seats for his confirmation.

Instead, CK focuses on me. "I thought you said literal answers need not apply," he teases, still not letting me off the hook for my highly inappropriate reaction to his *You push me over* answer.

"That's for writing prompts." I try to sound tough, but even I can hear the smile in my voice. "And it's not like I lied."

"Yeah, but you're making it sound like something it wasn't, Red."

"Red?" Kev asks.

"What happened to Q?" Alex adds.

I ignore the commentary from the peanut gallery, too busy

waving the metaphorical pom-poms over CK calling me Red in front of others for the first time.

"Fine." I huff like he's ruining all my fun when, in reality, I'm just getting started. "You wanna tell them all about my exceptional skill at *blowing a whistle*?" I add a seductive purr to the phrase, dirtying it up.

Alex does a spit take, onions, peppers, and beefsteak flying in all directions, while Kev ends up choking on his.

Having dealt with me on his own for weeks now, CK doesn't succumb to the tease. "Uh-huh, that's why I stole that damn whistle and tossed it off the balcony."

That he did. The jerk is lucky it didn't hit anybody.

"Wait...are we talking about a *literal* whistle?" Kev asks, then mimes bringing a whistle to his lips. "Like the shiny silver kind Coach Knight uses to pierce our souls when he calls out a new set of wind sprints?"

"Yup," I say longingly.

"Damn." Alex smacks the counter, the slap of his palm ringing out almost as loudly as the bleats of my whistle did that morning. "We're missing all the good stuff."

CHAPTER14

THE THUNDERING RUMBLE of bowling balls rolling down the wooden lanes followed by the crash and scattering of the corresponding pins toppling over has been the soundtrack of the evening.

Unfortunately, the cacophony inside Victory Lanes pales in comparison to the chaos inside my own head.

This was not at all how I thought tonight would go, and I imagined countless scenarios—ranging from the mundane to the mortifying—about how tonight's date with Julia would play out.

Sure, as far as dates go, this one hasn't been terrible. Though the bar was set pretty low since my most recent one ended with a bailout call.

Shifting around in the hard plastic seat, I do my best to get comfortable as Julia—just Julia, no Jules or any other godforsaken (her words, not mine) nicknames for this woman—walks up to take her next turn.

The white sundress she's wearing glows beneath the neon and black lights the bowling alley turned on at the start of cosmic bowling an hour ago.

Has it really been that long? We're three frames into our second game, so…probably. Look at that—a new record for me. Quinn would be so proud.

And…

Shit!

That's my problem right there—I shouldn't be thinking about Quinn while out with another woman. I need to put my focus back where it belongs—on my date, *not* my love coach, or how cozy she looked, laughing and joking with our other roommates.

Julia brings both her arms forward, holding her pink ball just below face level for a beat. Her shoulders rise and fall with the same measured breath I've seen her take every time she shoots the ball. Finally ready, she takes two steps forward, her right arm going into her backswing, her right leg shooting out diagonally behind her.

The ten pins at the end of the lane burst apart in an explosive strike—her third in a row.

There's zero fanfare when Julia returns. No shimmy of her shoulders or silly dance move to celebrate the turkey she just scored, and I don't bother holding up a hand for a high five. The first time I did that, she looked at me like I'd lost my mind, but thankfully refrained from adding any comments about me being lame.

Instead, I wait for her to slide her hands behind her thighs and smooth down the back of her dress so she can slide daintily into the seat beside me.

"Did you know the reason it's called a turkey is because turkeys were usually the prize for most bowling tournaments in the 1800s?" One of the random facts Quinn rattled off to me while hyping me up for tonight rolls off my tongue.

"Umm…" Julia blinks at me, and I hate how I notice that their brown hue isn't as deep and rich as Quinn's.

Shit, I'm doing it again.

"That's *interesting*?" Something inside me deflates at how Julia phrases her response as a question instead of a statement. We connected fine through text, but the practical application leaves a lot to be desired.

The whirr and clatter of Julia's ball returning from the automatic machine brings an end to the awkward moment, and I excuse myself to take my turn.

Standing at the end of the lane, I wish the only thing weighing on me was the weight of the fourteen-pound bowling ball cradled between my hands. This whole night has felt...off.

And honestly, I'm not sure why. A part of me wants to blame it on being distracted, and while, yes, I can admit that's part of the problem, that's not the crux of it. No, that's...

Well, when I figure it out, I'll let you know.

Hurling my ball down the lane, I successfully knock down eight of the ten pins.

Damn.

Of course, I end up with a split, and a 7-10 split, no less. Makes sense and fits with the current complicated theme of the night. It's a tough shot, one of the hardest to pick up statistically, but a feat I know I'm capable of accomplishing.

Excited shouts draw my attention to the lanes next to ours as I wait for the machine to deliver the bright green ball I selected earlier. The large group, chest bumping, ass slapping, and laughing, reminds me so much of the scene I left behind at home.

The slippery soles of my rented shoes slide across the wooden floor as the feeling of being on the outside looking in washes over me. I wonder if my friends are sad I'm not there for our group's impromptu reunion, or is my absence unnoticeable? I mean, Quinn is there. She's the fun one and fits in with them better than I could ever hope to.

Retaking my position, the remaining two pins taunt me with their existence. *Fuck me.* Those goddamn cylindrical pins only serve as a visual reminder of the architect behind the evening's festivities.

Quinn.

Quinn, who would be hurling all kinds of creative trash talk from behind me.

Quinn, who would be making a few questionable attempts to distract me from my shot. She wouldn't give a single damn if anyone looked at her sideways for them either.

Quinn was bumping and playfully shoving Kev the same way she's been doing to me for weeks as I was leaving earlier.

Fuck!

Why is it that last thought that has me squeezing my eyes shut until the lights flashing behind my lids could rival those reflecting in the high shine of the lanes?

Blowing out a breath, I ignore my constantly churning mind and stare down the "goalpost" setup of the revered 7-10 split. This is a challenge I can handle. Calculating where to aim and how much spin to put on the ball to pick up the spare feels far easier to figure out than this date itself.

I strike the 7 pin on the inside perfectly, the velocity enough to send it bouncing off the sidewall and rebounding out and across the deck into the 10.

There's a roar of cheers, *Oh shit*s and *Did you see that*s echoing over the thumping music from our lane neighbors.

Julia gives me a small smile, but that's it.

There are no shouted *woo*s.

She's not jumping into my arms with an exuberant *Did you see that?*

She's not bowing down to my accomplishment while following it up with a *Now watch me do it better.*

What does it say that the strangers next to us celebrated harder than my date?

More importantly…why am I comparing her to Quinn —again?

The rest of the night continues with more of the same. Julia wins the first two games, showing off her kingpin skills, with me squeaking out a win for our third.

Neither one of us says much as we wait to exchange our shoes at the rental counter, but an air of expectant tension builds between us.

I'm not quite sure what I'm supposed to do next. I think I worried so much about getting a date to stay for the whole time that I neglected to consider what would happen after it was over.

Do I ask her on a second date right now? Do I even want another one with her?

Do I tell her I'll text her?

Do I tell her I'll call her?

Do I kiss her? Is kissing on a first date too forward?

The closer we get to the exit, the faster my heart starts to beat, until each pulse feels like it pulls my skin tighter to my bones. My palms are sweaty as I rub my tingling fingertips together. Sweat drips down my back as we weave through the parked cars in the lot, though it has nothing to do with the balmy early summer heat.

Julia points to a gray Toyota Corolla. "This is me." She spins, putting her back to the driver's side door.

As if this night hasn't been awkward enough, I have to lean against the tan SUV in the next spot over to avoid crowding her. The vehicle's driver obviously failed coloring in kindergarten given how poorly they stayed inside the white painted lines.

Julia fiddles with her keys, her gaze watching each rotation of the music note key chain around her finger.

Unsure what to do with my own hands, I shove them into my pockets, worrying the tar of the payment with the toe of my all-white Adidas. A discarded cigarette butt lies inches from my shoe, the filter flattened as if run over instead of just crushed beneath someone's foot.

What would Quinn say if you told her you focused on someone's garbage instead of your date?

For the first time tonight, the thought of Quinn doesn't bring that pang of guilt. My subconscious is right. There's no *would* about it—it's a *will*. I'll be lucky if I make it off the elevator before she pounces and asks for a play-by-play. She cheers at too many football games not to Monday morning quarterback the first "official" date she arranged for me.

Unless…

What if she's too busy with the others when I get back? It's easy to hang out, to make me feel like a priority when I'm the only option around.

I know, I know—Quinn is my friend, and her friends are my friends. But friendship only extends so far. Plus…I'm pretty sure the main reason she even agreed to our arrangement is that Emma and Kay asked her.

After months spent listening to them harp about how much Quinn liked me, I should be relieved they enlisted her help in my dating endeavors instead.

They're finally moving on. And not a moment too soon.

I'll never tell them how close I came to believing them, how their words of encouragement bolstered me enough to…maybe… potentially, put aside my fears and take a chance with Quinn. Then I went home for winter break and was slapped back to reality.

Inside our town's coffee shop, I was cornered by my high school's old quarterback and his running back. They took great pleasure in scrolling through the UofJ411's Instagram in front of me, the football team's berth to the national championship game making Mason and the guys national news.

"Aww, if it isn't our valedictorian. Who knew nerding it up could get a person a social scholarship to go with an academic one."

"Wow. How do you apply for that, Chrissy?"

"Tell us, Chrissy…is nerd outreach one of the philanthropies for your school's Greek system?"

"Oh yeah, that has to be it, right? There's no way any of these people would willingly spend time with your loser ass."

I could hate my bullies, but I know this isn't like the movies. The nerd doesn't end up with the popular cheerleader. This is real life.

A hand touches my stomach, and I jump about four feet in the air.

Julia's watching me with a sheepish expression on her pretty face as I get my high-strung self to settle down.

"Sorry." She's still twisting her key ring around her fingers. "I wasn't sure if you were trying to work up the nerve to kiss me good night or not, but you haven't said anything for like three minutes." She shrugs, enough color creeping into her cheeks for me to make it out in the muted lighting of the parking lot. "So I figured, what the hell, I might as well initiate it."

Guess that answers my earlier question.

A good-night kiss is a go.

"No, I'm the one who should be apologizing." I work to clear my throat. "Give me a chance to…uhh…" I glance back at the bowling alley, the oversized illuminated sign of Victory Lanes giving me an idea. "Pick up a spare?"

Is that corny? Yes.

Is it awkward? As all damn hell.

Does it work? There's the tiniest tilt to Julia's lips, so unless she's having a mouth spasm all of a sudden, I'm going to say…*maybe?*

"You've been doing it all night. Why stop now?"

Oh my god.

She said yes.

You heard that too, right?

I used a punny bowling reference to ask if I could kiss this woman, and she said yes.

Oh-kay then.
I guess we're doing this.
Here goes nothing.

QUINN

"*OHMIGAH.*" I wave an arm around, my other banded around my middle. "Stop—no more—mercy—" I choke out, my laughter stealing both my breath and my words.

Trav continues to arm pump and hip thrust undeterred. "Am I turning you on, *mami*?" He moves across the deck until he's standing in front of me, the ends of his makeshift "grass" skirt hitting me with each forward pump of his lower body.

Just as Kev and Alex predicted, the others arrived shortly after CK left for his date—an unexpected distraction I'm now supremely grateful for.

Unable to breathe, I shake my head and clutch at my stomach, the muscles sore and screaming for a break. Conditioning work-outs have nothing on hours of continuous laughter when it comes to working out the core.

"I should have drowned your ass in the Pacific when I had the chance," Mason complains as Trav continues to dance around the balcony.

"Puh-lease." Trav shuffles over until he's giving Mason—and unfortunately for her, Kay as well, since she's snuggled in his lap

—a lap dance. "Your life would be incomplete without me, bruh."

"Keep telling yourself that, bro."

Livi giggles, contorting her body around to see her brother. "You do realize you were the one who picked him as your best friend, right?" She hooks a thumb at a now twerking Trav, another wave of giggles breaking the *Why you trying to act tough?* eyebrow arch she had going on.

And that's how my night has been. It started with a bro-hugging arrival, followed by macho man loving and trash-talking antics since.

The cheesesteaks didn't last very long. They were devoured like the guys were a swarm of piranhas and not the captains of the football team. Then Trav disappeared back inside the apartment, and that's when things really took a turn for the ridiculous.

It's a damn good thing I have no shame, otherwise QB1's QB2 —aka his dick, and yes, that's what he calls it—would be broken for pilfering clothes from my laundry.

Why?

Because when Mr. Quarterback reemerged to show off the hula dancing skills he learned in Hawaii, he used my underwear to make the "grass" skirt to help him get into character.

I hung them in the laundry room for CK to see, hoping the sight of my underthings would make him think of me *in* them.

Instead, now bright lace, satin, and spandex flutter with every swish of Trav's hips. I have to give him credit for his ingenuity, though. The way he threaded his T-shirt through the straps of my bras and panties to create the "belt" of his skirt was brilliant.

Plus, seeing a shirtless six-foot-plus man gesticulating like a drunk giraffe makes the annoyance of having to rewash every-thing totally worth it, not to mention the TikTok and Instagram gold I'm capturing on video for him to use as content later.

"I can't take it anymore." I push up, struggling to get up from my spot on the lounger. "I have to pee."

I step inside the apartment, the raucous sounds from outside instantly muted. Willing myself not to check the time, I make a beeline for the bathroom I share with Emma and take care of business. CK will get home when he gets home. No need to borrow trouble.

The elevator dings as I exit the bathroom. *CK's home.* I lean against the back of the couch to wait. For once, it seems like the universe is on my side with its timing, gifting me with the opportunity to put an end to my incessant wondering.

Except…

When CK makes his appearance, the front of his lightweight turquoise polo is stained with blood.

What the hell happened to him?

I gasp, rushing forward. "Superman, are you okay?"

Instantly I reach for his face, only for him to jerk away.

I'm not having it.

Protectiveness surges through me, and I grab him, cupping his face and holding him still. I need to see where he's hurt, how bad it is, and then figure out who I must kill.

"I'm fine," he says and tries to move out of my hold, but I don't relent.

"You're covered in blood, so I say that's far from fucking *fine*." I push onto my toes, trying to get closer.

CK sighs, refusing to meet my eye. "It's not mine."

"*Pinche mierda.*" I tuck my thumbs beneath his chin, pushing so he can see the glare I level him with. "You think *that* makes it any better?"

Still…

This frustrating-as-fuck man stays resolute in his silence. If I weren't so damn worried about him being injured, I'd throttle him myself.

He reaches up to fix his glasses, his arm brushing along mine as he does. Those butterflies, both his touch and that adjustment usually set free, remain dormant as he slides his gaze to the glass wall leading to the balcony.

His cheeks fill with color, and I do my best to finish my inspection of his person as quickly as possible, my concern for him palpable. Curling my fingers around his nape, I use my thumbs under his jaw as a pivot point and angle his head this way and that.

Satisfied that he was, in fact, telling the truth and there are no visible injuries, I lower to my heels. Casting my own glance toward the balcony, I'm grateful that the lighting allows me to see outside without them being able to see in.

Not wanting to be stumbled upon should they come looking to see what's taking me so long to come back, I link my hand with CK's and drag him in the direction of the laundry room. We have things to discuss, and we certainly do not need an audience.

I even go as far as shutting the pocket doors that close off the room behind us.

"Take off your shirt," I instruct, opening the cabinet housing the stain remover.

Spray bottle in hand, I turn, only to see a still-shirted CK looking at me like I've lost my mind.

"Why are you still wearing your shirt?" I make a *Come on, off with it* motion with my hands.

CK's eyebrows fly up his forehead, and still…his shirt stays on.

"*Ay dios mío*, Christopher." I slam the plastic bottle on the countertop above the two sets of washers and dryers and stalk toward the stubborn man, yanking on the end of his shirt.

"Why are you trying to get me naked?" There's a tiny hitch to CK's lips when he stares at my strangling hold.

Listen, it was either wring the cotton or his neck. I went with the option least likely to end up with me in the big house.

I scoff. "I didn't ask you to drop trou." I roll my eyes. "I asked you to take off your shirt, so it doesn't stain beyond repair."

"Don't worry about it, Q." CK wraps his hands around my wrists. "I'll just throw it out."

"Don't do that." I pout. I love this shirt on him. "It really makes your eyes pop." And it does. The greenish undertones in the turquoise pick up the darker navy that rims the outer edges of his irises, making the inner circles almost look like they're glowing.

"Maybe if I used lines like that, my date tonight would have gone better than it did."

A part of me is sad his date wasn't great, but another part—a piece slightly larger and one that wholly makes me an asshole— is happy.

What the hell am I doing to myself? I've never thought of myself as a masochist, but what else is there to explain my behavior?

If these past nine months have taught me anything, it's that getting CK to realize my feelings toward him are genuine is an uphill battle. Watching him go on dates, *helping* him go on those dates, is an exercise in insanity.

"Want to tell me about it?" I ask, purposely keeping my voice soft.

His mouth presses into a flat line and his nostrils flare.

I wait him out, wait for him to say something...anything. Hell, I'd play a round of *Blue's Clues* at this point if it'd give me any insight into what happened with...Julia? That was her name, right?

Oh, please. Don't try to pretend you didn't memorize every factoid on that chick's profile.

Shit!

I did. I totally did.

Julia Simon. Twenty-one years old. Member of her high school's national-winning debate team and valedictorian of her graduating class just like CK. Graphic design major about to start her senior year at the U of J.

Not only is she better suited for someone like CK on paper, she's also freaking gorgeous to boot.

Mamá constantly harps on about the importance of always looking one's best, insisting I should *never* leave the house without "putting my face on," but what's the use of being pretty if that's the only thing people see when they look at you?

I'm tired of the superficial, surface-level relationships I had before Emma brought me into her inner circle. These friendships I've formed over this last year are more meaningful than almost any others I've had before—at least outside of *Abuelita*.

Is it so wrong to want a similar connection with the person I share my heart with?

I worry the cotton of CK's shirt, twisting and bunching it in my fingers until I'm unable to handle the uncertainty of not knowing any longer. "Was she a sore loser or something?" I bite my lip, second-guessing the decision to suggest bowling for their date.

After learning CK used to play in a league with his gramps, I honestly thought it was a great suggestion. Bowling is one of those tried-and-true first date activities because it offers built-in conversation starters. It also happens to be an activity CK is already confident in, so it should have been a win-win.

"Or did you play the gentleman tonight and let her win?" I tease to disguise any of my own feelings.

"You mean like I did with you and *Dr. Mario*?"

My jaw drops, and I narrow my eyes at him, aghast. "You are *such* a *liar*, Christopher." A string of Spanglish nonsense spews out of me when the full weight of his insult hits.

"Uh-oh." CK moves to step away from me but can't because of the hold I still have on his shirt.

"Uh-oh is right, mister," I growl, stepping a foot between his, our chests bumping. "Blasphemous claims about my *Dr. Mario* skills will only have me seeking retribution."

I already know the perfect punishment. Thank god for Amazon Prime.

"Causing women to curse my name seems to be the theme of the night." I'd laugh, but the sadness coating CK's words tells me we're no longer joking.

"You wanna tell me about it?" I ask softly.

He shrugs, the action causing his shirt to tug inside my grip.

"Ugh...take this off." I unclench my hands and slip them beneath the hem, my fingers flexing at the feel of his warm skin.

CK sucks in a breath, the definition of his abdominals growing as his stomach goes concave at my touch.

We both freeze, our gazes crashing together through the lenses of his glasses.

Finally, he swallows, his Adam's apple bobbing, and I find myself mirroring the action—though it's a struggle for me because my hormones clog my throat.

Smoothing my palms around to CK's sides, I glide them up his torso, bringing the shirt with me. I have to bite down on my lip until the coppery taste of blood hits my tongue to restrain a moan at both the feel and sight of him. Inch by inch, his body is exposed to my gaze as I lift the cotton higher.

I may not be the shortest girl who lives here and he may not be the tallest guy, but still, I have to rise up onto my toes. This time when my chest brushes against his, I'm the one sucking in a shuddered breath, acutely aware of how hard my nipples are as they drag along his body.

I'm burning up, gooseflesh covering my skin as I imagine doing precisely this, helping CK disrobe, in an entirely different scenario...one where the door we're closed behind belongs to my bedroom and it hasn't been only minutes since he got home from a date with somebody else.

CK eventually bends, making it easier for me to ease the shirt off and over his head. His hands fall to my hips once free, the brush of his thumbs along the band of my shorts putting all kinds of ideas in my head.

Busying myself, I drop my gaze from the tempting man in front of me and pointedly focus on turning the polo right side out. The blood has already dried to a deep brown, and even after treating it with the stain solution, the shirt might be a lost cause.

Still…

Fixing it will give me something to do and hopefully help me remember what my role is here—love coach, not love interest.

Putting some much-needed distance between us, I move back to the counter and grab the spray bottle. "Okay, stop trying to avoid it." I glance back over my shoulder. "Give me the play-by-play."

CK's body is stiff, his hands shoved in the pockets of his linen shorts, his shoulders bunched up near his ears. "Why?"

I sigh, rolling my eyes at his petulant tone.

"Because any athlete worth their salt knows the only way to get better is to study game tape."

"I think it's more than obvious I'm not a jock."

My movements still, the plastic handle of the toothbrush I'm using to loosen the blood from the fibers of the shirt digging into my palm as I squeeze it tighter.

Meticulously setting everything down, I slowly spin to face CK. With the counter behind me, I lean against it, reaching back and curling my hands over the beveled edge of the countertop.

"I don't know…"

I give him one hundred percent of my attention, tracking my gaze from the top of his stylishly messy hair over those yummy sexy glasses, my heart cracking at the vulnerability swimming in the blue orbs behind them.

"I've seen you working out with the guys." Or more like shamelessly watched him.

My inspection continues down the length of his body, noting the unassuming muscle tone those sessions have crafted.

Physically he's hot as hell.

But…

Gah!

I wish he saw himself the way I see him.

His looks are the smallest piece of my crush on him. His wit.

His charm. The way he can explain and teach a person something without making them feel stupid. His unflinching loyalty to those he cares about. Those are the things I value most.

It's criminal how a person who has as much to offer as CK can become blinded to all the things that make them special, how insecure douchebags can twist their own shortcomings and project them onto those they deem weaker and unworthy.

"But I was speaking more metaphorically since I'm supposed to be your coach and all."

It's become sort of a bad habit of mine to remind him of my role in his life. I can't decide if it's a brilliant plan or pure stupidity. Yes, I've admitted that Tessa's strategy has been working in getting him to open up to me, but…why can't I shake the feeling that this is all just going to blow up in my face?

"Now tell me about your date."

He's silent for so long I begin to suspect he's going to continue with his evasion. "I think I broke her nose."

"What?!" I all but shout, not at all prepared for that to be what he says when he finally chooses to speak.

CK flinches, his answering nod so minuscule it could barely be classified as a confirmation.

"Sorry." I clasp my hands together, attempting to rein in my shock. "Umm…" I quickly cycle through bowling scenarios that could lead to a broken nose but come up empty. "You mean…like you didn't realize she was standing so close, and when you swung your arm back to shoot, you clocked her in the face?"

I have no clue if this is possible or not, but it's all I got. Honestly, a toe or a foot is more along the lines of the bones I could imagine being broken in a game of bowling. It's easy for a ball to slip and land on a foot, but a nose? Oof.

"I wish." His deadpan delivery has me laughing as I ask, "What?"

He sighs, his head tipping back on his shoulders. He keeps his gaze trained on the ceiling and says, "I think I broke her nose when I tried to kiss her good night."

I blink, stunned, speechless.

Umm…

I guess given the blood on his shirt, it sorta makes sense, but…

How?

"Okay…I'm going to need you to paint me a picture here, Superman."

As if my request pulled the plug on his reservations, the events of the night spill out of CK like a dam bursting.

He tells me how Julia bested him two games to one, how as impossible as it sounds, she seemed more reserved than him, and unlike him, she didn't seem to thaw when he tried to use my questions and fun facts on her.

I have to clamp my teeth together to not let out an audible squee upon hearing how he appreciates my randomness.

A rock of disappointed sadness settles in my gut when he tells me about the strangers at the lane next to them celebrating his 7-10 split more than Julia did. I make a mental note to tell the others when we get outside.

"I couldn't even tell you if she had a good time or not, so by the time the date was over, I was all—" He circles his hands by his head. It's something I've noticed he does any time he apologizes for zoning out on me when we hang out. "I even jumped when *she* tried to kiss me because I was all caught up in my own head."

"You jumped?" He nods. "How high?" I can't keep my smile from creeping into my voice.

"Why does that matter?" Oh, I know that exasperated tone of his well.

"Because I need it to gauge the severity of the situation. A little oh-my-god-you-scared-me jump like you do when you hear a loud noise in a scary movie is not the same as the feet fully losing-contact-with-the-ground type."

"What about the kind that has you splattering salsa all over a person?" Some of his embarrassment falls away as he turns the tease around on me, as does some of the space between us as he moves closer.

"You're never going to let me live that down, are you?" I hoist myself onto the counter, never taking my gaze off his twinkling one as I slide back and cross one leg over the other.

"Would you if the situation were reversed?"

I pretend to ponder the question but eventually shake my head with a laugh. Yeah, right.

I make a rolling motion with my hands. "Okay…get to the part where you think you broke Julia's nose. You didn't like"—I mime a palm strike to the face—"when she scared you, did you?"

He takes two more steps closer. "I wish."

Oh-kay.

"CK," I prod again.

"Umm…" He grips the back of his neck. "So after proving just how much of a geek I am—" I growl at the comment, but he ignores it, clearing his throat and taking another step closer. "I used a corny bowling pun to confirm permission…and…I…" He's now close enough that I can feel his body heat on my bare legs. "Uh…leaned in to kiss her but must have miscalculated the angle or something, and instead of us kissing…I…kinda… sorta…headbutted her."

"No." I breathe the word out in disbelief.

"Unfortunately, yes." His dry tone has the laugh I was desperately trying to restrain bursting free.

My hands come up to cover my mouth. "Oh, CK."

"Yeah…so…"

My mind starts to spin as his words trail off again. My gaze bounces between us, the height of the counter making it so I'm taller than usual and throwing off my calculations.

"Why do you look like you're trying to do math in your head?"

Ouch.

I shake off his accidental dig and turn it into a joke instead. "Well…I mean, I kind of am."

His head swivels around, glancing around the laundry room before coming back to me with a shrug. "Wouldn't chemistry be more fitting for this room than equations and limits?"

I hop down from the counter, my landing quiet thanks to my bare feet and years of experience dismounting stunts. "Listen, funny man…" I toss my hair back and poke CK in the chest. "Math may be the devil's work, but I'll have you know I squeaked out an A-minus in business calc."

He holds his hands up, stepping away from my touch as if expecting me to strike him. "I didn't mean any offense, Red."

He just had to go and call me Red, didn't he?

Dammit.

"It's your damn fault I'm over here thinking I need to bust out my protractor to figure out what angle you could have come in on that had you headbutting that poor woman's nose." Again I have to smother a giggle behind my hand as a slow-motion replay runs inside my head.

"It's not like they cover kissing angles in geometry." He tosses his arms in the air defensively.

A smile stretches my lips. We're quasi-arguing, and I'm over here grinning like a fool *because* we're arguing. Why? Because a month ago, CK would have *never* had the confidence to do so with me. With Em and Kay? Sure. Me? Not so much.

"See?" I pop him on the arm with a backhand. "And you're over there making fun of me for trying to figure it out."

He smirks and adjusts his glasses. He. Freaking. Adjusts. His. Glasses.

I'm done for. My brain cells are officially on lust overload.

Scrunching my toes, I dig them into the skinny rug placed in the center of the room and close the gap that has grown between CK and me.

"Show me," I suggest.

CK's brows dip below his frames. "Show you what?"

"Show me how you went in for the kiss."

He rears back. "What?"

Oh, that sputtering incredulity is so not good for the ego.

Bouncing a finger between us, I say again, "Show me how you went in for the kiss."

"*Why?*" He drags the question out to multiple syllables.

"Because I'm still having a hard time picturing how it was physically possible to do what you suspect you did." I clap my hands together, the sound ringing out in the acoustics of the room. "Now come on." I crook a finger. "Show me."

He shakes his head, a lock of his hair falling over his forehead, but he ignores it as he stares me down. "I don't want to hurt you."

"You won't," I say with complete certainty.

"You don't know that." He gives me another headshake. "I don't need your dad or someone flying out here to remind me how you don't mess with Texas if I inadvertently break his baby girl's nose."

I snort. I can't help it; the visual is too damn amusing. "For one"—I extend a finger—"it's *Abuelita* you should be scared of, not Daddy. And for two"—a second finger gets added—

"*Mamá* would probably buy you a thank you gift for *finally* creating the opportunity to make it *perfectly symmetrical*."

CK arches a brow at my tone but doesn't comment. Thank god because even I know I sounded a tad more sarcastic and bitter than I intended.

"Now stop stalling. You should know me well enough by now to know I'm not letting you out of this room until we do this."

He twists, looking toward the closed door as if he's contemplating making a run for it.

I stiffen, waiting for a rejection.

Instead, CK turns back to face me. His hands shake, then ball into fists at his sides before he draws in a deep inhalation.

Planting my heels, I wait him out. He needs to make the first move because if it's me, it'll only end with me throwing myself at him.

Finally, his hands rise to cup my shoulders, his hold not loose but not tight either; it's more like it's just…there.

I lift my chin, tilting my face toward CK, only to have him rapidly descend toward me. I can't think of any other way to describe it. There's no finesse, no buildup. It's like I'm Marsha Brady, and he's the football flying directly for my nose. Thank you, *TV Land*, for that pop culture reference.

"Whoa." I bob and weave out of harm's way.

"Sorry." A blush fills CK's cheeks.

"Don't apologize." I latch on to his forearm when he tries to slink away. "It showed me what I needed to know."

"Yeah, that I'm such a lousy kisser my lips don't even need to make contact to reveal that."

I give him a good smack to the shoulder, the skin-on-skin contact making the hit sound worse than it was. Whoops.

"Stop talking about my friend like that." I arch a brow, daring him to challenge me again.

And you know what he does? The stubborn man accepts my challenge. *Mierda.*

"Don't lie to me."

I huff out a breath. "I'm not."

"You are. It's fine. You can tell me the only angles I excel at are with billiards and bowling, not the babes."

"The babes?" I chuckle. "Points for alliteration, though."

"Don't make me laugh. This is serious, Quinn."

"Must be if you're back to calling me Quinn and using that extra-deep voice," I say, lowering the register of my own voice to mimic his. "Now, will you chill so I can show you where you went wrong?"

Oh, wow. If only Tessa could see me now. If she were in here instead of outside on the deck, she would slow-clap the move I'm about to make, it's that good.

"Okay," I say, more to psyche myself up after he nods.

I can totally do this.

Thumbs pressing along my fingers, I crack my knuckles, then shake out my hands before lifting them to rest on the curve of his shoulders.

"First, you wanna go slow." I glide my hands toward his neck. "They may know what's about to happen, but if you take your time, it helps build the tension."

My fingers fan out, touching as much of him as possible as I follow the curve of his throat up to the strong line of his jaw.

"Touching like this is always good." I cup the side of his face, the skin still smooth from when he shaved, preparing for his date tonight. "It helps show a sense of possession and a level of care you don't always get to experience outside of this moment."

Shifting closer, I press onto my toes, balancing on them with the same skill I employ at the top of a stunt.

"As long as our hair isn't in some elaborate updo laden with bobby pins galore"—I thread my fingers through his thick mane, the strands short but enough to grab onto—"a little hair tugging works too."

Feet turn to inches, which turn to centimeters, and finally millimeters as I grow closer to CK's mouth.

I lick my lips, the puffs of his warm breath blowing across the moisture. His pulse is erratic under the flat of my palm braced on his chest, my own a chaotic beat of *Oh my god, I'm going to do this, I'm really going to do this.*

I'm going to kiss CK.

I'm finally going to know what it's like to have his lips on mine.

It doesn't matter that it's in a laundry room or that it's after he had a date with somebody else.

No. I've dreamed about this moment more times than I can count, and *nothing* is going to ruin it.

My instruction stops. We don't need words to know what to do.

The tip of my nose skims along his, and just as my eyes start to slide closed, I catch sight of how wide his are and note the feel of his nostrils flaring.

Oh my god. What am I doing?

I drop down on my heels, the slam of the hard floor reverberating through my bones.

It doesn't matter.

Pinche mierda.

I was *this close* to kissing CK…

All my dreams about to come true…

But one look at the expression on his face, and it was clear to see *I* was the last person he wanted to be kissing.

Of course he doesn't want to kiss me. If he did, he would have done so already. He had more than ample opportunity to do so these last few weeks.

"Ay dios mío." My hands fly to my face, pressing over my mouth as I take two quick steps backward, my back slamming into the countertop behind me. "I'm so sorry, CK."

His brow is furrowed hard enough to cause deep wrinkles. "Sorry about what?"

Oh my god. The hair on one side of his head is all fucked up because I was gripping it like a saddle horn.

"I got carried away—caught up in the heat of the moment and all." My words run together, my laughter awkward as all get-out. "It won't happen again. Promise."

#THEGRAM

#CHAPTER16

SackMasterSanders22: *picture of Kev, Alex, and Trav biting into cheesesteaks*
Sorry @GreatestGrayson37 they were too good to save any for you #YummyInMyTummy
@GreatestGrayson37: You are an asshole #ImNotSpeakingToYou

QB1McQueen7: *reel of Trav hula dancing with a skirt made of unmentionables*
Picked up some new skills on vacation #CareerMove #TheseHipsDontLie
@bookbird2020: Whose underwear and bras are those? #VictoriaIsntTheOnlyOneWithASecret
@mylifethroughfiction: Most people bring home a shot glass from vacation #NotchedThatBedPost

UofJ411: *REPOSTED—TheGreatestGrayson37: TRAITORS. All of them #INeedNewFriends—picture of Kev, Alex, Trav, JT, and Quinn huddled together laughing*
Well, if you're accepting applications… #WhereDoISign
@madameizzy: OMG! I'll be your BFF @GreatestGrayson37 #PickMe

@Acolon1729: Anyone else curious about what they did? #AskingForAFriend

@sweer_rhi86: Who cares? #YouGotAFriendInMe

CK

#CHAPTER17

"HELLO." I clear my throat, trying to get rid of the sleep coating it.

"Dude." The deep boom of G's voice has me pulling the phone away from my ear, my closed eyes scrunching tighter together against the onslaught of sound. "I still can't believe you didn't save me a cheesesteak."

Releasing a groan, I bury myself deeper into my pillows. It's been four days since Kev and Alex made an unplanned pit stop at the apartment before they continued on to visit Kev's family the next day. Which means it's been four days of listening to Grant bitch about how all the cheesesteaks were gone by the time he caught a train to join us.

"Why aren't you over that yet?" I prop the phone against the side of my face and rub the crusties from my eyes. Oof, they burn like a mother from staring at a computer screen until the wee hours of the morning.

Grant gasps, the sound so over the top I'd bet good money he'd be feigning fainting if he were here. The almost-seven-foot giant certainly has a flair for the dramatic.

Sounds like somebody else you know.

And like she's done every day since we almost kissed, Quinn finds a way to be one of the first thoughts to pop up in my brain.

"It hurts that you can even ask me that," G complains, and I imagine he's miming being stabbed in the heart. "I should void my friendship card as punishment."

"Void it?" I scoff. "You're the one who forced it upon me in the first place." The reasoning behind such an action still escapes me to this day.

"You're goddamn right I did." There's the faint sound of someone shouting in the background on Grant's side of the line, and I swear I can hear him wince. "Sorry, Mama."

Not bothering to disguise my amusement, I let my laughter fly and climb out of bed. "Did she threaten to wash your mouth out with soap?"

"Fu—" He cuts off the curse, finishing with a "Screw you, man."

"Aww," I coo. "Mama G's still there, isn't she?" He makes a noncommittal grunt. "Tell me…does she prefer the classic bar soap, or does she embrace your dad's New York roots and go full-on savage with the liquid variety?"

I get a pained groan in response. "*Why* did I call you?"

I shrug despite him not being able to see me. "I've been asking myself that same question for the last five minutes."

We joke, but a weight I didn't realize I was carrying lightens as we carry on. It's not the most logical fear, but there's always the worry that extended separations will lead to me easily drifting out of the group, that my being out of sight will lead to me being out of mind.

The one time I tried saying as much to Kay, she gave me an eye roll that could end all eye rolls, and the subject was never broached again.

But…just because we don't talk about it doesn't mean I don't think about it. I do—all the time. It's a constant worry hovering in the back of my mind. It doesn't matter that I spent most of my life as a loner. Now that I know what it's like to be accepted into a group, it'll be impossible to go back to a solitary existence.

"Don't you live in the land of famed pizza and dirty water dogs?" I ask, shrugging on a shirt, preparing to hunt down a giant cup of coffee.

"Don't forget our epic bagel game." Grant's drooling is audible.

"Exactly." I wave a hand at him, proving my point before another thought hits me. "What does Mama G think about you pining over cheesesteak when she's cooking you gourmet feasts on the daily?"

"Be easy, bro." I can't help but grin at the panic tinging his words.

Grant may have played up missing out on the cheesesteaks as some great culinary tragedy, but we all know he's eating like a king, living his best life as the spoiled mama's boy he is.

"It's the price you pay for waking me up."

"Now you sound like Smalls." Grant's bark of laughter sounds more like he's trying to hack up a hairball and has me jerking the phone away from my ear again. "Unlike when Kay is being her anti-morning self, it's well after noon, so you have no excuse."

"I'll remember this moment the next time I'm looking for a beta tester for the new additions to the game."

G is the only person from our core group that has seen, let alone played, the video game I've spent the last few years of my life developing. The thing is like my baby. Giving someone a peek at what I've been working on is like giving them a glimpse at my soul.

Our call doesn't last much longer before I'm tossing my phone on my dresser and heading out of my room. As has been the case these last few days, there's nothing attached to my door when I pull it open.

Not only has it been four days since Grant didn't get his cheesesteak, it's also been four days since a colorful Post-it note pried into my business.

I understood the first day—most of our other roommates and a handful of our friends were here.

But…

Monday?

Tuesday?

Today?

What the hell is going on?

At first, I thought it was all in my head, thought after the abrupt end to our almost kiss, my insecurities were flaring up and causing me to imagine Quinn was pulling away.

Except…

The more days that go by without a note, the more withdrawn she seems to get.

She hasn't accepted any of my challenges in *Dr. Mario*.

I haven't seen her cook in days.

She's been spending more time at The Barracks than ever before.

It's weird, and I swear it feels like she's avoiding me.

QUINN

THE SUN BEATS down on my shoulders from above, the blistering heat of the summertime rays causing sweat to dot my skin before I finish unrolling my yoga mat out on the deck. I don't care. I need the intense rays to chase away the chill from my mother's words.

"You're not going to be young forever, Quinny linda.*"*

It took everything in me not to respond with the *No shit* that sat on the tip of my tongue. Annoyance simmers in my blood as I bring one of the chairs over to my chosen spot and set my iPad atop the cushion.

"How are other suitors supposed to know you're available if you're constantly seen in photos with other men?"

I'd block her from my Instagram if I thought it would help that particular issue. Except, thanks to the UofJ411's penchant for reposting *anything* that has to do with our crew—especially when it's connected to their favorite couple to report on—that wouldn't change anything.

Stepping to the top of my mat, my feet close together, I inhale along with the eight people on the screen. I can't really see them thanks to the glare from the sun, but I don't need to. I've practiced yoga long enough to follow along without it.

Mamá is actually the one who first got me into the practice, so it's kind of ironic that I'm doing it now to help me forget the last few of our phone calls I haven't been able to shake off.

In her defense, it's not her fault. She hasn't said anything I haven't heard before. And just like the fifty million other times she's used the same rhetoric, it's never with malicious intent.

"Your looks are your gift, mi niña. *They'll help you land a man who will treat you like a queen."*

Again, things would be far less complicated, my feelings far easier to sort out if there was a self-serving reason behind her thought process. Except...

There's not.

Instead, my mamá is a first-generation Mexican woman, the first person—male or female—in her family to go to college, and at a major American university to boot.

It was there she met and fell in love with Texas Longhorn cornerback Eli Thompson. Daddy's torn Achilles may have put an end to his NFL dreams, but it didn't stop him from receiving a hero's welcome when he moved back home.

Tom Landry once said, "Football is to Texas what religion is to a priest." It made sense that when hometown football star Elijah Thompson—the same Eli who helped bring two state titles to his high school team and followed those with a collegiate national title—returned after graduation, he still managed to be a very big fish in our small pond.

That same consideration extended to both his new wife and the baby girl—yours truly—they had on the way.

I didn't grow up overly wealthy by any stretch of the imagination, but we were more than comfortable. There was always plenty for my cheerleading, and for those of you who aren't aware, club, aka all-star cheerleading, is expensive as fuck.

That's the kind of life *Mamá* wants for me. She never wants me to have to worry about putting food on the table, and to her, that's a goal easily accomplished by landing a high-profile husband in college like she did.

I just wish she recognized that we have the same goal. The only difference? I want to be the one to give it to myself with a successful career. I want my future husband to be my partner, not my caretaker. And when she says things like that? It picks at the already lifted scab from old hurts and incorrect assumptions.

From my friends: *"You want to be class president? But you're the homecoming queen."*

Why couldn't I have been both?

However, my personal favorite came from my guidance counselor: *"Do you* really *think you should go out for student council? Isn't the prom committee more your speed?"*

Though that misogynistic asshole only had his job because of nepotism. By the end of my high school career, I learned to take his advice with a grain of salt…and then a shot of tequila at the bonfires the football team threw after their games on Friday nights.

Focusing on my breath instead of those spiraling thoughts, I drive into my palms, pedaling my feet to loosen up the downward dog of my first sun salutation. Sealing my lips, I take the breath in fully through my nose, drawing my belly button up and in. Lifting my tailbone as high as it will go, I hold for one more beat before exhaling both the air from my lungs and the negativity from my system.

I've just entered the final downward dog of sun salutation A when a set of bare feet enters my field of vision at the edge of my mat.

CK.

The reason behind why *Mamá's* words hurt more than usual.

"You're much better at this than Kay," he observes as I jump my feet back to the front of my mat, folding forward and reverse swan diving to stand.

"That's because I practice it three times a week, whereas Kay just fits it in when she can." Or it might have something to do with me being out here by myself. The hijinks tend to increase and your form tends to take a downturn when you're gossiping with friends during your workout.

Moving through chair pose, I follow the steps of sun salutation B to take me back down to the mat.

Could I pause the video instruction? Sure. Do I? Nope. I'm not out here glistening in the hot summer sun for my health. Well…okay, I sorta am, seeing as yoga has been proven to have numerous health benefits, but you're missing the point.

I'm a woman on a mission, trying to find my zen after being

the one to take the metaphorical sledgehammer—or in my case, an attempted what-the-hell-was-I-thinking kiss—to it.

Unfortunately, the weight of CK's gaze on me as I move through the poses until I'm back on my feet leaning into crescent pose and can make eye contact again isn't helping that endeavor in the least.

For close to a year, all I wanted was to have CK near me, to have him not run away any time it was only the two of us in a room.

Now?

Now for the sake of my heart and my sanity, I *need* him to go away.

CK

OKAY...WHO is this woman, and what did she do with the vivacious Quinn I'm used to living with?

Shielding my eyes, I glance toward the sky, searching for UFOs. I never thought there'd be a day I'd wish for a creepy, wrinkly, E.T.-type alien to appear in my life, but Quinn's behavior? Yeah, it's so off I'm starting to worry we've fallen into a real-life *Invasion of the Body Snatchers* situation. Being taken over by pod people is the only explanation I can come up with for the sudden shift in her personality.

I don't have the faintest idea what's up with her, but it ends now.

Spinning on my heel, I stalk toward the sliding door that leads to my bedroom.

The center drawer to my desk almost goes flying off its track when I yank it open. It's a clutter-filled mess as I sort through the contents.

Then, there, amongst the paper clips, highlighters, and too many pens to count, I spot the hint of yellow I knew would be hidden under the debris.

My Post-its may be the standard yellow and not the fluorescent shades Quinn seems to favor, but it'll do for what I have in mind.

My introverted nature typically makes it difficult for me to open up to others. It's a facet of my personality that contributes exponentially to my difficulty level when using Greet Geek. But with Quinn and her outrageous notes? Answering them has started to feel…natural.

Now it's my turn to ask the question.

Hmm…

Pad and pen in hand, I start to pace. What could I ask that will help break my friend out of this weird funk she's fallen into?

My gaze snags on the wall my bedroom shares with the living room, as if I can see past both and into the laundry room on the opposite side of the penthouse.

That freaking almost kiss.

Sonofabitch. That's when everything changed, and it sure as shit wasn't for the better.

No matter how many times I've imagined what it would be like to kiss Quinn, I've always known that's all it would ever be —a fantasy. If I had any delusions of them becoming a reality, those were put to rest the other night when she ran into the counter trying to get away from me.

"Would…you…teach me?"

What the hell was I thinking asking Quinn that? As if enlisting her help wasn't bad enough, then I went and asked her to be my freaking love coach.

"Well…yeah…you know…you've sorta been doing that already, but I thought maybe we can integrate a more practical approach…do a few mock date activities and stuff."

It's like I offered myself up on a silver platter for the universe to fuck with me.

Oh, damn. Forget the universe. I blurred the damn lines myself.

What a goddamn mess.

Where the hell are those Lysol wipes Kay jokes with Trav about when you need them?

I'm not saying Quinn and I need to revert back to how things were before the summer started, but we need a way to wash away the awkward lingering from the other night. If we don't, I fear it'll fester, eventually turning the dynamic in the house septic until the only solution would be for one of us to move out. And we all know Quinn wouldn't be the one asked to pack her bags if it came to that.

Welp, that took a depressing turn for a Wednesday afternoon.

I'm dealing with enough as is; there's no need to go looking for trouble.

Back to my note.

Whatever I write on this paper needs to create an opportunity for us to challenge each other. Nothing sparks Quinn's feisty side quite like telling her she can't beat me at something.

What can I use?

Dr. Mario is out. We've done that already. And I'm certainly not going to suggest bowling.

Hmm…

Ugh!

I need coffee. When I saw Quinn outside in all her matching baby pink leggings and sports bra glory earlier, I forgot to make myself a cup.

Leaning against the counter as the machine percolates, my gaze snags on the pool table Mason had delivered shortly after we all moved in.

That's it. There's a pool hall not far from campus we can go to. Anywhere is better than here. We need to put some distance between us and the scene of the crime.

I send another glare toward the laundry room, then quickly scrawl the words: *I'll buy the first round if you can beat me at a game of pool.*

Steamy mug of coffee in one hand, two-by-two piece of paper in the other, I make my way back outside.

Quinn's still doing her yoga thing, her workout having her in some weird backbend pose that has her resting on her forearms and lifted onto her toes. This should be a safer position than the face-down-ass-up-dog, whatever you call it she was doing the first time I interrupted her workout, but it isn't. Whereas the one from earlier showed off her spectacular ass, this one demonstrates the extreme flexibility I've witnessed her display on the sidelines at all the guys' football and basketball games.

Jesus.

Chicks think they have it rough with their periods and stuff, but at least they can hide if they're attracted to a person. They have no idea how hard—pun unintentionally intended—it can get being a dude, to constantly have the risk of your spot being blown up by an appendage that dangles between your legs—or worse, when that same body part tries to override your common sense.

Seriously, bro, didn't we just spend the last fifteen minutes coaching ourselves away from these kinds of imbecilic fantasies you're championing for? Quinn doesn't want us like that. Get. The. Memo.

And now I'm having conversations with my dick. *Awesome.*

Discretely adjusting myself inside my shorts, I pad across the warmed, bordering on hot-as-burning-coals Trex planks.

Without giving me a chance to second-guess myself, I place the Post-it on the bared strip of Quinn's toned stomach, pressing down on the adhesive to make sure it really sticks.

"Wha—" Quinn startles but doesn't fall. Instead, she draws her feet impossibly closer to her body, then rolls through the position until she can straighten onto her knees.

Oh my god.

What is she doing?

Does she have *any* idea what seeing her in that position does to me? Hell…maybe she does, and she's trying to put an end to our now awkward living arrangement by killing me off. That could be it if it were possible for a person to die of acute lust overload brought on by an influx of X-rated fantasies.

The instructor continues to call out moves from the iPad, but unlike before, Quinn stops following them as she stares up at me instead.

Neither of us speaks.

I'm honestly incapable of speech at the moment, my mind too busy to formulate words thanks to the onslaught of naughty images flashing through it.

Quinn glances from the paper to me and back again. Her brow furrows, a light sheen of sweat clinging to the bunched skin. Her lips start to move as she reads. I remember discovering that adorable quirk studying for finals during the fall semester.

Her eyes blaze hotter than the sun above when she lifts them back to me once she's done, the Post-it pinched tight between her fingers. "I think I'm going to have to start rethinking your nickname, Christopher."

Ahh…there she is. Missed you, friend.

Quinn's the only person who lives here who uses my full name with any regularity. I press my lips together. Now that she's back to acting like herself, I know her well enough to know she wouldn't appreciate me being amused when she's trying to scold me.

"And which one would that be?" I ask, folding my arms over my chest.

Her eyes narrow, and she huffs. I mean sucked in breath, nostrils flaring, hands forming fists, shoulders dropping huffs at me. She's so much fun to rile up. I can't believe I never realized how easy it is to do.

"What?" I challenge. "I may not have as many nicknames as Kay, but there's still more than one you'd have to choose from." Unfolding my arms when she continues to eye me dubiously, I tick off each moniker on my fingers. "Obviously, there's CK, but I also have Superman from you and what seems to be your *new* personal favorite, *Christopher*." I make sure to use the same inflection she typically uses.

"How is your given name considered a nickname?" Fiery Quinn is back, and she props her hands on her hips, her boobs jiggling from the aggressiveness.

Stop looking at her tits, bro.

Fuck me.

I rake a hand through my hair, dragging my gaze upward. What's it going to take for the *It's never going to happen* reality to sink in?

I clear my throat. "It is when it's wielded as a scold and spat like a curse," I add on the *Like you do* with a raise of my eyebrows.

"Eh." She reaches out, sticking the note on me. "You usually have done something to deserve it."

A smirk tugs at my lips, and I dip my chin, taking in the yellow square resting between my pectoral muscles. "Mmmhmm, whatever you say, Red." I pluck the paper from my shirt. "Just get your beer money ready."

QUINN

"YOU'RE ENJOYING this far too much." I send CK a glare, taking a healthy swallow of my beer. And, yes, before you ask, it was one *I* had to purchase thanks to Mr. Pool Shark over there, racking the balls for our next game.

"I'm sure I have no idea what you're talking about, Red."

Gah!

Why does such a simple statement have my belly throwing basket tosses?

Leaning back in my chair, I cross one leg over the other and watch CK as he does his thing. I could do this all night and not get bored.

Pinche mierda.

Why did I let him goad me into coming out tonight? I should have ignored the dare hidden in his note and continued to avoid him. I should have put off facing the reminder that he doesn't *like* me the way I *like* him until my feelings were less raw.

Maybe then it wouldn't hurt so much to be the only one getting turned on watching the other play.

Instead, I'm drooling over the confident way he plays this game of skill. Imagining how those long fingers of his currently sliding over the edge of the rack to steady the break would feel sliding inside me instead. Pondering if he would exhibit the same commanding focus to drive me insane with pleasure as he does when taking each shot.

And that right there is the crux of the issue.

I want CK to press me into the felt of the table and have his wicked way with me, and he just wants to wipe the table with me in another game of eight ball. The only form of spanking on his mind is the margin by which he wins and not connecting the flat of his palm to my ass.

It was a mistake coming here with him. This feels too date-like. It's making it difficult to remember that CK is my friend and only wants to be that—my *friend*.

"Do you wanna break?" A pool cue enters my field of vision.

I startle, beer spilling over the rim of my glass. When did CK get over here?

"But you won."

CK's lips twitch, and he dances the cue side to side. "Figured I'd give you a fighting chance."

"How gentlemanly of you."

His bark of laughter at my dry tone has my girly bits going haywire.

You're just friends, Quinn. Stop getting turned on by your friend.

I should listen to that voice inside my head, but I don't.

Instead, I keep my eyes locked with CK's and wrap my fingers around the skinny stick he has angled in my direction. I drag my thumb up and down the polished wood, pleased when I see the slow bob of CK's Adam's apple.

Because I'm a glutton for punishment, I turn my flirt factor up another notch, slipping off of the bar-height stool I'm on, sliding my body along CK's on my way down to stand.

There's a slight glaze to his blue eyes, but it's gone two seconds later.

Sighing, I head for the pool table but can't help adding an extra arch to my back as I bend over.

Hope blooms as CK's gaze does a quick pass over my body, but it dies just as quickly as it appears when he only calls out a correction of the placement of my hand. That's right, he calls it out. As in, stays all the way over there like he's some YouTube instruction video.

What more proof do I need that the man isn't interested in me that way? If he were, he'd be taking advantage of the situation and my shameless invitation to help me. He would be behind me, bending over to align his body with mine to *show* me, not *tell* me what to do.

Ugh!

I break, using more force than is probably necessary given the solid crack of the cue ball hitting the neat triangle of balls, sending them scattering across the table.

Despite my warring emotions, CK and I end up falling into that same comfortable rhythm we established before almost-kiss-gate.

We joke. We laugh. I ask him random questions he pretends to be annoyed by, but I see the hint of a grin he smothers before he answers them.

The tables around ours continue to fill with people as it gets later. Cries of disappointment, colorful swearing, and raucous cheering are the soundtrack of the night.

Eventually, CK and I draw ourselves a crowd. Well…okay, it's CK who does, but I think I deserve a little bit of credit because it was my dramatic bowing at his last trick shot that drew their attention.

"Alright, Superman." I lay my stick on top of the pool table after he ends our current game by sinking the eight ball in the corner pocket. "I'm tapping out."

His gaze flits around the people surrounding us. "You want to go?" His cheeks fill with color when our audience groans in disappointment.

"No." I giggle, skirting the bodies closest to us. "But I think I've more than earned the right to relax and watch you do your thing." I hoist myself onto my chair, settling in like it's my throne.

"My thing?" CK asks adorably, looking far too sexy—again—with his cue stick braced at his side.

"Yup." I roll my hand like a queen telling the jester to proceed with their show. "Now stop holding back and show me what you can really do."

"I wasn't holding back."

I roll my eyes. I've seen him play pool far too many times with the others not to notice how he was restraining himself.

"Much," he finally amends. "What?" He adjusts his glasses. "I was worried about hurting your feelings if I trounced you."

My jaw drops. "Hardy-har-har, *Christopher*."

His lips purse to the side, one brow lifting as if to say *See? I told you you do that.* Damn. He's right. I've totally turned his full name into a nickname.

"Enough trash talk." I clap my hands. "Time to earn all this beer you've made me buy."

"*Made* you?" Now he's the one rolling his eyes as he collects the balls from the catch and starts to rack them. "I'm pretty sure the deal was I would buy the first round if *you*"—he points to me—"beat me." He hooks his thumb at his own chest.

"And what about rounds two and three?" I throw my arms up, clipping the dude closest to me in the stomach, or at least I'm assuming it's a dude based on the defined washboard he has smuggled under his shirt. "*Ohmigod*, I'm sorry!"

Warm hazel eyes blink down at me in amusement, and… whoa. His face totally matches the *abs for days* he has going on. There's nothing butterface-y about it. "Don't worry about it, beautiful."

Ooo, and he's charming too.

"*And* I don't think we're going to need a fourth since now you're beating up the locals." CK slides my beer glass away from me.

When did he get over here?

"Aww…" I pout, creeping my hand toward my beer, wanting to keep the happy buzz warming my blood going. "Don't ruin my fun, Superman." I boop his nose.

A deep chuckle comes from my right, sending CK's gaze bouncing between Mr. Charming McHot Pants and me.

Umm…

"Like I told your girlfriend, it's cool, bro." Charming McHot Pants runs a *No harm, no foul* hand down those abs I'm just tipsy enough to be more than a little curious about.

Thankfully, the burst of happiness I feel at hearing him call me CK's girlfriend is enough to distract Tipsy Quinn's loose tongue.

I'm beaming like I'm at the top of a stunt. Fortunately for me, it's beer in the glass I have cradled to my chest like it's the stuffed teddy bear I used to sleep with as a kid and not tequila. If I were hanging with my homeboy Jose tonight, I'd be fluffing my pony-tail and vamping it up like I do during competitions. That would be bad, seeing as there aren't any judges around.

Charming McHot Pants called me CK's girlfriend. First, he was all, *No biggie* when I accidentally assaulted him, and now he's calling me CK's girlfriend. I should use my fake ID to buy *him* a drink because my night just got a whole lot better.

I really, *really* like the way that sounded—

"She's not my girlfriend." CK's uncomfortable chuckle is like nails on a motherflipping chalkboard.

Could he denounce me any quicker?

"You two aren't dating?" Mr. McHot Pants bounces a finger between CK and me, the former shaking so enthusiastically I worry his head will pop off like a broken Barbie—or I guess Ken—doll.

Meanwhile, I sit frozen in my seat, fighting the sudden heat prickling behind my eyeballs that denial causes. I refuse to be that girl in the bar—or pool hall, in this case—drunk crying.

Now it's his gaze doing the bouncing. "Are you sure? You two certainly sounded like a couple."

Aww…that prickling starts to fade as I consider CK's and my interactions. You know what? We do sort of bicker like Kay and Mase do—

CK starts to laugh—no…wait…that's not laughing. He's full-on guffawing, the arm not holding the pool cue even folding over his middle. Yup, somebody else is feeling his beers. Good thing I already called in the cavalry—aka Kaysonova and company—to pick us and the car up. Neither of us is fit to drive.

But…

Still…

Ouch.

I know he doesn't *like* me like that, but is the idea of us dating really *that* laughable? Geez.

It takes a solid minute for CK to compose himself enough to speak. "If you knew our crew, you'd understand. Trash talk and nicknames are how we show our love."

Mr. Charming McHot Pants glances around at the now dwindling crowd before returning his attention to us. "Are we talking a *Step Up/Stomp the Yard*-type crew or the type where I should be worried about somebody coming after me with a baseball bat?"

I snort. His humor reminds me a bit of Noah's and helps ease some of the sting from CK's appalled reaction to someone linking us romantically.

"We have to refer to our group of friends as a crew because the cheerleaders"—CK holds a hand out in my direction—"already belong to a squad."

"You're a cheerleader?" McHots seems to perk up at this revelation.

"Isn't it obvious?" CK eyes my high ponytail, his tone coming across as…annoyed? Maybe a tad bit angry? I don't know. That's probably the beer talking.

Time to redirect my brain before I start to wallow and overanalyze every little thing.

"Ooo, we should totally choreograph a dance." I tap my chin. "How difficult do you think it would be to teach y'all the "Bye Bye Bye" dance?"

"Don't even think about it, Red," CK cautions, but my mind is already churning with possibilities. I hope Tessa is with Kay when they get here. *Chica* will be all over this idea.

"Too late." I waggle my brows, tacking on a wink.

"You *sure* you two aren't a thing?" Charming makes a loop with his finger. The perplexed expression on his face is cute, but could he *maybe* stop twisting the knife I feel wedged between my ribs?

"No. No." Again, could CK have answered any faster? Then he adds, "Definitely not."

There's a shift in the atmosphere, one strong enough that not even the alcohol can dull it. McHot's very broad shoulders roll back, and he drapes a muscly arm across the back of my chair.

He chances one more peek at CK, who's watching the exchange stiffly, before focusing the full weight of his attention on me. A dimple pops out in his right cheek, then he asks, "Since you're available, would you be interested in going on a date with me this weekend?"

Ay dios mío.

#CHAPTER21

NO AMOUNT of coding in the world can distract me from the memory of Quinn agreeing to go on a date with *Grady*. How the hell could it? I was standing right there when he asked her out. Every word they exchanged imprinted on my brain like my very own 1s and 0s.

Why the fuck wasn't that Grady guy some jockhole douchebag? I mean, it was obvious he was a jock before he even told us he's a winger for the hockey team at BTU, the other major Division 1 university in the state. But in the few minutes he spent talking to both Quinn and me, it was also clear to see he falls more on the same side of the jock line as my roommates than that of those I grew up with.

Still…

I abhor the thought of Quinn going out with the guy. Don't ask me why. It's illogical, but I guess it makes sense, since emotions aren't generally logical in nature.

It's the only explanation I can come up with for why I did what I did.

Never drink and text people. I mean it. *Never* do it. Nothing good comes out of drunk texting. Hell, I barely have any success doing it sober, but intoxicated? Yeah, that doesn't end in good life choices.

Though I'll admit, my gravest miscalculation lay in the order in which I chose my textees.

Like an Edgar Allan Poe novel, the text message threads taunt me from my phone despite having powered it off.

What did I do? Why did I do it?

Sonofabitch.

Want to know the real kick in the crotch? I can already picture how Quinn would throw one of her mini-celebrations if I told her what I did.

She'd squeal and clap her hands, maybe even throw herself at me to squeeze the life out of me in a hug, so proud of me for taking the initiative. She'd be all, "Oh, Superman, look at you being all confident with your bad self."

Little does she know, the only reason I opened up the Greet Geek app last night and asked out the first person in my saved messages was because *she* accepted a date of her own.

Who does that? An asshole, that's who.

But…

Wait for it…

My assholery doesn't stop there.

Nope. That honor goes to how my thoughts have only spiraled more since I heard Quinn return home after her shift at The Barracks.

For the last thirty minutes or so, I've been forcing myself to remain in my gaming chair. If I get up, I'm liable to storm across the apartment and bang on her bedroom door.

Why would I do that? What would I say?

Don't go out with Grady; go out with me instead.

Yeah, okay. She'd probably pull a muscle laughing at the suggestion.

And if she didn't? There's also the issue of how I now have my own date tomorrow night as well. The difference is, I would cancel mine in a heartbeat if I thought I had a shot with Quinn.

Like I said, you shouldn't drink and text.

Why haven't the developers at Apple created an app that requires you to pass a breathalyzer before it lets you use your iPhone? Maybe I should switch from game design to app development. I'd probably make a mint if I could pull that off.

Drumming my fingers on the surface of my desk, I stare at the lines of code on the monitor, the numbers blurring into one giant blob.

Fuck, I need a break.

Removing my glasses, I rub at my tired eyes before sliding them back on.

I have no idea what Quinn is up to. Hopefully, she's in her room or outside, because I need something to drink, and if I see her, I don't know if I'll end up giving in to my chaotic musings.

The apartment is blissfully empty when I step out of my room. The loft-style vaulted ceilings and open concept make the absence of any sound besides the hum of the refrigerator almost eerie as I pad across the cold floor.

Light filters out beneath Quinn's bedroom door, confirming she is still home but not anywhere in sight.

I don't bother turning any lights on while I move through the kitchen. The ambient light from the moon streaming through the glass wall leading to the balcony is enough to guide my movements.

Hand gripping one of the vertical handles of the refrigerator, I down my first glass of water without bothering to move away.

A faint buzzing sound hits my ears as I'm filling my glass for the second time. Lifting the glass away from the door's water dispenser, I pause, straining to hear better.

What the…? What is buzzing like that?

Setting the half-full glass on the counter, I follow the noise, trying to determine where it's coming from so I can put a stop to it.

For some reason, I keep my focus on the ground as I walk, and it isn't until I step into the swatch of light stretching toward the kitchen that I realize the source of the sound is Quinn's bedroom. Of course she would pick the room closest to the kitchen—that room is her happy place.

Then it hits me.

Holy shit.

Tell me she's not…

Tell me I'm hearing things and my earlier frustration is causing my imagination to run wild.

The buzzing continues, the tempo increasing along with the pounding beat of my heart.

I move closer to the door, the shell of my ear touching the grain of the wood just as a moan drifts out from inside.

Oh, fuck.

Quinn is masturbating.

I rear back from the door, my gaze locked on the unassuming panel detailing hiding Quinn from view. A masturbating Quinn. A masturbating Quinn I can hear as she works herself over with a vibrator.

The hairs on the back of my neck rise as the full weight of what I'm hearing settles over me.

I should move. Hell, I *need* to move. But I'm frozen in place.

I shouldn't be hearing this. This is a private moment I have no right to encroach on. Yet…I can't seem to tear myself away.

Another moan filters out, and I have to bite down on a knuckle to keep from responding with one of my own.

My dick and I may not have been on the best of terms lately, but I can't fault him for pushing against the band of my boxer briefs.

I've just worked up the wherewithal to step away when the next moan has me rooted on the spot.

"CK…"

Holy fuck.

Did she just say my name?

It's fainter than faint, but I swear I hear the rustle of her sheets. Flashes of her naked body writhing on them assault me with staggering intensity. Chest heaving, nipples pebbled tight, one hand clutching at the sheets while the other works the vibrator between her spread legs, the limbs bronzed and toned and—

What the fuck am I doing?

CHAPTER22

BLOWING OUT A BREATH, I pocket my phone and pull open one of the heavy oak doors at Jonah's, a popular bar and grill not far from the U of J campus. My stomach rolls as soon as I step inside, though whether it's from nerves, my conflicting feelings, or the delicious aroma of the burgers this place is famous for is a toss-up.

When Kristy suggested we come here for our date, I was hesitant. The last time I chose a sit-down type of activity, it didn't end well for me. But Jonah's isn't your typical eatery.

There's the main restaurant area when you first walk in, then sectioned off of that, thanks to the clever placement of the large square padded booths, is the bar to the right and a game area to the left.

There's a couple battling it out over at the air hockey tables, a cluster of business types dressed in suits near the dartboards, and a group of friends gathered around the lone pool table.

The flat-screen TVs adorning the walls and above the bar showcase whatever sports are in season, leaving the volume turned up for whichever game Jonah's decides to use as its "fea-

ture" game of the night. That alone is why this place is one of our
main haunts to frequent when the U of J Hawks are playing on
the road.

Scanning the not-as-crowded-as-during-the-school-year-but-
still-packed space, I don't know if I'm hoping to find Kristy
waiting for me or dreading it.

I'm a few minutes early. I consider shooting her a text after
I'm done with my pass over the dining area, then my gaze spots
a familiar head of cherry-cola-red hair. And, yes, that's the actual
name of the color; I remember it from the countless times I've
heard the girls talking about it and something about how reds
fade.

Holy shit!

Quinn is here.

Quinn is on her date with Grady *here.*

You've got to be fucking kidding me.

How did I not know they were coming here?

*Oh, maybe because now you're the one avoiding her ever since you
ran away from her door like some chickenshit reverse Beetlejuice after
hearing her call out your name three times.*

Ugh!

Now is not the time to think about what I heard last night or
the fact that I listened to what I did for far longer than I should
have. I may not be any good at this dating thing, but I know
enough to know a person should not fantasize about their roommate rubbing one out to thoughts of them while they are out on a
date. Especially when their date is not that roommate.

Quinn's back is to me, but Grady is smiling like he's
endorsing toothpaste, his perfectly straight pearly whites on full
display. Aren't hockey players supposed to have smiles that
resemble a jack-o'-lantern?

A hand touches my back, and I jump before I realize it
belongs to Kristy.

"Chris?" I nod as her gaze bounces over the features of my
face.

I reach up to adjust my glasses, forgetting I didn't wear them.
What? I was feeling rebellious as the person who yelled at me for
not wearing them the last time is now on a date with another
man.

"Uh, yeah, sorry. Hi Kristy." I lean in like I'm going to hug her, but pull back at the last second, not sure if a hug is too personal at the beginning of the date. Then I reach out like I'm going to shake her hand, but that feels too formal, so I settle for this weird half-wave thing.

"Oh, good." Relief washes over her pretty features before she does this cute little nose scrunch. "It was hard to tell from the back, and then you turned around and you didn't have glasses on, so I wasn't sure."

She reaches up to adjust her own glasses. Looks like I'm not the only one nervous today, but her stammering is a whole lot more adorable and less awkward than mine.

Thankfully the hostess comes by then and shows us to a small booth. Being the gentleman my parents raised me to be, I hold out an arm for Kristy to go first. Unfortunately, my good manners bite me in the ass when she takes the bench seat facing the bar, because once I slide into the spot across from Kristy, I need to smother a curse.

Guess who has an optimal sightline to Quinn and her date with Mr. Perfect? Oh, wait, I apologize, that's Mr. Charming McHot Pants.

Hmm…

I wonder if Quinn told him of the little nickname she gave him. Lord knows I heard it *a lot* the other night. Quinn is talkative on a good day. Quinn with alcohol in her system? Watch out. Though…I can almost promise you would be highly entertained, making the trade-off worth it.

"Chris?" Kristy lays a hand on my forearm, and it isn't until she runs her thumb along the pronounced vein beneath my skin that I realize I, one, zoned out again, and two, am tense as hell. "Are you okay?" She shifts around in her seat, following my line of sight. "Do you know them or something?"

I use her question as an opportunity to study Quinn and Grady without it coming across as stalker-y weirdness.

Grady has his chin propped on his upturned fist, leaning in to listen as Quinn speaks. I can't see his expression given that his back is to me, but I imagine he's smiling because Quinn is most likely regaling him with a plethora of random facts. I've never wished I could read lips like Emma until this very moment, because Quinn's randomness has quickly become one of my favorite things about her.

Except…

I tilt my head, noting her arms aren't gesticulating like one of those wacky wavy arm guy things. *Wonder what's up with that?*

"Oh…umm…yeah, Quinn's one of my roommates," I finally answer as Kristy turns back around.

"How'd you get paired with an athlete? I thought the school typically kept all the jock types together."

How does she know Quinn is a jock? And why is the athlete part the thing that sticks out and not the more obvious fact that Quinn's female?

Unless…

"Oh, no, Quinn is the redhead," I explain. "But she cheers for the Red Squad, so your jock assessment is correct." *As was your assumption about me not being one.*

Kristy's eyes go as wide as the dinner rolls our server must have dropped off at some point during me being a bad date. "You live with a girl?"

I nod and hold up three fingers. "Three of them."

Kristy's jaw drops before she rests her elbows on the table, leaning in much the same way as Grady is with Quinn. "Like *Three's Company*, or I guess in your case, it's a four's company-type thing?"

Looks like Quinn isn't the only person with an appreciation for TV Land.

Shit!

You're doing it again. Stop thinking about Quinn when you're on a date with somebody else.

I feel like this time, it's not my fault. I mean…she's sitting right fucking there.

I chuckle as another one of my roommates comes to mind. "If we're going to go with a TV reference, a reboot of *The Real World* is probably more accurate." *Thanks for the comparison, Trav.* "There are nine of us total that share our place."

We're well aware of the unconventional nature of our living arrangement. I'm still in shock Mason was even able to find a place that could house us all.

"*Nine?*" I can't fault Kristy for the almost screeched way she responds, except now we've garnered the attention from our fellow diners. More specifically, the two diners I've utterly failed to pretend I haven't been well aware of since I entered the building.

"CK, dude," Grady calls out with a chin jerk while Quinn looks like someone just told her they don't like tacos.

"CK?" Kristy asks as I give Grady a wave. A part of me really fucking hates that the guy isn't an asshat.

"My one friend—well, she's more like family—has a thing for calling those she's closest to by a letter name."

"What does the K stand for?"

Ah, the impersonality of dating apps.

"Kent."

Kristy's brows knit together. "Aren't you from Kansas?" I nod. "And your last name is Kent?" I nod again, knowing exactly where this is going. "Huh." She falls back against the cushion of the booth. "Too bad your first name isn't Clark."

"I've heard that before." My eyes flit over her shoulder, a jolt coursing down my spine when I find Quinn's still staring this way.

"I bet." Kristy circles a finger in front of my face. "You definitely have that Superman's-alter-ego vibe when you have your glasses on."

Again, my gaze tracks to Quinn at the memory of how her Superman nickname had Grady thinking we were a couple.

It's ridiculous. Ludicrous even.

Still…

That doesn't stop the ache that's been pulsing inside me since I denied the claim from intensifying.

It isn't until their server arrives with their meals that Quinn finally pulls her attention off my date and onto her own.

Or so I thought until both my phone and Apple watch vibrate from an incoming text.

RED: Why didn't you tell me you had a date tonight?

When did she change her contact name in my phone? Better question, why am I surprised by this?

RED: She's pretty. *thumbs-up emoji*

Did she really just hit me with a thumbs-up? It's like she's telling me good job.

Thankfully, our server swings by to take our orders before any more texts can come through, and Kristy and I pick our conversation up from where it left off. Things are less stilted than they were with Julia, but still, my thoughts drift. Except it's worse because the object of my distraction is sitting three tables away and won't stop texting me. Isn't she supposed to be on her own date? What is she doing with all the commentary on mine?

Any time there's a lull in the conversation or a topic has the merest connection to Quinn, I'm looking her way. And when I do? That's when my own obsessing starts.

Despite her occasional—okay, constant—glances this way, she's still fully engaged with Grady.

Except...

Whenever I've looked over—which is way more often than I should be doing—she isn't doing any of the things she told me a girl would do if she liked a guy.

There's no touching of Grady's forearm like Kristy's doing to mine.

She's not playing with her hair like Kristy has done.

She's not leaning in close to Grady. Instead, she's sitting back in her chair, whereas Kristy has constantly had her forearm on the tabletop to eliminate some of the distance between us.

What is she doing?

And what's with all the texting? Keeping my arm angled in a way that has my wrist dangling over the edge of the table is annoying.

What kind of game is she playing?

Is she studying me? Making sure I'm following the tips she gave me throughout her "coaching"?

Though...

Except for helping me craft a few of my earlier text messages and that why-can't-I-stop-thinking-about-it-when-we-didn't-even-kiss lesson on how to not headbutt my date in the face, how much of what she's been doing can be even classified as love coaching?

My intelligence has always been something I've prided myself on. It's because I fostered it and nurtured it until it became the thing to save me from the unhappy life I was stuck living in my small town. Without it, I would never have earned a scholarship to the U of J. I would never have met Kay or gotten the chance to be a part of the kind of family I never knew existed.

So, not knowing something? Not understanding it? It slips under my skin like a splinter, and the longer I go on without getting answers, the worse it's going to fester.

Quinn stands from her table, and I watch until she disappears from view down the long hallway that leads to the restrooms.

Indecision wars inside me, but as soon as I see Grady pull his phone out, I'm reminded of how his date has been on her own phone most of the night texting me. Something inside me snaps, and I'm excusing myself before I even realize the words are out of my mouth.

The few people I pass on the way issue nods of acknowledgment, but I barely pay them any mind.

The ladies' room is the last door at the end of the hall, the rest of the sounds of Jonah's muted this far away. There's only the occasional whir of a hand dryer or flush of a toilet to break up the silence as I wait for Quinn to finish.

The bathroom door opens with a squeak, the shock of red peeking through the opening alerting me it's Quinn making her appearance and not another patron. She startles, jumping high enough that both her feet leave the ground when she spots me lurking in the shadows.

"CK!" She smacks a hand to her chest, massaging the area over her heart.

"What the hell do you think you're doing?"

"Well, hello to you too, CK. Fancy seeing you here. Small world, huh?"

Her teasing tone only ramps up my blood pressure.

"Don't try to be cute. Answer the question, Quinn."

She jerks at my harsh tone before she takes a step back and twists inside the opening of the door as if to say *Going to the bathroom.*

"Remember what you said about literal answers, Quinn."

"*Ay dios mío.*" Her dark eyes widen before they narrow at my continued attitude. "What the hell crawled up your butt and died?" She folds her arms over her chest. Since I've already been racking up the points in the *Worst Date Partner Ever* category, I don't bother stopping my gaze from taking in the way the move props up her cleavage.

"My butt?" I stab a thumb at my chest. "Maybe if you were a little less worried about my butt and a little more focused on your *date*"—I spit out the word—"we wouldn't be standing here right now."

She nods, and I toss my arms up. "Geez, *someone's* in a mood."

"And I wonder why that is?" I hum before we're interrupted by a pair of ladies in search of the restroom.

What is it with girls going to the bathroom in groups?

Quinn finally steps out of the doorway, and we move until we're tucked farther into the back corner. "Do you want to tell me what your problem is? Or would you rather I guess?"

"That shouldn't be too difficult for you since you've been watching me like you're a source for the UofJ411."

She sucks in a harsh breath, all the color draining from her face.

"Wow." She takes a step back, betrayed hurt turning her dark eyes flat. "I'm not even going to dignify that with a response."

"Shit." I automatically reach for her. I know that's a low blow considering everything that went down this past school year. "I'm sorry, Red."

"Mmmhmm." That hummed response does not sound good. It does not sound good at all. The way she pokes my sternum is not a great sign either. "Plus, don't pretend like you weren't constantly looking over at Grady and me."

"Ha." I bark out a laugh, the sound harsh and echoing down the long hall. "I love how you're conveniently neglecting to mention how you only know that because *you* were already looking at Kristy and me."

Quinn bristles, her shoulders rolling back. "I was just trying to see how things were going."

"Uh-huh, sure." I grip the back of my neck, the muscles knotted under my hold.

"What the hell is that supposed to mean?"

"I—" Whatever I was about to say dies on my tongue, my frustration with this inexplicable situation choking me.

Quinn shifts closer, bringing both her body heat and that

sweet scent of coconut with her. "CK." I hate how softly she says my name. All I hear is pity floating beneath the surface.

I bat away the hand reaching toward my face. "And what was with all the *texting*?"

"Wha—"

"Didn't Grady find it rude you were texting another dude during your date?"

"Uh…he knows we're friends."

"Friends," I scoff, having never hated the word more than I do at this moment.

Quinn's entire body deflates like a balloon slowly letting its air out. "Are you saying we're not friends?"

"I don't know, Quinn." I fold my arms to stop myself from reaching for her. "You tell me?"

"Stop calling me Quinn."

"Why? It's your name." Geez, if my gramps were here, he'd smack me upside the head for how petulant I sound.

"It is." She brings her hands to her hips, getting into that power pose of hers that never fails to make my dick twitch. *Not the time, buddy.* "But unlike how you're trying to pretend otherwise"—she pokes my stomach—"we *are* friends. And we're not the type of *friends*"—another poke—"who use formal names for each other, *Chris-to-pher*."

Dammit. Despite my best efforts, my lips twitch before I can smother the impulse.

Quinn rolls her eyes as if I'm the one being ridiculous when she's the one responsible for setting me off with her barrage of text messages.

"I wouldn't be a very good love coach if I wasn't shouting—or, I guess, texting—plays from the sideline."

Sonofabitch.

We're back to this love coach bullshit.

You only did that to yourself.

Yeah, yeah, I don't need the reminder, thank you very much.

"So…what? You didn't think I could handle it on my own?"

"What? No—"

"Did you tell Grady why you were texting me?"

"No—"

"Did you two share a good laugh over it?"

"Wha—"

Quinn keeps trying to interrupt, but I'm on a roll and continue to speak over her.

"Did you tell him all about how you've been spending the summer helping your nerdy *friend* date?"

"I—"

I rake a hand through my hair, yanking at the strands until my scalp burns, my chest tightening with a pending explosion.

"I can't do this anymore, Quinn." I wave a hand through the air. "I'm done being your charity case."

QUINN

CHAPTER 23

"MY *CHARITY* CASE?"

Even I wince at the piercing screech echoing off the walls of the narrow hallway. But...I am at a loss. Me, a person who can spout off facts like *Most cats are actually allergic to humans* has absolutely no idea what to say to the bullshit that just came out of this man's mouth.

"*Que chingados te pasa?*" is what I go with. Also, sidebar: I'm still shouting at a decibel better suited for Herkie and his brethren.

CK's eyes go wide enough that I could pluck them right out of his head and use them as replacement balls on the foosball table in the gaming area.

"It roughly translates to, what the fuck is wrong with you?" I answer his has-no-right-to-come-across-as-adorable-as-it-does-while-he's-spouting-dumb-shit confusion.

"How can you ask me that?" He slaps his chest, his palm connecting with an audible thump.

"Are you *serious* right now?" He continues to blink at me, those baby blues completely unobstructed, and *that* only ramps up my level of pissed off-ness. "Your glasses must be the key to that brilliant brain of yours because you sure think like a moron without them."

"Huh?"

Ugh, this man. I just want to smack him and kiss him, and I honestly couldn't tell you in what order.

I've been an utter basket case over him. First sitting idly, then not so idly by while he pursued and went out with women I'd never measure up against.

He thinks I think of him as a charity case? As if agreeing to the whole what-the-hell-was-I-thinking love coach thing didn't feel like it was scraping out a piece of my heart?

Dios santo!

He thinks I helped him because…I felt sorry for him? What the hell would he think if he knew my intentions didn't stem from pity but from one-hundred-percent self-serving selfishness?

Hell…his request was so earnest it should be criminal how impure my reasonings for accepting were.

"When are you going to open up those beautiful blue eyes of yours and see what's right in front of you?"

"Oh, don't worry, I saw all *that*"—he throws out an arm, gesturing down the hallway and out to the restaurant—"quite clearly."

"And what *exactly* do you think you saw?"

He goes to say something, but now I'm the one not letting *him* speak.

"Because I *promise* you *whatever* it is, you're wrong."

The defiant clench to his jaw shouldn't be hot, but it is. *Dammit.*

"How can you be sure?"

Lord, give me strength.

You know what? He wants to be stubborn? To keep being blind to what's right in front of him?

Well…

I'm done. I can't take any more. This ends now. No more games.

Sliding my foot across the floor, I move until our fronts are practically touching. I send a silent prayer of thanks to Jessica Simpson for designing the cute espadrille sandals adorning my feet. The additional four inches they're adding to my height are more than appreciated at the moment.

"Because, you stupid idiot—"

"That's redundant," he says, cutting me off.

I growl like some kind of feral animal, making *I want to strangle you* claw hands.

"*Ay dios mío.*" Shaking my head, I bring my hands to a prayer position, my fingers brushing along the buttons of his shirt. "Bless your big dumb heart, Christopher Kent." I link my fingers together, pushing them out until all my knuckles crack. "I can't take it anymore."

"I already said we should end the love coaching thing."

"THAT IS NOT WHAT THIS IS ABOUT," I shout, pushing off him and pacing away. I make it a step and a half before I hit the wall and have to turn around.

CK has his hands up, his voice lowering to help soothe the crazy girl in front of him.

One, you'd think he'd be used to my crazy by now, and two, *he's* the reason I snapped.

"Do you have *any* idea how frustrating it is that you are so blind to how amazing you are that it prevents you from seeing what's right in front of you?"

"You're starting to talk in circles."

My hands are in my hair, grasping at the strands like they're the tether to my sanity. "You're always spinning me in circles!"

Again, his tone is calm, cajoling even. "You're not making any sense, Q."

"That's because none of this makes sense." I circle my arms in the air, the back of my hand smacking the wall.

CK slides his hand beneath mine, lifting it to inspect my reddened knuckles, the touch of his thumb running over the backs of them a whole lot nicer than my own.

"I'm still not sure what you mean."

"You and me." I flounce my free hand between us.

He lets out a heavy exhalation, shifting until his back is resting against the wall behind him. He seems…almost resigned. "I know."

Oof…that stings.

"Why don't you go back to Grady." CK releases his hold on my hand. "I'm sure he's starting to wonder what's taking you so long."

"Grady?" Why is he bringing up Grady? "Have you not listened to a single word I've said?"

"What?"

"Ugh." Not wanting to risk further injury, I spin for another ineffective pace. "I can't even with you anymore."

"*Me?*" He straightens away from the wall. "What about you?" He points an aggressive finger at me.

"You're making me dizzy."

"You're the one walking in circles." His breaths come faster as his exasperation grows.

"*That's not what I mean.*" Great. I'm back to Screeching Quinn. Awesome.

"Well, this conversation is getting us nowhere."

"That's because you're constantly refusing to hear what I have to say."

Granted, I can admit the lines have blurred some with the hey-let-me-help-you-get-with-other-girls love coach thing, but for eight months before that, my flirting couldn't have been more obvious.

"What are you talking about?" He balks, clearly offended. "I always listen to what you have to say."

I relent. "Sure, you listen, but you don't *hear* me." I cup a hand around my ear.

"You're back to talking in circles, Red."

That does it.

I stomp the two steps it takes to close the distance between us, this time not stopping until we're pressed thigh to thigh, chest to heaving chest.

"Okay. Fine." Pushing up on my toes, I do my best to *really* get all up in his face until we're almost nose to nose. "You want straightforward?"

His nod is hesitant, his self-preservation probably telling him not to make any sudden movements.

"I like you."

He blinks, the slow rise and fall of his lashes infuriating. "I know. People typically aren't friends with people they don't like."

"UGH!" I hope Kay and Emma have bail money because this man is going to drive me to homicide. "No. I *mean* I. Like. You." I fall back on my heels, a sudden wave of sadness that he'll never reciprocate crashing over me.

"You like me?" He says the question like it's the first time he's ever strung those three words together.

"I know you don't feel the same way about me." I hold my arms out to the side. "I get it. But there it is."

He doesn't move or even breathe.

It's time to retreat and lick my wounds in private.

Turning, I take one step before a hand grips the back of my nape and yanks me back.

I don't even get the chance to reach out to steady myself before my shocked "What" is swallowed by CK's lips slamming into mine.

Holy guacamole.

I've kissed a lot in my short lifetime, but never, not once, have I been kissed like this.

CK and I release mutual groans, his mouth moving over mine. His fingers flex around my neck, the tips pressing along the pulse point now fluttering wildly along the side of my throat. He moves, shifting closer, the clean scent I've come to associate with him wrapping around us.

I'm almost afraid to move, like if I do, it'll spook him.

He licks at the seam of my lips, and I instantly open for him, the move finally enough to break me from my stunned daze. He kisses me as if *he* was the one pining for *me* for close to a year. It's heady and makes me dizzier than our fight that preceded it.

My tongue strokes along his, and the noise he makes in the back of his throat has my panties ruined in an instant before he delves deeper, using his hold on me to adjust our angle.

He nips at my lips, sucking my lower one into his mouth as his free hand skirts along the side of my hip. His arm coils around my back, tugging me in until the last hairbreadth of space between us is eliminated completely.

My hands are trapped between our bodies, but I'm able to rotate my wrists enough to clutch the front of his button-down, holding on while he takes me on the ride of my life.

Never would I have thought such an ardent kiss would come from shy CK.

We shouldn't be doing this. Not here. Not now. We both came

here with other people, yet we're kissing each other. By the flipping bathrooms, no less.

I don't care. Nothing has ever felt this right, despite the situation being oh so wrong.

My body throbs, sensations bombarding me from every angle. I'm lost to the chaotic pounding beat of his heart against my palm, the feel of his hard body pressing into mine, and the sheer possession in his touch.

I'm one more stroke of his tongue, one more nip of his teeth, one more guttural groan rolling around in the back of his throat from dragging him into the bathroom behind me and locking us in a stall when a singsonged "And that's how people end up pregnant" has CK ripping his mouth from mine.

His lips are swollen and shiny from our kisses and so damn tempting I don't give a damn about our new audience.

I rise onto my toes to kiss him again, but the shift has his gaze tracking over my shoulder at the pair of gawking college-aged ladies still standing there.

Annoyed that they interrupted the best kiss in the history of kisses—sorry, not sorry, all you trending #Kaysonova ones—I flick my hair over my shoulder and stare the two of them down until they hustle into the restroom.

I spin back around, more than ready to get back to sucking face with the man I've had a crush on for far too long, when, with four words, he sends me crashing harder than a botched pyramid transition.

"That shouldn't have happened."

#THEGRAM

#CHAPTER24

UofJ411: *picture of CK and Quinn standing close together in the bathroom hall at Jonah's*
Look what leftovers are out for a night at Jonah's #LeftBehind #DontYouTwoLookCozy
@strawbshortab: Wait? Is there another couple in the #Kaysonova circle? #IsThisTrue
@hbietsch: No way. Just look at her compared to him #OutOfYourLeague
@amberebooksandmore: Yeah, I don't buy it. #ShesHotYoureNot
@JenniferMarie119: That's not true. He's cute #Adorkable
@mrshanlon0128: Yeah, but it doesn't change the fact that she's a 10 and he's not. #DoTheMath

UofJ411: *picture of Quinn and Grady leaving Jonah's together*
Oh, no. THIS was her date for the night #HeyThereHottie
@TheQueenB: Isn't this the guy that just got drafted from BTU? #HockeyHunks
@briannas_bookshelf: Now THIS I believe #HotJock
@hmkerby: Oh 100% #TheCheerleaderAndTheJock

UofJ411: *REPOSTED—BTU_TitansHockey: So proud of our very

**own @GradySlapShot45 being drafted—picture of Grady in his
BTU hockey gear***

We gotta thank @TheQueenB always coming in clutch with the deets
#WeSeeYouBoo

@bsdmhutch: Why don't we have hockey at the U of J?
#ICouldBeAPuckBunny

CHAPTER 25

IT'S BEEN ROUGHLY thirty hours or so since I slept, but despite every minute that ticks by on the clock, I don't get any closer to sleep.

Last night has played on a constant loop in my mind. I can't seem to shut it off, no matter how hard I've tried. Kind of ironic, seeing as I'm pretty sure the catalyst behind blowing up life as I've known it, happened because I blacked out for a moment.

One minute I was arguing with Quinn—about what I'm still not entirely sure—and the next we were kissing.

No.

Wait.

Scratch that.

Then *I* was kissing Quinn.

I had dreamed of doing that for so long I'm still having a hard time comprehending that I actually made it a reality.

I let my emotions and the frustration of not understanding what I was feeling or how to correctly interpret...*any* of it push me into putting my lips on someone I had no right to put my lips on.

No matter how many times I recall Quinn kissing me back, it

doesn't change the fact that it should have never happened. Or that she went home with another man after.

I could pretend all I want, but the proof is out there in poorly captured photographs and hundreds of comments.

My phone vibrates for what feels like the millionth time, but again, I let the call from Grant roll over to voice mail. Unlike the others before it, he follows this one up with a text.

G: I SWEAR TO GOD, if you don't answer your GODDAMN phone, I'm getting on a train, and YOU can deal with Mama complaining about missing out on her "precious" baby boy time.

Heaving out a sigh, I stop pacing the living room and sit my ass down on the couch. Reaching for the remote, I pull up the video chat app. It takes all of point six seconds before the scowling face of the last person I would have thought would become my closest friend fills the flat-screen TV.

"You look like shit," Grant observes after carefully cataloging my appearance.

Thanks to the little box in the corner of the screen, I know exactly what he sees and squeeze my eyes shut against the visual.

My hair sticks out in every direction possible. My clothes— the same ones from last night—are rumpled and wrinkled beyond salvation, and the glasses I eventually put back on after ripping my contacts out of my eyes sit crooked on the bridge of my nose.

"Anyone ever tell you you say the sweetest things?" I sigh, pressing into the plushy cushions behind me.

"Maybe if you hadn't been avoiding my calls for the last seven-plus hours, I'd feel a little more sympathetic."

I start to speak, only to be cut off by yet another yawn. The exhaustion is like a heavy blanket settling over me, making my bones feel like they weigh a thousand pounds.

"Shit." Grant's curse has me lifting my gaze back to the screen to see his body folded over, searching the ground for something. "I'll be there in two hours," he says, coming up with one of his Jordans and tugging it onto one of his massive feet.

"What? Why?"

He freezes, his entire giant frame unmoving except for the slow blink of his eyes. "Are you for real?"

"Me?" Removing my glasses, I pinch the bridge of my nose. "You're the one getting all mama bear over a few missed phone calls."

"First off—" Grant's voice gets extra deep as he shifts forward, his feet slapping the ground. He leans close to the camera, his elbows resting on his spread knees, pinning me in place with a look I've rarely seen him use off the basketball court. "Em is the mama bear of our crew." He extends a finger, directing it to himself before pointing it at me. "I'm papa bear, and don't you forget it."

I roll my eyes at his absurdity.

Grant clears his throat. "Now tell me how you're holding up before I really do end up canceling my dinner date with Mama."

"G." I sigh, not wanting to talk about any of it.

Not how I ruined a perfectly nice date because I'm an asshole.

Not how I yelled at Quinn and accused her of things she would never do.

Not about how I went temporarily insane and kissed Quinn. How she stared at me heavy-lidded, touching tentative fingers to her puffy lips. How her dark red hair was a messy knot in the back or about the two strands that were coiled around my knuckles.

I especially don't want to think about how she left Jonah's with Grady after all...*that* went down.

"Don't you fucking *G* me." Grant's glare has returned when I blink back to the present, his long arms falling to hang between his spread legs.

Foreboding prickles at the base of my skull. Grant might be the most physically intimidating, but he's usually the most level-headed. So when he gets all intense like this, it's wise to heed the warning.

"This is the first time those fucknuggets turned their attention on you, and I wanna make sure it's not dredging up old memories."

My lips twitch, and I mouth the *word fucknuggets*.

"You can thank Dante for that gem," he says, referring to his younger brother. "Now, seriously...you doing okay?"

Oh, that's right. That's the other thing I've been doing my best to put out of my mind—the UofJ411.

"I'm fine," I start to say just as the elevator dings, announcing someone's arrival.

"Well, well, well, if it isn't the woman of the hour," G singsongs.

It takes everything in me not to leap over the back of the couch and rush Quinn, demanding answers I have no right to as she makes her appearance.

QUINN

CHAPTER 26

I'M DRAINED.

Emotionally.

Physically.

Hell, even spiritually, I'm spent.

I don't know where I thought CK would be when I got home from a double practice then clinics at The Barracks, but I certainly wouldn't have guessed he would be video-chatting with Grant in the living room.

I don't know what good deed I've done as of late—maybe it was the random act of kindness of paying for the coffee and smoothies for that mom and her three kids the other day at Espresso Patronum—but I'm more than grateful that I had already made plans to sleep at Kay's last night. Not only did my cherry-cola-red hair get a refresh, it allowed me to escape sleeping under the same roof as the guy who kissed the daylights out of me, then rejected me immediately after.

However, right now, I wish I had more than just my pajamas and work clothes in the bag I packed. How many questions do you think they would ask me if I showed up with a suitcase full of my crap? Too many. Could I handle the inquisition doing so would bring on? Probably not.

It takes considerable effort to pull my gaze away from a rough-looking CK and to Grant's smirking face. "Hey, G." I wave, moving into a better view of the camera but still managing to keep as much distance as possible from CK. Even with his *That shouldn't have happened* ringing in my ears all these hours later, I still don't trust myself.

"Sup, Insta-Famous."

I slick my tongue across my teeth, trying not to laugh and totally failing. "I hate you."

"No, you don't," he singsongs, shimmying his broad shoulders.

"Mmm." The unimpressed air I attempt to project only has Grant laughing harder. "Anyway…it was two pictures—Insta-famous that does not make."

The UofJ411 Instagram account is seen as more of an annoyance than an accomplishment, at least by us anyway. None of us want to be featured in their content, but the guys know it comes with the territory of being amongst the ranks of top athletes in the country. Why they decided people care about what CK and I were up to, though, I'll never know.

When Grant turns his attention back to CK, I use the opportunity to make my escape, spinning on my heel and heading for my room.

Kicking the door closed, I drop my bag and trudge to my bed, falling face-first onto the mattress, not giving a damn about the dried sweat coating my skin. My shower can wait.

The snick of my door opening has me rolling onto my side, the pillow lowering just enough for me to peer over the edge and make eye contact with CK.

Oof, rough looking might have been too nice of a descriptor.

His eyes are puffy as hell. The bags under them are big enough to hold all the makeup I need to be game day ready, and the dark circles could rival any eye black the football team uses. His dark hair is so twisted out of control it's almost impossible to tell Bette, Kay's sister-in-law, recently trimmed it.

Oh…and…he's still in last night's clothes.

Why is he still in last night's clothes?

Oh my god—did he go home with Kristy last night?

My stomach churns at the mere thought.

My gaze roves over him, taking in every detail while not really seeing anything. His sleeves are still rolled and cuffed at the elbows, the front a chaotic mess of wrinkles. But…all of the buttons are in their corresponding holes.

Dios santo!

I can't do this. It was one thing to help him date in the abstract sense.

But…

But…

Ugh!

Witnessing the evidence of the aftermath the morning after, the same night that he rocked my entire existence with a kiss…

Well…

I can't do it. It's too hard.

Tossing my pillow to the side, I stand. "What do you want, CK?" My tone is less than pleased.

He blinks slowly behind his glasses, and *damn him* for putting them back on.

"You didn't come home last night."

How would he know?

Annoyed, I wave a hand up and down his body. "Hi, Pot. I'm Kettle. It's nice to meet you."

He rears back, his brows dipping below his frames. "What's that supposed to mean?"

Oh my god, I'm so fucking sick of hearing him ask me that.

"Umm…I'm not the one standing here in last night's clothes." I make a window with my fingers, framing him in all his walk-of-shame glory. "Besides…how would you even know if I came home or not when you weren't here?"

"What are you talking about?" He looks down at his outfit as if only just realizing what he has on. "I was here all night, waiting for you."

I scoff. "*Riiiight.*" All the fight drains out of me. "I can't do this with you anymore, CK." I move around him, sucking in a breath when my arm brushes his as I reach for the overnight bag I dumped near the door.

"What do you mean?"

I squeeze my eyes shut hard enough to see spots, clutching at my bag until the teeth of the zipper bite into my palms and I have to pause opening it.

"I swear to god, if I have to hear you ask me that one more time, I'm liable to snap." I grit my teeth, tossing my clothes from yesterday in the direction of my hamper, not bothering to check if they actually go in.

CK doesn't say a word. I would have thought he left if I didn't feel the weight of his gaze tracking my every movement.

Stepping into my walk-in closet—a glorious perk I'll surely miss if I do end up moving out permanently—I start to throw clothes toward the bed. I don't even look at what I'm grabbing. I'm pretty sure the cocktail dress I wore to my last ring ceremony for my old all-star team is in the giant pile I'm creating.

"What are you doing?" CK eyes me like I'm a crazy person. I can't blame him. I am feeling particularly unhinged.

"Packing." My answer is clipped.

"Where are you going?" His confusion wraps itself around my heart and squeezes.

"Kay's." That's it. That's all I say. No added explanation.

"Weren't you just with her?" He gestures to my outfit of black cheer shorts, blue camouflage NJA Coach racerback tank, and matching oversized bow.

I nod. "I'm going to stay with her for a while."

"A while?" CK's brow furrows, and I know he's doing calculations in his head. His gaze tracks to the books I have stacked neatly on my desk. "But what about your classes?"

"I'll commute." I shrug as if turning a five-minute drive into an almost-hour-long one isn't a dumb decision or a giant pain in the ass.

"What? Why? That's dumb."

Maybe so, but it's necessary.

"I need some space."

"Because the almost eight thousand square feet of this place are suddenly too small for just the two of us?"

"Yes."

He rears back. "I was kidding."

I continue packing, still not really looking at what I'm shoving into the bag. "Well, I wasn't."

Feet shuffling along the floor is the only warning I get before one of CK's hands is cupping my elbow, guiding me around to face him. "What's going on, Quinn?"

God, I hate that he calls me Quinn. And…that's a problem. It shouldn't matter what he calls me—not when he's too embarrassed by me to call me his.

"I can't keep living with you. At least not right now." I go to turn around, but he squeezes my elbow, holding me in place.

"What?" This time there's an edge of panic to the question. "Is this because of what happened last night?"

"Yes," I say point-blank. There's no use beating around the bush anymore. What's done is done. There's no taking it back.

"I already told you I was sorry."

"Yes, and that's the problem."

I want to shake him. If it were physically possible, I'd haul him down to Home Depot and have them shove him into a paint mixer just to shake some sense into him.

"I know." He hangs his head, finally releasing me. "I know it shouldn't have happened."

I whirl right back around. "No!" I shout, poking him above one of the more prominent wrinkles in his shirt. "See? *That's* the problem right there."

"Huh?"

"You think it shouldn't have happened, and *I* think it should have happened forever ago."

"Wha—"

"So…no." I speak right over whatever he was about to say. "After that, I can't stay here. It hurts too much."

"I don't understand."

"And I can't make you understand."

"Why not?"

I huff, tossing the shirt balled in my fist behind me. "You can lead a horse to water, CK, but you can't force them to drink."

"What the fuck does that proverb have to do with any of this?"

"It means, no matter how much I like you, I can't make you feel the same way about me."

"You like me?"

"Yes."

"You like me as a friend?"

"Duh." I roll my eyes. "But that's not what I'm talking about here."

"You like me as more than a friend?"

"Yes."

"But you went out with Grady last night."

Not my best decision, I can admit that. "He caught me in a weak moment when he asked me out."

"Because we were drinking?"

I shake my head. "No. Because he asked me right on the heels of you vehemently denying being connected to me in *any* way as more than a friend."

He's too close. His scent fills my lungs. His body heat warms my front. It's too much.

Again I move to step away, and again he stops me, his long fingers curling over the curve of my hip.

"I thought we already established we're friends...didn't we?" His question is so earnest it makes me feel guilty for being so utterly frustrated with him.

"We are." I sigh, my head falling forward until my forehead is resting against his middle. "But I can't keep pretending I don't want to be more than that."

Heat prickles at the back of my eyes, my emotional well tapped out. A finger notches under my chin, and I have to blink to keep the frustrated tears at bay.

"It was one thing when I had a crush on you and you were just this guy I knew and sometimes hung out with because he was friends with my friends." I blow out a breath, tipping my head back, glancing toward the ceiling. "I would get these little glimpses into your personality whenever you would forget to be wary of the rest of us. Seeing the way you would interact with Kay, Em, and G showed me this whole side of you that you keep hidden beneath your hot shy-nerd exterior."

The jerk reaches up to adjust his glasses before daring to ask, "You think I'm hot?"

"Yeah." My mouth presses into a flat line, and I meet his gaze head-on. "Except for when you're refusing to believe me when I tell you how I feel about you. Yeah, I think you're hot."

There are maybe three inches of space between us, but I shuffle closer, closing the tiny gap.

Grabbing the front of his shirt, I twist the material and tug until he's forced to crane his neck.

"I. Like. You."

Without giving him the chance to chime in with another stupid *Yeah, like a friend* comment, I lift up on my toes, using my grip on his shirt to bring us together until my lips brush his.

"*Yo te quiero.*"

I swear I hear him swallow.

"I don't know how many different languages I have to say it in, but it translates to the same thing in all of them."

"You like me?"

I roll my eyes but end up answering with a nod anyway.

Here we are, at the same standstill we found ourselves at last night. This is why I need space. I can't keep putting myself out there if he's going to continue to stubbornly play dumb in response to the words I'm saying. My heart can't take it anymore. I've reached my limit.

I've started to move away, to finally put that distance between us, then his words freeze me in place.

"I like you too."

#CHAPTER27

THERE'S the distinct possibility I'm in the midst of a sleep-deprivation hallucination. The mental fatigue I feel rivals that of any finals week, except instead of spreading out the topics, I crammed them all into one night.

Obsessing over the fact that I kissed Quinn.

Remembering the shocked disbelief of the college co-eds who found us tucked in the corner near the bathrooms.

Grady coming to look for Quinn because she had been gone for so long.

Then, what kept me awake and unable to do anything but pace around the apartment like I was casing the joint: wondering and imagining all the things Quinn could be doing with Grady that would keep her out all night.

Sure, now I realize Quinn may have left with Grady, but she wasn't with him. Instead, she slept at Kay's. Maybe if I hadn't been avoiding her, I would have known that was her plan.

Or...who knows? Maybe that wasn't her original plan, but I made her feel forced into running.

And why would she assume that I...what? Spent the night with Kristy?

Me going home with Kristy is as unlikely as Quinn telling me she likes me, yet here we are: Quinn once again standing toe to toe with me, her mouth skimming mine with every unbelievable but no less amazing word she utters.

You know what?

I just don't care anymore.

"I like you too."

Holy shit. Did I just admit that?

I tense, waiting for her to laugh in my face. As if me returning the words will suddenly make her realize she didn't mean them when she said them herself.

Except…she doesn't.

There's no laughter. She's not pulling away.

Instead, she sucks in a breath, her dark eyes going wide.

Then…the tip of her tongue skims my lips when she licks hers, and I'm done.

No more teasing.

Real or not, I'm shutting my brain off for once and letting instinct take over.

Using my teeth, I latch on to Quinn's lower lip, biting down and sucking it into my mouth, swallowing down the ball-tingling whimper she expels as I seal our mouths together properly. Her nails scratch my chest as her hold on my shirt turns strangling. I don't care. The pain barely registers.

Moving my mouth over hers, I hook an arm around her middle until it's impossible to distinguish my body from hers. Quinn's hands slide up my chest, her arms lopping around my neck, her fingers driving into my hair.

I return the favor, fisting her long ponytail, using it as leverage as I move along her jaw, then down the line of her neck. Her pulse flutters against my lips, a hint of saltiness lingering on her skin.

Bringing my mouth back to Quinn's, I lick at the seam of her lips, loving the way she automatically opens for me, just like she did last night.

Her hold on me turns frantic, an edge of pain creeping into her grip. She pulls me closer, kissing me harder, as if stopping will only end with me rejecting her again.

I won't. I'm done with that.

We may not make sense together, but I'm going to enjoy it, going to enjoy this for as long as possible.

I'll find a way to mitigate the consequences of when this inevitably ends.

I couldn't tell you how long Quinn and I kissed before she put a stop to it, claiming she needed to shower off all the grossness (her word, not mine) from The Barracks.

I used the reprieve to get in a shower of my own. I needed the space to think about the fact that I admitted to liking her, that I opened myself up to that kind of rejection. Yes, I know she told me—multiple times—that she liked me first, but there's still this underlying part of me that has trouble accepting it past face value. I also wanted to wash off my sleepless night and take care of myself before joining Quinn on the couch like we agreed.

Thank god I did too.

Because as soon as Quinn emerged from her bedroom, dressed in a pair of tiny plaid sleep shorts and this cross-strapped sports bra thing, my dick took notice. If I hadn't just made myself come minutes before, it would have been glaringly obvious the effect she has on me.

I had a momentary flash of panic when she said she wanted to cuddle, but then she tossed this oversized fuzzy pillow of hers in the corner of the sectional and beckoned for me to be the one to lie on her.

I tried to argue, but surprise, surprise, she wasn't having it. She only propped her hand on her hip and cursed—in Spanish, of course—about how I looked like I was ready to keel over. Granted, I didn't know what she said to me until she translated, but in the month where the majority of the time it's just been the two of us living here, she's figured out I'm a sucker for when she goes bilingual on me.

I held back a bit longer, but when she smacked the cushions in front of her, inviting me toward her, I found my feet moving of their own accord.

She smirked with this half-smug tilt to her lips until I lifted one of her legs and sat down with it draped over my lap instead. I got one of those challengingly annoyed narrowing of her eyes, but she let it go, scrolling through Hulu until she found the show *Bones*.

When I asked why she was watching something she had clearly watched before, given the complete green status bars showing on all the episodes, she shushed me. Like full out, finger covering her still slightly swollen lips shushed me.

Then she pushed me until I was slouched against the couch and started running her fingers through my hair. Needless to say, I didn't even make it through Bones and Booth's first exchange of sexually charged witty banter before my eyes were closing.

I have no clue how long ago that was, but I suspect it's been a few hours given that Hulu's binge-shaming prompt is now blurrily displayed on the television. Where are my glasses?

Wanna know what else I'm clueless about? How I ended up with my face using Quinn's stomach—her *bare* stomach—as my pillow.

Tilting my chin, I glance up at a slumbering Quinn. Unlike last night, she doesn't have an ounce of makeup on, and her hair hangs in a messy ponytail dangling over the side of the pillow, but still, she's achingly beautiful.

She likes me.

It hasn't quite set in that she told me that, but there's something about seeing her like this that makes me believe maybe, just *maybe*, I have a real shot with her. Her hands are tangled in my hair as if, even in sleep, she couldn't resist toying with the strands, and I gotta admit, I like it.

"Hey," Quinn says in this sexy as hell sleepy rasp when I lift my head, searching for my glasses.

My apology for falling asleep on top of her dies on my tongue the instant she starts to scratch my scalp with her nails.

"Hey," I say instead, reaching for my glasses.

"You crashed hard."

I nod, practically purring as she continues to rake her fingers through my hair, my glasses completely forgotten. "I didn't sleep last night," I admit, though that was probably obvious.

"Why not?" I feel her tense beneath me. Does she really think I went home with Kristy?

"First, it was because I couldn't stop thinking about you leaving with Grady"—a flash of how she glanced back over her

shoulder right before they rounded the end of the hall hits me—
"or the sad look on your face as you did."

I have to pause to clear the sudden lump from my throat when a mirroring expression crosses her face now. I doubt the rest of what I have to say will help ease it at all.

"Then sometime around three in the morning when it became evident you weren't coming home…" I grip the back of my neck. "I started to imagine all the things you could be doing while not home and—"

"I get it." She cuts me off.

Gliding her hands down the white undershirt I changed into earlier, she pushes on my chest. Then, with the aid of the leg hooked over my hip, she maneuvers us around until I'm once again sitting on the couch. She continues the movement, straddling me and settling in my lap. The blanket that was covering us is now a tangled mess, bunched uncomfortably under my ass, but I barely pay it any mind when her center lines up against me. Even through the material of her shorts and my sweatpants, I can *feel* how hot she is.

Her hands come up to frame my face, her fingers tracing over my eyebrows, then outlining my eyes, still unobstructed without my glasses. Her touch is soft, almost reverent as she explores my features until she slides her fingers back through my hair, resting her thumbs at my temples, her gaze boring into mine the entire time.

"I wasn't in a good headspace when I first got home. And… when I saw you still dressed in the same clothes as last night…" Her throat moves with a swallow as her words trail off. "My mind instantly went to the same place…and…it…*hurt*."

I don't want to piss her off, but I got to know. "Why?"

"Did you forget how I told you I liked you a few hours ago?" She points over my shoulder at her bedroom.

My hands fall to her hips when she rocks into me, as if to reiterate her point.

"No. I remember it." I give her a warning squeeze when she rolls her hips again. "I still have a hard time believing it, but I remember it quite well."

She stills, freezing in my hold, before shifting back until the curve of her butt rests on my knees. She braces her hands at my collarbones, her fingers digging into my trapezius muscles.

"Why?" There's an edge to her question.

I haven't shared the details of what I went through in high school with anyone outside of the original trio who adopted me into the group. I've long since suspected Quinn has heard some of the details, but telling her is a lot harder than telling the others.

My high school experience is filled with more memories I'd rather forget than remember, but there is one I can tell her about that might help her understand.

"In my experience…" I have to pause to swallow again. "The only reason a girl who looks the way you do would talk to me was that she was trying to distract me while her star jock boyfriend and his friends either fucked with my locker or were waiting to ambush me in some way."

"Those jackholes you went to high school with better *pray* to *La Virgen María* that they never run into me." There's zero hint of a tease in her tone. "I hate that because of them, you can't see how amazing you truly are, CK."

I start to fidget, focusing on the spandex band of Quinn's bra top, toying with the material. She's not the first person to say something of the sort to me, but coming from her? There's a bit more weight to it.

Except…

"If you think I'm so great and like me so much"—I swallow and meet her gaze head-on—"why did you try to help me get with other girls? Why not keep me for yourself?"

QUINN

#CHAPTER28

OOF. Look at CK coming in with the hard-hitting questions.

Now…

Do I deflect or admit the truth?

Ugh!

Heat crawls up the back of my neck, and I look away, no longer able to stare into his penetrating blue gaze.

My heart gives a mini cheer when CK pinches my chin in his fingers, my belly swooping at the uncharacteristic command of my attention.

"Tell me."

Gah! When he talks in that deep, gravelly voice, I want to stand up and let him know I'll tell him *anything* he wants to know.

"I was desperate."

"Desperate?" he questions.

I nod, my ponytail slipping over my shoulder. "I've had a crush on you for so long, but it always seemed like you were purposely finding ways to keep a certain amount of distance from me that you didn't keep from the others."

Now he's the one looking away because we both know what I

said is true. Any time we've had a moment that remotely showed the connection we shared, he doubled downed on his avoidance techniques.

Yet…

I can't seem to quit him.

Except for the two times he's kissed me, everything about us has been entirely one-sided. It may not have been until recently that I've truly put my feelings, put *myself* on the line, but there's always been this innate sense of vulnerability about CK that keeps drawing me in.

"I had hoped if you thought I was helping you with other women, you'd end up being less hesitant with me. And…then… maybe…you might fall for me instead."

See what I mean? See that silver platter? Oh, yes, here, let me serve myself up on it.

"What?"

"I don't just like you, Superman." I shrug, bringing my hands to my chest. "*I* want to be the one *you* date." I motion between us. "It *killed* me any time you went out on a date with one of those other women. It was completely irrational, and I know they're probably better suited for you than me…but…*ay dios mío!*" I grip my skull with both hands, digging my nails into my scalp. "The night you went out with that *puta* who bailout called you, I was going out of my *damn* mind at The Barracks. I legit had to be talked down by a high school student." It's been weeks since that night, but still, that battery-acid bubble of crazy percolates inside me. "*Me estaba volviendo loca,*" I shout when I can't swallow it down.

CK's palms glide up the length of my arms, his fingers carefully working mine from where they are tangled in my hair. My hands held in his, he slowly lowers my arms between us, his thumbs ghosting back and forth along the backs of my knuckles.

"Why were you going crazy?" The sincerity in the question is one of those things that tug at me.

"Aw, look at you knowing what I said without translation," I tease, needing to lighten the heavy. "I'll make a bilingual man out of you yet, Superman."

"Not that I want to ruin your Spanish-speaking dreams for me, Red"—I have to clamp my teeth together to hold in the squee at him calling me Red—"but you use that phrase quite a bit."

Sonofabitch.

I slick my tongue across my teeth but can't help but laugh.

"While I'm sure that statement is factually accurate"—I shake off one of his hands, pressing a finger to his chin and tilting his face up to mine for a change—"I find it prudent to point out it was your insistence on being stubbornly blind to me and my charms"—I lift my hand under my chin, creating a shelf with the back of my hand as if presenting said charms—"that tested the limits of my sanity on the reg."

My phone vibrates on the coffee table, and the extended buzzing tells me it's a phone call instead of another Instagram notification. When I glance over my shoulder at it, I groan at Tessa's smiling face lighting the screen. "I swear that chick has some freaky voodoo sixth sense for when she's being talked about."

CK pushes forward to see who I'm talking about, all of his hard muscles rippling around me and pressing into me. "Tessa Taylor is the one who talked you off the ledge?"

I understand his disbelief. People may use the adjectives *perky* and *bubbly* when describing me, but Tessa? I don't think there's a person on God's green earth more extra than she is.

"I was in *bad* shape, *mmkay*." My voice turns breathy when his large hands cup my ass, holding me steady.

His cheek brushes mine, the smell of his evergreen shampoo stronger thanks to his recent shower. I nuzzle into him, breathing in that intoxicating scent.

"I like you too." His warm breath caresses the shell of my ear with his whispered confession.

It's not the first time he's finally admitted as much, but things have been so one-sided between us it's going to take a bit before it sinks in.

"You do?" Is that my voice that sounds like a strangled sob? *Gah!* I'm such a girl.

CK pulls back, his eyes bouncing over my face, my breathing hitching at the dilated heat banked in them. It's the first time he's ever looked at me with such naked want. It's heady, but not nearly as much as what he says next.

"Of course I like you, Quinn." He drags a knuckle over the apple of my cheek. "I don't think I've ever met a more kindhearted, effervescent person than you." He cups the side of my throat, his thumb stroking down the center with my heavy swallow. "You also scare the shit out of me."

"Because of my fiery temper?" I tease, but his expression remains stoic.

"I kinda like that side of you, Red." His fingers flex around my nape. "But, no…you scare me because I could easily become addicted to you."

Oh.

My.

Word.

I'm not exactly sure how to respond to that.

Neither of us says anything, the only sound in the room the continuous buzzing of my cell phone. The thing has been going off nonstop thanks to the damn UofJ411 account. I have a whole new appreciation for what Kay and Mason deal with.

CK's gaze tracks to my mouth when I lick my lips. The corners of his eyes flare fractionally as he watches the motion.

"You're too fucking beautiful for me," he says in a guttural admission.

I'm self-aware enough to recognize that, yes, by society's warped beauty standards, I'm considered very pretty. I get it. My features are symmetrical, and I inherited the killer Bautista bone structure along with their curves. I may have issues with the emphasis and single-minded importance others have placed on my looks, but I'm not blind to it.

But…

The open candor in CK's statement gives me an entirely new appreciation for them.

Until the last part of his sentence registers.

"Bullshit," I counter. "No one, no *fucking* one is too *anything* for you, Christopher."

The corner of his mouth twitches at my use of his full name, but for the first time ever, I don't return his amusement. I'm dead fucking serious about this.

Cupping his handsome face in my hands, I hold him in place and say, "You…are beautiful inside and out. You could have turned bitter and cold after everything you've been through, but instead, your heart is as kind and loyal as they come. *That*"—I smush his cheeks until his lips pucker like a fish

—"is why I've crushed on you for an embarrassingly long time."

He takes me by the wrists, lowering my hands to rest on either side of his neck. "*How* long?"

I shake my head, refusing to answer, my ponytail whipping us both in the face.

CK reaches up, fingering the ends. "Is this brighter than it was yesterday?"

I can't see it, but based on how it feels, my grin is cheesy as hell at him noticing. "Yeah, Bette gave me a refresh while the others bugged me for a status update."

He continues to absentmindedly twirl my hair. "Status update?"

"On us." I let my tone imply the *Duh* I leave off.

"On us?"

I look toward the vaulted ceiling. "Is there an echo in here?"

CK tugs on my hair. "Smartass."

"Dumbass," I counter with a tilt of my head.

We grin at each other until the joking atmosphere settles and is replaced by a simmering intensity.

CK brushes his knuckle along my lips. "You like me?"

I place a kiss on that knuckle and respond with my own question. "You like me?"

"This is crazy."

"Maybe." I shrug. "But life's too short to try to be anything but happy."

I shift closer again, sliding down his thighs until I'm pressed against the bulge straining against his gray sweatpants. "I want you, CK," I whisper against his lips.

He emits this groan from the back of his throat that has my hormones sighing, and this time, *I'm* the one who kisses him.

His strong arms band around me, bringing me back with him as he falls against the cushions, my hips oscillating of their own accord.

He's hard, and based on how long it takes me to slide along his length, a ripped torso isn't the only thing CK hides under his clothes.

My breathing hitches and my stomach flutters. My body undulates, my fingertips tracing the outline of his handsome face, using my sense of touch to see him with my eyes squeezed shut. I'm lost in a sea of sensation.

His hand cups my rib cage, squeezing to help guide my movement.

CK may have frustrated the fuck out of me with his inability to see what was right in front of him, but when he kisses me? Whoa. It's like he was made for it.

The Christopher Kent model of human: specializes in kissing Quinn Thompsons.

His lips are soft, but the pressure he wields with them is insistent, commanding even.

I arch my back, my breasts pressing against his hard chest as his other hand skims down my body to grip my ass, his fingertips slipping under the hem, riding high on my butt cheek.

"CK." He freezes when I moan his name. "More," I plead, those jumping-jack firecrackers sparking through my veins when I rub my clit against him just so.

"Quinn." He thrusts against me, and I whimper, "CK."

My touch turns frantic. The need to touch more of him, to remove any barriers between us thrums through my bloodstream.

His kisses travel across my jaw and down my neck, his tongue flicking out to lick at the erratic pulse hammering in my throat.

He nips at my collarbone, and I rip at his shirt, clutching the soft cotton and yanking it up over his head with enough force to have dislodged his glasses if he were wearing them. For the first time ever, I'm actually grateful he doesn't have them on. If I ended up being the one to break those babies, there's a legitimate chance I would cry.

His eyes have deepened to the same color as the darkening night sky outside, and his chest heaves in gulping breaths.

"*Dios*, you are deceptively sexy." I run my hands over his torso, flicking his tan nipples with my thumbs and biting my lip when that sound of his makes another appearance in the back of his throat.

"Me?" he chokes out. "Fuck, Quinn." His fingers dig into the nip of my waist, a roughness hovering on the edge of the grip. "Have you *seen* yourself?"

I attempt to grind on him again, but he holds me in place, his eyes boring into me with an intensity I can't quite name.

"If this somehow is just one of my dreams, don't you dare fucking wake me up."

Happiness blooms behind my rib cage and radiates outward. "You dream about me?" I ask shyly, dipping my chin.

CK notches a finger under my jaw, waiting to speak until I meet his burning gaze. "Every. *Fucking*. Night."

My mouth falls into a stunned O. Any restraint I might have had evaporates on the spot, and I throw myself at him with an unmatched fervor.

My actions turn sloppy, touching and groping any part of him I can get my hands on. By the time I cross my arms in front of me to remove my own top, there's not an ounce of grace to my movements. I'm running on pure lust and pent-up sexual frustration.

I'm so keyed up that I jolt when CK stills me by covering my hands with his own.

"Huh?" I ask as his thumbs slip under my palms, prying my grip from the tight spandex.

Color stains CK's cheeks, but it's the measured bob of his Adam's apple that makes me think his isn't a horny blush like the one I feel burning on my chest.

An edge of trepidation slithers beneath my skin as he lowers our hands between us. It isn't until his fingers thread through mine, linking us together, that it starts to ease.

"What? Why are we stopping?"

Again he swallows thickly.

"CK?" I bring our conjoined hands up to stroke along his clenched jaw.

"There's something I need to tell you."

An ugly and probably irrational thought pops into my brain, but there's no stopping it or the question it inspires. "You don't want me?"

"The fuck?" He startles, his fingers pinching around my knuckles. "Of course I want you," he's quick to confirm.

Irrational assumption or not, my body sags under the weight of relief his confirmation makes me feel.

"Fuck do I want you, Quinn."

"But…" I prod, hearing the but in the statement.

"But I'm afraid I'm not going to measure up to what you're used to."

I bite my lip and shake a hand free, cupping him through his pants. "I'd say you *measure* up just fine, Superman." I squeeze, relishing his groan. "Talk about a man of steel."

His chuckle is pained, but there's no denying the tension easing out of his bunched muscles.

"I adore your crazy." He wraps his arms around me, hugging me close.

"Keep saying sweet things like that, and you're gonna make me cry." My voice comes out smaller than usual because I wasn't lying; I'm choking back a flood of tears.

"That wasn't meant to make you cry, but what I tell you next just might."

I straighten, sitting up but refusing to climb off his lap. If this is all going to come crashing down around me, I want to enjoy every second of it I possibly can before it does.

"I'm a virgin."

I stare at him, waiting for the rest, because he made it sound like he had this bomb to drop on me.

"Umm…" I'm kind of at a loss for what to say. It feels wrong to be all *Yeah, I figured as much*, but in the same breath, the longer I go without saying anything, the more awkward the moment grows. So instead, I go with, "Why do you say that like it's a bad thing?"

CK blinks at me, crinkles forming in the corners of his eyes. "You're saying it's not?" I shake my head. "Most people find it weird for someone our age not to have had sex before."

"Who the fuck cares what anyone else thinks?" I run my fingers through his hair, sensing the need to soothe him.

"It doesn't bother you?"

This man will forever create fissures in my heart with his shy vulnerability. "No. I actually find it kind of hot," I answer honestly.

"What?"

Oh, I kinda love that I'm knocking him off balance.

"Ooo," I singsong, twisting around on his lap as I search the room for something I know isn't here but still seek regardless.

CK steadies me before I can take a header. "Why does your *Ooo* scare me more than admitting I was a virgin?"

I pinch the tip of my tongue between my teeth with a grin. "Because you may have fought it at first, but you, sir, know me quite well." I give him a wink.

"Dare I ask what you're looking for?" He sighs, as if resigned to his fate. It doesn't bother me in the least. I'm just happy he's not focusing on things he should have never seen as short-comings.

I waggle my eyebrows. "Oh…you know…my whistle."

"What?" He barks out a laugh, and the sound is music to my ears. "Why?"

"Because being your love coach just got a whole lot more fun for me."

#CHAPTER29

THE SHRILL OF A WHISTLE—*THE* whistle, because no surprise, Quinn managed to retrieve it—greets me the second I step off the elevator.

I can't see her yet, thanks to my vantage point, but I know the second I find Quinn, she's going to have that teasing, taunting, troublemaking grin firmly in place on her pretty face.

How do I know? It's the same one she's given me for the past six days.

Not even a whole week has passed since I fell into this alternate universe where I go to sleep every night with Quinn snuggled in my arms, and wake up to her psychotically energetic morning-person self, rousing me without shame. Yet, like Quinn abandoning her room in favor of mine, playful greetings like this have just as easily become my new normal.

Setting my bag down on the kitchen island, I do a quick inspection of the penthouse, searching for the feisty redhead.

"Umm…" I blow out a breath, my cheeks puffing out when I spot her perched atop the pool table, long legs dangling over the edge, silver whistle pinched between red-painted lips, enough layers of clothing on her body to rival Joey in that episode of *Friends* when he wears all of Chandler's clothes. "You do realize it was almost ninety today, right, Red?"

The whistle falls from her mouth, and *that* grin makes its appearance. A bolt of anticipation shoots down my spine and settles below my belt.

Quinn crosses one—*Are those Grant's snap-away warm-ups?*—pant-covered leg over the other, folds her arms over the top, rests one elbow on her knee, and props her chin on her fist, shooting me a wink.

"Guess it's a good thing we have central air, hmm?"

Oh, that hum is just as much trouble as that grin.

She's definitely up to something, and I am here for it because I dig her crazy.

"Why do I always feel like I need to gird my loins with you?" I ask, closing the distance between us.

"Oh, I have *plans*"—she purrs the word—"for your loins, Christopher." She uncrosses her legs and wraps them around my waist when I reach her, said loins going instantly hard.

Quinn Thompson, as a love coach, is an experience in and of itself.

Quinn Thompson as both the love coach and the recipient of the results of all of said coaching? Well…let's just say things have gotten a whole lot more *hands on*, if you catch my drift.

It's become natural for me to greet Quinn with a kiss, and I place a quick one on her upturned lips as a hello.

Of course, I'm not naive enough to believe this happy bubble we have going on will last once we start telling people we're… dating? But I'm perfectly content living in Delusionville for as long as I can.

Truthfully…I think I might have been more nervous to ask Quinn if we could keep what's been happening between us a secret—at least until we figure it out—than I was to tell her I'm still a card-carrying member of the v-train. I'm still a bit stunned by how well she took both those things.

Keeping Quinn and me well…between Quinn and me has been…an exercise in creative deflections—more so on her end than mine.

Shockingly, it hasn't been our way-too-damn-many-of-them roommates butting into our business. Of course, that could be because they're still mostly doing their own things and aren't here. But…I suspect it has more to do with the UofJ411 targeting us.

Now…Tessa Taylor? That's a horse of a different color. The romance novels she devours—even more so now that it's summer vacation—have made her more than mildly obsessed with what Quinn has told me she refers to as our *forced proximity golden opportunity*.

While I could do without all her prying, I can admit I've been more than happy reaping the benefits—yes, *those* kinds of benefits—of all her brainstorming to "help" Quinn get me to "notice" her.

"Dare I ask what plans you could have that have you wearing half your closet?" I tug on the strings of the zippered hoodie she has on.

Quinn stretches her arms overhead, her back arching in that lithe way that keeps me transfixed any time she does yoga at home. It's a crying shame she has so many damn layers on because I know exactly what that position does for her cleavage, cleavage I'm now more than allowed to ogle. Hell, it's practically encouraged.

She loops her arms around my neck, pulling me in and pressing a kiss of her own to my mouth. "You and I are about to have a do-over." She presses her palms to my chest, pushing me away and hopping down from the table.

"A do-over?" I ask as she rounds the table, arm extended behind her, fire-engine nails trailing along the felt. My gut clenches, feeling that touch as if it were dragging down my abdominals like she's been prone to do.

"Yup." She gives me her back as she studies the rack of pool cues hanging on the wall. She glances over her shoulder, her long red hair falling like a curtain, shielding part of her face from view, but there's no missing the naughty promise twinkling in the single eye maintaining contact with mine as she wraps her fingers around one of the cues.

"Hmm," she hums, rolling it along her fingers. "Not as *thick* as the things I'm used to handling."

My mind flashes to last night, my dick perking up, remembering how it felt the moment she boldly took it in her hand.

"How is giving a hand job to a pool cue a do-over of last night?"

"It's not." Her eyebrow waggle confirms her mind went to the same place mine did. "*That* deserves a repeat performance, *not* a do-over."

Her total confidence in everything she does makes it easy for me to forget about my lack of experience with members of the opposite sex and live in the moment with her.

Quinn stands the cue on the ground, leaning against it. "No, Superman, we are taking a mulligan on the night we played pool last week."

I move so I'm standing across from her with only the pool table between us. "Still haven't gotten over losing to me, Red?" I ask, curling my hands over the side rail and leaning in with my taunt.

"Keep talking shit like that, and you'll be waking up with a stuffed E.T. in your bed instead of me." Her gaze flits toward my bedroom.

I run my tongue across my teeth to keep my reaction to the threat from showing as a shudder racks my body. After finding one of those Funko Pop! dolls hidden with my Beats headphones, I don't doubt she has a whole arsenal of E.T.s to torture me with.

"I only *lost*—"

The arch of one of her dark brows is my only clue to how close her fiery side is to the surface. It probably shouldn't make my dick hard, but it does.

"—because you, you silly man, were too blind to all my attempts at getting you to *properly* teach me how to shoot."

"I wasn't blind to them, Red." I just had a hard time believing they were anything more than her typical flirting. I wanted nothing more than to *show* her in that *proper* way she's implying, but the lines had already blurred between us by then. It felt too risky to act so couple-ly.

"Yet you did nothing about them."

My skin starts to feel too tight, and I grip the back of my neck. "Can you imagine how fast pictures like that would have hit the UofJ411?"

The posts of us at Jonah's pop into my brain, and in those, we were only standing together. Ones of me standing behind her, showing her how to shoot? Yeah, those definitely would have hit the Gram.

Understanding fills Quinn's dark eyes. I hate how she can be so empathetic to my request to keep us a secret when it's born from insecurities and an attempt to put off our inevitable end for as long as possible.

"I don't know how Kay and Mase deal with that bullshit all the time." Quinn sighs and comes around to my side of the table. "Whoever runs that account really needs to find a hobby."

"Agreed." I loop my arms around her middle, letting my hands rest on the top curve of her ass—or at least where I think the curve of her ass would begin. It's hard to tell with all the layers of clothing.

My thoughts turn to my friends. Kay and Mason may be an almost daily post on the school's gossip account, but my concerns about being featured are a bit different from theirs. My problem isn't so much *being* the story as it is for Kay, but more about the attention cutting into the already borrowed time I feel I have with Quinn. I don't know how many posts it will take for her to realize what I already know—she's too good for me.

"We'll figure it out." Quinn kisses the underside of my jaw. "For now, I'm going to use us flying under the radar to my advantage."

She's smiling when she steps out of my hold, but there's an edge to it that has me asking, "You're sure you're still okay with us keeping this"—I bounce a finger between us—"a secret?"

She ups the wattage of her smile, but...still, it doesn't quite reach her eyes. "Yeah."

Why don't I feel entirely convinced?

Quinn steps back to me, and I widen my stance so she can fit herself between my legs. "Plus, it's kind of fun torturing Tessa with noncommittal answers."

"Hmm. Now I understand the true reason your hair is red." I tuck a wayward piece of it behind her ear.

"Why's that?" Her eyes glitter like they do any time she can sense I'm gearing up to tease her.

"It's because you're really the devil." I smooth my thumbs along her scalp. "Hmm, no horns."

Quinn bursts out laughing, the musical sound wiping away any of my earlier worries. "Sorry to break it to you, Superman, but I get my hair from a box of dye, not the ruler of hell. Though..." She taps her chin. "If he were inclined to give me anything, I wouldn't turn down tacos."

My laughter echoes her own. "You are an absolute nut." I kiss the tip of her nose. "Now…do you wanna tell me how you plan on using us being on the down low to your advantage? And does it have anything to do with me sweating just looking at you in all those clothes?"

"Why yes." She steps back again, circling her arms around before propping her hands on her hips, presenting her comically bulky self. "You and I are going to play us some pool." She taps the table as if that part of the plan wasn't already obvious.

"And we couldn't do that at the pool hall because…" I let my sentence trail off because she's so much fun to bait.

"Because, *Christopher*…" See what I mean? "For every shot either of us makes, the other has to remove an article of clothing."

"Ha! And you think making those the stakes when you're so *clearly* stacking the odds against your own pending nudity"—I wave a hand up and down her bundled form—"is going to get me to help you learn how to play better?"

"No." Quinn shakes her head. "This"—she fluffs the sweat-shirt serving as her outermost layer—"is for today's coaching lesson: *delayed satisfaction*." She had to purr the last part, didn't she? "Your incentive for getting all up close and personal *for* my lesson is that for any shot you *help* me make, it earns you a kiss to any place of your choosing."

"Don't go writing checks your mouth can't cash," I warn. I have imagined her mouth on every inch of my body.

"Please, CK." She rolls her eyes. "Every day, I want to attack your mouth with my mouth. Do you really think I'm going to be sad having to kiss you anywhere else?"

Annnnd…playing pool with a boner should be interesting.

Quinn insists on breaking, beaming when she sinks a ball and I have to remove my *Nerd? I prefer the term intellectual badass* T-shirt. And yes, before you ask, it was a gift from Kay.

"This is categorically unfair," I say, holding the shirt pinched between my fingers before dropping it. "I'm going to be naked in like"—I do some quick math—"four shots."

"Socks and shoes count as two each," Quinn says offhandedly as she scopes out her next shot, which, thankfully, she misses.

Looking at her, it's impossible to determine how many layers she donned before issuing this challenge.

"So you're saying you could potentially have me naked in one game, but I'll have to risk playing in my birthday suit to even have a *chance* of getting you naked?"

"Delayed satisfaction, Superman."

"I'll give you delayed satisfaction," I mutter and sink a striped ball in a side pocket. "Now strip, Red."

She's all Cheshire cat grinning as she slowly tugs the tab on the silver zipper holding her U of J Red Squad sweatshirt closed. Unlike me, she just shrugs out of it, letting it pool on the floor at her feet before kicking it away.

I mutter a curse at the unbuttoned flannel shirt and U of J Cheerleading T-shirt now on display. That's a minimum of three layers—if you count her bra—before I get to see her boobs.

"Alright." I suck in my teeth, eyeing her ensemble like it personally offends me. "I see how it's gonna be."

Cracking my neck to loosen up, I ignore the temptress taunting me and make quick work of sinking my next six shots without even pausing for her to strip until I'm eyeing which pocket would be best for the eight ball.

Without any fanfare, Quinn toes off both her shoes, her socks —because of course she wouldn't be wearing her typical flip-flops—the flannel, and the T-shirt.

"Evil," I singsong under my breath, narrowing my eyes at the white crop top she's revealed as yet another layer.

Blowing out a breath, I use the sight near the foot string, call out my shot, and bank the eight ball off the cushion, sinking it into the corner pocket with a smooth roll.

"Off." I snap for the shirt.

Quinn being Quinn only smirks and grabs the front of Grant's snap-away warm-ups. Unfortunately, the pants don't come off like they do for our friend before a game because she had to roll them over half a dozen times to not trip over them.

"Not a word," she cautions with an extended finger.

"I know you said math is your bestie's work—"

"My bestie?" Her face scrunches up before her jaw drops. "I'm going to start calling your punk ass Lucifer if you keep this devil shit up, mister."

"What?" I shrug. "Just saying this"—I point to the pants she's still struggling to remove—"is what happens when you're a five-foot-two cheerleader and you borrow clothes from a six-foot-eight basketball star."

"Look at the funny man with the jokes." Quinn finally huffs in defeat, her hands slapping her thighs before she shimmies the pants down her legs. "God, I imagined that being *way* sexier than it was."

I take a slow perusal up the long length of her toned legs, now bared to my view, with her clad in another pair of those plaid sleep shorts. "You're sexy, Red."

Color stains her cheeks, and she peers at me from beneath her lashes. "I like that you tell me what you think now."

She never shies away from telling me how she feels.

"What?"

"Huh?" I scratch at my jaw.

"You made this…face."

Her ability to read me as well as she does is a skill I wasn't aware she had until we started spending so much time together. "I was just thinking how much I admire your ability to be so vulnerable with telling me how you feel."

She licks her lips and dips her chin, hiding behind the shield of her hair. Witnessing a bashful Quinn Thompson is as rare as seeing a unicorn, and no less magical.

She recovers quickly, unabashedly watching my every movement as I collect and rerack the balls for our second game.

I break, landing a solid, but end up scratching from a bad ricochet, sending the cue ball rolling into one of the other corner pockets.

I don't even care that Quinn institutes a new penalty that has me toeing off both my Chucks because now that crop top is gone, and Quinn is standing before me in a sexy-as-fuck black-lace bra.

My mouth goes dry while simultaneously filling with drool at the sight before me. The delicate material cups Quinn's breasts, the generous swells of her cleavage pushed high and tight together and begging me to bury my face in them.

The bronzed hue of her skin looks as warm and inviting as I know it is to touch and highlights the nip of her waist and the toned muscles she's honed from years of cheerleading. She's the perfect contradiction of womanly curves with her flared hips and powerful athletic build.

It takes me a solid minute to work my way down to the

toenails painted a matching fire-engine red and back up to the lust-filled brown eyes studying me.

I remain rooted to my spot, my knuckles turning white as I strangle my pool cue, unable to move as I watch Quinn slip a finger under the strap hooked over her shoulder. She lifts it away from her body, teasingly lowering it down her arm before putting it back in place.

I need my hands on her in any way I can get them on her. And I need them on her now.

"Let's see if I can't help you perfect your shot," I suggest, making my way toward her.

"I thought you'd never ask, Superman," Quinn says with an arch of her back, the long line of her spine curving in and popping out the bubble of her butt and swell of her breasts in a way that has me adjusting myself in my shorts.

Last summer, before I went home to Kansas, JT had the brilliant idea for us to celebrate my going away in style, and by style, I mean going to some shady pool hall down the shore to hustle people we had no business cheating out of their money. We made it out alive by the skin of our teeth, and *still*, this right here feels like the most dangerous game of eight ball I'll ever play.

Stepping behind Quinn, I spread my legs and press my front to her back. "Chalk your cue, Red."

With trembling fingers, she does as I ask, picking up the tiny paper-wrapped cube of blue chalk and rubbing it around the end of her cue. From over her shoulder, I watch, any lingering softness in my dick gone the instant her red-painted lips purse to blow the excess chalk off the tip.

"*Fuuuck* me, Quinn," I groan.

"All in good time, Christopher." She bends forward, her ass pushing against my erection with a swivel of her hips.

With a feral growl, I fold myself over her back, my thighs pressed along the backs of hers, her ass nestled against my groin. Quinn grinds into me, and I still her with a squeeze of her hip. I glide my palm up her side, feeling each bump of her rib cage before her smooth skin gives way to the scalloped edge of her bra.

She sucks in a breath, her chest expanding under mine. I trail my fingertips along the outline of her bra before I dip inside and tweak her nipple.

"*CK.*" The husky gasp of my name falling from her parted lips is everything, spurring me on further.

I just barely let the tips of my fingers skim the length of her arms, following the cut of her triceps over the jut of her elbow, and finally cupping her forearm before threading my fingers with hers from over the top of her hand.

Quinn shakes her hair out of her face, looking at me out of the corner of her eye.

"You ready for your lesson, Q?" I ask, my cheek pressed to hers.

"Mmmhmm." Her hum reverberates through me.

I nip at the back of her shoulder, then push into her more. "One of the biggest mistakes I've seen you make with your shots is trying to put too much power behind them."

Sliding my left arm so it lies under her, I maneuver her right back and forth in the same motion needed to take a shot. "Too much power can make the ball travel too fast."

"Yeah, *nobody* likes fast balls," she quips, her chest rumbling as she laughs at her own joke.

"Pay attention, smartass." I nibble the side of her throat, sucking at her pulse point, when she drops her head to grant me better access. "The pocket is actually bigger when the ball travels at slower speeds."

"Most guys like their *pockets* small and *tight*."

"Quinn!"

She giggles, relishing how close she has me to snapping. This is not going at all like I hoped. I'm the one who is supposed to be teasing her, yet she keeps turning it around on me.

Flexing my fingers around her, I exhale a long breath and take our shot on the two ball. It rolls perfectly into the side pocket, with the cue ball rolling to the center of the table like I intended.

Quinn whoops in glee, spinning in my hold. She touches the tip of her tongue to one of her incisors, pure mischief radiating in her eyes.

"Where do you want my lips?"

Wrapped around my cock, I think, but shove that thought down…for now.

"How about shooter's choice," I offer, not trusting myself not to voice my earlier thought. The first time we move the bases along to oral is not going to be because I won having her mouth on my dick in a game.

That intoxicating scent of coconut I just spent the last few minutes inhaling wraps around me again as she moves in close. Quinn walks her fingers up my abs, her mouth curling at the corners right before it disappears from view. Warm breath hits the skin at the base of my throat before the soft pillow of her lips follows. It's light, gentle even, yet so fucking erotic it's a miracle I'm not coming in my shorts like the virgin I am.

I move away as soon as she pulls back, needing distance immediately. "You're on your own for the next one."

She smirks, having heard the lust coating my voice as much as I did. Following my advice, she takes advantage of the premier placement I left her with and sinks two more shots, winning my socks with them.

Linking my fingers together, I push my hands out, cracking my knuckles as I survey the spread on the table. I move into position, lifting my gaze to Quinn as I pause before taking my shot.

"Get ready to sing happy birthday, Red."

Her response is delayed as she tracks the path of the green ball rolling down the felt. "Huh?"

"You're about to be in your birthday suit, baby." I motion for her to drop her shorts.

Fuck me. Her panties match the bra.

Done messing around, I clear the five remaining solids from the board and the eight. But I don't stop there. Instead, I take care of the rest of Quinn's and then toss the pool cue on the table.

Quinn's eyes are wide, her dark brows pinched together as she tries to work out why I didn't stop when she should have been naked eight shots ago.

I stalk toward her, not bothering to answer the unasked question. Hooking my hands under her arms, I lift her and hoist her onto the pool table.

"Wha—"

I nudge her knees open, stepping between them, and cut off whatever she was about to say by crashing my mouth into hers.

There's nothing sweet about this kiss. It's pure need and banked lust, every bit of teasing from our games colliding and combusting.

I nip, lick, and suck at Quinn's lips. Her jaw. Her throat.

My arms wrap around her, the sweet smell of coconut filling my lungs as I pant against her skin while working the clasp of her bra open.

"Beautiful," I whisper as soon as I toss her bra off to the side, cupping and lifting her breasts to my mouth.

Quinn gasps as I suck on her nipple, flicking the hardened peak with my tongue. She goes slack as I suckle, the arm I left banded behind her back the only thing keeping her upright as I alternate lavishing attention on one breast then the other.

She starts to writhe, her nails scraping along my scalp as she tugs at my hair.

Needing more of her, I kiss a path down the plane of her body, following the zigzag pattern of beauty marks dotting her skin on the way down. I ease her down until her shoulder blades hit the felt and splay her out on the table like a feast waiting to be devoured.

Hooking my fingers under the band of her underwear, I take great care as I roll the lace over her hips and down her legs. Quinn's arms flail around as her hands search for purchase before slapping down on the felt, unable to reach me as I follow the path of her panties.

"CK…" She sighs when I place a kiss to the back of her knee and over the quivering muscles of her thighs on my way back up.

"So fucking beautiful." I speak against her skin, kissing the jut of her hip bone, inching closer and closer to her apex. "So fucking perfect."

"*Ay dios mío*," she calls out as I lick up her seam. This isn't the first time I've tasted her—that happened the other night when I sucked my fingers clean after I made her come all over them— but this is the first time I've gotten to drink from the source. She smells just as sweet down here, with a hint of musk mixed in.

Her hips arch toward me, and I wrap my hands around them, pinning her down as I fuck her with my tongue. My name is a litany of whisper curses as I eat her like no man has eaten a woman before.

"CK," she whimpers.

My glasses fog, but I can still make out the way her head is thrown back as she writhes in pleasure, the long column of her throat arched toward the ceiling, her nipples pebbled peaks swaying with every shuddered inhalation.

I want this to be good for her.

I *need* this to be good for her.

I...

Fuck me.

My dick has never been this hard in my life, but all I care about is getting her to come down my throat.

"What do you need to come?" My voice is muffled by her pussy.

"Just—" She moans. "*Más.*"

More. I can give her more.

Wedging my shoulders under her legs, I let the limbs drape over my back and straighten to the full height my kneeled position allows. Her lower half folds upward, her ass lifting off the edge of the table as I lick her from clit to asshole and back.

This may be my first time going down on a woman, but I've watched a lot of porn in my life. Quinn's reactions have consistently confirmed that I was a good study with everything else we've done.

I splay a hand over her concave belly and reach the other up to toy with her nipples, squeezing and kneading her breasts to a chorus of mewls spilling from her mouth.

Quinn's hands are all over me. In my hair, on my shoulders, grabbing on and anchoring herself on my biceps.

"CK...*more*. Mmm."

I give her everything I've got, sweat dripping down my back, my lungs screaming for air as I bury my face hard against her.

I listen to her sounds. To her gasps. To her moans. To the wailing mewls that serve as a prelude to her indistinguishable Spanish mutters, and...then...she's coming.

She's crying out my name, chanting it over and over, and I am here for it.

I'm more than aware of how out of my league Quinn is. But here? Inside these walls? Kneeling between her legs? This is the one place I don't worry about not being good enough for her, and I'll keep us here as long as I can if it means I can hold on to her that much longer.

QUINN

I ROLL over with a growl as the increasingly steady beat of *duunn-dunn duuunnnn-duun duunnnn-dun-dun-dun-dun* invades my dreams.

"And you said I was the evil one," I mumble, burying my face into CK's side. He's damn lucky I'm too busy being a content pile of girly goo to get mad at him for setting the *Jaws* theme song as my alarm's ringtone.

His arms tighten around me, one of his hands smoothing down my back, slipping under the hem of his T-shirt I slept in to cup my bare ass. "You're the one who set my text tone to *E.T. Phone Home*." He pulls me even closer, breathing me in and pressing a soft kiss to the crown of my head. "Turnabout is fair play, Red."

"Mmm." I dot kisses along his naked chest. "I've created a monster."

CK's laughter has always affected me, but hearing it so carefree and extra rumbly from sleep shifts something elemental inside of me.

"What can I say?" He moves his hand lower, my back arching

as his fingers graze my slick center before he cups me from behind, enjoying my commando self. "Your pussy is a lot more tempting than the simple apple your mentor went with."

My laughter gets choked by my moan as he teases my entrance. The confident way he handles me makes it extremely difficult to believe I'm the first woman to experience this side of him, but I'm honored by it nonetheless.

"I don't want to get up." I snuggle deeper, lifting and hooking a leg over CK's hip to grant him better access to do whatever he wants with my body.

He slips two fingers inside me with a muttered *"Fuck"* before he scissors them, pumping lazily. "That's high praise coming from you."

He's not wrong. Usually, I'm up with the sun, bounding out of bed, ready to start my day before my previously non-*Jaws*-themed alarm has a chance to go off. Not even sleeping in CK's bed for the last week has changed that facet of my personality.

Apparently, that ends today. My brain is probably still melted from what he did to me on the pool table, not that I'm mad about it. Far from it.

"When do you have to leave for The Barracks?"

I groan at the reality check his question brings with it. "Too soon." My eyes fall shut as need vibrates inside me.

My job at The Barracks has been a source of pride for me. Despite being a cheer gym, it's been an unexpected but welcome opportunity to prove myself outside of the world of cheerleading. So why is it this morning has me cursing that job? Why do I want to say fuck it all and spend the day in bed? Is it lust? A primal need to sate my sexual desires? Or...is it because here, alone in this bed, room, apartment, is the only place I don't have to hide my feelings for CK?

Oof. I may be a morning person, but even that feels like too much to unpack so early in the day.

"Then we better make the most of the time we've got." CK twists his wrist, keeping his hand in place inside me as he uses his hold on me to maneuver me around. "Straddle me, Red."

My body unconsciously does as he asks. "Mmm, CK." His erection is hard and thick between my legs when I settle on his lap.

"*Fuck* me, you're a sight like this." His blue eyes are almost black through his heavy-lidded sweep of me.

"*Mm*, you too." I rock back and forth, rubbing my greedy clit on his length.

His black hair is a disheveled mess from both sleep and my hands clutching at it as he brought me to multiple orgasms with his mouth. His shoulders, biceps, and chest all sport fading scratch marks I hope he'll wear like badges of honor.

His abs ripple with each labored breath he takes, and the glistening head of his cock peeks out from the band of the boxer briefs he pulled on to sleep.

He removes his fingers from inside me, and I whimper at the loss. Wetness trails in the wake of his touch as his bruising grip on my ass cheeks guides my movements.

"Quinn."

The cords of his neck stand out in stark relief, and there's a distinct jut to his jaw with each increasingly relentless grind of me on him.

He moves his palms down my thighs, his knuckles and my skin blanching of color at his punishing hold. "Fuck me, Quinn." It's not an exclamation. This time it's a command.

I shake my head, my own hair a mass of messy waves as it moves around my shoulders. "I'm not going to *Slam, purr, thank you, sir* you for your first time."

With him bracing a palm on the mattress, all those sexy lines of his ripple and flex as he pushes to sit up. We're nose to nose, his hand taking me by the nape. "I don't need candles and rose petals."

His thumb strokes down the line of my throat, and I swallow against the touch. "I'm not saying that." I shake my head again. "But first time or not, you deserve more than me having to rush out the door as you're tying off the condom."

His displeased growl has me tossing my head back as a new wave of desire rolls through me.

"Fine." He flops back down, only mildly huffing but wildly cute.

I adore this side of him. He's playful and uninhibited in a way I never could have imagined he could be with me.

He hooks his hands under my thighs and lifts, my ass losing contact with his body. Gravity has my shirt falling with me as he tilts me forward, the well-worn cotton pooling on my lower back. Goose bumps sprout along my skin as the cool air caresses it.

"Ride my face then, beautiful."

My body goes molten, my core pulsing with both the memory of last night and how surprisingly deliciously alpha I've discovered CK to be.

"No," I deny him, slipping out of his hold and shifting down his body. "Today, it's my turn to have you in my mouth."

That sound I love rolls through the back of his throat, and he's fisting my hair in both hands. My scalp burns, and the sting of pain sends a bolt of pure lust pinballing through my nipples to my clit.

Slipping beneath the band of his boxers, I inch the material down, revealing him to my greedy gaze one inch at a time. With a similar squeeze of his hips like he's done to me, I urge CK to lift up and tug the boxers over the curve of his ass.

I've grown more than acquainted with CK's cock over the last week, but this is the first time I've gotten to be eye to eye with his one-eyed beast. My sigh is audible as I take in the shiny-with-precum head stretching toward his navel.

Balancing on my elbows, I make myself at home between CK's spread legs, tilting my chin up to find his gaze already trained on me.

A bolt of apprehension hits me in the solar plexus and has me swallowing thickly.

"What's wrong?" CK runs a thumb across my lower lip, his handsome features shifting when he reads something in mine.

"I want this to be good for you," I admit.

"Isn't that supposed to be my line?" He smirks.

"I'm serious. I don't want you to be disappointed."

He stretches his arm out, cupping the side of my face. "One, I'm embarrassingly close to coming by you just *breathing* on me. And, two, no matter what we do, I couldn't be disappointed because I'm doing it with you."

My jaw goes slack, and a pressure I'm quick to blink away builds behind my eyes. I know the famous movie quote is there's no crying in baseball, but there's no crying in blow jobs either. Well…I guess maybe there is if you've worked up one hell of a deep throat, but—

What the fuck?

I have a penis in my face, and this is where my mind goes? Shit, you would think I was the virgin.

Focus, Quinn.

And I do.

I open up my mouth, mentally shove my gag reflex to the side, and swallow every glorious inch of CK's dick, delighting in every curse, hiss, and groan slipping off his tongue.

Talk about a cock-a-doodle-doo in the morning.

When most people think of cheerleaders, they think of pretty girls with high ponytails and short skirts waving pom-poms on the sidelines of sporting events. We're the fluff, the added entertainment meant to accessorize the *real* sport you're there to watch —football, basketball, etc., etc.

Now, sure…

Some of those facts are accurate.

My hair *is* tied back in the highest of ponytails, and I completed my hairstyle with a badass sequin-covered blue camouflage bow in front to match the sports bra I have on. And when I dress for game day as a member of the U of J Red Squad, my uniform does consist of a skirt and pom-poms.

But…

What *those* people don't necessarily see is the athleticism that goes into crafting the routines they watch between downs played on the field.

Nothing irks me more than when a person tries to tell me cheerleading isn't a sport. However, after cheering for over seventeen years, I know better than to listen to them. Plus, now cheerleading is an Olympic sport, so those naysayers better watch out.

Because when you get to the competition aspect of cheer? Well, that's a whole different ball game.

Any amount of time spent in a gym for a club team, or what is more commonly referred to as all-stars, would prove it. The Barracks, the cheer wet dream of a gym, home to the New Jersey All-Star Cheerleading teams, or NJA for short, is a prime example of where to go. This place is a hundred-thousand-square-foot cheer mecca of excellence, and even having been an official employee of it for two months, it's still hard to believe I'm standing inside it.

All around me, cheerleaders of various ages ranging from twelve to eighteen are spread across the blue mats working on their skills. For five-plus hours, I've helped coach them on their tumbling, jumps, pyramids, dance, and stunts alongside some of the best coaches in the sport. Seriously, I'm still struggling to accept that I'm considered one of those coaches as well.

"That's great, Livi," Kay says as she dismounts from the full toss stunt her twin brother Olly threw her into.

"Just watch your toss line on the way up, Olly." JT automatically finishes the instruction for the pair.

"Again." Kay circles a finger in the air, then counts them off.

My two friends work as one cohesive unit, training the next duo to take over the champion mantel they held for years. The whole process happens in a matter of seconds.

On Olly and Livi's next attempt at a trick few partner stunt duos can even do, its execution is flawless.

I slow-clap and bow at my friends.

"When are you going to cut that shit out?" Kay rolls her eyes at my antics.

"Oh, leave her alone, PF." JT slings a slightly sweaty arm around my shoulders, overenunciating Kay's cheer nickname to a drawn out *Pfff*. "You know Q is my favorite fangirl."

My cheeks heat, but I can't deny the title. It's strange to say I grew up idolizing Kay and JT since we're the same age, but... that's essentially the truth. In all my years of cheering, I have never seen a partner stunt pairing as solid and accomplished as them.

And now I work with them. *Eep!*

I *may* have had a mini—and by mini, I mean total, full-blown —freak-out when I realized the hot auburn-haired—genetic, not from a box like mine—guy my new roommate was video chatting with was *the* JT Taylor.

Annnd, when I realized said new roomie was his stunt partner, PF Dennings, I might have done a bad impression of Meredith Blake in *The Parent Trap* being confronted with two Hallies.

It wasn't my fault, I swear. How else is a person supposed to react when presented with the fact that she was unexpectedly living with cheer royalty? I mean, covering my mouth with my hands and jump-bouncing my gaze between the two of them seems like a perfectly acceptable reaction to me.

Not going to lie—it still hurts my heart a bit that they aren't my Red Squad teammates. However, coaching alongside them this summer has gone a long way to healing that hurt.

Epic…that's really the only adjective I can think of to describe the experience.

"Did you get all the footage you needed?" JT asks, motioning to the GoPros I have set up along the perimeter of our practice floor.

"Yup. I can edit the content later," I confirm, thinking of my unofficial favorite part of my job here helping revamp NJA's social media presence.

"Okay then." JT finger snaps at me as most of the NJA senior level athletes head for the locker rooms at the back of the gym. "Let's have some fun."

"Wha—" I mumble around a mouthful of Gatorade.

"I'm about to make all your dreams come true, Q."

I see Kay roll her eyes at JT dialing up his flirt level.

"Why am I scared to ask what you mean by that?" I move cautiously in JT's direction, waving at Mason, Trav, and Savvy, making their way onto the floor now that practice is over.

"Dunno." He shrugs. "Unless you're suddenly scared to get tossed around."

"*OHMIGAH!* We're stunting together?" I screech and just don't care.

JT nods, and I drop to the mat, immediately starting to stretch, watching as Mason hooks an arm around Kay as soon as he's close enough. Then, he lays a kiss on her mouth that's so hot it has *my* toes curling inside my cheer shoes.

Sighs chorus at the sight, my own included.

While I admit it's been fun keeping my and CK's relationship a secret, I can't help but feel irrationally angry at a whole bunch of people I've never met over all the damage they inflicted on the man I'm falling for.

After folding over in a straddle split, my gaze finds its way back to a canoodling Kaysonova.

I have to admit, I am looking forward to the day that will be CK and me—kissing each other no matter where we are. That day is coming soon, seeing as most of our roommates are moving back into the apartment when camp for the football team starts.

#CHAPTER31

"AH, *TRAITOR!*"

I carefully set aside the tablet I've been using to tweak some of the graphics for my video game as Quinn hustles into the living room. I expected a reaction like this out of her when I put on *Bones* without her. Honestly, I think I was practically begging for it.

"Don't act like you haven't seen this episode before, Red," I say, tracking her progress toward me and noticing the hitch in her gait.

"Irrelevant, *Christopher.*"

There's my girl.

Shit!

Those kinds of thoughts are dangerous. I know we've been messing around for the last week, and sure, we've done some *couple-ly* things, as Quinn would call them, but I'm under no delusions that this is anything more than a friends-with-bennies type situation. Quinn is no more *my* girl than she is JT's or Grady's, as has been speculated on the Gram.

Though...I can't help finding myself agreeing with some of the comments I read. A hunky (their words, not mine) male cheerleader or future NHL-playing hockey player makes much more sense as Quinn's match than a shy computer nerd.

That fact is one of the main reasons keeping us a secret has been so important. There's no need to worry about the others feeling pressured to choose between us when we inevitably end if they never knew about us in the first place. Eviction would be nothing compared to the excommunication from the group, something I truly fear.

Quinn flops onto the couch, toeing off her flip-flops and kicking her legs up to rest in my lap with a groan.

"Sore?" I lift one of her feet and knead the arch.

"Oh, god." She tosses her head back, much the same as she did on the pool table last night. My dick, which had already perked up at the sight of Quinn in her tiny black cheer shorts and NJA-emblazoned sports bra, goes from half-mast to full-fledged at the guttural sound.

"Feel good?" I dig into the ball of her foot.

"Mmm, if you keep doing things like that, I envision lots more blow jobs in your future."

"Is that so?" I massage up the length of her calf, her skin warm and soft over the hard muscle.

"Mmmhmm," she hums, eyes squeezed shut, dark lashes fanned across her flushed cheeks.

"And what do those clairvoyant abilities of yours see if I tell you I turned up the temperature on the hot tub once I saw the video of you stunting at practice?"

Quinn's head lolls on the back of the couch, her dark eyes slowly peeling open to hazily blink up at me. "You didn't."

I smirk. "I did."

Her gaze flits to the wall of glass leading to the balcony. "Then I'd say..." She pushes up, folding forward, stretching an arm out toward me. I suck in a breath as she walks her fingers up my thigh, slipping them beneath the hem of my T-shirt. "How do you feel about joining me for a dip?"

"I'd say"—I gesture to the board shorts I have on—"why else do you think I'm wearing these?"

"Oh, Superman." Quinn giggles and bites down on her lip. "I love that you think you're going to need your bathing suit."

Sure enough, fifteen minutes later, Quinn is eyeing my Superman-printed board shorts like they're the enemy.

"You do realize you were the one who gifted me these for Christmas, right?" I step out of the way so she can set the tray with the charcuterie board she quickly put together on one of the lounge chairs surrounding the hot tub.

"Yeah, yeah, yeah." She waves a dismissive hand at me. "I'm an excellent gift giver. Now take them off."

I run my gaze over the practice gear she still has on.

"Fine." She huffs, throwing her arms up before wiggling to remove her top. Then, as if I'm not already struggling to breathe at the sight of her full tits topped with dark hard nipples, she hooks her thumbs in her shorts and shoves them down her legs.

Kicking the material to the side, she straightens and assumes her favorite superhero hands-on-hips pose. There's zero care that we are outside, the warm evening air blowing gently around us, the fading light of the early evening sun casting a glow on her tanned skin. It's not like anyone can see us. None of the other buildings around are as tall as ours.

I wish I could bottle up some of her confidence for myself. If I had just an ounce of it, we might have a fighting chance.

"Jesus, Quinn." I rub a hand over my mouth, taking her in. It shouldn't be humanly possible for a person to be as beautiful as she is. She is literal perfection from the top of her cherry-cola-red hair down to her tiny fire-engine-red toes.

"You like what you see?" There's an edge to her question, but all I really notice is the playful tilt to her lips and the jiggle of her breasts as she shifts around.

"You are the most gorgeous person I have ever had the privilege of setting eyes on."

The long column of her throat works with a swallow as my words settle over her. She starts to fidget, toying with the ends of her fingers and biting her lip more than before.

Then, with a toss of her ponytail over her shoulder, Quinn steps into the hot tub and lowers herself onto one of the built-in seats. The *Well, what about you?* eyebrow raise she gives me as the water bubbles around her, hiding her nakedness from view, is what finally spurs me into action.

Quinn keeps her gaze shamelessly locked on me as I remove my shirt, lips twitching as she runs it over my torso.

I know I'm not the same lanky nerd as I was in high school thanks to Grant dragging me along to the gym with him, but Quinn has a way of looking at me like I really am the *goddamn swan* Em and Kay try to tell me I am. And, yes, they use those exact words.

My hands go to the tie of my shorts, and Quinn's tongue peeks out, licking across the swell of her bottom lip as she watches me work the knot free. I didn't think it was possible, but my dick hardens even further, pushing against my fly and grazing my knuckles at her hungry expression.

"Wait!" Droplets of water sprinkle the deck and hit the top of my foot as Quinn thrusts a hand up in the universal sign for stop.

I instantly move my hands to cover my junk, insecurity making my skin feel too tight.

"What are you doing?" Quinn shouts, slapping the water. "It's my turn to admire the goods—don't cover them up."

It takes me a second before I comply and lower my hands.

"Much better." Quinn beams, then circles her finger. "Give us a twirl?"

I roll my eyes and, *without* twirling, climb into the hot tub, taking the seat beside a pouting Quinn.

"You're no fun," she complains.

"You'll live," I counter, used to her dramatics.

The steam rising off of the water causes my glasses to fog. I should have put my contacts in when I turned up the temperature, but unless we're in bed, Quinn tends to yell at me if I don't have them on. Removing my glasses, I dip them into the water to warm up the lenses and shake them dry as best I can.

Quinn watches me the entire time, a tiny tilt to her mouth as I slide them up the bridge of my nose.

"This might be the best idea you've ever had." Quinn sighs, sagging against the side of the hot tub.

"Rough day at the gym?"

"Yeah." She grunts. "Oh, that's the spot." She shifts closer to whatever jet is working for her. "Camp is always harder."

Folding one of my legs beneath me, I turn so I'm facing her, trying valiantly to forget about the fact that I'm sitting here naked while she tells me all about camp.

Quinn explains how they're more hands on with their athletes as they teach them new skills and help them to perfect others. I already know all about how Kay's ability to jump in to see why a stunt isn't working or personally demonstrate a skill makes her a special kind of coach, so it doesn't surprise me in the least that Quinn's been using the same method with her coaching.

I get a little lost in the technical jargon when Quinn tells me about the stunts I saw her and JT doing on Instagram earlier, but there's no missing the gushy fangirl edge that tinges the retelling.

"You're lucky we didn't bring any alcohol out with us. Otherwise, you'd be drunk right now," I tease, swallowing down my unwarranted jealousy toward JT.

Quinn buries her face in her hands. "I still can't believe you guys made a drinking game about me."

"If the fangirl bow fits."

My pun earns me a beaming smile. "Well…you may not believe me, but getting to stunt with a cheer god wasn't even the best part of my day."

"Of course not." I tug on her ponytail. "That was this morning." I shrug. "Or at least it was for me."

Now I'm the one grinning like a fool, thinking about the blow job that started my day.

Under the surface of bubbling foam, Quinn curls her hand over my thigh, my body heating hotter than the water. "While I did have fun licking your lollipop…"

"Jesus." I bark out a laugh.

"The best part was the job Coach Kris offered me."

Coach Kris is the owner and main coach for all of NJA.

"Isn't that what she did when she hired you as a summer coach?"

"Yeah, but this one is even better." Quinn's sentence is more squeal than words by the end.

She's practically vibrating from excitement as she tells me all about how Coach Kris asked her if she wanted to become NJA's official social media curator. She would be responsible for choosing and creating all the content for the gym itself and for each NJA team.

Social media is a hot-button issue for most of us that live here —each of us having our own reasons—but I know Quinn has been more instrumental than she's let on in helping Kay dip her toes back into those shark-infested waters.

"Not only did Coach Kris offer to pay me, we're also going to see if I can use it for course credit."

"That's awesome, Q." I know the whole reason she stayed in Jersey for the break was to squeeze in as many summer classes as possible to help lighten her academic load during cheer season.

The thought is a reminder of the invisible clock counting down our time together. It's there, ticking away whether we want to acknowledge it or not. We can pretend all we want, but I'm not naive enough to think things won't change once our roommates return for good.

Our pending ending pulses through me, and I need Quinn as close to me as possible until that moment comes. Decision made, I take her hand in mine, thread my fingers between hers, and pull. She comes willingly, grinning happily as she straddles my lap.

Cupping the back of my head, she keeps her gaze locked with mine and eases onto me at such a maddeningly slow pace I have to flex my fingers around her hips to keep from yanking her down.

The frothy waterline plays peekaboo with her nipples, seducing me with every flash of the erect buds. My mouth waters, the need to have them against my tongue intensifying.

I've thought of, dreamed of, and fantasized about Quinn more times than can be counted, but each real-life experience we've had this last week has put every last one of them to shame.

"Your hands feel so good on me," Quinn says as I glide them along her rib cage and up to her breasts, weighing them. They're perfect, just like the rest of her, filling my palm and then some.

"And you feel even better in them." I squeeze, leaning forward and sucking one nipple, then the other into my mouth, flicking and swirling my tongue around the hard bud.

"*Dios.*" Quinn arches into me, holding me to her chest. "Why are you so good at this?"

I grin against her skin, pleased to be pleasing her.

"You make it easy," I admit. With Quinn, my lack of experience has never been an issue. She makes it easy to read her body and translate her sounds. "Your bilingual switch is by far my favorite gauge to tell if you like something or not."

She does this gasp-moan, and then her thumbs are pressing

on the underside of my jaw, lifting my face for a kiss. It's lazy but ardent.

Jets pulse against my back, but it's the squeeze of her knees on my sides that I never want to lose. We kiss and kiss some more while I let my hands explore every curve and valley of her body.

Quinn scoots closer, her slit making contact with the head of my dick, eliciting a hiss at a heat that feels hotter than the hundred-and-three-degree water. "Shit."

I thrust my hips up to meet hers, my dick gliding through her wetness and bumping along her clit. "You're soaked, Quinn."

Her hands fall to my shoulders, clawing at me. "Mmmhmm." Eyes squeezed shut, she tosses her head back, her long hair floating along the surface of the water. "It's because of you."

Talk about giving a guy an ego boost.

Taking her ass in my hands, I grip her hard enough I worry I'm going to bruise her, but Quinn's whispered "*Más*" shuts those worries down before they can fully form.

We're both panting as our bodies toy with each other.

I pull her forward and push toward her.

Lift her up and pull her down.

Angling her while I move against her.

On and on it goes.

Her nails bite into my skin, her nipples grazing my chest with every pitch of her body.

"CK."

"Yeah…"

"Mmm," she hums, bearing down, increasing the friction of our wet humping. "You're going to make me come."

I chuckle, splaying my fingers to hold her to me tighter. "Isn't that the point?"

She nods wordlessly. Back and forth she moves, her clit riding the ridge surrounding the head of my dick. Her toes curl against my legs, the angle shifting just slightly, just enough for my tip to slip inside her.

Twin hisses echo in the night air, and Quinn's forehead falls to mine. Our eyes lock, and neither of us moves.

"CK?" She digs her fingers into me, sucking in a shuddering breath. "We can stop."

I'm shaking my head before she finishes her offer. "I want to fuck you."

"It certainly feels like you do," she quips, but this is one situation I won't let her turn into a joke.

Taking her by the back of the neck, I sit up, lengthening my spine so she knows I'm serious. "I want *this. With. You.*"

QUINN

CHAPTER 32

OH, be still my beating heart.

I know, I *know* things have been progressing in this direction, but hearing the words *I want this with you* coming from CK has my heart two-stepping.

"Are you sure?" I have to ask. I may have spent months nursing a major crush on him, but I don't want him to have regrets about how quickly our physical relationship has progressed.

Not for him.

Not for his first time.

"I've never been more sure about anything, about any*one* in my life."

Well, shit. If I wasn't already half in love with him from crushing on him, hearing that would undoubtedly do it.

"Not in here," I say, referring to the hot tub. "Water isn't always a friend to the hippity-dippity."

CK's chest rumbles with his laughter. "You certainly have a way with words, Red," he says, but he's already nodding his agreement. "Plus, the condoms are in my room."

"Umm…" I bite my lip, hoping I'm not about to get judged. "There are a few mixed in with the charcuterie."

My heart sinks when he shakes his head, his chin dipping toward his chest.

Mierda.

Is he judging me for my presumptuousness?

"Only you, Red."

Is that a good thing or a bad thing?

But then he holds out a hand for mine, and all my worries melt away as our fingers link together. He helps me climb out of the sunken hot tub, quickly tucking one of the towels we brought out around his waist before wrapping me up in another one.

Looping my arms around CK's neck, I push up on my toes and cover his mouth with mine. He immediately meets my kiss with one of his own, stoking the flame we started in the hot tub to a burning blaze.

One second I'm standing on the deck feeling the grain of the Trex planks, then the next my feet are off the ground as CK lifts me into his arms. I wrap my legs around him, hooking my ankles together behind his back, kissing him even deeper. My ponytail finally gives way to the weight of the water soaking the strands and CK's rough treatment of them as he thrusts a hand through my hair.

"Right here," I whisper against CK's mouth when I feel him take a step backward.

He growls, stepping forward this time, lowering me onto one of the empty lounge chairs, following me down with his lips still on mine.

A hand follows the line of my leg, skirting over my calf, dipping into the bend of my knee then up and around my thigh. CK's thumb presses into the space between my muscles, and I'm arching into him as he pulls away, kneeling between my splayed legs.

His glasses sit crooked on his nose, his eyes burning me with a want that sears me from the inside out. "Are you sure?"

Pushing up onto my elbows, I nod. "As long as you are."

He grunts as if I'm insane, then shifts onto one foot, reaching toward the lounger beside us, rooting around on the tray until he comes up with a foil packet. I may not have been a Girl Scout, but you can't say I'm not always prepared.

I shiver as his hands snake under the poorly wrapped terry cloth, holding my breath as he slowly drags it up, then pulls it open to expose my naked body to the night air and, more importantly, to him.

"Goddamn it, Quinn." He drags a hand over his mouth.

Indecision hums beneath my skin. "We don't have to do this if you want to wait." I offer him another out.

He shakes his head. "That's not it." He rips the packet open with his teeth, sheathing himself before tentatively touching my knees. His touch is reverent as it glides up my legs and over the jut of my hip bones.

His Adam's apple bobs and his tongue peeks out to wet his lips as he watches his hands spread over my body, his thumbs meeting at my pubic bone before following the line of my slit, parting my lips.

His groan is guttural as he stares at my exposed pussy. It's so fucking erotic I'm about to come without a single touch. He circles my clit, and I latch on to his forearms, not sure if I want to knock his touch away or hold him there so he'll never be able to stop.

"You're absolutely sure about this?" His question holds a hint of hesitation, but his actions are pure confidence as he drags his fingers down to my entrance and plunges them inside me.

I can hardly breathe, let alone speak at the pleasure whipping through my system. I nod, clutching at him to bring him closer.

CK's large frame hovers over me, his elbows bracketing my head as he leans in for the sweetest kiss.

"*Tómame.*" I whisper for him to take me as I hook my legs around him.

"*Fuck.*" His curse is primal. His biceps flex as he twists an arm between us, his knuckles grazing my inner thigh as he fists his length.

Grabbing the back of his neck, I lever my body up to his. "*Hazme tuya.*" I beg him to take me when I feel him fit himself at my entrance.

"Fuck, Quinn." He may not know what I said, but he still does as he's asked.

I gulp, knowing what is about to happen, hissing at the delicious burn of him stretching me as he fills me with his length.

My inner muscles ripple around CK, my body doing its best to suck him in, desperate to have all of him.

"Jesus Christ." CK unleashes the unholiest of curses, despite crying out for the son of God. "Oh fuck." His fingers dig into my hips as he holds himself still, only halfway inside me.

Jesus is right. How the hell does he have this much control when I'm about to come out of my skin?

"I want this to be good for you." CK pushes in another inch, his forehead falling to my shoulder, sweat making his skin slick.

"It is," I promise. Everything with him has been beyond compare. If he wasn't who he is, I'd probably think he was lying about being a virgin because it almost seems impossible for him to be *this* good.

"I don't know how long I'll be able to last because you feel fucking incredible."

"You do too." I run my hands down the length of his spine, my fingers dancing over each bump of his vertebra.

CK grunts, biting the side of my throat, and I mewl.

"Touch my clit," I moan, writhing under him.

He does, and I slip into Spanish as he mutters about how wet I am, blinding need making the world around us fade.

I grind against him once he's fully seated inside me, his hand trapped between us, creating an erotic experience in itself. My breasts are crushed against his muscular chest. I kiss his lips, his jaw, his neck, anywhere I can get my mouth on.

"CK," I beg. I need more.

"I got you." And he does. He pulls out, then pushes all the way back in, holding my hips down as he pumps inside me.

Hooking my feet around his legs, I anchor myself and meet him thrust for thrust. My skin comes alive. The residual heat from the hot tub steams off it, and goose bumps form as the air blows across the water droplets dotting it.

"Harder," I moan, biting down on his shoulder.

The lounge chair groans, the wrought iron legs knocking against the deck with our movements but too heavy to actually move.

His heartbeat hammers wildly against me, and when he lifts his head, cupping the back of mine, the expression on his face slays me. His features are drawn taut as pleasure ravages us both. Neither of us is going to be the same after this. I can feel it. It's elemental.

"*Dios*," I cry out, clutching him impossibly tighter as euphoria bursts throughout my system.

CK grasps me much the same, each tip of his finger branding me as we both gasp in pleasure.

My pussy squeezes his hard shaft with my orgasm, and he follows me over the edge.

"Quinn…shit…mmm…Red, so good."

My own mutterings are as nonsensical as he snaps his hips forward one last time before stilling over me.

His glasses are askew, his brows drawn together, his jaw clenched tight like he's in pain, but he's not. If he's feeling anything like I am, he's experiencing a pleasure so intense it's bordering on pain, but it's the best kind.

He starts to shift off of me, but I latch on to him like a koala, keeping him with me for a moment longer while I do my best to get myself under control.

Pinche mierda.

CK may have just been the one to lose his virginity between us, but I think I may have lost something more vital, something I question if he even wants—my heart.

Fifteen minutes later, dressed in a pair of my favorite plaid sleep shorts, a cropped tank—sans bra—and a jersey cotton cardigan, I'm sprawled out on the couch like I'm one with the cushions. It's incredible what a soak in a hot tub and fantastic sex can do for sore muscles or one's ability to human.

A noise in the distance has my head lolling on the pillow, my cheek falling into the wet spot my haphazard messy bun has been creating for the last few minutes.

"Umm…you look"—CK's gaze rakes over my relaxed form, snagging on the exposed skin of my stomach for an extra beat—"comfy."

I sigh, taking in the sight of him in a white undershirt and gray sweatpants. "I find your lack of nudity disturbing, Christopher."

He barks out a laugh, shaking his head at me. "I'll show you mine if you show me yours," he counters, lifting my legs to sit and draping them across his lap.

"Mmm…if I wasn't in some seriously epic delayed postcoital bliss, I would totally take you up on your offer. Because while I like you for your personality"—I snap finger guns at his crotch—"that dick is a *really* nice bonus."

His teeth bite into his lower lip, and I know, just *know,* he's holding in a laugh. "Why do I feel like I'm going to be reading that on a Post-it note soon?"

"I love how well you know me now." I fling my arms out happily. If I had the energy, I would one-hundred-percent get up and twirl, but I don't.

Color fills CK's cheeks. It's cute how he can still feel embarrassed by me simply telling him the truth.

"I'm shocked I didn't come out here to find you watching *Bones.*" He gestures to the dark television in the perfect deflection.

I flop a hand out toward the coffee table. "I forgot to grab the remote before I sat down. Now it's too late. The cushions have already accepted me as one of their own."

"Does this turning-into-furniture condition of yours prevent you from doing anything?" He pulls a flash drive from the pocket of his sweats.

Any lethargy evaporates out of my cells at the sight of the rectangular orange object. I know what that is. It's CK's *precious.*

I just barely manage to miss kicking him in the balls as I shoot up from my reclined position.

"Oh my god! Is that what I think it is?" I clap my hands in front of my chest, twisting my fingers together to keep from reaching for the flash drive and yoinking it out of his hold.

CK side-eyes me like he's suddenly regretting opening this can of my crazy. "It is," he finally confirms.

"But G's the *only* one you've let see it." I can feel how wide my eyes are as I stare at the drive like it'll disappear if I take them off of it.

"Are you saying you don't want to play?"

"*Ay dios mío.* Are you flipping *crazy*?" I shove at his shoulder. "Plug it in, plug it in." I make gimme hands.

He chuckles, shifting my legs the rest of the way off of him. He moves to plug the drive into the side of the TV before retrieving a set of universal game controllers from the storage unit.

"*Eep*. This is the best day ever!" I clap again, because of course I do.

CK smirks as he makes his way back to me. I love that I'm able to put such a carefree expression on his face now.

He settles into the corner of the couch, holding one of the controllers out to me as he stretches his legs out along the cushions. I accept the controller and move to settle between his spread legs, resting my back against his chest.

I tense for a beat, but when his arms come around me, holding his own controller just above my boobs, I know he isn't going to ask me to move.

His fingers press buttons and toggle the thumbsticks to navigate the game, handling the controller with the same confidence he did my body out on the balcony.

Did the air conditioning just fail? No? *Hmm.* It certainly feels hot in here all of a sudden.

I finally pull my gaze off his hands and stifle the thoughts of all the magical orgasms they can dish out like candy on Halloween, then promptly suck in a breath.

Lighting up the television screen is what looks like the menu screen for the game, but the graphics are stunning.

"That looks just like Mason's car." The gleaming silver 1967 Ford Shelby GT500 idles behind the menu options.

"That's because it is."

My jaw drops, and I shift until my head is propped in the hollow where CK's arm connects to his side. "Wow."

"Thanks." CK dips his chin, adjusting his glasses. "I had some help with some of the graphics and gameplay development, but it's still coming out better than I could have originally hoped."

"Does Mase know?" I point at the avatar version of his car.

"No."

I blink. "You've used his car as inspo but haven't even shown him the game?"

"No. Only G."

"And now me?" I touch a tentative hand to my chest.

"And now you, Red."

I mouth the word *Wow* as I try to process what this all means.

This game is CK's baby. He guards it like the country does nuclear launch codes.

The fact that he's sharing it with me…it means…like…*whoa*.

Trying not to let the heaviness of that thought resonate too much after my other revelation out on the balcony, I refocus my attention back to the game. "Okay, teach me how to play this thing so I can kick your ass, Superman."

His chest reverberates against my back with his amusement. "It's adorable how delusional you are."

I make a noncommittal sound but listen intently as he explains the game's premise, committing all the details to memory. It's a racing game where players need to win the races to unlock the subsequent races. There are also mini challenges where they can unlock mods for their vehicle of choice. It sort of reminds me of a hybrid between *Mario Kart* and the *Cruis'n USA* arcade game, with a dash of *The Fast and the Furious*.

"The game sounds like it has the Royals written *all* over it."

CK goes still at my mention of Savvy and Carter King's crew, then avoids all eye contact when I tip my head back to look at him.

"CK…"

He grips the back of his neck, and I'm momentarily distracted by the pop of his bicep straining against the sleeve of his shirt. "Carter has been…a…consultant of sorts."

"Oh, I can't wait to talk to him about it next time we go to one of his parties."

CK smirks. "You're going to be the worst secret keeper ever, aren't you?"

I shrug. "I mean…I'm not going to spill the beans on King, but I sure as shit will be bragging about having sampled your goods." I waggle my eyebrows with the double entendre.

CK's answering chuckle is music to my ears.

"Ooo," I say as a thought hits me. "Kay is gonna be mad if she ever finds out you let someone from an outside crew see your baby before us," I singsong and can't help but laugh, picturing her reaction. "You know what story I've never heard?" I ask as I choose a badass black and purple Camaro as my vehicle.

"What's that?" CK selects the Shelby.

"How Kay and the others managed to 'force their friendship'"

—I make air quotes around the words—"on you in the first place."

Maybe if I know how they slipped past his defenses, I can figure out how to do the same for myself permanently. Because now that he's allowed me off the metaphorical bench he kept me on, I never wanna go back to riding that pine.

#CHAPTER33

THE ONLY THING that surprises me about Quinn's question is that she hasn't already heard the story. I would have thought Kay and Em would have jumped to tell it.

"You want to play while I tell you, or will you claim I'm cheating by distracting you?" I give her *I dare you to say you wouldn't say something like that* side-eye.

"Oh no, I want to play." She wiggles around, snuggling into me more. She's so excited it makes the fact that I feel like I'm going to puke because I'm showing her my game worth it.

"Alright, bring it on, Red." I hit the start button, and the game counts down to the start of the race.

"Aww, look at you with the cheer movie reference."

I roll my eyes. The ladies say that *every time* one of us says "Bring it on" to them.

On the screen, the light turns green. Our cars peel out, white and gray smoke billowing around as our tires spin for a few seconds.

"Well…I fell into this crazy rabbit hole"—I wing my elbows out, gesturing at the apartment—"because I had a chemistry lab with Kay our first semester of freshman year."

Even now, I have a hard time believing that was almost two years ago.

"Were you assigned as lab partners?" Quinn's body shifts to the left as her car takes a sharp right turn.

"Not assigned." I groan when she moves back to her original position. Maybe letting her lie on me while playing was a mistake. "But Kay was surprisingly not shy in assigning me to the role anyway."

I still remember how I was arranging my slides to test that day when Kay asked if the spot next to me was open.

"I was such a dick to her at first," I admit as I cut Quinn's Camaro off before our next turn.

"I have a *really* hard time believing that," Quinn says, then she growls. I can feel the tension in her arms as she tries to catch me.

"Oh, trust me, it happened. I was such a judgmental douche when we met."

I took one look at how pretty Kay was, and all I saw was the perfect, popular, head cheerleader shine those who made my life miserable in high school had.

"I judged her by her looks and assumed she was just like all the others I went to high school with."

Quinn nods. "I get that. *Chica* does have that cheerleader shine to her, even though she tries to hide it."

I smother my laugh on the crown of her head. Why? Why doesn't it surprise me she picked up on the precise wording I used without voicing it?

"I kept expecting Kay to want something from me, but every week we'd show up for class, she'd do her work, and I'd do mine."

"You thought she would try to sweet-talk you into doing her work for you by batting those pretty gray eyes of hers and flipping her blonde and rainbow curls?"

"It's almost scary how much you can read my mind," I say as my car crosses the spray-painted finish line of the race.

"Shit." Quinn tosses her arms up but doesn't automatically start the next race like I would have assumed. Instead, she repositions herself until she can see me while we talk.

"But, yes...that's what I thought. I was bullied into writing more than one term paper that wasn't mine in high school."

A murderous gleam enters Quinn's dark eyes before she blinks it away. "So, what changed?"

I blow out a breath, thinking about Kay bombarding me in the library and telling Quinn about it. Kay was all crazy eyes and wild hair.

"She asked me something about being really good at this whole science thing and then didn't give a damn about how I hedged my response."

"And yet, despite all your reservations, you agreed to help her."

I nod. "I held firm at first, but she started rambling and talking so fast I could barely keep up. Then, somewhere in that mess of words, I heard her offer to return the favor in any other class and how if I didn't help her, she could lose her scholarship."

Quinn giggles. "You know she used it as an in to get you to open up, right? She could have gone to the tutoring center."

I nod. I do. I didn't see it at the time, but Kay admitted as much to me. "She's told me it's because she felt we were kindred spirits, which was a miracle because I spent the entire first month of knowing her assuming she was just another vapid girl based on her looks." I rake a hand through my hair, guilt still eating at me over how stereotypical I was. "I had people judge me by their perceived notions of me my entire life, and yet there I was doing the exact same thing. I should have known better."

Quinn slides a hand over mine, threading our fingers together. "Sometimes, it's those old wounds that cut the deepest."

I squeeze her knuckles. "Why does it sound like you're speaking from experience?"

She clucks her tongue. "No, no. It's story time for you tonight, not me."

That's probably for the best. I'm already admitting to how judgmental I was with our friends; no need to address that I was still doing it over a year later when I met her too.

"What about Em and G?" she asks, bringing us back.

"By the time midterms rolled around, Kay was comfortable enough to tell me she invited her roommate and friend to meet us after they got out of practice."

"Let me guess, you panicked."

I glare at her for once again guessing correctly. "That's starting to get annoying."

"Uh-huh." She makes a rolling motion with her hand.

"It was when I tried to leave that Kay told me about her own history. It was like after knowing what she went through...I don't know...kind of like she vouched for Em and G. I about shit a brick when I realized this guy she kept calling G was Grant freaking Grayson."

I may have avoided the jock set, but any student at the U of J would be able to recognize him on sight. There are twenty-foot banners of him and other members of the basketball team hanging around campus.

"It was G who actually called Kay out on not giving me a letter nickname."

Grant was also the person to drive home how rare it is for Kay to offer her friendship to people. He told me no matter how much help Kay said she needed in class, she would have never asked *me* to be the one to help her if she didn't see something special in me.

And now here I am, almost two years later, hoping maybe yet another cheerleader might end up feeling the same.

#THEGRAM

CHAPTER34

UofJ411: *picture of Quinn getting coffee in The Nest*
Anyone else hearing Bieber's "Lonely Girl"? #TheOnlyOneLeft
#HopeTheySentAPostCard
@reiersonreads4u: She's not the only one here. That other guy is
still hanging around #RememberJonahs #LetMeScrollBack
@jess_giles_: Oh yeah, the geeky guy with the glasses, right?
#NerdIsTheWord

**UofJ411: *REPOSTED—BTU_TitansHockey: Keeping the skills
fresh in the off-season—reel of Grady and some of his
teammates practicing trick shots***
I think I could totally be a hockey fan #LookAtThoseThighs #NewFan
@bama2182: Same, girl, same! #IDontWantToBlink
@serenity_nikki: Good thing BTU is super close
#WeShouldGetTickets

CK

#CHAPTER35

"YOU JUST LET us know if you need bail money because I got you, booboo."

Those were not the words I expected to greet me when I returned home on a Thursday night, and I certainly didn't think snooping through Quinn's phone for *Abuela Lupe's* number was an arrestable offense.

I'm about to say as much when I hear the sound of Emma's voice responding. "I feel like I should be offended that you think I would leave enough evidence to require being held on bail."

You know what? I don't even wanna know what they're talking about.

Instead, I pretend I can't hear them while I set the grocery bags on the counter and start to unpack my purchases.

"CK," Emma calls out, the first to spot me.

I have a package of tortillas in my hand when I look up at the television to see Emma waving. Is she…

"Where are you?" I ask, unable to decipher exactly what I'm seeing beyond some seriously hideous flower-print wallpaper.

"She's in *hiding*," Quinn answers for our friend, eyes dancing with mirth.

Oh yeah, there's definitely a story here if Quinn's amused. I hold up my hands and back away. "I don't wanna know."

Emma snorts. "Aww...where's your sense of adventure, CK?"

"Safely tucked away at the words 'bail money'," I deadpan.

"Ugh." Emma tosses her head back, falling to lean against that god-awful wallpaper. "And here I hoped living with Quinn for most of the summer would have loosened you up a little." She shifts forward, narrowing her eyes at me. "You're making the rest of us look like delinquents or something."

Out of the corner of my eye, I see Quinn watching me, my spine straightening at her sudden interest. "He did break this chick's nose almost three weeks ago," she supplies, and my jaw drops.

"This I *gotta* hear," Emma singsongs at the same time I shout, "What the hell, Q?"

Quinn lifts a pillow to her face, her shoulders shaking with smothered laughter as she folds in half.

I round the end of the island while Quinn is distracted at my expense, picking up the remote for the TV.

"Oh, wait..." I cup my hand around my ear, craning my neck to the side. "Is someone calling you, Em?"

A prickle of guilt makes the back of my neck itch at the way Emma jolts and presumably lowers her phone into her stomach if the sudden blackness on the TV is any indication.

When Emma's back in view, it's from an underneath angle, and she's lowered her voice to a whisper. "I'm freaking counting down the hours until this weekend when I can move back home with you guys."

"Ugh! I can't believe I'll be leaving the day after you get back," Quinn complains.

A pang of something I don't wholly recognize hits at the reminder that she's going to be gone for six days.

"Gotta love those parental guilt trips that have us rearranging our own plans." If Emma's sarcasm were any thicker, it would be a physical entity sitting beside her on the screen. Not that any of us can blame her since she's been spending her summer shuffled between different events for her father's political career.

Emma's gaze rises to stare at something in the distance before flitting back to me. "And if you think I'm not plopping my ass in the middle of your bed the second I get home and demanding you tell me this story, you've forgotten all about how we became friends in the first place." Then without ceremony or even a goodbye, she ends the call.

Quinn recovers from her fit, cuddling the pillow to her middle and looking at me with such naked joy it makes my stomach clench.

I'm growing addicted to having her look at me this way. It's a problem on any day ending in Y, but on the heels of a direct reminder that I'm about to have to go almost a week without seeing it...

I shake my head before those thoughts can take root. I have plans for tonight, and I'm not going to let Emma—or myself—get in the way of them.

Quinn bounds from the couch, skipping over to me and planting an arms-thrown-around-my-neck, smacking kiss on my mouth. "Where were you?"

I bookend her hold by looping my arms around her waist. "I had to get stuff for dinner."

"I thought we were having tacos." Quinn abandons me to scope out the grocery situation.

"Did you honestly think I could still have tacos after the Post-it you left stuck to my computer monitor this morning?"

Quinn bites down on her tongue, the tip peeking out when she can't contain her grin any longer. "I thought that was some of my best work."

I shake my head with a roll of my eyes. She would think that about her *You are the only meat for my taco* note. Hell, she even added a little sticker of a taco on it for good measure.

"You know I dig your crazy." I start to close the distance between us.

"Is that so?" She slides a foot across the floor in one giant step toward me.

"Mmmhmm." I back her into the counter, caging her in with my arms and nuzzling the curve of her neck. "But I'm not eating tacos tonight."

She tips her head to the side, giving me more space to work with. "Why not?"

I nibble along her soft skin, keeping my lips pressed to it, and say, "Because eating dinner with a boner isn't my idea of a good time."

"You say tomato, I say to—"

The rest of her smartass comment cuts off with a gasp when I bite down, sucking on her fluttering pulse point.

"Blame yourself, Red." I drag my teeth along her skin. "Because now any time I eat tacos, I'm going to think about stuffing your pussy full of my cock."

Quinn throws an arm up. "Check, please."

She's a nut, but it's my favorite thing about her.

It takes a Herculean effort not to lift her onto the counter and follow through on that statement. Eventually, I manage to step away from her to get back to my original plan.

Quinn snuggles in close, watching over the curve of my biceps as I pull out all the ingredients for her *abuelita's* enchiladas recipe.

"Enchiladas?" she exclaims.

"Yup."

One arm banded behind my back, she stretches the other out, tapping the tops and picking up the container of chili powder. "This is *Abuelita's* brand of choice."

I nod. "It is her recipe."

Quinn goes silent, and I angle around so we're face to face. "How…" she trails off.

"I texted her and asked."

Her eyes bug out. "What?"

"I gotta say, she's much hipper than my gramps when it comes to texting. Did you know her GIF game is on point?"

Quinn gives me a *Who do you think taught her?* eye roll. "We're going to ignore the fact that you must have snooped through my phone to get her number and cut straight to the important question."

My mouth hitches at her attempt to sound serious, but the glimmer in her dark eyes gives her away.

Folding my arms across my chest, I lean back against the counter, adopting a position to match her tone. "And what's that, Red?"

"Why risk a bilingual inquisition"—she holds up a hand to stop any comments—"and before you try to lie and say that woman didn't ask you a million and one questions *before* she gave up the goods, just *remember*"—she arches one of her dark brows—"I talk to her *every* day. I *know* there's *no way* that didn't happen."

Pulling my phone from my pocket, I unlock it and pull up the text thread. Sure enough, above the recipe is a litany of questions. What I don't tell Quinn about is the twenty-minute phone call that also took place. That'll be our secret for now.

Tucking my phone away, I hook an arm around Quinn and maneuver her until she's standing in front of me, her back to my front. "Remember when I showed you how to play pool?"

She hums, rocking back into me, my semihard dick more than on board with things heading in that direction, but my grumbling stomach tells him to slow his roll.

"I thought maybe you'd want to show me how to do something you're incredible at."

Her weight sags against me, and I kiss the top of her head, hugging her to me tighter.

"I love this idea." She spins in my hold, looping her arms around my neck again and rising up onto her toes. "And I know *just* what you need to conquer the kitchen."

There's a whisper of caution out in the distance. "I'm almost afraid to ask."

Quinn winks, then prances toward the pantry, opening the door with a similar flourish. Her dark gaze licks across my body, heating my blood hotter than the oven I'll need to preheat.

"Strip, Superman," she orders, emerging with her apron dangling from her finger.

"I said nothing about this being strip cooking, Red." I eye her cautiously. "That's just not sanitary."

Quinn's eyes fall closed with a shiver. "*Mmm*, but that visual, though."

I don't strip naked, but I do remove my shirt before donning the apron. Sure, I know I don't have to, but it makes her smile, and I like making Quinn smile. Having watched her cook more times than she probably realizes, it's easy for me to follow her orders while she flits around the kitchen like a pro.

At one point, I'm so distracted by how radiant she is here in her element, I almost clip the tip of my finger off while chopping onions. Thankfully I only nick the skin.

My distraction only increases by a thousand when Quinn lifts my hand to inspect the damage, then sucks the abraded tip into her warm mouth.

Every brush of her arm along mine as we work side by side…

Every sweet kiss of approval to my bare shoulder blade when I follow a direction correctly…

Every playful hip bump…

All of it adds to the lust in my system until it feels like I've gone from a simmer to a rolling boil. By the time Quinn bends over to put the pan in the oven to bake, I'm about ready to snap.

When I take her hips against mine, she yelps, and I grind into her, growling out, "How long?"

"Fifteen minutes," she answers breathily.

I spin her around, one hand hooking around her knee to lift her to me, and then her phone rings with a FaceTime call.

"Mierda." Quinn's head falls forward until her forehead rests on my chest. "It's like that woman *knows* we were about to defile her precious enchiladas."

I don't know if we would have defiled them, but there was a damn good chance they would have been burned beyond recognition by the time I got done doing all the dirty things I want to do to her granddaughter.

Quinn pulls herself away from me with a groan, moving to the living room to connect the call that way. Hmm. I think this is the first time I can recall her taking a call from her family there.

"Ah, *hola, mija.*" *Abuela Lupe* fills the screen, her face instantly breaking into a smile when she sees her granddaughter. *"Como estás?"*

I'm completely lost as Quinn responds in rapid-fire Spanish, but I'm hard. Highly, inappropriately, *uncomfortably* hard at every rolled R coming off Quinn's very talented tongue.

Quinn glances over her shoulder at me, the messy topknot she tied her hair in listing to the side before she winks at me. She. Winks. At. Me.

Sonofabitch.

She *knows.*

If I had any doubts that she knows I'm standing here with a boner that could rival the goalpost at the football stadium while she casually talks to her grandmother, well…those are put to rest the instant she drops her gaze to where the counter hides my lower half.

"CK!" *Abuela Lupe's* hot pink lips spread into an even bigger grin when she spots me, if that's possible. "*Ven aquí, ven aquí.*" She makes a *Come here* motion with her hands.

I follow her command. It seems I can't deny any female who shares DNA with Quinn.

Her eyes are the same shade of dark brown as her grand-daughter's, and they hold an all too familiar sparkle in them as they take in my bare arms and naked chest beneath the apron.

"Oh, *mija...*" There's one more pass over my body before *Abuela Lupe* returns her attention to her mischievous protégé. "Now that's the sort of thing you should get the *mitoteros* of an Instagram account to post."

Quinn's gaze, naughty and full of sexy promise, dips down my body. Holy shit, she's blatantly checking me out in front of her grandmother.

And...

Now I have to resort to running lines of code in my head to keep the erection I barely managed to get under control at bay.

The touch of Quinn's tongue to her teeth tells me she's doing this to me on purpose.

Quinn visibly stiffens when a different feminine voice calls out something off-screen. I wish I knew what was being said and am mentally cursing my lack of knowledge of the Spanish language for my inability to understand what could cause Quinn to react the way she is.

That feeling of *What the hell?* only grows stronger when it's Quinn's mother who joins our conversation. "Quinny, *linda*, hi, baby."

"Hi, *Mamá.*" Quinn returns the greeting, but her posture remains stiff as hell.

Why does she seem...apprehensive about talking to her mom?

"You and *Abuelita* aren't talking about that Grady boy, are you?" Mrs. Thompson visibly brightens at the possibility of the hockey player being the topic of discussion.

Now it's my shoulders locking up at the mere mention of him.

"You're not still dating him, are you, *mi niña*?"

Quinn's gaze slides my way, and for some unexplainable reason, bile crawls up the back of my throat. I know she hasn't been out with Grady again. All our time not spent attending summer classes or working has been spent together.

But…

Could they still be talking? Is that why she didn't fight me when I asked if we could keep things just between us for now? Was it her way of hedging her bets? To see if the crush claimed to have on me panned out while keeping Grady on the hook if it didn't?

What the fuck am I thinking?

Quinn isn't like that…right?

No.

No, she's not.

Again I wish Grady were a jerk. It would be so much easier to despise the future NHL player and shut down these nonsensical thoughts if he were a major douchecanoe. The fact that he seems like a genuinely nice guy only makes it all the more unbelievable that Quinn would choose someone like me over him. And from the sound of things, it seems her mother agrees.

Maybe if her mom knew she was dating you, she would feel differently?

"No, Mom, I'm not dating Grady. I'm—"

"Oh good," Mrs. Thompson says before Quinn finishes speaking. "Because Lindsey Davis and I got to talking at last night's Hoedown Throwdown planning meeting."

"*Mamá*," Quinn starts as if she can already tell what her mom is about to say.

"Don't *Mamá* me, *linda*." Mrs. Thompson's mouth presses into a flat line. "You remember how much money the kissing booth raised at last year's Throwdown."

A kissing booth? Quinn's going home to help run a kissing booth? Other guys are going to be kissing lips that belong to me? Why didn't she tell me?

Quinn's eyes fall closed, and I can feel the weight of her next measured inhalation like I'm the one taking it into my lungs.

"Mom." She sighs, rubbing her forehead. "I told you I'm not working the booth this year."

"Nonsense. What better way to increase the numbers than to have both the *beautiful* cheerleader *and* the hunky UT football star running it?"

Quinn's lips move with what I assume is a curse, but whatever she says is spoken too softly for me to make out the words. Her frustration, though? That's more than clear to see to anyone paying attention.

The timer of the oven dings and Quinn jumps all over the interruption, saying a hasty goodbye before rushing into the kitchen.

I hang back and watch her for a minute. It doesn't take a genius to see she's agitated. She yanks open the oven with a clang. It isn't until I shout that she even realizes she's about to reach for the pan with bare hands. With an absentminded glance around, she locates the potholders in the same place we've always kept them—the drawer next to the oven—removes the dish, and turns off the oven.

I don't know what is happening right now, but something is most definitely going on. I may not fully understand what all just went down, but I know Quinn well enough to recognize this isn't normal behavior for her. This isn't the same woman who gave me the space to get to know her without pressure because she was empathetic toward my history. Gone is the woman who wasn't afraid to yell at me because she liked me, the one who seduced me with her own charming awkwardness.

I'm usually the one hiding behind my shy shell. I despise this absence of her crazy.

My feet eat up the distance between us, my strides double their typical length as the need to reaffirm my girl is still in there somewhere pulses through my veins.

She startles when I curl my fingers around the backs of hers and take her hands in mine. That's all I need to prove how utterly lost she is inside her head.

"What's wrong, baby?"

Quinn's eyelashes twitch, her mouth pressing into a flat line at my question.

Adjusting my hold, I cuff both of her hands in one of mine and cup the side of her neck with my freed hand.

Stroking along the underside of her jaw, I tilt her face to mine. "Where'd my feisty spitfire go?"

"I'm sorry," she whispers.

I roll my shoulders back at her apology. "What in the world are you sorry for?"

Quinn blinks up at me, a crinkle forming between her brows. "For my mom."

I make a noise in the back of my throat that only has that crinkle deepening.

"Your mother is her own person and an adult at that. *You* are not responsible for anything she does or does not say."

"I know." Quinn's shoulders sag as she expels a breath, her eyes dropping to the left. I bring them back to me with a tap on her jaw. "She's always saying stuff like that. You'd think I'd be used to it by now."

My insecurities want to latch on to that as if it's all the proof I need that every thought I've had about how Quinn would be nothing more than a fantasy for me was correct and it's best to cut bait now before I'm in this any deeper than I already am.

But…

Somewhere in the deep recesses of my mind, the second part of what she said registers: *You'd think I'd be used to it by now.* That certainly sounds like it's something that's been happening for more than the two weeks or so we've been…*together*?

I link our hands together and start for the living room. This doesn't feel like a standing-in-the-middle-of-the-kitchen type of conversation.

"What about the food?" Quinn asks, looking back over her shoulder.

"Later," I answer, settling us together on the couch in that her-legs-draped-over-mine way that has become our standard.

"Wanna talk about it?" I ask after she remains silent for a while.

Quinn sags to the side, her head resting on the back of the couch. Her eyes peer up at me with a naked vulnerability I'm not used to seeing from her, creating fissures in my heart.

"You have to promise not to think less of me, or"—she jumps to add before I even get a chance to agree to the first part—"lump me in with the likes of Bailey."

I trace circles over her kneecap. "What have I ever done to make you believe I would do either of those things?"

"I'm serious, CK." Both her tone and the fact that she is calling me CK have me straightening. Again, I momentarily wonder if I should retreat instead of walking further along this road we're on.

"Okay…first off"—I wait for her eyes to come back to me—
"the only thing you have in common with Bailey is that you're
both cheerleaders. If *any*one thought differently, there wouldn't
have been a chance Mason would invite you to live here. He's
way too protective of Kay."

She doesn't say anything, so I continue.

"As for the other thing"—I ghost a knuckle across her cheek
—"I could never. You may have a tendency to let your crazy fly
with your temper"—those eyes of hers narrow as said temper
flares—"but you are still easily one of the most compassionate
and kindhearted people I've ever been fortunate enough to
know."

She sniffles, blinking rapidly. "Do not make me cry, Christopher. It's not a good look on me."

There's some of that spark. I give her a grin and link my hand
with hers again. "Tell me what you meant."

"I want you to know I love my mom, and I've never doubted
that she loves me."

Oh-kay. Not where I thought this was going, but I nod
anyway.

"I know she only wants the best for me, but…" She trails off,
fiddling with the seam at the top of the cushion. "Her idea of
what that means differs from mine."

"Explain."

"It's not even all her fault, either. People would take one look
at me—a mini replica of my mother—and assume I would follow
in her footsteps. All my life, I was the pretty one. *That's* what
people focused on."

My gut clenches as I think of all the times I've told her she's
beautiful and the idea that she would lump me in with all the
others.

"That was *all* people focused on," she continues. "No one
ever really seemed to believe I was capable of things beyond the
superficial. And, my mom"—she puffs out a breath—"she's
always leaned into that mindset by preaching the importance of
having 'the right man'"—I can feel the sarcasm in her one-
handed finger quotes—"to take care of me. Though that's probably Daddy's fault for making sure she's never wanted for
anything. Damn him for treating her like a queen." She shakes a

fist at the sky, an air of humor edging its way back into the moment. "This job Coach Kris offered me…"

She waits for my nod of acknowledgment, as if I could forget the pure, unfiltered excitement pulsing off of her when she told me about it, or the hours she spent cuddled against my chest detailing all of her plans for continuing to revamp NJA's social media.

"It's the first time someone saw me as capable of being more than fluff."

Wow. It amazes me how she can be so wrong about herself.

Pressing into some of the space separating us, I slide a hand into her hair and say, "You are anything but fluff, Quinn."

She nuzzles her head against my palm, lips parting, anticipating my kiss. I don't leave her hanging and press a slow, lingering kiss to her mouth.

It physically pains me to break the kiss, but I do, pulling back and holding her head between my hands. "The only thing that conversation had me curious to know is if you're planning on kissing a bunch of dudes for charity when you're home."

"No." Her answer comes without a hint of hesitation, and any worries about that particular topic vanish.

"Good." I drag my thumb across her lower lip until it separates from the upper. "Because these lips are mine."

I prove my statement by retaking them, licking at the seam until she opens for me. Our tongues stroke and she whimpers softly, the sound traveling straight to my dick.

She shifts around, sliding her own fingers into my hair with an edge of desperation that has me yanking her over me. That beast is back, roaring and clawing to claim her, to own her as much as I can, for as long as I can.

Guiding her legs to straddle my waist, I hook my hands under her thighs and stand with her wrapped around me. Quinn's chest is flush with mine, her elbows digging into the top of my back as she latches on.

I waste no time carrying her to my bedroom and laying her out on my bed.

Her hair came loose somewhere between the living room and here, the dark red strands fanning out across my pillows. Fitting myself between her legs is easy, seeing as they are still wrapped tightly around my waist, but I still prop myself on an elbow, holding most of my weight off her.

Her eyes search my face as I hover above her, searching for what I don't know. It doesn't matter. Not when she's looking at me like I can take all the pain away.

"I won't deny that I think you are beautiful." I caress the side of her face, then drag my hand down her body until my palm is flattened over her heart. "But this is where your true beauty comes from."

She chokes out a sob, biting down on her lip until I fear she'll make herself bleed.

Reaching up, I use my thumbs to free her lip from her teeth, smoothing the pad over the abraded skin. Slipping my hand under her neck, I tilt her head and kiss her sweetly.

"CK," she whispers against my mouth. "I need you."

I swallow thickly, nodding. I need her too.

Reaching back, I fumble with the tie of the apron, muttering a curse when I pull in the wrong direction and create a knot I don't want to deal with.

Quinn giggles at my frustrated growl, and the sound warms me down to my bones.

Her hands skim down my naked spine, deftly working the mess I created free, then helping to rid me of the apron. I return the favor, easing her tank over her head, and then, miracle of miracles, unhook her bra without issue and toss it over the side of the bed.

We're back to kissing as soon as we're both topless, as if it's impossible for our lips to stay apart.

I suck my belly in as our hands fumble between us, each racing to be the first to undo the other's shorts.

Quinn's heels dig into the top curve of my ass, pushing and nudging my shorts down and over my hips. The length of my arms is the only reason I rid her of her bottoms first, except whereas she double played with my boxer briefs going the same way as my shorts, her tiny green panties remain, covering her mound from view.

I'm not having it and rip them from her body, the shredding of the satin ripping the sweetest symphony.

Quinn gasps, back bowing off the mattress. "I just knew you had a kinky side."

I stare down at her, sure I heard her wrong. "What?" I shake my head. "Never mind, you can tell me later. That's not important right now." I draw a line between her breasts, stretching my pinkie and thumb out to tease her nipples before continuing down to circle her clit.

She's wet. She's always wet when I touch her, and I love that about her.

"I'm going to taste every inch of you, Quinn." I start to ease myself down her body when she yanks me up by my ear.

"No."

I arch a brow. "I thought you said you love it when I eat your pussy."

"Oh god." She throws her head back. "Yes, yes I do." She hooks an arm around my neck, anchoring herself to me to pull herself close. "But I *need* you *in* me."

Again, same.

I drop a kiss to her lips and reach to the nightstand for a condom.

Quinn takes the foil square from me when I move to kneel between her spread thighs. She slips a hand under my dick as she tears the wrapper open with her teeth, then she rolls the condom down my length. Her heels are back to digging into my ass, tugging me forward before positioning me at her entrance.

Inch by inch, I sink into her slowly, savoring the feel of her surrounding me.

I used to judge myself for being a virgin, as if the fact that I'd never been with a woman proved all the bullies of my past right.

But then Quinn happened.

No sexual history is needed to know that what I experience with her is unmatched on every level.

I kiss every bare, coconut-scented inch of her while I pump into her with leisurely strokes. When I feel myself start to get close, I drag my hand up her forearm, reaching for the hand she has coiled around my nape, stilling us as I stretch her arm overhead.

She writhes under me, calling out my name between those perfect, *perfect* Spanish mutterings. Thrust after thrust, I feel myself hovering on the edge, but back off any time I get too close.

Pressing her arm more firmly to the pillows, I link my fingers with hers and hold her hand while an orgasm rolls through her, pulling back just enough to watch the ecstasy bloom across her features.

Hooking an arm around her middle, I roll to my back, bringing her with me until she's straddling me. Gone is the haunted glaze from earlier, in its place a lust-drunk gaze.

"Now that's what I call a beautiful sight." It's my turn to anchor myself with a hand on her nape, drawing her down until we're nose to nose. "Seeing you come undone is by far my favorite thing to witness."

Quinn's dark eyes take me in with a sense of awe before popping wide as I drive up into her harder and harder until I'm coming with her pussy clenching around me with her second orgasm. Our mouths fuse together, my glasses knocked askew, but it doesn't matter.

Nothing else matters but this right here.

The high of the moment starts to wane as exhaustion from earlier starts to creep in. I rid myself of the condom, tying it off and dropping it unceremoniously and unhygienically onto the floor. I'll worry about cleaning it up later.

Instead, I tuck Quinn close to my side and pull the covers over us. Her breath hits my neck in little warm puffs, the intervals between them slowing as she drifts into sleep.

I try to think about how good she feels against me and how natural it seems for her to be with me this way. I'm going to miss the shit out of this while she's gone.

Then I remember our friends start to move home tomorrow. For as much as I'm excited about their return, I fucking hope it doesn't ruin what we have here.

QUINN

CAREFULLY FOLDING THE CUTE SUNDRESS, I set it inside the small rolly bag on my bed, only to have Emma yank it out and toss it behind her.

"Em!" I shout, giving her the hairy eyeball. She couldn't give two shits.

"What?" She shrugs, as if she hasn't been unpacking everything I've been trying to pack for the past five minutes.

"How am I supposed to know if I have everything I need if you keep taking things out of my bag?"

"But if you're missing stuff, then you can't go." She holds out her hands as if it were that simple.

"No. All that's gonna happen is I'm going to get to Texas and end up having to go commando or something because one of my best friends stole all my underwear."

"Who's panty poaching?" Kay asks, entering the room and tossing a bag of frozen peas at Emma before taking the open spot next to her.

Em waves an accusatory hand at me. "Q here doesn't appreciate my efforts to keep her home with us."

"Ahh." Kay strokes her chin and nods. I don't need her to say anything to know I'm about to be outnumbered. I'm never going to finish packing at this rate.

"Don't you have your own packing to do?" I ask Em, trying to redirect her attention. Everyone may have only just moved back, but we're all spending the night at Kay's family home in Blackwell because it's easier to Uber from there to Carter King's place later.

"Puh-lease. We're spending the night, not the week. I'm done."

I huff, annoyed I have no way to distract her when I *do* have to pack for a week since I'll have to leave stupid early in the morning for the airport.

"Can you put those on your face already?" I point to the peas, currently not doing anything to help the shiner I accidentally gave Emma sitting on her thigh. "And you act like I haven't spent pretty much every waking and unwaking hour with you since you guys got back yesterday."

Because I'm the *bestest* friend ever in existence, I spent my first night in two weeks *not* sleeping in CK's bed slumber partying it up with these two last night. Hell, I was barely back in my own room long enough to get a change of clothes yesterday morning before Emma tackle hugged me down to the bed.

Homegirl pretty much hasn't left mine or Kay's side since. Well, more so me than Kay, because Mason has stolen his girlfriend back a time or two. There hasn't even been a chance to talk to CK about when we're going to tell everyone about us, let alone allow for moments for him to steal me away.

Emma pouts but listens to my earlier order. She stares me down with her good eye, looking like some cross between an eye-patched pirate and a *Phantom of the Opera* reject with the rectangular white bag covering half her face. "You know, it's just *rude* of you to leave after injuring me."

And they say *I'm* the dramatic one of the group? Emma's approaching crown-fitting levels of drama queen.

"It's a black eye, not a broken leg." I narrow my eyes as I place another dress in my suitcase, daring her to remove it.

And you know what happens? The biotch does.

Ay dios mío.

Changing tactics, I straighten and sweetly ask, "Do you have your phone on you?"

"Why?" I grin at the caution that bleeds into her question.

Batting my lashes, I play up the innocent angel act. "Because maybe you should call Matthew back over here."

Emma rears back like she's reenacting when I clocked her with an elbow during our pyramid clinic at The Barracks this morning. "Why would I willingly call Captain Buzzkill?"

"Because if you don't stop trying to stop me from packing, I'm going to kill you dead."

"Ugh! Fine." She flops back onto the mattress. "Also, remind me to leave my phone at Kay's later so Mr. Captain Buzzkill himself can't track me to the party."

"Aww." Kay pokes her in the side, blessedly leaving me alone long enough to get three whole items into my suitcase. "You mean you don't want to risk him cockblocking you with King again?"

"*What?*" I screech, tossing the shorts in my hand somewhere and jumping onto the bed, all pretense of packing over.

Emma covers the non-injured side of her face with her free hand, groaning. "Thanks, Kay," she mumbles through her fingers dryly.

"I *knew* there was something you weren't telling us." I motion to Kay, then flop my hand back at me. "Well, I guess just me since Kay seems to be in the know."

Emma peers at me from over the tips of her fingers before sighing in resignation. She extends a pinkie out to me, knowing there's not a chance in hell I'll be leaving this room without hearing this story now that its existence is confirmed.

I link our pinkies together as fast as humanly possible and swear the most sacred of all girl promises.

I may have only just learned the juicier details of what went down between Emma and the man dubbed the leader of The Royalty Crew—a fascinating Blackwell social experiment in my eyes—hours ago, but I've been looking forward to tonight's party since we received the text about it yesterday.

It should come as no surprise that when the nine of us were

splitting into our Ubers for the drive to Carter King's place, Emma all but demanded Kay and I ride with her.

It also shouldn't shock you that Mason danced on the border of throwing a tantrum over it. But then Trav hooked his beefy throwing arm around his neck, dragging him into their own Uber with a "Short Stack loves you because you're a caveman, not a clingy baby."

That didn't stop Mason from texting Kay during the short ten-minute trip, though. I think they exchanged over a dozen or so messages by the time we pull into the acre-sized parking lot making up Carter King's property.

There are a few dozen vehicles parked haphazardly in the lot, but it feels more like an unorganized tailgate party than the staging area for a *Fast and Furious* movie, like the last time I was here.

The guys wait for us before heading toward the three-story black warehouse building that serves as Carter's residence and the bonfire set up not far from it. My ladies and I link arms, *Wizard of Oz*-ing it, as we weave our way through the mishmash of vehicles to join the guys by the roaring bonfire.

We pass a few tables featuring beer pong and flip cup along the way. There are also other classic tailgate activities like cornhole and our group's personal favorite, giant Drunk Jenga.

As expected, we find JT, Carter, and who I'm told are the other four members of the Royalty Crew holding court in black camping chairs surrounding the bonfire. The last time I was here, I didn't understand, nor did I get to fully appreciate all things Royal. But now? Holy damn, talk about tattooed, muscly, broody, sorta scary, bad boy hotness.

I've met and been around Carter and his number two, Wes, a handful of times, but the others I only know from the stories I've heard from Tessa and Savvy when they come around. That's not all that surprising since Kay considers Carter more JT's friend than her own. Though…I guess we should add CK to that mix.

I don't see either of the two high school troublemakers around the fire, but then I remember they keep their distance because of Savvy's asthma and spot them holding a court of their own with Mason's siblings and a few other high school-aged peeps across the lot.

I spot one more familiar and completely shocking-to-see face in the group we're approaching, but JT is out of his seat, stealing Kay away from us before I can finish wondering why Grady, of all people, is here.

Mason is back to his grumpy, grumbling self at yet another person keeping Kay from him, but JT isn't the least bit intimidated by the six-five tight end.

"Keep your club-swinging, chest-beating caveman self in your pants," JT teases.

"What does that even mean, Cheer Boy?" Mason tries to sound stern, but everyone can hear the amusement creeping into his voice.

"It means relax, Mr. Tight End." JT smacks his ass at his own lame joke about Mason's football position. "You get her back all to yourself the day after tomorrow."

"Careful, bruh." Trav extends a fist out for JT to bump. "Mase is on his period because Em's been turning the girl time up to eleven."

"Fact." I wave my still-linked-with-Emma's elbow like a dilapidated chicken wing. "Peter Pan's shadow ain't got nothing on Emma Logan after a stint with the senator."

JT winks, approving my reference to his late mom's favorite story.

"What the fuck happened to you?" Carter barks, danger pervading the atmosphere as he storms up to Emma.

"*Excuse* me?" Em holds her ground, meeting Carter's murderous glare with one of her own.

I slip my arm free of Emma's and back away slowly to not spook the animals, though I doubt either of them is aware of anything besides each other.

Carter grips Emma's chin between his fingers, tilting her face this way and that way to inspect the bruising makeup didn't completely cover. "Tell me who the fuck did this to you so I know who I have to kill."

I shrug when Em's gaze slides my way. Is it wrong I find it anticlimactic that I'm the one who gave her the black eye? If it is, I don't want to be right, because I personally think it might be fun to see what this violent edge of Carter's might lead to.

"I don't see how that's any of your business," Emma says instead of giving me up.

I highly doubt it's because she's worried about what King

would do to me. Nope, she's doing it just to get a rise out of him, only further proving why our friendship was so easy to form. We live for poking the bear, or the Royal, as the case may be.

"You are my fucking business, Emma."

Even with the few steps I've taken, I can tell she's rolling her eyes. "I'll tell you the same thing I tell Matthew—"

"Don't you fucking say his name around me."

"Puh-lease." She pats him on the chest. "I don't have a ruler on me for a dick measuring contest. Besides"—she shrugs—"at least Captain Buzzkill's concern is bought and paid for, whereas yours is misplaced."

A familiar presence steps up behind me, causing my skin to come alive. Shifting back, I lean into CK like I've done a million times before and angle my chin around to whisper, "When do you think would be a good time to tell him it was me?"

CK's rumbly chuckle hits my ears as he, too, takes in the scene in front of us. "The fact that she didn't choose to tell him as soon as he asked makes me suspect you all have devil horns hidden under your cheer bows."

I smother a giggle, butterflies sprouting to life at the playful twinkle I see behind his lenses. "Why are you pretending you didn't *personally* confirm I am horn-free?"

"Hmm, you're right. But maybe I should check again." CK looks over my head at King's place. "Carter does have a pool table."

My entire body heats at the suggestion. From the way CK's gaze tracks to my mouth, I'd say he's thinking about how every game of pool we've played since the first time I suggested strip pool has played out.

"Do you—"

Whatever CK was about to say gets cut off by the arrival of Grady. "Hey. Small world, huh?"

CK straightens, and I'm pretty sure I pout when my body loses contact with his.

What was he going to say?

Do you want to find a dark corner and take advantage of me?

Do you want to tell our friends about us?

The possibilities are endless.

Instead, I turn to Grady and ask, "What are you doing here?"

Savvy is the one who answers as she and Tessa come over to

snoop on the Carter and Emma situation, still happening mere feet away.

"He's teammates with Lance." She points to one of the Royals before jerking a chin at her brother. "If he doesn't bang her and put us all out of their sexual tension–fueled misery, I swear I'm going to have Wes start taking bets on when it'll happen."

"It's either that or they'll spontaneously combust," Tessa adds. "Fifty-fifty on which will happen."

"Preach." Savvy links an inked pinkie with Tessa's, the two continuing the rest of their conversation silently.

"Speaking of combustible sexual tension…" Tessa turns, training her midnight blue eyes on CK and me.

"Ugh!" Emma stomps into our small cluster before Tessa can begin inquisition three thousand and forty-eight about the status of my relationship with CK.

I don't know how to feel about the interruption, nor do I get the opportunity to examine it. Emma has gone from *I missed my bestie* needy, to *Distract me with something before I commit homicide* annoyed, and so we answer the call.

That was hours ago.

I had to settle for kicking CK's butt in cornhole instead of getting bent over a pool table. *Le sigh* Another time.

Since then, though, it feels like he's avoiding me, like it's become his mission to keep as much space as physically possible between us without it seeming like that's what he's doing. It's driving me batty.

My only saving grace has been Emma and her mission to ignore all things Carter King, which now has me pleasantly buzzed from all the beer pong and flip cup we've been playing. Otherwise, I would be obsessing about the fact that CK is standing across the table from me—again. It wasn't said, but I swear he refused to be on my team.

However, our most current game has been on pause in favor of recording TikTok dances.

"No, no, no." Grady waves his arms, cutting into Trav's latest pathetic attempt to copy my booty pop. "Geez, you'd think you'd football players would have better dance skills."

I double over in a fit of laughter. Trav has been trying to emulate the touchdown dance I created for him to use in the TikTok #SaveIt4TheEndZone challenge for the last ten minutes. I say trying, because it's been nothing short of an epic failure. Homeboy can throw a football like none other, but he can't dance for shit.

"You gotta use the hips, man." Grady demonstrates with a surprisingly fluid oscillation.

"Ooo yeah!" I toss my arms up, copying his movements and moving in closer. "The puck head's hips don't lie."

Emma snorts, joining in and sandwiching Grady from the other side. "Better step up your dance game, QB1."

Trav pouts before shouting across the lot to Livi to show him some moves since we're being jerks.

Our impromptu dance party comes to an end as we crowd together for selfies, but when I spin to reach for CK to join us, my heart sinks because now he's gone.

Where'd he go?

"We need more beer?" Alex says, holding up the empty pitchers.

Latching onto the distraction, I reach for the empty.

I'm at the keg, finally refilling one of the pitchers for our next game of flip cup, when Grady joins me at the tap with the other one.

"Glad to see things worked out with you two." Grady jerks his chin, and I finally spot where CK made off to, sitting with Carter around the bonfire. You know, all the way on the other side of the lot because the opposite side of the table wasn't far enough away. It feels wrong to be annoyed by this, but I can't seem to help it.

Shaking it off, I tilt my head to look up at Grady. "Have I said I'm sorry for how shitty of a date I was to you?"

He waves my apology off. "Nah. I should have never asked you out in the first place. It was obvious there was more between you two than he was willing to admit."

His comment should make me feel better, but it does the opposite, only serving to remind me of how quick CK was to deny any attachment to me.

These last couple of weeks have been amazing, but now that our friends are back, it feels like we're reverting back to the detachment. I know we haven't had a moment alone to talk about how we would tell them about it, but...why does it have to be a big thing? It's not like they don't know how I feel about CK.

The man himself was the only one who was clueless when it came to my feelings. Us being a couple isn't going to be much of a surprise.

Really…

I should just march over there, plop myself in CK's lap, and kiss him.

Why don't I?

What's stopping me?

Except…

I can't seem to fully quiet that small voice inside my head telling me he'll only reject me if I do that. I'd probably have more luck telling that voice to shut the fuck up if it didn't feel like CK has been purposely staying away from me. Because, except for when we first got here, that's *exactly* what it feels like he's been doing.

He's watched me, though. Even now, as Grady and I return to the flip cup table, falling back into the trash talk of the game and the hip bumps of celebration when our team wins, I can feel the weight of CK's eyes on me.

I make it through three more rounds before my bladder complains about all the beer I've consumed. I excuse myself, letting someone else take my place, and head for the bathrooms inside the auto garage located on the back of the lot.

A pacing figure scares the crap out of me as I step out of the building, my hand flying up to keep my heart from jumping out of my chest. It takes one heavy exhale before my pulse starts to race for an entirely different reason.

"Superman," I coo, automatically reaching for him, only to be met with dead air when CK steps out of reach. "Wha—"

"I bet your mom will be happy to see the pictures of you and Grady together," he says, cutting off my question and confusing me further.

"You're mad I took a selfie with him?" I've taken pictures with a lot of people tonight. It's a party—that's what we do. "I wanted to take pictures with you too, but you had just up and left us."

CK's jaw works side to side, but he remains silent. Thanks to all the alcohol pumping through my system, each second that ticks by without him saying anything cranks my temper higher.

"Is it just Grady you have a problem with, or do you suddenly have an issue with Trav and Alex too?"

Again…nothing. Not a single word.

"You're the one who's been avoiding us all night."

"Don't be dramatic, Quinn."

I suck in a breath, the air whistling through my teeth. "*Excuse* me?"

A muscle ticks on the side of his jaw, and I get an overwhelming urge to slap him.

"You're acting like we all haven't been together all night. And now you're freaking out because I missed a few selfies?"

Now I'm the one not saying a word, literally biting down on the tip of my tongue to help rein in my temper. But…Jesus! No one triggers it worse than CK.

"You could have joined us, you know." I wish he would have joined us. I know he's been here, but I miss him.

He glances back over his shoulder, but the party, which has tripled in size since we arrived, is too far away for anybody to pay us any mind. "No, I couldn't."

"Why not?" Annoyance creeps into my tone.

"Because…" He grips the back of his neck, and I'm momentarily distracted by the pop of his biceps.

"Because why?" I take another step closer, only for him to step back again. "You're not making any sense, CK."

His cheeks puff as he blows out a breath, his eyes scanning me from head to toe. "Because any time I'm near you, I want to touch you."

"And that's a bad thing, why?" If I had my way, we'd be touching as much as is socially acceptable. Hell, I would take a page out of Mason's playbook and push that envelope.

"Because—"

Ay dios mío. I'm really getting tired of hearing that word come out of his mouth.

"—then everyone will know we're"—he circles a hand between us—"you know."

He can't be serious right now.

"Again," I mutter through gritted teeth, "I ask, why would that be a bad thing?"

"Because."

"Jesus fucking Christ, CK," I shout, shoving my hands into

my hair and yanking at the strands. "We're back to talking in fucking circles."

He drops his chin to his chest. "I'm sorry."

Great, now I feel like an asshole. "I don't need an apology," I say, softening my tone. "But I do need to know why we're not just telling them about us. If we do that, then you can touch me all you want."

"What would we even tell them about us?"

I fall back a step, the question damn near knocking me on my ass. "Umm…that *we're dating*." My tone is pure *Duh, it's not rocket science.*

"They're never going to believe that." It may be the alcohol talking, but I swear as his eyes take me in, they're filled with disgust.

"Oh my god! You're kidding me, right?" He flinches back when I step to the side to see around, and I growl. God forbid I get close enough to touch. Geez. "They know I like you."

"Knowing you like me and believing we would actually be together are two entirely different things."

I cross my arms in front of my chest, tucking my hands inside the bend of my elbows to keep myself from reaching out and strangling him. "It blows my mind how, for such a smart guy, you can say the dumbest things."

"You say that, but only an idiot would believe I could be with you when you're so clearly not on my level."

CHAPTER 37

I'M A FUCKING IDIOT.

This whole night—hell, the last thirty-six hours have been a test of patience that has only helped push me into making one mistake after the other.

It was one thing when Quinn's time was being monopolized by Emma and Kay. It was entirely another when I started putting purposeful distance between all of us because of my own insecurities.

What the fuck is wrong with me? Why is it that I let the sight of Grady push me into acting like not just a moron, but an asshole as well?

And, as if karma didn't take a big enough pound of flesh via Quinn reining in her temper instead of coming at me like she typically would, it's now coming at me for the dickish shit I said to her by having Grady be the one to find me hiding out where the Drunk Jenga is set up.

"Umm…you do know your girlfriend is pissed as fuck at you, right?" Grady nudges me with his elbow.

I'm not sure which fact I want to be true more—Quinn being my girlfriend or her being pissed at me. That hot-poker-slicing-between-my-ribs feeling is back because, again, I'm reminded that Quinn just walked away. No yelling. No cursing. No fiery temper putting me in my place.

That hurt.

That tells me just how badly I fucked up.

"I told you, Quinn's not my girlfriend."

I mean…she's not, right?

"Yeah, oh-kay." Out of the corner of my eye, I see Grady smirk before lifting his Solo cup to his mouth.

"She's not," I reiterate.

"And why is that?" he challenges.

"Because," I hedge noncommittally, keeping my focus off him and on the teetering Jenga tower in front of me.

"Oh, wow, things are so much clearer now." I roll my eyes at Grady's sarcastic comment. His sarcasm is amateur at best compared to those I live with.

Oh, shit!

It's actually a goddamn miracle that Grady is the first person to approach me in the last two hours. There is *no way* the others—at the minimum, the ladies—are going to let what I said go, especially now that I realize how misconstrued it was.

I think Quinn had taken four steps away from me when I realized she thought I was talking about her not being good enough for me when that was the complete opposite of what I meant.

Fuck me.

"So is it because she's not your '*girlfriend*'"—I do *not* appreciate the air quotes Grady puts around the word girlfriend, nor the fact that he is pulling me out of my thoughts—"that you're all the way over here while she's all the way over there?" He hooks a thumb somewhere behind him where I assume Quinn is.

I shrug, but Grady annoyingly waits out my stubbornness until I admit, "I can't be around her right now."

"Why not?"

Fuck! What is it with people asking me a million questions tonight?

"You mean besides the fact that she probably wants to ram a pom-pom down my throat?" I run a hand through my hair, straightening to give him my full attention as he nods. "If I'm around Quinn any more tonight, I'm liable to grab her and kiss her."

"Bro." Grady clamps a hand over my shoulder. "There ain't no problem with that."

And that's the *real* issue. There isn't a problem with it. I was just so busy being a chickenshit and chose avoidance as a method of hiding.

"Our friends"—I cast an arm out at the party going on around us, turning back to the tower—"don't know we're together."

Grady snorts. "Bullshit."

"What?" I whip back around.

"Didn't your roommates move back *yesterday*?" He enunciates each syllable of the word as if I can't tell how long of a time frame it is.

"Yup."

"Then they know." He shrugs as if what he said is no big deal when it's anything but.

"No, they don't," I argue.

"Bro…" Grady claps me on the shoulder, meeting my eye. "I spent most of that night at the pool hall thinking you were a couple."

And yet, he asked her out.

I put my focus back on our game. "There's no way you believed that."

"I did." He chuckles.

"No way you thought I was dating Quinn."

"I did," Grady retorts again.

I pause, my hand hovering over a Jenga block, then slowly spin around again. "You don't think—" My stomach rolls thinking about how I even dared to voice to Quinn something similar to the question I'm about to ask him. God, how could I after hearing how so many people didn't value her for everything she is? Then I went and alluded to the exact same thing when I was actually talking about myself.

I clear my throat. "You didn't think to yourself that I needed to be with somebody more on my level?"

"What the fuck does that mean?" There's a hint of laughter in Grady's question.

"Umm…you've seen her."

He nods. "I have eyes."

Frustration and something I can't quite name cause a tightness in my chest. "The issue isn't just that Quinn's the most beautiful woman on the planet on the outside. It's that I'll never be able to match who she is on the inside."

Don't even get me started on how pissed I am that others have ever made her feel like she's anything less than extraordinary. And now…I fucking went and made her think I think the same.

How the fuck am I supposed to fix this?

More importantly, how am I supposed to fix this with her about to be in Texas for the next six days?

"Has she said that to you?" Grady asks, eyeing the crushing grip I have on my Solo cup, the plastic creaking in my hold.

"No." I snort. "She'd probably smack me for even thinking something like that."

Whether or not Quinn would commit physical harm is a toss-up, but I would for sure find some kind of new E.T. figurine hidden somewhere. Oh…and the whistle. She would definitely bust out that whistle.

"Do you love her?" Grady's question pulls me up short.

"Huh?"

"The question is simple enough." He pops a brow, holding my gaze. "Do you love her?"

Do I love her?

Um…

Holy shit!

I fucking love Quinn Thompson.

#CHAPTER38

THE STACK of folded blankets topped by a blue sheet and pillow mocks me as I stare at the empty couch in Kay's living room.

Where the hell is Quinn? Did she already leave for the airport?

No. It's too early, right?

An urgency I should have felt last night but was too stubborn to acknowledge pumps through my veins.

Whipping around, my socks slip on the tile floor as I rush to the front door, yanking it open, then sagging against it when I confirm Emma's car is still parked in the driveway.

Quinn has to still be here because Emma is her ride, right?

I slam the door closed and come to an abrupt halt at the sight of Grant standing in the kitchen. How did I not see him there?

"Dude, you're gonna wake the beasts making all that noise." He looks toward the ceiling where the bedrooms are located.

"I'll be fine. Mase will keep Kay in bed."

"Nah, bruh," Trav says, making his way down from upstairs, also dressed and ready for a run. "Em's the one you gotta worry about. Baby girl is going to be hungover as fuck when she finally drags herself out of the guest room."

That brings me up short. "Isn't she up already?" I check the time on my watch. "Quinn needs to leave soon."

"Q's gone," Grant says, moving around the kitchen. "She was ordering an Uber while I made my protein shake."

I shove my glasses out of the way and pinch the bridge of my nose. "Shit."

My stupidity has compounded itself, and now Quinn is gone.

First, I picked an unnecessary fight with her and didn't go and apologize for being an ass. Then I realized I loved her, and instead of tracking her down and telling her, I doubled down on avoiding her, choosing to wait until I could get her by herself. Now I lost my chance to talk to her in person altogether.

Why?

What was I so afraid of?

"You two didn't kiss and make up before she left?" Trav asks as he pops a pod in the coffee machine.

I freeze; the only part of me moving is my heart beating inside my chest.

"Pay up." Grant holds out one of his dinner plate–sized hands to Trav.

"I'll get you later." Trav low-fives his palm.

I bounce my gaze between them. "Huh?"

Neither of them acknowledges me. Instead, they hit their fists against their palms, rock, paper, scissoring until Trav's rock loses to Grant's paper.

Trav shoves off the counter with a sigh before trudging toward the stairs. "Make sure you say nice things about me at my funeral."

"Where are you going?" I ask, utterly lost.

Trav presses his hands to his heart. "To risk life and limb waking up Short Stack and Miss M&M."

Yeah, his explanation doesn't help clear things up in the least.

"We let you off the hook long enough." Grant pulls out one of the barstools, settling in at the counter. "We want the deets about you and Q." A slow grin forms on Grant's face as he takes in my befuddled expression. "I love how you think we didn't know."

"You've gotta be fucking kidding me." I stab my hand through my hair.

"Nah." He shakes his head, chuckling. "We're all just happy it finally happened since you spent this last year refusing to believe us when we told you she liked you."

Jesus Christ. I'm even more of a moron than I thought.

Here I was, so damn worried about what others would think that I asked Quinn to keep our relationship—and yes, I admit that's exactly what we had, a relationship—a secret. All that did was cause a fight that should have never happened in the first place. Not when everyone was only waiting for us to get together.

Sure, the whole not going out on public dates thing was more us trying to limit our chances of appearing on the UofJ411's feed and the subsequent comments from trolls than anything else.

But…

Keeping it from our friends? The same people who love to joke about how they thought I was so awesome they decided to force their friendships on me? Yeah, they would never think, let alone say to Quinn, that I'm not good enough for her.

I don't know what the greater disservice was: not trusting our friends to know about Quinn and me or not trusting in the feelings Quinn never shied away from admitting she had for me in the first place.

It's pathetic that despite how much I've grown, I still somehow managed to let the assholes from my past cause me to devalue those who mean the most to me in my present.

I don't know why I didn't realize any of it sooner, or why it took a veritable stranger like Grady last night to really drive the point home and make me recognize the depths of my feelings. Maybe if I hadn't been so blind and afraid, I would have stopped feeling like I was stuck on the sidelines watching life pass me by.

Now Quinn is gone for six days, and worse…she'll be spending that time around people who don't value her for everything that makes her spectacular. And then worse still, those same people are the ones responsible for her ever feeling like she's less than.

Yup, it all makes me regret not being out with our relationship. If I wasn't hiding us, we would have never fought, and even better, I could have gone with her to Texas.

Adrenaline pumps through my system as I aimlessly spin in circles.

Why did she have to leave for the airport early? She didn't even say goodbye.

Now not only is she gone, she also thinks I don't care about her, thinks I don't reciprocate her feelings when, in reality, I'm in love with her.

Fuck me.

Okay…

First things first, I have to tell our friends—our makeshift family—about us. Then I need their help figuring out what I'm going to do to ensure there is even still an us to tell them about.

QUINN

GOING to a party and getting drunk with my friends the night before I had to be up at five to catch an eight a.m. flight to Texas might not have been the best life decision I've ever made.

Why?

Well…

Shit.

Where the hell are my Post-its when I need them? I could give you a whole damn list of reasons.

First off, in a hungover and possibly still slightly buzzed state, the hum of the jet engines will lull you to sleep for the four hours it'll take you to arrive in the Lone Star State from Jersey. Then, you'll wake up with dried drool on your chin and a crick in your neck. It's not a good look. Trust me.

What the hell am I saying? Maybe I'm still drunk.

Not gonna lie…I sorta wish I was.

Alcohol definitely helped numb the pain of CK's rejection.

Fuck.

I can't think about that right now; otherwise, I'll cry.

Being drunk would also undoubtedly go a long way to making this day bearable.

Instead, I'm sober while suffering through a Hoedown Throwdown planning meeting. Why I'm here, I don't even know. Any time I've tried to offer up a suggestion or pitch an idea I learned in one of the marketing classes I've taken, I'm blown off. I've received more palliative smiles, condescending pats on the hand, and *Bless your hearts* than are possible to count.

It's nothing at all like how Coach Kris has treated me at The Barracks. In one week, she has listened to me and implemented my ideas more times than these people have my entire life.

I knew I shouldn't have given in to *Mamá's* guilt-trip. Coming home for this event has been a giant waste of time. All it's done is remind me that I'm just Pretty Quinn Thompson here.

Sonofabitch.

No wonder CK doesn't want me as anything more than a friend with benefits. If the people I've known all my life only see me this way, how could I expect him to ever believe we are on the same level?

Day two in Texas is pretty much a rinse and repeat of day one, right down to the hangover I'm nursing while sitting in this pointless meeting.

Damn *Abuelita*. That woman is evil. She wielded the power of frozen tequila goodness until I wasn't only sharing her special jalapeño margaritas with her, but also the details of what went down with CK.

"Oh, that's wonderful. It will coordinate perfectly with the white sundress I purchased for Quinny to wear." The cooed comment from my mom has me tuning in to the committee's meeting for the first time in over an hour.

"What?" I feel like I should feel bad for not paying attention, but honestly, what's the point?

"Nothing, *linda*." *Mamá* waves off my question like it's inconsequential. "I was just commenting how perfect you and the Davis boy will look all color coordinated while working the kissing booth."

Dios.

I thought we cleared this up already. "*Mamá*, I'm not working the booth this year."

CK may have been why I initially said I wouldn't participate, but unlike *Abuelita*, *Mamá* has no idea we were even together, let alone broke up. So, my refusal should still be valid in her eyes.

"Nonsense, *linda*. Think of how much good your pretty face can do for the charity."

I don't know what it is that pushes me over the edge, but something inside me finally snaps.

I didn't lose my shit on CK like he deserved, but that was because I was too in shock and heartbroken hearing that he really does believe I'm nothing more than fluff, despite anything else he said.

No more.

I'm done feeling undervalued, done letting my opinions and ideas be treated as less than.

I am so much more than my looks.

"And maybe if you actually *listened* to me for once, you'd realize it's my ideas that could probably help double donations."

"Oh, Quinny." I hate how my mom can simply brush me off with a shake of her head. "Your little Tickytocky and Bookface things aren't going to help raise money for charity."

I grind my teeth together. How this woman can practically stalk my life through Instagram yet be so unknowledgeable about other forms of social media is mindboggling.

"It's a hybrid form of advertising and word of mouth. It's a powerful tool when utilized correctly."

"And think of the interest you would get if that word of mouth was about someone as beautiful as you sitting inside the booth."

"Oh my god!" I throw my hands up, done with this conversation. I can't handle her tunnel vision. "I don't know how many times you need me to say it, but I'm not doing the kissing booth."

I push out of my chair with enough force that the legs screech like nails on a chalkboard. A dozen sets of wide eyes are locked on my movements, watching my exit like I'm some kind of telenovela.

I'm done letting their bullshit affect me. Their opinions couldn't matter less to me.

CHAPTER 40

BY THE TIME I make it back home, I'm so drained from everything that happened these past few days that my bones feel heavier. I'm not sure how I will survive being here another four days, given my level of frustration toward my mother.

On the flip side, changing my flight to return early only means I would have to face CK and all...that. I'm not sure how I'll handle being around him, especially when it's taking everything in me *not* to ask Kay and Em if he's said anything.

You know what? That is a problem for future Quinn. Present Quinn is going to take a nap because I need a redo on this day.

My feet drag along the floor with every step toward my bedroom.

What the—

Did a 3M factory explode in here?

Neon-colored Post-it notes in every shade cover the entire wall behind my dresser and part of the rectangular mirror hanging above it. It looks like a murder mystery author broke into the room and borrowed my wall to plot out their next book.

Remember when I was wondering where my Post-its were yesterday? This is not what I meant.

Except…

After rubbing my eyes to make sure this isn't my hangover manifesting in a way one never has before, I realize the glitter gel pen writing isn't mine, but a different scrawl I'm more than familiar with.

CK?

What?

How?

Why?

Cautiously, I approach the dresser but chicken out as soon as I'm in front of it, squeezing my eyes shut.

"I used to do the same thing when you first started tacking these things all over the place."

I jump at the sound of his voice, cursing and slapping a hand over my now racing heart.

Oh my god.

My eyes fly open, immediately spotting CK's reflection in the mirror.

I don't turn around to face him, too afraid if I do, I'll only find out he's a mirage or finally lose control of my temper and go off on him.

Instead, I use the mirror as my conduit to keep my gaze trained on him. My hormones sigh because, despite being on my shit list, he really is the most perfect hot nerd. His black hair is messy, his blue eyes blazing and cautiously studying me from behind his black frames, his jaw clenched. But what makes him most attractive is the brain I know he has under his good looks.

"You're here?" My voice comes out more question than statement. Yes, I know I recognized his handwriting and I'm looking at him standing there, but still…I'm struggling to believe this is real.

"I'm here." He nods.

"Why?" I fold my arms across my chest.

"Read the notes, Red." He jerks a chin at the wall he decorated.

"Why should I?"

His mouth curves up on one side at my petulant tone. "I'm hoping you'll be less inclined to maim me if you do."

I growl because now I'm the one smirking. What a jerk he is making me grin when I'm mad at him.

Swallowing down the lump of emotion clogging my throat, I unfold my arms, brace my hands on the dresser, and then look up at the white note closest to me.

I'm sorry.

My heart squeezes at those two simple words, and I have to blink away tears before moving to the green square directly above his apology.

If she hasn't shown you her crazy, she's just not that into you.

Gasping, I go to whirl around, but then CK's warmth is at my back, his evergreen scent filling my lungs.

"You're a jackass." I meet his gaze in the mirror again.

He chuckles, the sound reverberating through my back and straight to all my fun parts. "I am, for a few reasons lately. But on this"—he jerks his chin at the wall—"I dare you to try to tell me that's not true."

I narrow my eyes. Damn him.

"Keep going." His warm breath caresses my cheek as he prods me to read the blue one next to the set.

If she doesn't scare the hell out of you a little, she's not the one.

"I scare you?" I ask, my voice small.

"You terrify me. I'm damn near Quinnaphobic." He places the gentlest of kisses on my cheek. "But that's how I know how special you are."

My eyes grow hot. I blink the sensation away, already searching out the next note without having to be told.

I just want you to know that when I picture myself happy, it's with you.

"Even before you were mine, it was always you I pictured by my side." His arms come around to circle my middle, holding me to him tighter as if to illustrate his statement.

Oh my god.

I press my lips together and read a hot pink note.

Sometimes I wonder how you put up with me. Then I remember, oh, I put up with you. So, we're even.

"Even-shmeven," I complain. "Mr. Let Me Pick A Useless Fight With My…" My words trail off, the incomplete sentence hanging in the air. I'm at a loss for how to describe my role in his life.

"Girlfriend. The word you're looking for is girlfriend, Red."

My pom-pom is suddenly back in my throat, and it takes me a

moment to clear it. "If I'm your girlfriend, as you claim, what the hell do you mean you put up with me?"

He buries his face in the curve of my neck, chuckling against my skin when I gasp. "Do I need to remind you of the two different E.T. figurines I now own, or your whistle?"

"Do *I* need to remind you how I practically had to beat the fact that I like you into you?" I counter. "Not that it mattered much."

"Oh, it mattered." He nips at my skin. "But that's one of the reasons why the note says we were even."

I finally give in and lean into him, scanning the wall again.

The best relationships start off as friendships.

"Oof, Kaysonova might argue that one." I point to the purple paper, thinking of those early days when Kay would just walk away from Mason.

I feel CK shrug more than I see it, too busy hunting out another note.

I'm shy at first, but I do the most random things once I get comfortable with someone.

He props his chin on my shoulder, reading along with me. "I adore how no one day is the same as another."

Oh…these are getting good. Look at CK coming in with the swoon.

"You *didn't*." I choke-laugh when I read the yellow *You remind me of my pinkie toe because I know I'm eventually going to bang you on every piece of furniture in our apartment* note.

"I figured it was best to go with the body part you value the most if I wanted to try my hand at naughty notes like the ones you've been leaving me more recently."

Turning my head, I press a kiss to his chin. "And what makes you think my pinkie toe is the MVBP in my life?" I ask, getting creative with the acronym.

"You were willing to eliminate all bed corners out of existence for it."

"And to think…" I nod to the wall. "If you had gotten your way in that category, you wouldn't have been able to do all this."

His *You make me realize I don't have to stay where I came from* note makes me want to take an eight-hour road trip to Kansas and find his old bullies. CK must sense the violence in me because he runs his hands down my forearms, covering my hands and linking them with his.

Then the orange paper next to it has me flopping to the mushy side of the emotional spectrum.

A true relationship is two imperfect people refusing to give up on each other.

"I'm hoping that is just as much true now as it was when you refused to give up on me when I wouldn't admit I liked you," he whispers in my ear. "And I promise I won't ever give up on you."

Jesus. Who is this swoony confident man? More importantly, why did he keep him hidden for so long?

Together we shuffle to the right so I can read the notes on the opposite side.

My heart skips a beat as I read *You're the one who forced me to level up*, and I immediately spin in CK's hold, my jaw unhinged.

"*That's* what you meant when you said I wasn't on your level?"

I drop my head, my forehead resting over his erratically beating heart.

Most days, I'm convinced my guardian angel drinks, but thank god I was the tipsy one the other night and not her. Luckily she was on point and reined in my crazy when he said that. I one-hundred-percent could have flown off the handle, but instead, I spun on my heel and walked away, irresponsibly getting drunker to help me not think about it.

Hands thread into my hair and cup my face, tilting it up until I'm drowning in blue irises. "I'm sorry I ever made you think I meant you." I nod and try to look away, but he's not having it. "Fuck, baby." His fingers tighten around me, tugging on my hair. "I was talking about *me. Not* you."

He glides his hands down my neck, his palms causing shivers as they ghost over my skin before taking me by the shoulders and spinning me around to face the Post-its again.

The tip of his finger bends back as he stabs at a blue *I realized I have two options: 1, Live with regret, or 2, Fight for what I want* note.

"I'm here because I'm choosing option number two."

There's nothing to fight. I'm willingly his.

"This is my promise to you." The sinew of his forearm

distracts me for a moment as it brushes my face, rising to point at the next note.

I can't go back and change our beginning, but I can start where we are and change our ending.

"If we're lucky, our ending won't be for quite a few decades."

"CK…"

He kisses my temple. "I think I may have channeled a bit of you for this one." He taps the orange *I love who you are on the inside…all that sexy on the outside is just a bonus* square a little further down.

"You love me?" Hope strangles my voice down to a whisper.

CK says nothing. Instead, he takes my hand in his and lays them on one last Post-it. *I love everything about you, except the fact that you're not mine.*

He allows me to spin around this time, and I jump him, my arms circling his neck, my legs wrapping around his middle. I kiss him, my nose bumping his glasses, but I don't care.

"I've always been yours, Superman," I say against his lips.

He takes over the kiss, moving us until my back hits one of the walls of my bedroom and pinning me against it. I'm not sure how long we make out, but it's long enough that his glasses have fogged and his lips are swollen. He widens his stance, balancing me more with his lower body as he palms one side of my face.

"I've spent my life watching it from the sidelines, letting things pass me by because I was too afraid to take a chance or put myself out there." He runs a thumb over my cheek, his blue eyes boring into me. "Then I met you."

If my heart were a game day cheerleader, it would be holding up a sign with SWOON printed on it because that's precisely what I'm doing.

"You came in with your big smile and even bigger personality and forcibly pushed me out of my comfort zone."

I can't help but smile at that. Probably a bit too proudly, if I'm being honest.

"You not only showed me what it's like to be in love, but how to show it in return. I'm done being too afraid to go after what I want, done sitting on the bench while others go after what *I* want. I want you, Quinn. I *love*. You, Quinn. It's time for me to officially come off the bench and make a play for your heart. It's time I take all those love coaching lessons of yours and use them to get the only thing that matters…you."

I blow out a breath, my head thunking against the wall. Yeah, no more love coaching for this man. I don't think I'll survive it if he gets any swoonier than this.

"I love you too, CK." Clenching my thighs, I leverage my body tighter against his. "So damn much."

His smile is blinding in its intensity then slips a bit when I say, "But…there's one thing I need to know before I can *really* commit to us."

He swallows hard, his Adam's apple doing that bobbing thing I could watch all day long. "What's that, Red?"

"What does your ruler collection look like?"

He starts to answer but stops, his brows dipping beneath his frames. Oo, how I love knocking him off balance.

"What do my school supplies have to do with anything?" He jerks his chin at the Post-its stuck to the wall. "Don't you have that category covered for us?"

It gives me butterflies hearing him call us an us.

"Well, you see…" I twirl my finger around the slightly longer strands of his hair. "I have this recurring fantasy where I'm a naughty cheerleader and you're the dirty professor in charge of my…detention."

He barks out a laugh, and I feel the joy radiating into each of my cells.

"You're crazy, and I am fucking here for it."

QUINN

"WE'RE NEVER GOING to be alone, you know that, right?" CK says without stopping his drugging kisses as the elevator takes us up to the penthouse.

"Kay and Mase seem to manage just fine," I answer, hooking my legs around his calf and pushing in closer.

He hums, the sound vibrating my lips. "Mase is a hell of a lot scarier than I am." He pauses, pulling back to peer down at me with a hand curled around the side of my head. "Though, I do have a secret weapon."

I narrow my eyes, suspicion pushing me to say, "Oh yeah? And what's that?"

CK kisses the tip of my nose, his lips spreading into a teasing smile. "I share my bed with you."

Yeah, he does. Looks like our place just gained a second guest room.

Pushing up on my toes, I kiss the underside of his jaw, skimming my lips down to his ear and whispering, "Because of my crazy?"

He nods. "I love your crazy."

Swooping in, he steals another kiss, walking me back until I'm pressed against the wall of the elevator.

Man, I love his kisses.

He sips at my lips, nipping and sucking until I'm completely lost to anything else around us.

And...

That is how we end up getting caught by four of our seven roommates, still lip-locked, my leg hitched high on CK's hip and his hand up my shirt.

I feel CK smile against my mouth when I whimper from him flicking my nipple one last time before trying to covertly remove his hand from my top. Based on the Cheshire grins Trav, Kev, Alex, and Emma sport, I'd say it's safe to say CK didn't come close to pulling that off.

The four of them part down the middle, Trav and Emma on one side, Kev and Alex on the other, greeting CK and me, exiting the elevator as if we're making a game-day entrance. Their whoops and exaggerated catcalls follow us and draw the attention of our remaining three friends.

Grant, the most subtle of any of these idiots, jerks a chin in greeting.

"Welcome home," Kay says from her perch, snuggled in Mason's lap. "How was your trip?"

"Better after CK got there and I wasn't mad at him for being a stupid idiot anymore," I answer, CK glancing down at me with a wink.

The others filter back into the living room, claiming spots on the sectional as CK and I do the same, my boyfriend—*Eep, can we pause for a girly moment over being able to say that word officially?*—draping his arm over me until I'm snuggled back against his side.

"Oh my god, look how cute they are!" Emma does a poor job whispering as she leans into Grant, not an ounce of subtlety in the way she points at CK and me cuddled together.

"Wait." Kay holds up a hand, angling her head in a way that allows her to look at Emma and us at the same time. "We're for sure going to be talking about *that*, but how'd things go with your mom?"

Linking my hand with CK's, I settle in and relay the story, detailing everything from my blowup at the Hoedown Throwdown meeting to when *Mamá* and I made up.

It was hard as hell, but CK being there went a long way to making it feel just a bit better. It wasn't even that he flew across the country to declare his love for me—though that did help—but more him telling me all about how it was my self-confidence and fearless attitude that made him fall in love with me in the first place.

I channeled all that into pushing myself to finish a difficult conversation to get to a resolution. Fighting with *Mamá* nearly made me sick, but it was worth it in the end. For the first time in as long as I can remember, it actually felt like she heard me when I told her about my plans for the future.

"I'm so proud of you," CK whispers just for me, pressing his lips to the crown of my head.

"About that." Kay glances at Mason, who nods before kissing her temple. "How would you feel about helping me too?"

My brows draw together. "Huh?" A part of me wonders if she's going to ask if I'll stay on as a coach for the season, but I doubt it. Kay knows full well I wouldn't be able to commit the time once my own season starts.

She blows out a breath, her cheeks puffing out with the action. "So you know how you've been unofficially helping me navigate what and how much I show on social through NJA and you guys?"

I nod. Not gonna lie—any time she asks for my advice or opinion, I get little giddy butterflies.

"Well…I was thinking…seeing as your stint as a love coach worked out so well for you…"

Kay winks at us, and CK whispers about not daring to share my whistle. I shush him and give my full attention back to Kay.

"Maybe you wouldn't mind being my social media coach."

I blink, stunned silent.

My gaze bounces around the room, smiles and nods of encouragement coming from all those who make up my U of J family.

"What about Jordan?" I ask, referring to the revered sports publicist her brother is signed with.

"E's her client, not me." Kay shrugs. "I don't want to hassle her with this."

"You could have Mase deduct the cost of your help from your rent," Trav suggests, falling over laughing.

All of us roll our eyes at that. None of us pay rent. Mason used his trust fund to buy it outright as his own swoony—okay, caveman-motivated gesture.

"Are you sure you want to do this? It's a big step."

Just being featured on our accounts, Mason's especially, was a massive step for her. This is…wow.

"Not even a little bit." Kay shakes her head. "But…if I'm going to have a chance of handling all the changes coming this year, I figure…maybe…going with the motto of the best offense is a good defense might help me survive."

"Are you sure?" I ask again, because, again…this is *huge*.

"Nope. But we're doing it anyway."

Okay then. Bring on junior year.

Randomness For My Readers

Whoop!

Wow, *finally* a U of J book that doesn't end on a cliffy...well, a big one anyway, lol.

But...I mean good news is Kay and Mase are getting more books! Yay! *spirit fingers*

So now for a little bullet style fun facts:

- I absolutely loved writing Quinn and CK. Yes, I had to keep crazy hours to finish them, but they were by far the fastest I've ever written a book.
- Quinn was a lot easier to write than shy CK. At least until she started breaking him out of his shell, and then he got talkative. Though, not gonna lie, I was a little surprised by his alpha-ness.
- Most of the IG handles you see in the comments are from my reader Covenettes. So many are great bookstagrammers to check out.
- Tacos! OMG, do I love tacos! So, of course, my girl Q had to love tacos. And margaritas! TEQUILA for life! Even if Mr. Alley isn't a fan, lol.
- All the props go to my own personal Quinn, Marisol, for keeping Quinn as authentic as possible. We will pretend that we weren't schooled in the middle of (my)

night by your ten-year-old daughter. (you don't need that many coats in Southern California)

- The number of times I listened to *Shivers* while writing this book was so high I'm shocked my Spotify didn't shame me. But the middle royal is obsessed now lol.
- Quinn's fear of sharks because of *Jaws* and CK's *E.T.* fear are both true stories about yours truly. I really don't suggest watching shark movies on a waterbed. It's not a good idea.
- It should come as no surprise if you've read my BTU Alumni books, but Mr. Alley and I also battle it out in *Dr. Mario*. Oh, the trash talk!

If you don't want to miss out on anything new coming or when my crazy characters pop in with extra goodies make sure to sign up for my newsletter! If my rambling hasn't turned you off and you are like "This chick is my kind of crazy," feel free to reach out!

Lots of Love,
Alley

Acknowledgments

This is where I get to say thank you; hopefully, I don't miss anyone. If I do, I'm sorry, and I still love you and blame mommy brain.

I always start with Mr. Alley, who still bitches about not having a book dedicated to him yet. I try to tell him I always mention him first in the acknowledgments lol.

Also, I'm sure he would want me to make sure I say thanks for all the hero inspiration, but it is true (even if he has no ink *winking emoji*)

To Jenny, the other half of my brain, the bestest best friend a girl could ask for. Why the hell do you live across the pond? I live for every shouty capital message you send me while you read my words 97398479 times.

To Britt and Melissa, who have helped Jenny keep my crazy ass in line and even went all "Hold my beer" when Jenny passed the PA role over to them. I would seriously be lost without these two.

To Jen, my publicist for helping me despite my crazy.

To Rebecca for seriously still being my friend after all our insane voice memos trying to get this beast done. Though, the same can absolutely still be said about Julia and Laura too and all their beta help. Seriously, why are you guys still my friends lol.

To Marisol, I know I mentioned you in randomness, but thank you so much for being my Quinn expert/sensitivity reader to keep her as authentic as possible. And for your endless voice memos to all my random Spanish question, followed by me saying, "Okay, but now spell it."

To my group chats that give me life and help keep me sane: The OG Coven, The MINS, The Tacos, The Book Coven, and Procrastinating & Butt Stuff (hehe—still laugh at this name like a 13 year old boy).

To all my author besties that were okay with me forcing my

friendship on them and now are some of my favorite people to talk to on the inter webs.

To Sarah and Claudia the most amazing graphics people ever in existence. Yeah I said it lol.

To Jules my cover designer, for going above and beyond, then once more with designing the cover. I can't even handle the epicness of it.

To Jess my editor, who is always pushing me to make the story better and giving such evil inspiration that leads to shouty capitals from readers, even if you demand the conflict while telling me you live for harmony.

To Caitlin my other editor who helps clean up the mess I send her while at the same time totally getting my crazy.

To Dawn and Rosa for giving my books their final spit shine.

To my street team for being the best pimps ever. Seriously, you guys rock my socks.

To my ARC team for giving my books some early love and getting the word out there.

To every blogger and bookstagrammer that takes a chance and reads my words and writes about them.

To my fellow Covenettes for making my reader group one of my happy places. Whenever you guys post things that you know belong there I squeal a little.

And, of course, to you my fabulous reader, for picking up my book and giving me a chance. Without you I wouldn't be able to live my dream of bringing to life the stories the voices in my head tell me.

Lots of Love,
Alley

For A Good Time Call

Do you want to stay up-to-date on releases, be the first to see cover reveals, excerpts from upcoming books, deleted scenes, sales, freebies, and all sorts of insider information you can't get anywhere else?

If you're like "Duh! Come on Alley." Make sure you sign up for my newsletter.

Ask yourself this:
* Are you a Romance Junkie?
* Do you like book boyfriends and book besties? (yes this is a thing)
* Is your GIF game strong?
* Want to get inside the crazy world of Alley Ciz?

If any of your answers are yes, maybe you should join my Facebook reader group, Romance Junkie's Coven

Join The Coven

Stalk Alley
Join The Coven
Get the Newsletter
Like Alley on Facebook
Follow Alley on Instagram
Hang with Alley on Goodreads
Follow Alley on Amazon
Follow Alley on BookBub

Subscribe on YouTube for Book Trailers
Follow Alley's inspiration boards on Pinterest
All the Swag
Book Playlists
All Things Alley

Sneak Peek of Savage Queen

SAVVY- CHAPTER 1

Senior year.

It's supposed to be epic. Filled with parties, prom, and all sorts of debauchery.

God! I was *so* looking forward to living out my teenage drama dreams.

Yeah…

Now though…

Not so much.

All thoughts of what I envisioned my first day of senior year would be like dissolve as our driver pulls through the wrought iron gates of Blackwell Academy and the butterflies in my belly turn into fire-breathing dragons. I shouldn't be here. This isn't me.

The luxury vehicle, the uniform, the most expensive private school on the east coast—*all* of it, wrong.

This isn't my school. No, mine is on the other side of town. Why the hell do I have to spend my last year of high school at this uptight prep school instead of Blackwell Public? Just thinking about it has the potential to make me rage like the Hulk.

I have friends at BP.

A crew.

A legacy.

I was Savvy-fucking-King.

Here? I have nothing, am nothing.

Actually…if I'm being honest, it might even be a little bit dangerous for me to be here, though I expect that thought is more my brother's paranoia rubbing off on me than actual reality.

I get it. At BP, my name alone demands respect, not to mention there's a system in place to help remind those who need it that being an asshole for assholerly's sake is an automatic way to get yourself canceled.

Here at BA? Who the hell knows. For all I know, I could be walking into a *Lord of the Flies*-type situation. Fun times.

"Miss?" The voice of Daniel, my stepfather's driver, startles me. Looks like I was lost in my thoughts and didn't hear him open my door.

It's going to be a *long* day; I can already feel it.

"Ready, Samantha?" asks Mitchell St. James, my new stepdad.

I grit my teeth. Why *she* insists on people calling me by my legal name is *beyond* me.

"Yes. Coming." I loop the strap of the black Nappa leather messenger bag—another insistence from *her*—over my shoulder and slide out, using my hand to smooth my pleated schoolgirl-style skirt that hits me mid-thigh.

Ugh. This damn uniform. Like seriously? What am I, auditioning to be in a Britney Spears music video?

I do have to give credit where it's due. The pretentious people who run this place picked some high-quality materials for us to wear. The white button-up is silk, and my gray blazer is made of the softest cashmere. I was also surprised by the staggering number of possible combinations for a school with a uniform.

I walk around the back of the Bentley, the silver shiny enough I can see my reflection in it, and join the reason for my upheaval.

Okay, I may be acting a tad dramatic from still being salty about this latest development, but who the hell wants to be uprooted from their school *senior* year? *points with both thumbs* Not this girl.

Things would be a lot easier if I hated Mitchell St. James, but alas, I don't. And…

To be fair, *he* isn't the *real* reason for this life change. Nope.

That honor falls firmly on *her*—Natalie King. For a woman who didn't give two shits about me for most of my life, this demand— threat—to have me fall in line and live with her straight-up pisses me off.

The thing I haven't figured out yet—and yes, let me tell you, it frustrates the fuck out of me that I haven't—is why the sudden push to act like mom of the year? I honestly have a hard time recalling an instance when I saw her as a parental figure. When he was alive, it was Dad, then the Falco family and my older brother Carter after his death.

It's actually quite fascinating to watch how Natalie transforms into what most people would think is a "normal" human being when Mitchell is around versus the devilish bitch we've always known her as.

Her attempts at rewriting history have also been commendable. Make no mistake, her pretending *she* was the one who made sure I was cared for, ensured I always had my meds, took care of me if I got sick, and taught me how to take care of myself is *precisely* that—pretending. Try as she might, she can't greenscreen herself into a role filled by Carter and others.

I'm seventeen years old, a few months shy of being an adult, and capable—at least legally—of making my own decisions. So why? *Why* is it *now* that Natalie King, now St. James, insisted— again, made threats—I fall in line and pretend to be a model daughter? *She's* the real person I'm pissed at. The only good thing that woman has done for me was giving birth to me instead of aborting me.

"This will always *be your home whether you live here or not."* My brother's promise echoes in the back of my mind. It's one I've been playing on repeat since Natalie called us to the house neither one of us has called home to drop her bombs like Blackwell was all of a sudden the Middle East.

"I got married." She wiggles the fingers of her left hand, the giant rock on the fourth one practically blinding us.

To say Carter and I were surprised would be the understatement of the century. Sure we aren't the sit-down-to-dinner-together type of family, at least not with her, but we weren't even aware she was *dating* someone, let alone seriously enough for him to put a ring on it.

"Who did you sucker into marrying you, Natalie?" My lips twitch

at the way she bristles at Carter using her first name. I don't blame him; even when I think of her as 'Mom,' the sarcasm is thick.

Marrying into a founding family of Blackwell, Natalie had grown used to a certain level of status. The grass hadn't had a chance to grow over Dad's grave before she started her hunt for husband number two all those years ago.

I dip my chin to study my new stepdad out of the corner of my eye. I gotta hand it to her—it took her *years* to reel in husband number two, but she certainly landed herself a whale in Mitchell St. James. In a custom-tailored suit that must have easily cost five figures, the hotelier radiates luxury and power. *Gossip Girl* is my go-to show to rewatch with my bestie Tessa, and he gives off massive Bart Bass vibes.

"Samantha"—Natalie has always refused to call me by my Savvy nickname—"you will be moving to the St. James with me, and I'll be transferring your enrollment to Blackwell Academy."

I tried to fight it, but it was no use. Within two weeks, I was moved out of my brother's place and into the penthouse residence at the St. James and was a registered senior of Mitchell's alma mater.

"Follow me," Mitchell instructs, and again, I do as I'm told.

The BA campus is like something out of a movie. The stone steps at the entrance have to be a hundred feet wide, and the three-story gray stone building beyond them is equally impressive. The doorway I follow Mitchell through is big enough to drive a truck through.

Geez, are we overcompensating for something?

My dark purple Chucks—a nod to my Blackwell Public roots—squeak on the white marble floors, because of course they're marble. Yes, I'm aware I sound like a judgy bitch, but in my defense, *everything* about the place *drips* money. There's no fake lemony scent of floor cleaner here, only a fresh one that manages to make me feel like I'm still outside. Even the hallway's metal lockers look more like high-end appliances than a place for students to store their belongings.

Also…we're late.

Classes started thirty minutes ago, and not one person is in the hall as I follow Mitchell to Headmaster Woodbridge's office. Of *course* they have a headmaster. God forbid they went with a simple principal like BP.

I snort, and out of the corner of my eye, I can see Mitchell's mouth twitch at the sound.

Fuck I'm so bitter about having to be here.

We step inside a room that is—unsurprisingly given everything else so far—beautifully decorated. There are two tufted black leather couches mirroring each other and a large desk set up in front of a wall of windows overlooking the state-of-the-art football stadium and hockey arena. That's what happens when the average person would have to sell their soul to afford the cost of tuition here—though I can't help but smirk thinking of how both places looked the last I saw them. If you ever need to know how much toilet paper is required to TP a football stadium or the best paint to use on ice, I'm your girl.

Actually…

I wonder how the BP start-of-the-school-year prank is going over. I also need to remember to pay extra-close attention to the bathrooms when I need to use one.

"Ah, Mitchell." Headmaster Woodbridge rises, rounding his desk.

"Jonathan."

They shake hands, and by the use of first names, I can only assume the leader of my new school is golfing buddies with my stepfather. *Awesome*—not.

"Samantha." Their attention turns to me. "It's a pleasure to meet you. And let me say, we are honored to have you joining the ranks of our student body."

Honored? Laying it on a little thick, don't you think?

"Umm…thank you?"

"Jonathan." Mitchell speaks to cut the awkwardness. He may be pulling me from everything I've known, but unlike Natalie, he is perceptive enough to read me. "How about we let my daughter"—just daughter; I've noticed he never uses 'step' when he speaks of me—"get settled in before you start any sales pitches."

"You're right, you're right." Headmaster Woodbridge claps him on the back in a good-ol'-boys way. "I've arranged for one of our top students to show you around—teach you the ropes of BA, if you will." He flicks his wrist, checking the gold Rolex on it for the time. "She should be here any minute."

Again I'm hit with a wave of *I shouldn't be here.* I don't want to "learn the ropes." BP is my turf, my kingdom to rule. I want to be sitting in class, passing notes to Tessa. Instead, I'm stuck here in a place where it feels like my Royalty status could bring on a wave of *Off with her head* as opposed to the *Oh shit, Savvy's coming* I'm used to.

For all the stories I've heard about the great pranks of the past, I never fully understood how the *Romeo and Juliet*-esque feud started. I always assumed it was mostly a case of a school that could afford to recruit some of the best athletes from across the country being butthurt because the public school could claim more alumni playing in the NFL.

After I was told I would be transferred to this place that mostly boards—and let's not forget how it boasts about having—some of the brightest and most connected young minds on the east coast, I decided it was time I needed all the facts if I were to come up with a proper plan of attack.

My brother and his friends may have nicknamed me Savage —Savvy for short—for my boss bitch personality, but I know how to turn on the girl-next-door charm when needed. My connections may not come from being a child of the upper one percent like my new school chums, but I *am* a child of a Blackwell founding family, and I exploit the shit out of it.

Not to bore you with too much detail, but here is the gist of Blackwell's history.

The town was founded in 1866 by five families: the Falcos, the Princes, the Castles, the Salvatores, and my family, the Kings. Together they worked toward creating one of the oldest munici-palities in the state. Even today, it is a major bedroom suburb of New York City.

Blackwell, at its core, is a town deeply rooted in its citizens. It's why generations later, those founding families are held in such high regard. It also helps that the great-great-grandfathers of the Kings, Princes, and Castles banded together to create Royal Enterprises, a technology and industrial research powerhouse that employs hundreds of locals while giving back to the community.

I also learned from the mayor, my "Uncle Chuck," that most of the town's residents look down on how uninvolved Blackwell Academy is and how it doesn't give back to the community it resides in. Not one of the limited scholarships the school earmarks for Jersey residents has ever gone to someone from Blackwell.

Knock-knock.

"Ah, there she is now." The headmaster holds an arm out like he's a game show host presenting us with the grand prize. "Samantha St. James, I'd like you to meet Arabella Vanderwaal. Miss Vanderwaal is student body president and the *perfect* person to be your tour guide."

We eye each other warily. She's exactly what I would have expected given my past interactions with the student body of BA —aka Prep School Barbie. She's pretty, gorgeous even, with long chestnut waves that could make a shampoo commercial jealous. She wears the same uniform configuration, but unlike me, her shirt is tucked in where I left mine to drape over my skirt. Her tie is cinched tight at her throat instead of the knot hanging between my breasts. She also has on a killer pair of Mary Jane stilettos— the same ones Natalie tried to get me to change into.

And yes, before you ask, I totally stole my sense of style for the day from my girl Serena van der Woodsen (Blake Lively's character on *Gossip Girl*). What can I say? I'll conform, but only to a point. *Sorry not sorry, Natalie.*

The way Arabella's highly glossed lips twist into a frown, I can tell she too finds my appearance lacking. Too bad, so sad for her—I don't give a fuck.

Keep reading for free in KU.

Also by Alley Ciz

Stay connected with Alley

Sign Up for Alley's Newsletter

Bloggers Join Alley's Master List

Join Alley's Facebook Reader Group

.

About the Author

Alley Ciz is an internationally bestselling indie author of sassy heroines and the alpha men that fall on their knees for them. She is a romance junkie whose love for books turned into her telling the stories of the crazies who live in her head…even if they don't know how to stay in their lane.

This Potterhead can typically be found in the wild wearing a funny T-shirt, connected to an IV drip of coffee, stuffing her face with pizza and tacos, chasing behind her 3 minis, all while her 95lb yellow lab—the best behaved child—watches on in amusement.

- facebook.com/AlleyCizAuthor
- instagram.com/alley.ciz
- pinterest.com/alleyciz
- goodreads.com/alleyciz
- bookbub.com/profile/alley-ciz
- amazon.com/author/alleyciz

Printed in Poland
by Amazon Fulfillment
Poland Sp. z o.o., Wrocław